Peter Straub

Peter Straub was born in Milwaukee, Wisconsin. His bestselling novels include *Ghost Story*, *Shadowland*, *Floating Dragon*, *The Talisman* and its sequel *Black House* (with Stephen King), *Koko*, *Mystery*, *The Throat*, *The Hellfire Club* and most recently *Mr X*. He has won the British Fantasy Award, two Bram Stoker Awards and two World Fantasy Awards. Among the prizes won by the seven stories collected in *Magic Terror* are the 1993 World Fantasy Award for 'The Ghost Village' and the 1998 Bram Stoker Award for 'Mr Clubb and Mr Cuff'. Peter Straub lived for a decade in Ireland and England and now lives in New York City.

MAGIC TERROR

'Mixing stark realism with black comedy, and reverberating with echoes of Conrad, Melville and the Brothers Grimm, these excursions to the dark side of life set a high standard for the literature of contemporary magic terror.'   *Publishers Weekly*

'Psychological insights and memorable phrasing . . . intelligent . . . inventive.'   *TLS*

'If there is a more brilliant writer of suspense, horror or weird terror than Peter Straub, I've never read him. No one writes better prose, but it is impossible to categorize. There is a taste of horror, a soupçon of the supernatural, a generous helping of crime, a hint of mystery. The delicious mix is unique to American letters; if you haven't read *Ghost Story* or *Mr X* or *Koko*, *Magic Terror* is a great place to start reading Straub. It is a compilation of several novellas and short stories, each different, yet all imbued with Straub's magical talent. From the creeping realization of the horrible truth in "Ashputtle" to the lyric beauty of "Porkpie Hat" and the shockingly dark revenge comedy "Mr Clubb and Mr Cuff", Straub shows herein a range of originality rarely matched among even the most gifted writers.'

OTTO PENZLER, *Amazon.com*

'Clever exercises in horror.'   *New York Times*

By Peter Straub

NOVELS

Marriages
Under Venus
Julia
If You Could See Me Now
Ghost Story
Shadowland
Floating Dragon
The Talisman (with Stephen King)
Koko
Mystery
Mrs God
The Throat
The Hellfire Club
Mr X
Black House (with Stephen King)

POETRY

Open Air
Leeson Park & Belsize Square

COLLECTIONS

Wild Animals
Houses Without Doors
Peter Straub's Ghosts (editor)
Magic Terror

Peter Straub

MAGIC TERROR

[7 tales]

HarperCollins*Publishers*

Grateful acknowledgement is made to Georges Borchardt, Inc., for permission to reprint six lines from 'Down by the Station, Early in the Morning', from *A Wave*, by John Ashbery (New York: Viking, 1984). Copyright © 1981, 1982, 1983, 1984 by John Ashbery. Reprinted by permission of Georges Borchardt, Inc., for the author.

All of the pieces in this work have been previously published: 'Ashputtle' was originally published in *Black Thorn, White Rose*, edited by Ellen Datlow and Terri Windling (William Morrow, 1994); 'Isn't It Romantic?' was originally published in *Murder on the Run*, by the Adams Round Table (Berkley, 1998); 'The Ghost Village' was originally published in *The Mists from Beyond*, edited by Robert Weinberg, Stefan R. Dziemianowicz, and Martin H. Greenberg (ROC, 1993); 'Porkpie Hat' was originally published in *Murder for Halloween*, edited by Michele Slung and Roland Hartman (Mysterious Press, 1994); 'Bunny Is Good Bread' was originally published, under the title 'Fee', in *Borderlands 4*, edited by Elizabeth E. Monteleone and Thomas F. Monteleone (Borderlands Press, 1994); 'Hunger, an Introduction' was originally published in *Ghosts*, edited by Peter Straub (Borderlands Press, 1995); and 'Mr Clubb and Mr Cuff' was originally published in *Murder for Revenge*, edited by Otto Penzler (Delacorte Press, 1998).

HarperCollins*Publishers*
77–85 Fulham Palace Road,
Hammersmith, London W6 8JB
www.**fire**and**water**.com

This paperback edition 2002
1 3 5 7 9 8 6 4 2

First published in Great Britain by
HarperCollins*Publishers* 2001

First published in the USA by
Random House 2000

Copyright © Peter Straub 2000

The Author asserts the moral right to
be identified as the author of this work

ISBN 0 00 710991 1

Typeset by Palimpsest Book Production Limited,
Polmont, Stirlingshire

Painted and bound in Great Britain by
Omnia Books Limited, Glasgow

For Lawrence Block

The result is magic, then terror, then pity at the emptiness,
Then air gradually bathing and filling the emptiness as it leaks,
Emoting all over something that is probably mere reportage,
But nevertheless likes being emoted on.
.   .   .   .

                                        . . . the light
From the lighthouse that protects us as it pushes us away.

'Down by the Station, Early in the Morning.'
JOHN ASHBERY

Contents

MAGIC TERROR

Ashputtle

People think that teaching little children has something to do with helping other people, something to do with service. People think that if you teach little children, you must love them. People get what they need from thoughts like this.

People think that if you happen to be very fat and are a person who acts happy and cheerful all the time, you are probably pretending to be that way in order to make them forget how fat you are, or cause them to forgive you for being so fat. They make this assumption, thinking you are so stupid that you imagine that you're getting away with this charade. From this assumption, they get confidence in the superiority of their intelligence over yours, and they get to pity you, too.

Those figments, those stepsisters, came to me and said, *Don't you know that we want to help you?* They came to me and said, *Can you tell us what your life is like?*

These moronic questions they asked over and over: *Are you all right? Is anything happening to you? Can you talk to us now, darling? Can you tell us about your life?*

I stared straight ahead, not looking at their pretty hair or pretty eyes or pretty mouths. I looked over their shoulders at the pattern on the wallpaper and tried not to blink until they stood up and went away.

What my *life* was like? What was *happening* to me?

Nothing was happening to me. I was *all right.*

They smiled briefly, like a twitch in their eyes and mouths, before they stood up and left me alone. I sat still on my chair and looked at the wallpaper while they talked to Zena.

The wallpaper was yellow, with white lines going up and down through it. The lines never touched – just when they were about to run into each other, they broke, and the fat thick yellow kept them apart.

I liked seeing the white lines hanging in the fat yellow, each one separate.

When the figments called me *darling*, ice and snow stormed into my mouth and went pushing down my throat into my stomach, freezing everything. They didn't know I was nothing, that I would never be like them, they didn't know that the only part of me that was not nothing was a small hard stone right at the center of me.

That stone has a name. MOTHER.

If you are a female kindergarten teacher in her fifties who happens to be very fat, people imagine that you must be truly dedicated to their children, because you cannot possibly have any sort of private life. If they are the parents of the children in your kindergarten class, they are almost grateful that you are so grotesque, because it means that you must really care about their children. After all, even though you couldn't possibly get any other sort of job, you can't be in it for the money, can you? Because what do people know about your salary? They know that garbage men make more money than kindergarten teachers. So at least you didn't decide to take care of their delightful, wonderful, lovable little children just because you thought you'd get rich, no no.

Therefore, even though they disbelieve all your smiles, all your pretty ways, even though they really do think of you with a mixture of pity and contempt, a little gratitude gets in there.

Sometimes when I meet with one of these parents, say a fluffy-haired young lawyer, say named Arnold Zoeller, Arnold and his wife, Kathi, Kathi with an *i*, mind you, sometimes when I sit behind my desk and watch these two slim handsome people struggle to keep the pity and contempt out of their well-cared-for faces, I catch that gratitude heating up behind their eyes.

Arnold and Kathi believe that a pathetic old lumpo like me must love their lovely little girl, a girl say named Tori, Tori with an *i* (for Victoria). And I think I do rather love little Tori Zoeller, yes I do think I love that little girl. My mother would have loved her, too. And that's the God's truth.

I can see myself in the world, in the middle of the world. I see that I am the same as all nature.

In our minds exists an awareness of perfection, but nothing on earth, nothing in all of nature, is perfectly conceived. Every response comes straight out of the person who is responding.

I have no responsibility to stimulate or satisfy your needs. All that was taken care of a long time ago. Even if you happen to be some kind of supposedly exalted person, like a lawyer. Even if your name is Arnold Zoeller, for example.

Once, briefly, there existed a golden time. In my mind existed an awareness of perfection, and all of nature echoed and repeated the awareness of perfection in my mind. My parents lived, and with them, I too was alive in the golden time. Our name was Asch, and in fact I am known now as Mrs Asch, the Mrs being entirely honorific, no husband having ever been in evidence, nor ever likely to be. (To some sixth-graders, those whom I did not beguile and enchant as kindergartners, those before whose parents I did not squeeze myself into my desk chair and pronounce their dull, their dreary treasures delightful, wonderful, lovable, above all *intelligent*, I am known as Mrs Fat-Asch. Of this I pretend to be ignorant.) Mr and Mrs Asch did dwell together in the golden time, and both mightily did love their girl-child. And then, whoops, the girl-child's Mommy upped and died. The girl-child's Daddy buried her in the estate's church yard, with the minister and everything, in the coffin and everything, with hymns and talking and crying and the animals standing around, and Zena, I remember, Zena was already there, even then. So that was how things were, right from the start.

The figments came because of what I did later. They came from a long way away – the city, I think. We never saw city dresses like that, out where we lived. We never saw city hair like that, either. And one of those ladies had a veil!

One winter morning during my first year teaching kindergarten here, I got into my car – I *shoved myself* into my car, I should explain; this is different for me than for you, I *rammed myself* between the seat and the steering wheel, and I drove forty miles east, through three different suburbs, until I got to the city, and thereupon I drove through the city to the slummiest section, where dirty people sit in their cars and drink right in the middle of the day. I went to the department store nobody goes to unless they're on welfare and have five or six kids all with different last names. I just parked on the street and sailed in the door. People like that, they never hurt people like me.

Down in the basement was where they sold the wallpaper, so I huffed and puffed down the stairs, smiling cute as a button whenever anybody stopped to look at me, and shoved myself through the aisles until I got to the back wall, where the samples stood in big books like the fairy-tale book we used to have. I grabbed about four of those books off the wall and heaved them over onto a table there in that section and perched myself on a little tiny chair and started flipping the pages.

A scared-looking black kid in a cheap suit mumbled something about helping me, so I gave him my happiest, most pathetic smile and said, well, I was here to get wallpaper, wasn't I? What color did I want, did I know? Well, I was thinking about yellow, I said. Uh-huh, he says, what kinda yellow you got in mind? Yellow with white lines in it. Uh-huh, says he, and starts helping me look through those books with all those samples in them. They have about the ugliest wallpaper in the world in this place, wallpaper like sores on the wall, wallpaper that looks like it got rained on before you get it home. Even the black kid knows this crap is ugly, but he's trying his damnedest not to show it.

I bestow smiles everywhere. I'm smiling like a queen riding through her kingdom in a carriage, like a little girl who just got a gold and silver dress from a turtledove up in a magic tree. I'm smiling as if Arnold Zoeller himself and of course his lovely wife are looking across my desk at me while I drown, suffocate, stifle, bury their *lovely, intelligent* little Tori in golden words.

I think we got some more yellow in this book here, he says, and fetches down another big fairy-tale book and plunks it between us on the table. His dirty-looking hands turn those big stiff pages. And just as I thought, just as I knew would happen, could happen, would probably happen, but only here in this filthy corner of a filthy department store, this ignorant but helpful lad opens the book to my mother's wallpaper pattern.

I see that fat yellow and those white lines that never touch anything, and I can't help myself, sweat breaks out all over my body, and I groan so horribly that the kid actually backs away from me, lucky for him, because in the next second I'm bending over and throwing up interesting-looking reddish goo all over the floor of the wallpaper department. Oh God, the kid says, oh lady. I groan, and all the rest of the goo comes jumping out of me and splatters down on the carpet. Some older black guy in a clip-on bow tie rushes up toward us but stops short with his mouth hanging open as soon as he sees the mess on the floor. I take my hankie out of my bag and wipe off my mouth. I try to smile at the kid, but my eyes are too blurry. No, I say, I'm fine, I want to buy this wallpaper for my kitchen, this one right here. I turn over the page to see the name of my mother's wallpaper – Zena's wallpaper, too – and discover that this kind of wallpaper is called 'The Thinking Reed'.

You don't have to be religious to have inspirations.

An adventurous state of mind is like a great dwelling-place.

To be lived truly, life must be apprehended with an adventurous state of mind.
But no one on earth can explain the lure of adventure.

Zena's example gave me two tricks that work in my classroom, and the reason they work is that they are not actually tricks!

The first of these comes into play when a particular child is disobedient or inattentive, which, as you can imagine, often occurs in a room full of kindergarten-age children. I deal with these infractions in this fashion. I command the child to come to my desk. (Sometimes, I command two children to come to my desk.) I stare at the child until it begins to squirm. Sometimes it blushes or trembles. I await the physical signs of shame or discomfort. Then I pronounce the child's name. 'Tori,' I say, if the child is Tori. Its little eyes invariably fasten upon mine at this instant. 'Tori,' I say, 'you know that what you did is wrong, don't you?' Ninety-nine times out of a hundred, the child nods its head. 'And you will never do that wrong thing again, will you?' Most often the child can speak to say *No*. 'Well, you'd better not,' I say, and then I lean forward until the little child can see nothing except my enormous, inflamed face. Then in a guttural, lethal, rumble-whisper, I utter, 'OR ELSE.' When I say 'OR ELSE,' I am very emphatic. I am so very emphatic that I feel my eyes change shape. I am thinking of Zena and the time she told me that weeping on my mother's grave wouldn't make a glorious wonderful tree grow there, it would just drown my mother in mud.

The attractiveness of teaching is that it is adventurous, as adventurous as life.

* * *

My mother did not drown in mud. She died some other way. She fell down in the middle of the downstairs parlor, the parlor where Zena sat on her visits. Zena was just another lady then, and on her visits, her 'social calls', she sat on the best antique chair and held her hands in her lap like the most modest, innocent little lady ever born. She was half Chinese, Zena, and I knew she was just like bright sharp metal inside of her, metal that could slice you but good. Zena was very adventurous, but not as adventurous as me. Zena never got out of that town. Of course, all that happened to Zena was that she got old, and everybody left her all alone because she wasn't pretty anymore, she was just an old yellow widow-lady, and then I heard that she died pulling up weeds in her garden. I heard this from two different people. You could say that Zena got drowned in mud, which proves that everything spoken on this earth contains a truth not always apparent at the time.

The other trick I learned from Zena that is not a trick is how to handle a whole class that has decided to act up. These children come from parents who, thinking they know everything, in fact know less than nothing. These children will never see a classical manner demonstrated at home. You must respond in a way that demonstrates your awareness of perfection. You must respond in a way that will bring this awareness to the unruly children, so that they too will possess it.

It can begin in a thousand different ways. Say I am in conference with a single student – say I am delivering the great OR ELSE. Say that my attention has wandered off for a moment, and that I am contemplating the myriad things I contemplate when my attention is wandering free. My mother's grave, watered by my tears. The women with city hair who desired to give me help, but could not, so left to be replaced by others, who in turn were replaced by yet others. How it felt to stand naked and besmeared with my own feces in the front yard, moveless as a statue, the same as all nature, classical. The gradual disappearance of my father, like that of a figure in a cartoon who grows increasingly transparent until total transparency is reached. Zena facedown in her garden, snuffling dirt up into her nostrils. The resemblance of the city women to certain wicked stepsisters in old tales. Also their resemblance to handsome princes in the same tales.

She who hears the tale makes the tale.

Say therefore that I am no longer quite anchored within the classroom, but that I float upward into one, several, or all of these realms. People get what they need from their own minds. Certain places, you can get in there and rest. The classical was a cool period. I am floating within my cool realms. At that moment, one child pulls another's hair. A third child hurls a spitball at the window. Another falls to the floor, emitting pathetic and mechanical cries. Instantly, what was order is misrule. Then I summon up the image of my ferocious female angels and am on my feet before the little beasts even notice that I have left my desk. In a flash, I am beside the light switch. The Toris and Tiffanys, the Joshuas and Jeremys, riot on. I slap down the switch, and the room goes dark.

Result? Silence. Inspired action is destiny.

The children freeze. Their pulses race – veins beat in not a few little blue temples. I say four words. I say, 'Think what this means.' They know what it means. I grow to twice my size with the meaning of these words. I loom over them, and darkness pours out of me. Then I switch the lights back on, and smile at them until they get what they need from my smiling face. These children will never call me Mrs Fat-Asch; these children know that I am the same as all nature.

*   *   *

11

Once upon a time a dying queen sent for her daughter, and when her daughter came to her bedside the queen said, 'I am leaving you, my darling. Say your prayers and be good to your father. Think of me always, and I will always be with you.' Then she died. Every day the little girl watered her mother's grave with her tears. But her heart was dead. You cannot lie about a thing like this. Hatred is the inside part of love. And so her mother became a hard cold stone in her heart. And that was the meaning of the mother, for as long as the little girl lived.

Soon the king took another woman as his wife, and she was most beautiful, with skin the color of gold and eyes as black as jet. She was like a person pretending to be someone else inside another person pretending she couldn't pretend. She understood that reality was contextual. She understood about the condition of the observer.

One day when the king was going out to be among his people, he asked his wife, 'What shall I bring you?'

'A diamond ring,' said the queen. And the king could not tell who was speaking, the person inside pretending to be someone else, or the person outside who could not pretend.

'And you, my daughter,' said the king, 'what would you like?'

'A diamond ring,' said the daughter.

The king smiled and shook his head.

'Then nothing,' said the daughter. 'Nothing at all.'

When the king came home, he presented the queen with a diamond ring in a small blue box, and the queen opened the box and smiled at the ring and said, 'It's a very small diamond, isn't it?' The king's daughter saw him stoop forward, his face whitening, as if he had just lost half his blood. 'I like my small diamond,' said the queen, and the king straightened up, although he still looked white and shaken. He patted his daughter on the head on his way out of the room, but the girl merely looked forward and said nothing, in return for the nothing he had given her.

And that night, when the rest of the palace was asleep, the king's daughter crept to the kitchen and ate half of a loaf of bread and most of a quart of homemade peach ice cream. This was the most delicious food she had ever eaten in her whole entire life. The bread tasted like the sun on the wheatfields, and inside the taste of the sun was the taste of the bursting kernels of the wheat, even of the rich dark crumbly soil that surrounded the roots of the wheat, even of the lives of the bugs and animals that had scurried through the wheat, even of the droppings of those foxes, beetles, and mice. And the homemade peach ice cream tasted overwhelmingly of sugar, cream, and peaches, but also of the bark and meat of the peach tree and the pink feet of the birds that had landed on it, and the sharp, brittle voices of those birds, also of the effort of the hand crank, of the stained, whorly wood of its sides, and of the sweat of the man who had worked it so long. Every taste should be as complicated as possible, and every taste goes up and down at the same time: up past the turtledoves to the far reaches of the sky, so that one final taste in everything is *whiteness*, and down all the way to the mud at the bottom of graves, then to the mud beneath that mud, so that another final taste in everything, in even peach ice cream, is the taste of *blackness*.

From about this time, the king's daughter began to attract undue attention. From the night of the whiteness of turtledoves and the blackness of grave-mud to the final departure of the stepsisters was a period of something like six months.

I thought of myself as a work of art. I caused responses

without being responsible for them. This is the great freedom of art.

They asked questions that enforced the terms of their own answers. *Don't you know we want to help you?* Such a question implies only two possible answers, 1: no, 2: yes. The stepsisters never understood the queen's daughter, therefore the turtledoves pecked out their eyes, first on the one side, then on the other. The correct answer – 3: person to whom question is directed is not the one in need of help – cannot be given. Other correct answers, such as 4: help shall come from other sources, and 5: neither knowledge nor help mean what you imagine they mean, are also forbidden by the form of the question.

Assignment for tonight: make a list of proper but similarly forbidden answers to the question *What is happening to you?* Note: be sure to consider conditions imposed by the use of the word *happening*.

The stepsisters arrived from the city in grand state. They resembled peacocks. The stepsisters accepted Zena's tea, they admired the house, the paintings, the furniture, just as if admiring these things, which everybody admired, meant that they, too, should be admired. The stepsisters wished to remove the king's daughter from this setting, but their power was not so great. Zena would not permit it, nor would the ailing king. (At night, Zena placed her subtle mouth over his sleeping mouth and drew breath straight out of his body.) Zena said that the condition of the king's daughter would prove to be temporary. The child was eating well. She was loved. In time, she would return to herself.

When the figments asked, *What is happening to you?* I could have answered, *Zena is happening to me*. This answer would not have been understood. Neither would the answer, *My mother is happening to me.*

Undue attention came about in the following fashion. Zena knew all about my midnight feasts, but was indifferent to them. Zena knew that each person must acquire what she needs. This is as true for a king's daughter as for any ordinary commoner. But she was ignorant of what I did in the name of art. Misery and anger made me a great artist, though now I am a much greater artist. I think I was twelve. (The age of an artist is of no importance.) Both my mother and Zena were happening to me, and I was happening to them, too. Such is the world of women. My mother, deep in her mud-grave, hated Zena. Zena, second in the king's affections, hated my mother. Speaking from the center of the stone at the center of me, my mother frequently advised me on how to deal with Zena. Silently, speaking with her eyes, Zena advised me on how to deal with my mother. I, who had to deal with both of them, hated them both.

And I possessed an adventurous mind.

The main feature of adventure is that it goes forward into unknown country.
Adventure is filled with a nameless joy.

Alone in my room in the middle of Saturday, on later occasions after my return from school, I removed my clothes and placed them neatly on my bed. (My *canopied* bed.) I had no feelings, apart from a sense of urgency, concerning the actions I was about to perform. Perhaps I experienced a nameless joy at this point. Later on, at the culmination of my self-display, I experienced a nameless joy. And later yet, I experienced the same nameless joy at the conclusions of my various adventures in art. In each of these adventures as in the first, I created responses not traceable within the artwork, but which derived from the conditions, etc., of the audience. Alone and unclothed now in my room, ready to create responses, I squatted on my heels and squeezed out onto the carpet a long cylinder of fecal matter, the residue of, dinner not included, an entire loaf of seven-grain bread, half a box of raisins, a can of peanuts, and a quarter pound of cervelat sausage, all consumed when everyone else was in bed and Zena was presumably leaning over the face of my sleeping father, greedily inhaling his life. I picked up the warm cylinder and felt it melt into my hands. I hastened this process by squeezing my palms together. Then I rubbed my hands over my body. What remained of the stinking cylinder I smeared along the walls of the bedroom. Then I wiped my hands on the carpet. (The *white* carpet.) My preparations concluded, I moved regally through the corridors until I reached the front door and let myself out.

I have worked as a certified grade-school teacher in three states. My record is spotless. I never left a school except by my own choice. When tragedies came to my charges or their parents, I invariably sent sympathetic notes, joined volunteer groups to search for bodies, attended funerals, etc., etc. Every teacher eventually becomes familiar with these unfortunate duties.

Outside, there was all the world, at least all of the estate, from which to choose. Two lines from Edna St Vincent Millay best express my state of mind at this moment: *The world stands out on either side / No wider than the heart is wide*. I well remember the much-admired figure of Dave

Garroway quoting these lovely words on his Sunday-afternoon television program, and I pass along this beautiful sentiment to each fresh class of kindergartners. They must start somewhere, and at other moments in their year with me they will have the opportunity to learn that nature never gives you a chance to rest. Every animal on earth is hungry.

Turning my back on the fields of grazing cows and sheep, ignoring the hills beyond, hills seething with coyotes, wildcats, and mountain lions, I moved with stately tread through the military rows of fruit trees and, with papery apple and peach blossoms adhering to my bare feet, passed into the expanse of the grass meadow where grew the great hazel tree. Had the meadow been recently mown, long green stalks the width of caterpillars leapt up from the ground to festoon my legs. (I often stretched out full length and rolled in the freshly mown grass meadow.) And then, at the crest of the hill that marked the end of the meadow, I arrived at my destination. Below me lay the road to the unknown towns and cities in which I hoped one day to find my complicated destiny. Above me stood the hazel tree.

I have always known that I could save myself by looking into my own mind.

I stood above the road on the crest of the hill and raised my arms. When I looked into my mind I saw two distinct and necessary states, one that of the white line, the other that of the female angels, akin to the turtledoves.

The white line existed in a calm rapture of separation, touching neither sky nor meadow but suspended in the space between. The white line was silence, isolation, classicism. This state is one half of what is necessary in

17

order to achieve the freedom of art, and it is called the Thinking Reed.

The angels and turtledoves existed in a rapture of power, activity, and rage. They were absolute whiteness and absolute blackness, gratification and gratification's handmaiden, revenge. The angels and turtledoves came streaming up out of my body and soared from the tips of my fingers into the sky, and when they returned they brought golden and silver dresses, diamond rings, and emerald tiaras.

I saw the figments slicing off their own toes, sawing off their heels, and stepping into shoes already slippery with blood. The figments were trying to smile, they were trying to stand up straight. They were like children before an angry teacher, a teacher transported by a righteous anger. Girls like the figments never did understand that what they needed, they must get from their own minds. Lacking this understanding, they tottered along, pretending that they were not mutilated, pretending that blood did not pour from their shoes, back to their pretend houses and pretend princes. The nameless joy distinguished every part of this process.

Lately, within the past twenty-four hours, a child has been lost.

A lost child lies deep within the ashes, her hands and feet mutilated, her face destroyed by fire. She has partaken of the great adventure, and now she is the same as all nature.

At night, I see the handsome, distracted, still hopeful parents on our local news programs. Arnold and Kathi, he as handsome as a prince, she as lovely as one of the figments, still have no idea of what has actually happened to them – they lived their whole lives in utter abyssal ignorance – they think of hope as an essential component of the universe. They think that other people, the people paid to perform this function, will conspire to satisfy their needs.

A child has been lost. Now her photograph appears each day on the front page of our sturdy little tabloid-style newspaper, beaming out with luminous ignorance beside the columns of print describing a sudden disappearance after the weekly Sunday school class at St-Mary-in-the-Forest's Episcopal church, the deepening fears of the concerned parents, the limitless charm of the girl herself, the searches of nearby video parlors and shopping malls, the draggings of two adjacent ponds, the slow, painstaking inspections of the neighboring woods, fields, farms, and outbuildings, the shock of the child's particularly well-off and socially prominent relatives, godparents included.

A particular child has been lost. A certain combination of variously shaded blond hair and eyes the blue of early summer sky seen through a haze of cirrus clouds, of an endearingly puffy upper lip and a recurring smudge, like that left on corrasable bond typing paper by an unclean eraser, on the left side of the mouth, of an unaffected shyness and an occasional brittle arrogance destined soon to overshadow more attractive traits will never again be seen, not by parents, friends, teachers, or the passing strangers once given to spontaneous tributes to the child's beauty.

A child of her time has been lost. Of no interest to our local newspaper, unknown to the Sunday school classes at St-Mary-in-the-Forest, were this moppet's obsession with the dolls Exercise Barbie and Malibu Barbie, her fanatical attachment to My Little Ponies Glory and AppleJacks, her insistence on introducing during classtime observations upon the cartoon family named Simpson, and her precocious fascination with the music television channel, especially the 'videos' featuring the groups Kris Kross and Boyz II Men. She was once observed holding hands with James Halliwell, a first-grade boy. Once, just before naptime, she turned upon a pudgy, unpopular girl of protosadistic tendencies named Deborah Monk and hissed, 'Debbie, I hate to tell you this, but you *suck*.'

A child of certain limitations has been lost. She could never learn to tie her cute but oddly blunt-looking size 1 running shoes and eventually had to become resigned to the sort fastened with Velcro straps. When combing her multishaded blond hair with her fingers, she would invariably miss a cobwebby patch located two inches aft of her left ear. Her reading skills were somewhat, though not seriously, below average. She could recognize her name, when spelled out in separate capitals, with narcissistic glee; yet all other words, save *and* and *the*, turned beneath her impatient gaze into random, Sanskrit-like squiggles and uprights. (This would soon have corrected itself.) She could recite the alphabet all in a rush, by rote, but when questioned was incapable of remembering if *O* came before or after *S*. I doubt that she would have been capable of mastering long division during the appropriate academic term.

Across the wide, filmy screen of her eyes would now and then cross a haze of indefinable confusion. In a child of more finely tuned sensibilities, this momentary slippage might have suggested a sudden sense of loss, even perhaps a premonition of the loss to come. In her case, I imagine the expression was due to the transition from the world of complete unconsciousness (Barbie and My Little Ponies) to a more fully socialized state (Kris Kross). Introspection would have come only late in life, after long exposure to experiences of the kind from which her parents most wished to shelter her.

An irreplaceable child has been lost. What was once in the land of the Thinking Reed has been forever removed, like others before it, like all others in time, to turtle-dove territory. This fact is borne home on a daily basis. Should some informed anonymous observer report that the child is all right, that nothing is happening to her, the comforting message would be misunderstood as the prelude to a demand for ransom. The reason for this is that no human life can ever be truly substituted for another. The increasingly despairing parents cannot create or otherwise acquire a living replica, though they are certainly capable of reproducing again, should they stay married long enough to do so. The children in the lost one's class are reported to suffer nightmares and recurrent enuresis. In class, they exhibit lassitude, wariness, a new unwillingness to respond, like the unwillingness of the very old. At a schoolwide assembly where the little ones sat right up in front, nearly every one expressed the desire for the missing one to return. Letters and cards to the lost one now form two large, untidy stacks in the principal's office and, with parental appeals to the abductor or abductors broadcast every night, it is felt that the school will accumulate a third stack before these tributes are offered to the distraught parents.

Works of art generate responses not directly traceable to the work itself. Helplessness, grief, and sorrow may exist simultaneously alongside aggressiveness, hostility, anger, or even serenity and relief. The more profound and subtle the work, the more intense and long-lasting the responses it evokes.

Deep, deep in her muddy grave, the queen and mother felt the tears of her lost daughter. *All will pass*. In the form of a turtledove, she rose from grave-darkness and ascended into the great arms of a hazel tree. *All will change*. From the

21

topmost branch, the turtledove sang out her everlasting message. *All is hers, who will seek what is true.* 'What is true?' cried the daughter, looking dazzled up. *All will pass, all will change, all is yours,* sang the turtledove.

In a recent private conference with the principal, I announced my decision to move to another section of the country after the semester's end.

The principal is a kindhearted, limited man still loyal, one might say rigidly loyal, to the values he absorbed from popular music at the end of the nineteen sixties, and he has never quite been able to conceal the unease I arouse within him. Yet he is aware of the respect I command within every quarter of his school, and he has seen former kindergartners of mine, now freshmen in our trisuburban high school, return to my classroom and inform the awed children seated before them that Mrs Asch placed them on the right path, that Mrs Asch's lessons would be responsible for seeing them successfully through high school and on to college.

Virtually unable to contain the conflict of feelings my announcement brought to birth within him, the principal assured me that he would that very night compose a letter of recommendation certain to gain me a post at any elementary school, public or private, of my choosing.

After thanking him, I replied, 'I do not request this kindness of you, but neither will I refuse it.'

The principal leaned back in his chair and gazed at me, not unkindly, through his granny glasses. His right hand rose like a turtledove to caress his graying beard, but ceased halfway in its flight, and returned to his lap. Then he lifted both hands to the surface of his desk and intertwined the fingers, still gazing quizzically at me.

'Are you all right?' he inquired.

'Define your terms,' I said. 'If you mean, am I in

reasonable health, enjoying physical and mental stability, satisfied with my work, then the answer is yes, I am all right.'

'You've done a wonderful job dealing with Tori's disappearance,' he said. 'But I can't help but wonder if all of that has played a part in your decision.'

'My decisions make themselves,' I said. 'All will pass, all will change. I am a serene person.'

He promised to get the letter of recommendation to me by lunchtime the next day, and as I knew he would, he kept his promise. Despite my serious reservations about his methods, attitude, and ideology – despite my virtual certainty that he will be unceremoniously forced from his job within the next year – I cannot refrain from wishing the poor fellow well.

Isn't It Romantic?

N steered the rented Peugeot through the opening in the wall and parked beside the entrance of the auberge. Beyond the old stable doors to his left, a dark-haired girl in a bright blue dress hoisted a flour sack off the floor. She dropped it on the counter in front of her and ripped it open. When he got out of the car, the girl gave him a flat, indifferent glance before she dipped into the bag and smeared a handful of flour across a cutting board. Far up in the chill gray air, thick clouds slowly moved across the sky. To the south, smoky clouds snagged on trees and clung to the slopes of the mountains. N took his carry-on bag and the black laptop satchel from the trunk of the Peugeot, pushed down the lid, and looked through the kitchen doors. The girl in the blue dress raised a cleaver and slammed it down onto a plucked, headless chicken. N pulled out the handle of the carry-on and rolled it behind him to the glass enclosure of the entrance.

He moved through and passed beneath the arch into the narrow, unlighted lobby. A long table stacked with brochures stood against the far wall. On the other side, wide doors opened into a dining room with four lines of joined tables covered with red-checkered tablecloths and set for dinner. A blackened hearth containing two metal grilles took up the back wall of the dining room. On the left side of the hearth, male voices filtered through a door topped with a glowing stained-glass panel.

N moved past the dining room to a counter and an untidy little office – a desk and table heaped with record books and loose papers, a worn armchair. Keys linked to numbered metal squares hung from numbered hooks. A clock beside a poster advertising Ossau-Iraty cheese said that the time was five-thirty, forty-five minutes later than he had been expected. *'Bonjour. Monsieur? Madame?'* No one answered. N went to the staircase to the left of the office. Four steps down, a corridor led past two doors with circular windows at eye level, like the doors into the kitchens of diners in his long-ago youth. Opposite were doors numbered 101, 102, 103. A wider section of staircase ascended to a landing and reversed to continue to the next floor. *'Bonjour.'* His voice reverberated in the stairwell. He caught a brief, vivid trace of old sweat and unwashed flesh.

Leaving the carry-on at the counter, he carried the satchel to the dining room doors. Someone beyond barked out a phrase, others laughed. N walked down the rows of tables and approached the door with the stained-glass panel. He knocked twice, then pushed the door open.

Empty tables fanned out from a door onto the parking lot. A man in a rumpled tweed jacket and with the face of a dissolute academic; a sallow, hound-faced man in a lumpy blue running suit; and a plump, bald bartender glanced at him and then leaned forward to continue their conversation in lowered voices. N put his satchel on the bar and took a stool. The bartender eyed him and slowly came up the bar, eyebrows raised.

In French, N said, 'Excuse me, sir, but there is no one at the desk.'

The man extended his hand across the bar. He glanced back at his staring friends, then smiled mirthlessly at N. 'Mr Cash? We had been told to expect you earlier.'

N shook his limp hand. 'I had trouble driving down from Pau.'

'Car trouble?'

'No, finding the road out of Oloron,' N said. He had driven twice through the southern end of the old city, guessing at the exits to be taken out of the roundabouts, until a toothless ancient at a crosswalk had responded to his shout of 'Montory?' by pointing toward the highway.

'Oloron is not helpful to people trying to find these little towns.' The innkeeper looked over his shoulder and repeated the remark. His friends were nearing the stage of drunkenness where they would be able to drive more confidently than they could walk.

The hound-faced man in the running suit said, 'In Oloron, if you ask *"Where* is Montory?" they answer, *"What* is Montory?"'

'All right,' said his friend. 'What is it?'

The innkeeper turned back to N. 'Are your bags in your car?'

N took his satchel off the bar. 'It's in front of the counter.'

The innkeeper ducked out and led N into the dining room. Like dogs, the other two trailed after them. 'You speak French very well, Mr Cash. I would say that it is not typically American to have an excellent French accent. You live in Paris, perhaps?'

'Thank you,' N said. 'I live in New York.' This was technically true. In an average year, N spent more time in his Upper East Side apartment than he did in his lodge in Gstaad. During the past two years, which had not been average, he had lived primarily in hotel rooms in San Salvador, Managua, Houston, Prague, Bonn, Tel Aviv, and Singapore.

'But you have spent perhaps a week in Paris?'

'I was there a couple of days,' N said.

Behind him, one of the men said, 'Paris is under Japanese occupation. I hear they serve raw fish instead of *cervelas* at the Brasserie Lipp.'

They came out into the lobby. N and the innkeeper went to the counter, and the two other men pretended to be interested in the tourist brochures.

'How many nights do you spend with us? Two, was it, or three?'

'Probably two,' said N, knowing that these details had already been arranged.

'Will you join us for dinner tonight?'

'I am sorry to say that I cannot.'

Momentary displeasure surfaced in the innkeeper's face. He waved toward his dining room and declared, 'Join us tomorrow for our roasted mutton, but you must reserve at least an hour in advance. Do you expect to be out in the evenings?'

'I do.'

'We lock the doors at eleven. There is a bell, but as I have no desire to leave my bed to answer it, I prefer you to use the keypad at the entrance. Punch twenty-three forty-five to open the door. Easy, right? Twenty-three forty-five. Then go behind the counter and pick up your key. On going out again the next day, leave it on the counter, and it will be replaced on the rack. What brings you to the Basque country, Mr Cash?'

'A combination of business and pleasure.'

'Your business is . . . ?'

'I write travel articles,' N said. 'This is a beautiful part of the world.'

'You have been to the Basque country before?'

N blinked, nudged by a memory that refused to surface. 'I'm not sure. In my kind of work, you visit too many places. I might have been here a long time ago.'

'We opened in 1961, but we've expanded since then.' He slapped the key and its metal plate down on the counter.

N put his cases on the bed, opened the shutters, and leaned out of the window, as if looking for the memory that had escaped him. The road sloped past the auberge and continued uphill through the tiny center of the village. On the covered terrace of the cement-block building directly opposite, a woman in a sweater sat behind a cash register at a display case filled with what a sign called 'regional delicacies'. Beyond, green fields stretched out toward the wooded mountains. At almost exactly the point where someone would stop entering Montory and start leaving it, the red enclosure of the telephone booth he had been told to use stood against a gray stone wall.

The innkeeper's friends staggered into the parking lot and left in a mud-spattered old Renault. A delivery truck with the word *Comet* stenciled on a side panel pulled in and came to a halt in front of the old stable doors. A man in a blue work suit climbed out, opened the back of the truck, pulled down a burlap sack from a neat pile, and set it down inside the kitchen. A blond woman in her fifties wearing a white apron emerged from the interior and tugged out the next sack. She wobbled backward beneath its weight, recovered, and carried it inside. The girl in the blue dress sauntered into view and leaned against the doorway a foot or two from where the delivery man was heaving his second sack onto the first. Brown dust puffed out from between the sacks. As the man straightened up, he gave her a look of straightforward appraisal. The dress was stretched tight across her breasts and hips, and her face had a coarse, vibrant prettiness entirely at odds with the bored contempt of her expression. She responded to his greeting with a few grudging words. The woman in the apron came out again and pointed to the sacks on the floor. The girl shrugged. The delivery man executed a mocking bow. The girl bent down, slid her forearms beneath the sacks, lifted them waist-high, and carried them deeper into the kitchen.

Impressed, N turned around and took in yellowish-white walls, a double bed that would prove too short, an old television set, a nightstand with a reading lamp, and a rotary phone. Framed embroidery above the bed advised him that eating well would lead to a long life. He pulled the carry-on toward him and began to hang up his clothes, meticulously refolding the sheets of tissue with which he had protected his suits and jackets.

A short time later, he came out into the parking lot holding the computer bag. Visible through the opening, the girl in the blue dress and another woman in her twenties, with stiff fair hair fanning out above a puggish face, a watermelon belly, and enormous thighs bulging from her shorts, were cutting up greens on the chopping block with fast, short downstrokes of their knives. The girl lifted her head and gazed at him. He said '*Bon soir.*' Her smile put a youthful bounce in his stride.

The telephone booth stood at the intersection of the road passing through the village and another that dipped downhill and flattened out across the fields on its way deeper into the Pyrenees. N pushed tokens into the slot and dialed a number in Paris. When the number rang twice, he hung up. Several minutes later, the telephone trilled, and he picked up the receiver.

An American voice said, 'So we had a little hang-up, did we?'

'Took me a while to find the place,' he said.

'You needum Injun guide, findum trail heap fast.' The contact frequently pretended to be an American Indian. 'Get the package all right?'

'Yes,' N said. 'It's funny, but I have the feeling I was here before.'

'You've been everywhere, old buddy. You're a grand old man. You're a star.'

'In his last performance.'

'Written in stone. Straight from Big Chief.'

'If I get any trouble, I can cause a lot more.'

'Come on,' said the contact. N had a detailed but entirely

speculative image of the man's flat, round face, smudgy glasses, and furzy hair. 'You're our best guy. Don't you think they're grateful? Pretty soon, they're going to have to start using Japanese. *Russians*. Imagine how they feel about that.'

'Why don't you do what you're supposed to do, so I can do what I'm supposed to do?'

N sat outside the *café tabac* on the Place du Marche in Mauléon with a nearly empty demitasse of espresso by his elbow and a first edition of Rudyard Kipling's *Kim* in near-mint condition before him, watching lights go on and off in a building on the other side of the arcaded square. He had used the telephone shower in his room's flimsy bathtub and shaved at the flimsy sink, had dressed in a lightweight wool suit and his raincoat, and, with his laptop case upright on the next chair, he resembled a traveling businessman. The two elderly waiters had retired inside the lighted café, where a few patrons huddled at the bar. During the hour and a half N had been sitting beneath the umbrellas, a provincial French couple had taken a table to devour steak and *pommes frites* while consulting their guidebooks, and a feral-looking boy with long, dirty-blond hair had downed three beers. During a brief rain shower, a lone Japanese man had trotted in, wiped down his cameras and his forehead, and finally managed to communicate his desire for a beef stew and a glass of wine. Alone again, N was beginning to wish that he had eaten more than his simple meal of cheese and bread, but it was too late to place another order. The subject, a retired politician named Daniel Hubert with a local antiques business and a covert sideline in the arms trade, had darkened his shop at the hour N had been told he would do so. A light had gone on in the living room of his apartment on the next floor and then, a few minutes later, in his bedroom suite on the floor above that. This was all according to pattern.

'According to the field team, he's about to move up into the big time,' his contact had said. 'They think it'll be either tonight or tomorrow night. What happens is, he closes up shop and goes upstairs to get ready. You'll see the lights go on as he goes toward his bedroom. If you see a light in the top floor, that's his office, he's making sure everything's in place and ready to go. Paleface tense, Paleface know him moving out of his league. He's got South Americans on one end, ragheads on the other. Once he gets off the phone, he'll go downstairs, leave through the door next to the shop, get in his car. Gray Mercedes four-door with fuck-you plates from being Big Heap Deal in government. He'll go to a restaurant way up in the mountains. He uses three different places, and we never know which one it's going to be. Pick your spot, nice clean job, get back to me later. Then put it to some *mademoiselle* – have yourself a ball.'

'What about the others?'

'Hey, we love the ragheads, you kidding? They're customers. These guys travel with a million in cash, we worship the camel dung they walk on.'

The lights at the top of the house stayed on. A light went on, then off, in the bedroom. With a tremendous roar, a motorcycle raced past. The wild-looking boy who had been at the café glanced at N before leaning sideways and disappearing through the arcade and around the corner. One of the weary waiters appeared beside him, and N placed a bill on the saucer. When he looked back at the building, the office and bedroom lights had been turned off, and the living room lights were on. Then they turned off. N stood up and walked to his car. In a sudden spill of the light from the entry, a trim silver-haired man in a black blazer and gray slacks stepped out beneath the arcade and held the door for a completely unexpected

31

party, a tall blond woman in jeans and a black leather jacket. She went through one of the arches and stood at the passenger door of a long Mercedes while M. Hubert locked the door. Frustrated and angry, N pulled out of his parking spot and waited at the bottom of the square until they had driven away.

They did this more than they ever admitted. One time in four, the field teams left something out. He had to cover for their mistakes and take the fall for any screwups. Now they were going two for two – the team in Singapore had failed to learn that his subject always used two bodyguards, one who traveled in a separate car. When he had raised this point afterward, they had said they were 'working to improve data flow worldwide'. The blond woman was a glitch in the data flow, all right. He traveled three cars behind the Mercedes as it went through a series of right-hand turns on the one-way streets, wishing that his employers permitted the use of cell phones, which they did not. Cell phones were 'porous', they were 'intersectable', even, in the most delightful of these locutions, 'capacity risks'. N wished that one day someone would explain the exact meaning of 'capacity risk'. In order to inform his contact of M. Hubert's playmate, he would have to drive back to the 'location usage device', another charming example of bureaucratese, the pay telephone in Montory. You want to talk capacity risks, how about that?

The Mercedes rolled beneath a streetlamp at the edge of the town and wheeled left to double back. Wonderful, he was looking for a tail. Probably he had caught sight of the field team while they were busily mismanaging the data flow. N hung back as far as he dared, now and then anticipating the subject's next move and speeding ahead on an adjacent street. Finally, the Mercedes continued out of Mauléon and turned east on a three-lane highway.

32

N followed along, speculating about the woman. In spite of her clothes, she looked like a mistress, but would a man bring his mistress to such a meeting? It was barely possible that she represented the South Americans, possible but even less likely that she worked for the buyers. Maybe they were just a lovely couple going out for dinner. Far ahead, the Mercedes's taillights swung left off the highway and began winding into the mountains. They had already disappeared by the time he came to the road. N made the turn, went up to the first bend, and turned off his lights. From then on, it was a matter of trying to stay out of the ditches as he crawled along in the dark, glimpsing the other car's taillights and losing them, seeing the beams of the headlights picking out trees on an upward curve far ahead of him. Some part of what he was doing finally brought back the lost memory.

From inside the telephone booth, he could see the red neon sign, AUBERGE DE L'ÉTABLE, burning above the walled parking lot.

'Tonto waiting,' said the contact.

'I would have appreciated a few words about the girl-friend.'

'White man speak with forked tongue.'

N sighed. 'I waited across from his building. Hubert seemed to be doing a lot of running up and down the stairs, which was explained when he came out with a stunning young lady in a motorcycle jacket. I have to tell you, I hate surprises.'

'Tell me what happened.'

'He dodged all over the place before he felt safe enough to leave Mauléon. I followed him to an auberge way up in the mountains, trying to work out how to handle things if the meeting was on. All of a sudden, there's this variable, and the only way I can let you know about it is to turn around and drive all the way back to this phone, excuse me, this location usage device.'

'That would have been a really terrible idea,' said his contact.

'I waited for them to go into the lot and leave their car, and then I pulled up beside a wall and climbed uphill to a spot where I could watch their table through the glasses. I was trying to figure out how many reports I'd have to file if I included the girl. Remember Singapore? Improvising is no fun anymore.'

'Then what?'

'Then they had dinner. The two of them. Basque soup, roast chicken, salad, no dessert. A bottle of wine. Hubert was trying to jolly her up, but he wasn't getting anywhere. The place was about half full, mainly with local people. Guys in berets playing cards, two foursomes, one table of Japanese guys in golf jackets. God knows how they found out about the place. When they drove out, I followed them back and waited until all the lights went out. In the midst of all this wild activity, I remembered something.'

'Nice. I understand people your age tend to forget.'

'Let me guess. You knew about the girl.'

'Martine is your background resource.'

'Since when do I need a backup?' Seconds ticked by in silence while he struggled with his fury. 'Okay. Fine. I'll tell you what, that's dandy. But Martine does all the paperwork.'

'Let me work on that one. In the meantime, try to remember that we've been mainstreaming for some time now. Martine has been in field operations for about a year, and we decided to give her a shot at learning from the old master.'

'Right,' N said. 'What does Hubert think she is?'

'An expert on raghead psychology. We positioned her so that when he needed someone to help him figure out what these people mean when they say things, there she was. Doctorate in Arab studies from the Sorbonne, two years doing community liaison for an oil company in the Middle East. Hubert was so happy with the way she looks, he put her up in his guest room.'

'And Martine told him that his partners would have him followed.'

'He never laid eyes on you. She's impressed as hell, Kemo sabe. You're her hero.'

'Martine should spend a couple of days with me after we're done,' N said, almost angry enough to mean it. 'Let me advance her education.'

'You?' The contact laughed. 'Forget it, not that it wouldn't be educational for both of you. If you could handle encryption programs, you wouldn't have to use LUDs.'

It took N a moment to figure out that the word was an acronym.

'I hope you realize how much I envy you,' the contact said. 'When you came down the trail, this business was a lot more individual. Guys like you made up the rules on the fly. I was hired because I had an MBA, and I'm grateful to help rationalize our industry, move it into the twenty-first century, but even now, when you have to dot every *i* and cross every *t*, fieldwork seems completely romantic to me. The years you've been out there, the things you did, you're like Wyatt Earp. Paleface, I was honored to be assigned your divisional region controller.'

'My what?'

'Your contact person.'

'One of us is in the wrong line of work,' N said.

'It was a pleasure, riding through the Old West with you.'

'To hell with you, too,' N said, but the line was already dead.

*   *   *

Thirty-odd years ago, an old-timer called Sullivan had begun to get a little loose. A long time before that, he had been in the OSS and then the CIA, and he still had that wide-shouldered linebacker look and he still wore a dark suit and a white shirt every day, but his gut drooped over his belt and the booze had softened his face. His real name wasn't Sullivan and he was of Scandinavian, not Irish, descent, with thick coarse blond hair going gray, an almost lipless mouth, and blue eyes so pale they seemed bleached. N had spent a month in Oslo and another in Stockholm, and in both places he had seen a lot of Sullivans. What he had remembered during the drive into the mountains was what had brought him to the French Pyrenees all that time ago – Sullivan.

He had been in the trade for almost a year, and his first assignments had gone well. In a makeshift office in a San Fernando Valley strip mall, a nameless man with a taut face and an aggressive crew cut had informed him that he was getting a golden opportunity. He was to fly to Paris, transfer to Bordeaux, meet a legend named Sullivan, and drive to southwest France with him. What Sullivan could teach him in a week would take years to learn on his own. The job, Sullivan's last, his swan song, was nothing the older man could not handle by himself. So why include N? Simple – Sullivan. He seemed to be losing his edge; he wasn't taking care of the loose ends as well as he once had. So while N absorbed the old master's lessons, he would also be his backstop, make sure everything went smoothly, and provide nightly reports. If Sullivan was going to blow it, he would be pulled out, last job or not. The only problem, said the man with the crew cut, was that Sullivan would undoubtedly hate his guts.

And to begin with, he had. Sullivan had barely spoken on the drive down from Bordeaux. The only remark he made as they came up into the mountains was that Basques were so crazy they thought they were the sole survivors of Atlantis. He had dropped N off at the hotel in Tardets, where he had a room and a waiting car, with the suggestion that he skip coming over for dinner that night. N had spoken of their instructions, of his own desire to be briefed. 'Fine, I give up, you're a Boy Scout,' Sullivan had snarled, and sped off to his own lodgings, which were, N remembered once more as the Peugeot rolled downhill from the telephone booth, the Auberge de l'Étable.

Though the inn had been roughly half its present size, the dining room was the same massive hall. Sullivan had insisted on a table near the lobby and well apart from the couples who sat near the haunch of mutton blackening over the open fire. Alternately glaring at him and avoiding his glance, Sullivan drank six marcs before dinner and in French far superior to the young N's complained about the absence of vodka. In Germany you could get vodka, in England you could get vodka, in Sweden and Denmark and Norway and even in miserable Iceland you could get vodka, but in France nobody outside of Paris had even heard of the stuff. When their mutton came, he ordered two bottles of Bordeaux and flirted with the waitress. The waitress flirted back. Without any direct statements, they arranged an assignation. Sullivan was a world-class womanizer. Either the certainty that the waitress would be in his bed later that night or the alcohol loosened him up. He asked a few questions, endured the answers, told stories that made young N's jaw drop like a rube's. Amused, Sullivan recounted seductions behind enemy lines, hair-raising tales of OSS operations, impersonations of foreign dignitaries, bloodbaths in presidential palaces. He spoke six languages fluently, three others nearly as well, and played passable cello. 'Truth is, I'm a pirate,' he said, 'and no matter how useful pirates might be, they're going out of style. I don't fill out forms or itemize my expenses or give a shit about reprimands. They let me get away with doing things my way because it almost always works better than theirs, but every now and again, I make our little buddies sweat through their custom-made shirts. Which brings us to you, right? My last job, and I get a backup? Give me a break – you're watching me. They told you to report back every single night.'

'They also said you'd give me the best education in the world,' N told him.

'Christ, kid, you must be pretty good if they want *me* to polish your rough edges.' He swallowed wine and smiled across the table in what even the young N had sensed as a change of atmosphere. 'Was there something else they wanted you to do?'

'Polishing my rough edges isn't enough?' asked the suddenly uncertain young N.

Sullivan had stared at him for a time, not at all drunkenly but in a cold curious measuring fashion. N had known only that this scrutiny made him feel wary and exposed. Then Sullivan relaxed and explained what he was going to do and how he planned to do it.

Everything had gone well – better than well, superbly. Sullivan had taken at least a half dozen steps that would have unnerved the crew-cut man in the strip mall, but each one, N took pains to make clear during his reports, had saved time, increased effectiveness, helped bring about a satisfactory conclusion. On the final day, N had called Sullivan to see when he was to be picked up. 'Change of plans,' Sullivan had said. 'You can drive yourself to the airport. I'm spending one more night with the descendants of the Atlanteans.' He wanted a farewell romp with the waitress. 'Then back to the civilian life. I own thirty acres outside Houston, think I'll put up a mansion in the shape of the Alamo but a hundred times bigger, get a state-of-the-art music room, fly in the best cellist I can get for weekly lessons, hire a great chef, rotate the ladies in and out. And I want to learn Chinese. Only great language I don't already know.'

On a rare visit to headquarters some months later, N had greeted the man from the strip mall as he carried stacks of files out of a windowless office into a windowless corridor. The man was wearing a small, tight bow tie, and his crew cut had been cropped to stubble. It took him a couple of beats to place N. 'Los Angeles.' He pronounced it with a hard *g*. 'Sure. That was good work. Typical Sullivan. Hairy, but great results. The guy never came back from France, you know.'

'Don't tell me he married the waitress,' N had said.

'Died there. Killed himself, in fact. Couldn't take the idea of retirement, that's what I think. A lot of these Billy the Kid-type guys, they fold their own hands when they get to the end of the road.'

Over the years, N now and again had remarked to himself the elemental truth that observation was mostly interpretation. Nobody wanted to admit it, but it was true anyhow. If you denied interpretation – which consisted of no more than thinking about two things, what you had observed and why you had observed it – your denial was an interpretation, too. In the midst of feeling more and more like Sullivan, that is, resistant to absurd nomenclature and the ever-increasing paperwork necessitated by 'mainstreaming', he had never considered that 'mainstreaming' included placing women in positions formerly occupied entirely by men. So now he had a female backup: but the question was, what would the lady have done if M. Hubert had noticed that N was following him? Now there, that was a matter for interpretation.

A matter N had sometimes weighed over the years, at those rare times when it returned to him, was the question Sullivan had put to him before he relaxed. *Was there something else they wanted you to do?*

In institutions, patterns had longer lives than employees.

The parking lot was three-quarters full. Hoping that he still might be able to get something to eat, N looked at the old stable doors as he took a spot against the side wall. They were closed, and the dining room windows were dark. He carried the satchel to the entrance and punched the numerical code into the keypad. The glass door clicked open. To the side of the empty lobby, the dining room was locked. His hunger would have to wait until morning. In the low light burning behind the counter, his key dangled from the rack amid rows of empty hooks. He raised the panel, moved past the desk to get the key, and, with a small shock like the jab of a pin, realized that of the thousands of resource personnel, information managers, computer jocks, divisional region controllers, field operatives, and the rest, only he would remember Sullivan.

The switch beside the stairs turned on the lights for a carefully timed period which allowed him to reach the second floor and press another switch. A sour, acrid odor he had noticed as soon as he entered the staircase intensified on the second floor and worsened as he approached his room. It was like the smell of rot, of burning chemicals, of a dead animal festering on a pile of weeds. Rank and physical, the stench stung his eyes and burrowed into his nose. Almost gasping, N shoved the key into his lock and escaped into his room to discover that the stink pursued him there. He closed the door and knelt beside the bed to unzip his laptop satchel. Then he recognized the smell. It was a colossal case of body odor, the full-strength version of what he had noticed six hours earlier. 'Unbelievable,' he said aloud. In seconds he had opened the shutters and pushed up the window. Someone who had not bathed in months, someone who reeked like a diseased muskrat, had come into his room while he had been scrambling around on a mountain. N began checking the room. He opened the drawers in the desk, examined the television set, and was moving toward the closet when he noticed a package wrapped in butcher paper on the bedside table. He bent over it, moved it gingerly from side to side, and finally picked it up. The unmistakable odors of roast lamb and garlic penetrated both the wrapper and the fading stench.

He tore open the wrapper. A handwritten sheet of lined paper had been folded over another, transparent wrapper containing a thick sandwich of coarse brown bread, sliced lamb, and roast peppers. In an old-fashioned girlish hand and colloquial French, the note read: *I'm hoping you don't mind that I made this for you. You were gone all evening and maybe you don't know how early everything closes in this region. So in case you come back hungry, please enjoy this sandwich with my compliments. Albertine.*

N fell back on the bed, laughing.

The loud bells in the tower of the Montory church that had announced the hour throughout the night repeated the pious uproar that had forced him out of bed. Ignoring both mass and the Sabbath, the overweight young woman was scrubbing the tiled floor in the dining room. N nodded at her as he turned to go down into the lounge, and she struggled to her feet, peeled off a pair of transparent plastic gloves, and threw them splatting onto the wet floor to hurry after him.

Three Japanese men dressed for golf occupied the last of the tables laid with white paper cloths, china, and utensils. N wondered if the innkeeper's drunken friend might have been right about the Brasserie Lipp serving sushi instead of Alsatian food, and then recognized them as the men he had seen at the auberge in the mountains. They were redistributing their portion of the world's wealth on a boys-only tour of France. What he was doing was not very different. He sat at the table nearest the door, and the young woman waddled in behind him. *Café au lait. Croissants et confiture. Jus de l'orange.* Before she could leave, he added, 'Please thank Albertine for the sandwich she brought to my room. And tell her, please, that I would like to thank her for her thoughtfulness myself.'

The dread possibility that she herself was Albertine vanished before her knowing smile. She departed. The Japanese men smoked in silence over the crumbs of their breakfast. Sullivan, N thought for the seventh or eighth time, also had been assigned a backup on his last job. Had he ever really believed that the old pirate had killed himself? Well, yes, for a time. In N's mid-twenties, Sullivan had seemed a romantic survivor, unadaptable to civilian tedium. Could a man with such a life behind him be content with weekly cello lessons, a succession of good meals, and the comforts of women? Now that he was past Sullivan's age and had prepared his own satisfactions – skiing in the Swiss Alps, season tickets to Knicks and Yankees games, collecting first editions of Kipling and T. E. Lawrence, the comforts of women – he was in no doubt of the answer.

Was there something else they wanted you to do?

No, there had not been, for Sullivan would have seen the evidence on his face as soon as he had produced his question. Someone else, an undisclosed backup of N's own, had done the job for them. N sipped his coffee and smeared marmalade on his croissants. With the entire day before him, he had more than enough time to work out the details of a plan already forming in his head. N smiled at the Japanese gentlemen as they filed out of the breakfast room. He had time enough even to arrange a bonus Sullivan himself would have applauded.

Back in his room, he pulled a chair up to a corner of the window where he could watch the parking lot and the road without being seen and sat down with his book in his lap. Rain pelted down onto the half-empty parking lot. Across the road, the innkeeper stood in the shelter of the terrace with his arms wrapped around his fat chest, talking to the woman in charge of the display case stocked with jars of honey, bottles of Jurançon wine, and *fromage de brebis*. He looked glumly businesslike. The three Japanese, who had evidently gone out for a rainy stroll, came walking down from the center of the village and turned into the lot. The sight of them seemed to deepen the innkeeper's gloom. Wordlessly, they climbed into a red Renault L'Espace and took off. An aged Frenchman emerged and made an elaborate business of folding his yellow raincoat onto the passenger seat of his Deux Chevaux before driving off. Two cars went by without stopping. The cold rain slackened and stopped, leaving shining puddles on the asphalt below. N opened *Kim* at random and read a familiar paragraph.

He looked up to see a long gray tour bus pulling up before the building on the other side of the road. The innkeeper dropped his arms, muttered something to the woman at the register, and put on his professional smile. White-haired men with sloping stomachs and women in varying stages of disrepair filed out of the bus and stared uncertainly around them. The giant bells set off another clanging tumult. The innkeeper jumped down from the terrace, shook a few hands, and led the first of the tourists across the road. It was Sunday, and they had arrived for the Mutton Brunch. When they were heavy and dull with food and wine, they would be invited to purchase regional delicacies.

Over the next hour, the only car to pull into the lot was a Saab with German plates, which disgorged two obese parents and three blond teenagers, eerily slim and androgynous. The teenagers bickered over a mound of knapsacks and duffel bags before sulking into the auberge. The muddy Renault turned in to park in front of the bar. Dressed in white shirts, red scarves, and berets, the innkeeper's two friends climbed out. The hound-faced man was holding a tambourine, and the other retrieved a wide-bodied guitar from the back seat. They carried their instruments into the bar.

N slipped his book into the satchel and ran a comb through his hair and straightened his tie before leaving the room. Downstairs, the fire in the dining room had burned low, and the sheep turning on the grill had been carved down to gristle and bone. The bus tourists companionably occupied the first three rows of tables. The German family sat alone in the last row. One of the children yawned and exposed the shiny metal ball of a tongue piercing. Like water buffalos, the parents stared massively, unblinkingly out into the room, digesting rather than seeing. The two men in Basque dress entered from the bar and moved halfway down the aisle between the first two rows of tables. Without preamble, one of them struck an out-of-tune chord on his guitar. The other began to sing in a sweet, wavering tenor. The teenagers put their sleek heads on the table. Everyone else complacently attended to the music, which migrated toward a nostalgic sequence and resolved into 'I Hear a Rhapsody', performed with French lyrics.

Outside, N could see no one at the kitchen counter. The air felt fresh and cool, and battalions of flinty clouds marched across the low sky. He moved nearer. *'Pardon? Allô?'* A rustle of female voices came from within, and he took another step forward. Decisive footsteps resounded on a wooden floor. Abruptly, the older woman appeared in the doorway. She gave him a dark, unreadable look and retreated. A muffled giggle vanished beneath applause from the dining room. Softer footsteps approached, and the girl in the bright blue dress swayed into view. She leaned a hip against the door frame, successfully maintaining an expression of indifferent boredom.

'I wish I had that swing in my backyard,' he said.

'*Quoi?*'

In French, he said, 'A stupid thing we used to say when I was a kid. Thank you for making that sandwich and bringing it to my room.' Ten feet away in the brisk air, N caught rank, successive waves of the odor flowing from her and wondered how the other women tolerated it.

'Nadine said you thanked me.'

'I wanted to do it in person. It is important, don't you agree, to do things in person?'

'I suppose important things should be done in person.'

'You were thoughtful to notice that I was not here for dinner.'

Her shrug shifted her body within the tight confines of the dress. 'It is just good sense. Our guests should not go hungry. A big man like you has a large appetite.'

'Can you imagine, I will be out late tonight, too?'

Her mouth curled in a smile. 'Does that mean you'd like another sandwich?'

'I'd love one.' For the sake of pleasures to come, he took two more steps into her stench and lowered his voice. 'We could split it. And you could bring a bottle of wine. I'll have something to celebrate.'

She glanced at his satchel. 'You finished what you are writing?'

She had questioned her boss about him.

'It'll be finished by tonight.'

'I never met a writer before. It must be an interesting way of life. Romantic.'

'You have no idea,' he said. 'Let me tell you something. Last year I was writing a piece in Bora Bora, and I talked to a young woman a bit like you, beautiful dark hair and eyes. Before she came to my room, she must have bathed in something special, because she smelled like moonlight and flowers. She looked like a queen.'

'I can look more like a queen than anyone in Bora Bora.'

'I wouldn't be surprised.'

She lowered her eyes and swayed back into the kitchen.

After parking in a side street off the Place du Marche, N strolled through shops, leafed through *Kim* and sipped *menthe à l'eau* at cafés, watched pedestrians and traffic move through the ancient town. In a shop called Basque Espadrilles he saw the Japanese from the auberge swapping their golf caps for yellow and green berets that made them look like characters in a comic film. They paid no attention to his smile. Caucasians all looked alike. Passing the extensive terrace of what seemed to be the best restaurant in town, he observed elegant M. Daniel Hubert and adventurous Martine in intense discussion over espresso. M. Hubert's black silk suit and black silk T-shirt handsomely set off his silver hair, and Martine's loose white sweater, short tan skirt, and oversized glasses made her look as if she had come from delivering a lecture. Here the reason for his observation was no mystery, but how might it be interpreted? N backed away from the terrace, entered the restaurant by its front door, and came outside behind them. He drank mineral water at a distant table and let their gestures, their moves and countermoves, sink into him. After a sober consideration of his position in the food chain, M. Hubert was getting cold feet. Smiling, intelligent, professorial, above all desirable Martine was keeping him in the game. What can we conclude, knowing what we know? We can, we must conclude that the object of N's assigned task was not poor M. Hubert himself but the effect the task would have upon his buyers. N pressed button A, alarmingly closing a particular door. Another door opened. All parties profited, not counting the winkled buyers and not counting N, who no longer counted. A series of mechanical operations guided money down a specific chute into a specific pocket, that was all. It was never anything else. Not even now.

N trailed along as they walked back to M. Hubert's building, and his wandering gaze sought the other, the hidden player, he whose existence was likely as unknown to Martine as it had been to his own naive younger self. Hubert had settled down under Martine's reassurances. Apparently pausing in admiration of some particularly impressive window embrasures, N watched him unlock his great carved door and knew that the little devil was going to go through with it. Would a lifetime's caution have defeated ambition had his 'consultant' been unattractive? Almost certainly, N thought. Hubert had not come so far by ignoring his own warning signals. They knew what they were doing; Hubert would not permit himself to exhibit weakness before a woman he hoped to bed. But N's employers had their own essential vulnerability. They trusted their ability to predict behavior.

In the guise of a well-dressed tourist absorbed by sixteenth-century masonry, N drifted backward through the arches and found lurking within the *café tabac* the proof of his evolving theory.

Standing or rather slumping at the back of the bar, the feral-looking boy with messy shoulder-length blond hair was tracking him through the open door. His motorcycle canted into the shadow of a pillar. As one returning to himself after rapt concentration, N looked aimlessly into the square or across it. The boy snapped forward and gulped beer. With a cheering surge of the old pleasure, N thrust his hands into his jacket pockets and walked into the square, waited for cars to pass, and began to amble back the way he had come. The boy put down his beer and moved to the front of the café. N reached the bottom of the square and turned around with his head raised and his hands in his pockets. The boy struck an abstracted pose between the pillars.

If his job had been to instruct the boy in their craft, he would have told him: *Never close off an option until the last moment. Roll the bike, dummy, until I tell you what to do.* The kid thought making up your mind was something you did minute by minute, a typical hoodlum notion. N strolled away, and the boy decided to follow him on foot. A sort of cunning nervous bravado spoke in his slow step forward. All he needed was a target painted on his chest. Enjoying himself, N sauntered along through the streets, distributing appreciative touristy glances at buildings beautiful and mundane alike, and returned to the restaurant where Martine had coaxed M. Hubert back into the game. He pretended to scan the menu in its glass case. Two shops away, the boy spun to face a rack of scenic postcards. His sagging, scruffy leather jacket was too loose to betray his weapon, but it was probably jammed into his belt, another thuggish affectation. N strolled onto the terrace and took a table in the last row.

The boy sidled into view, caught sight of him, sidled away. N opened his satchel, withdrew his novel, and nodded at a waiter. The waiter executed a graceful dip and produced a menu. The boy reappeared across the street and slouched into a café to take a window seat. That wouldn't have been so bad, if everything else had not been so awful. N spread the wings of the menu and deliberately read all the listings. *Can't you see? I'm telling you what to do. You have time to go back for your motorcycle, in case you'll need it when I leave.* The boy plopped his chin on his palm. N ordered mushroom soup, lamb chops, a glass of red burgundy, a bottle of Badoit *gazeuse*. He opened his book. Plucky Kimball O'Hara, known as Kim, presently in the Himalayas, was soon to snatch secret papers from a couple of Russian spies. The boy raked his hair with his fingers, stood up, sat down. A bowl of mushroom soup swirled with cream sent up a delicious, earthy odor. The boy finally slouched off up the sidewalk. N returned to Kim, the Russians, and the wonderful soup.

He had begun on the lamb chops when he heard the motorcycle approach the terrace, blot out all other sounds, and cut out. N took a swallow of wine. Across the street and just visible past the front of the restaurant, the boy was dismounting. He shook out his hair and knelt beside his machine, an old Kawasaki with fat panniers hanging from the saddle. After a sketchy pretense of fussing with the engine for a couple of minutes, he wandered away. N cut open a chop to expose sweet, tender meat precisely the right shade of pink.

When he had paid for his lunch, he made certain the boy was out of sight and ducked into the restaurant. The men's room was a cubicle in a passageway alongside the kitchen. He locked the door, relieved himself, washed and dried his hands and face, and sat down on the lid of the toilet. Five minutes went by while he ignored the rattle of the handle and knocks on the door. He let another two minutes pass, and then opened the door. The frowning man outside thrust past him and closed the door with a thump. N turned away from the dining room and continued down the passage to a service door, which let him out into a narrow brick alley. A vent pumped out heat above overflowing garbage bins. N moved toward the top of the alley, where a motorcycle revved and revved like a frustrated beast. The boy was supposed to carry out his instructions at night, either in the mountains or on the little roads back to Montory, but after having seen N, he was in a panic at losing him. The sound of the motorcycle descended into a low, sustained rumble and grew louder. N faded backward. Maybe the kid would want to see if the restaurant had a back door – that wouldn't be so stupid.

N ducked behind the garbage bins and peered over the refuse as the walls amplified the rumble. The boy stopped short with his front wheel turned into the alley. The bike sputtered, coughed, died. *'Merde.'* The boy looked into the alley and repeated himself with a more drastic inflection. What he had figured out meant *merde* for breakfast, lunch, and dinner, as far as he was concerned. N waited to see what he would do next, plod to the nearest approved telephone to report failure or come down the alley in search of whatever scraps he might salvage from the ruin.

The kid pushed his bike into the alley and mooched along for a dozen feet. Muttering to himself, he propped the bike against a wall. N braced his legs and reached into the satchel. He closed his hand around the grip of the nine-millimeter pistol, fitted with his silencer of choice, and thumbed the safety up and the hammer down. The kid's footsteps slopped toward him from maybe twenty feet away. The boy was uttering soft, mindless obscenities. The sullen footsteps came to within something like ten feet from the far end of the garbage bins. N drew out the pistol, tightened the muscles in his legs, and jumped up, already raising his arm. The kid uttered a high-pitched squeal. His blunt face went white and rubbery with shock. N carried the gesture through until his arm extended straight before him. He pulled the trigger. A hole that looked too small to represent real damage appeared between the kid's eyebrows at the moment of the soft, flat explosion. The force of the bullet pushed the kid backward and then slammed him to the ground. The casing pinged off brick and struck concrete. A dark spray of liquid and other matter slid down the face of the wall.

N shoved the pistol back into the satchel and picked up the cartridge case. He bent over the body, yanked the wallet out of his jeans and patted for weapons, but found only the outline of a knife in a zippered pocket. He moved up to the Kawasaki, unhooked the panniers on their strap, and carried them with him out of the alley into an afternoon that seemed sharp-edged and charged with silvery electricity.

A tide of black-haired priests with boys' faces washed toward him from five or six feet away, their soutanes swinging above their feet. One of them caught his mood and smiled at him with teeth brilliantly white. He grinned back at the priest and stepped aside. A red awning blazed like a sacred fire. Moving past, the boy priests filled the sidewalk, speaking machine-gun South American Spanish in Ecuadorean accents. Another noticed N and he, too, flashed a brilliant smile. It was the Lord's day. The priest's sculpted coif sliced through the glittering air. N nodded briskly, still grinning, and wheeled away.

By the time he got back to the Peugeot, his forehead was filmed with sweat. He unlocked the car, tossed the panniers inside, climbed in, and placed the satchel next to his right leg. He wiped his forehead with his handkerchief and fished the boy's wallet from his jacket pocket. It was made of red leather stamped with the Cartier logo. Three hundred francs, about sixty dollars. A driver's license in the name of Marc-Antoine Labouret, with an address in Bayonne. A prepaid telephone card. A membership card from a video rental store. The business card of a Bayonne lawyer. A folded sheet of notepaper filled with handwritten telephone numbers, none familiar. A credit card made out to François J. Pelletier. Another credit card made out to Rémy Grosselin. Drivers' licenses in the names of François J. Pelletier and Rémy Grosselin of Toulouse and Bordeaux, respectively, each displaying the image of a recently deceased young criminal. The forgeries were what N thought of as 'friend of a friend' work, subtly misaligned and bearing faint, pale scars of erasure. He withdrew the money, put the wallet on the dash, and pulled the panniers toward him.

The first held only rammed-in jeans, shirts, underwear, socks, a couple of sweaters, and everything was crushed and wrinkled, filthy, permeated with a sour, poverty-stricken smell. Disgusted, N opened the second pannier and saw glinting snaps and the dull shine of expensive leather. He extracted an alligator handbag. It was empty. The next bag, also empty, was a black Prada. He took four more women's handbags from the pannier, each slightly worn but serviceable, all empty. Fitting them back into the pannier, N could see the kid roaring alongside his victims, ripping the bags from their shoulders, gunning away. He had stripped the money and valuables, junked everything else, and saved the best to peddle to some other rodent.

Either N's employers were getting desperate, or he had misidentified a would-be mugger as his appointed assassin. The latter seemed a lot more like reality. Irritated, concerned, and amused all at once, he went over the past twenty-four hours. Apart from the boy, the only people he had seen more than once were Japanese tourists who went out for walks in the rain and bought garish berets. His contact had said something about Japanese labor, but that meant nothing. A siren blared behind him. Immediately, another screamed in from his left. He shoved the Cartier wallet into one of the panniers and wound back through the one-way streets.

A boom and clatter of bells louder than sirens celebrated the conclusion of another mass. The traffic slowed to pedestrian speed as it moved past the restaurant, where uniformed policemen questioned the remaining diners on the terrace. Two others, smart in their tunics and Sam Browne belts, blocked the entrance of the alley. The traffic picked up again, and soon he was breezing down the wide, straight road toward Montory.

At Alos, an abrupt turn took him over an empty bridge.

Halfway across, he halted, trotted around the front of the car, opened the passenger door, and in one continuous motion reached inside, thrust his hip against the railing, and sent the panniers whirling out over the swift little Saison River.

The contact took twenty minutes to call him back.

'So we had a little hang-up, did we?' N asked, quoting his words back to him.

'I'm not in the usual place. It's Sunday afternoon, remember? They had to find me. What's going down? You weren't supposed to call in until tonight.'

'I'm curious about something,' N said. 'In fact, I'm a pretty curious guy, all in all. Humor me. Where did they find you? A golf course? Is it like being a doctor, you carry a beeper?'

There was a short silence. 'Whatever you're unhappy about, we can work it out.' Another brief silence. 'I know Martine came as a nasty surprise. Honestly, I don't blame you for being pissed. You need her like a hole in the head. Okay, here's the deal. No reports, no paperwork, not even the firearms statements. You just walk away and get that big, big check. She handles all the rest. Are you smiling? Do I see a twinkle in your eye?'

'You were at your health club, maybe?' N asked. 'Did you have to leave a really tense racquetball match just for me?'

The contact sighed. 'I'm at home. In the old wigwam. Actually, out in back, setting up a new rabbit hutch for my daughter. For her rabbit, I mean.'

'You don't live in Paris.'

'I happen to live in Fontainebleau.'

'And you have a beeper.'

'Doesn't everyone?'

'What's the rabbit's name?'

53

'Oh, dear,' the contact said. 'Is this how we're going to act? All right. The rabbit's name is Custer. Family joke.'

'You mean you're a real Indian?' N asked, and laughed out loud in surprise. 'An honest-to-God Red Man?' His former image of his contact as a geek in thick glasses meta-morphosed into a figure with high cheekbones, bronze skin, and straight, shoulder-length black hair.

'Honest Injun,' the contact said. 'Though the term Native American is easier on the ears. You want to know my tribal affiliation? I'm a Lakota Sioux.'

'I want to know your name.' When the contact refused to speak, N said, 'We both know you're not supposed to tell me, but look at it this way: You're at home. No one is monitoring this call. When I'm done here, no one is ever going to hear from me again. And I have to say, telling me your name would reinforce that bond of trust I find crucial to good fieldwork. As of now, the old bond is getting mighty frayed.'

'Why is that?'

'Tell me your name first. Please, don't get tricky. I'll know if you're lying.'

'What on earth is going on down there? All right. I'm putting my career in your hands. Are you ready? My name is Charles Many Horses. My birth certificate says Charles Horace Bunce, but my Indian name was Many Horses, and when you compete for government contracts, as we have been known to do, you have to meet certain standards. Many Horses sounds a lot more Native American than Bunce. Now can you please explain what the hell got you all riled up?'

'Is someone else down here keeping an eye on me? Besides Martine? Someone I'm not supposed to know about?'

'Oh, please,' the contact said. 'Where's that coming from? Ah, I get it – sounds like you spotted somebody, or thought you did anyhow. Is that what this is all about?

I guess paranoia comes with the territory. If you did see someone, he's not on our payroll. Describe him.'

'Today in Mauléon, I noticed a kid I saw hanging around the café last night. Five-ten, hundred and fifty pounds, late twenties. Long blond hair, grubby, rides a Kawasaki bike. He was following me, Charles, there is no doubt at all about that. Where I went, he went, and if I weren't, you know, sort of reasonably adept at my job, I might never have noticed the guy. As it was, I had to run out of a restaurant by the back door to ditch him. Okay, call me paranoid, but this sort of thing tends to make me uncomfortable.'

'He's not ours,' the contact said quickly. 'Beyond that, I don't know what to tell you. It's your call, champ.'

'Okay, Charles,' said N, hearing a murky ambiguity in the man's voice. 'This is how it goes. If I see the kid again tonight, I have to deal with him.'

'Sounds good to me,' said the contact.

'One more thing, Charles. Have we, to your knowledge, taken on any Japanese field people? You mentioned this possibility yesterday. Was that an idle remark, or . . . no. There are no idle remarks. We hired some Japanese.'

'Now that you mention it, a couple, yeah. It's impossible to find people like you anymore. At least in the States.'

'Are these the Japanese gentlemen I'm seeing wherever I go, the past couple of days?'

'Let me ask you a question. Do you know how strong the yen is against Western currencies? It's a joke. If you fly first-class on Air France, they give you sushi instead of escargots. Busy little Japanese tourists are running around all over Europe, the Pyrenees included.'

'Sushi instead of snails.' The knowledge that he had heard an almost identical remark not long before set off a mental alarm which subsided at the recollection of the drunken Basques.

'It's about money, what a shock. Walk right in, right?

You want it, we got it. Just ask Tonto. What's our revenge against the palefaces? Casinos. That'll work.'

'Like an MBA,' N said. 'You're too embarrassed to admit you went to Harvard, but you did.'

'Now, just how . . .' The contact gave a wheezy chuckle. 'You're something else, pardner. Heap proud, go-um Harvard, but people assume you're an asshole. Anyhow, lay off the Japs. You see the same ones over and over because that's where they are.'

'Neat and tidy, peaceful and private. Just Hubert, Martine, and me.'

'See how easy it gets when you dump your anxiety? Try not to mess up his car. Martine'll drive it back to town. The mule who's bringing her car down from Paris is going to drive the Mercedes to Moscow. We have a buyer lined up.'

'Waste not, want not.'

'Or, as my people say, never shoot your horse until it stops breathing. I'm glad we had this talk.'

Neat and tidy, peaceful and private. Lying on his bed, N called a private line in New York and asked his broker to liquidate his portfolio. The flustered broker required a lengthy explanation of how the funds could be transferred to a number of coded Swiss accounts without breaking the law, and then he wanted to hear the whole thing all over again. Yes, N said, he understood an audit was inevitable, no problem, that was fine. Then he placed a call to a twenty-four-hours-a-day-every-day number made available to select clients by his bankers in Geneva, and through multiple conferencing and the negotiation of a four-and-a-half-point charge established the deposit of the incoming funds and distribution of his present arrangements into new accounts dramatically inaccessible to outsiders, even by Swiss standards. On Monday, the same accommodating bankers would ship by same-day express to an address in Marseilles the various documents within a lockbox entrusted to their care. His apartment was rented, so that was easy, but it was a shame about the books. He stripped down to his shirt and underwear and fell asleep watching a Hong Kong thriller dubbed into hilarious French in which the hero detective, a muscly dervish, said things like 'Why does it ever fall to me to be the exterminator of vermin?' He awakened to a discussion of French farm prices among a professor of linguistic theory, a famous chef, and the winner of last year's Prix Goncourt. He turned off the television and read ten pages of *Kim*. Then he put the book in the satchel and meticulously cleaned the pistol before inserting another hollow-point bullet into the clip and reloading. He cocked the pistol, put on the safety, and nestled the gun in beside the novel. He showered and shaved and trimmed his nails. In a dark gray suit and a thin black turtleneck, he sat down beside the window.

The lot was filling up. The German family came outside into the gray afternoon and climbed into the Saab. After they drove off, a muddy Renault putted down the road and turned in to disgorge the innkeeper's friends. A few minutes later the red L'Espace van pulled into the lot. The three Japanese walked across the road in their colorful new berets to inspect the food and drink in the display case. The blond woman offered slivers of cheese from the wheels, and the Japanese nodded in solemn appreciation. The girl in the blue dress wandered past the kitchen doors. The men across the street bought two wedges of cheese and a bottle of wine. They bowed to the vendor, and she bowed back. An eager-looking black-and-white dog trotted into the lot and sniffed at stains. When the Japanese came back to the auberge, the dog followed them inside.

N locked his door and came down into the lobby. Mouth

open and eyes alert, the dog looked up from in front of the table and watched him put his key on the counter. N felt a portion of his anticipation and on the way outside patted the animal's slender skull. At the display counter he bought a wedge of sheep's-milk cheese. Soon he was driving along the narrow road toward Tardets, the sharp turn over the river at Alos, and the long straight highway to Mauléon.

Backed into a place near the bottom of the arcade, he took careful bites of moist cheese, unfolding the wrapper in increments to keep from dropping crumbs on his suit. Beneath the yellow umbrellas across the square, an old man read a newspaper. A young couple dangled toys before a baby in a stroller. Privileged by what Charles (Many Horses) Bunce called its fuck-you plates, M. Hubert's Mercedes stood at the curb in front of the antique shop. A pair of students trudged into the square and made for the café, where they slid out from beneath their mountainous backpacks and fell into the chairs next to the couple with the baby. The girl backpacker leaned forward and made a face at the baby, who goggled. That one would be a pretty ride, N thought. A lot of bouncing and yipping ending with a self-conscious show of abandonment. An elegant woman of perhaps N's own age walked past his car, proceeded beneath the arcade, and entered the antique store. He finished the last of the cheese, neatly refolded the wrapping paper, and stuffed it into an exterior pocket of the case. In the slowly gathering darkness, lights went on here and there.

There were no Japanese golfers in Basque berets. The backpackers devoured *croque-monsieurs* and trudged away, and the couple pushed the stroller toward home. An assortment of tourists and regulars filled half of the tables beneath the umbrellas. A man and a woman in sturdy

English clothing went into Hubert's shop and emerged twenty minutes later with the elegant woman in tow. The man consulted his watch and led his companions away beneath the arcades. A police car moved past them from the top of the square. The stolid man in the passenger seat turned dead eyes and a Spam-colored face upon N as the car went by. There was always this little charge of essential recognition before they moved on.

Obeying an impulse still forming itself into thought, N left his car and walked under the arches to the window of the antique store. It was about twenty minutes before closing time. M. Hubert was tapping at a desktop computer on an enormous desk at the far end of a handsome array of gleaming furniture. A green-shaded lamp shadowed a deep vertical wrinkle between his eyebrows. The ambitious Martine was nowhere in sight. N opened the door, and a bell tinkled above his head.

Hubert glanced at him and held up a hand, palm out. N began moving thoughtfully through the furniture. A long time ago, an assignment had involved a month's placement in the antiques department of a famous auction house, and, along with other crash tutorials, part of his training had been lessons in fakery from a master of the craft named Elmo Maas. These lessons had proved more useful than he'd ever expected at the time. Admiring the marquetry on a Second Empire table, N noticed a subtle darkening in the wood at the top of one leg. He knelt to run the tips of his fingers up the inner side of the leg. His fingers met a minuscule but telltale shim that would be invisible to the eye. The table was a mongrel. N moved to a late-eighteenth-century desk marred only by an overly enthusiastic regilding, probably done in the thirties, of the vine-leaf pattern at the edges of the leather surface. The next piece he looked at was a straightforward fake. He even knew the name of the man who had made it.

Elmo Maas, an artist of the unscrupulous, had revered

an antiques forger named Clement Tudor. If you could learn to recognize a Tudor, Maas had said, you would be able to spot any forgery, no matter how good. From a workshop in Camberwell, South London, Tudor had produced five or six pieces a year for nearly forty years, concentrating on the French seventeenth and eighteenth centuries and distributing what he made through dealers in France and the United States. His mastery had blessed both himself and his work: never identified except by disciples like Maas, his furniture had defied suspicion. Some of his work had wound up in museums, the rest in private collections. Using photographs and slides along with samples of his own work, Maas had educated his pupil in Tudor's almost invisible nuances: the treatment of a bevel, the angle and stroke of chisel and awl, a dozen other touches. And here they were, those touches, scattered more like the hints of fingerprints than fingerprints themselves over a Directoire armoire.

M. Hubert padded up to N. 'Exquisite, isn't it? I'm closing early today, but if you were interested in anything specific, perhaps I could . . . ?' At once deferential and condescending, his manner invited immediate departure. Underlying anxiety spoke in the tight wrinkles about his eyes. A lifetime of successful bluffing had shaped the ironic curve of his mouth. N wondered if this dealer in frauds actually intended to go through with the arms deal after all.

'I've been looking for a set of antique bookcases to hold my first editions,' N said. 'Something suitable for Molière, Racine, Diderot – you know the sort of thing I mean.'

Avarice sparkled in Hubert's eyes. 'Yours is a large collection?'

'Only a modest one. Approximately five hundred volumes.'

Hubert's smile deepened the wrinkles around his eyes. 'Not so very modest, perhaps. I don't have anything here that would satisfy you, but I believe I know where to find precisely the sort of thing you are looking for. As I stay open on Sundays I close on Monday, but perhaps you could take my card and give me a call at this time tomorrow. May I have your name, please?'

'Roger Maris,' N said, pronouncing it as though it were a French name.

'Excellent, Monsieur Maris. I think you will be very pleased with what I shall show you.' He tweaked a card from a tray on the desk, gave it to N, and began leading him to the door. 'You are here for several more days?'

'Until next weekend,' N said. 'Then I return to Paris.'

Hubert opened the door, setting off the little bell again.

'Might I ask a few questions about some of the pieces?'

Hubert raised his eyebrows and tilted his head forward.

'Is your beautiful Second Empire table completely intact?'

'Of course! Nothing we have has been patched or repaired. Naturally, one makes an occasional error, but in this case . . . ?' He shrugged.

'And what is the provenance of the armoire I was looking at?'

'It came from a descendant of a noble family in Périgord who wanted to sell some of the contents of his château. Taxes, you know. One of his ancestors purchased it in 1799. A letter in my files has all the details. Now I fear I really must . . .' He gestured to the rear of the shop.

'Until tomorrow, then.'

Hubert forced a smile and in visible haste closed the door.

Ninety minutes later the Mercedes passed beneath the streetlamp at the edge of town. Parked in the shadows beside a combination grocery store and café a short distance up the road, N watched the Mercedes again wheel sharply left and race back into Mauléon, as he had expected. Hubert was repeating the actions of his dry run. He started the Peugeot and drove out of the café's lot onto the highway, going deeper into the mountains to the east.

Barely wide enough for two cars, the winding road to the auberge clung to the side of the cliff, bordered on one side by a shallow ditch and the mountain's shoulder, on the other a grassy verge leading to empty space. Sometimes the road doubled back and ascended twenty or thirty feet above itself; more often, it fell off abruptly into the forested valley. At two narrow places in the road, N remembered, a car traveling up the mountain could pull over into a lay-by to let a descending car pass in safety. The first of these was roughly half the distance to the auberge, the second about a hundred feet beneath it. He drove as quickly as he dared, twisting and turning with the sudden curves of the road. A single car zipped past him, appearing and disappearing in a flare of headlights. He passed the first lay-by, continued on, noted the second, and drove the rest of the way up to the auberge.

The small number of cars in the wide parking lot were lined up near the entrance of the two-story ocher building. Two or three would belong to the staff. Canny little M. Hubert, like all con men instinctively self-protective, had chosen a night when the restaurant would be nearly empty. N parked at the far end of the lot and got out, the engine still running. His headlights shone on a white wooden fence and eight feet of meadow grass with nothing but sky beyond. Far away, mountains bulked against the horizon. He bent down and stepped through the bars of the fence and walked into the meadow grass. In the darkness, the gorge looked like an abyss. You could probably drop a hundred bodies down into that thing before anyone noticed. Humming, he jogged back to his car.

N turned into the lay-by and cut the lights and ignition.

Far below, headlights swung around a curve and disappeared. He straightened his tie and patted his hair. A few minutes later, he got out of the car and stood in the middle of the road with the satchel under his arm, listening to the Mercedes as it worked its way uphill. Its headlights suddenly shot across the curve below, then lifted toward him. N stepped forward and raised his right arm. The headlights advanced, and he took another step into the dazzle. As two pale faces stared through the windshield, the circular hood ornament and toothy grille came to a reluctant halt a few feet short of his waist. N pointed to his car and raised his hands in a mime of helplessness. They were talking back and forth. He moved around to the side of the car. The window rolled down. M. Hubert's face was taut with anxiety and distrust. Recognition softened him, but not by much.

'Monsieur Maris? What is this?'

'Monsieur Hubert! I am absolutely delighted to see you!' N lowered his head to look in at Martine. She was wearing something skimpy and black and was scowling beautifully. Their eyes met, hers charged with furious concentration. Well, well. 'Miss, I'm sorry to trouble the two of you, but I had car trouble on the way down from the auberge, and I am afraid that I need some help.'

Martine tried to wither him with a glare. 'Daniel, do you actually know this man?'

'This is the customer I told you about,' Hubert told her.

'*He* the customer?'

Hubert patted her knee and turned back to N. 'I don't have time to help you now, but I'd be happy to call a garage from the auberge.'

'I only need a tiny push,' N said. 'The garages are all closed, anyhow. As you can see, I'm already pointed downhill. I hate to ask, but I'd be very grateful.'

'I don't like this, Daniel,' Martine said.

'Relax,' Hubert said. 'It'll take five seconds. Besides, I have a matter to discuss with Monsieur Maris.' He drove forward and stopped at the far end of the lay-by. N walked uphill behind him. Hubert got out, shaking his head and smiling. 'This is a terrible place for car trouble.' Martine had turned around to stare at N through the rear window.

'Finding you was good luck for me,' N said.

Hubert came up to him and placed two fingers on his arm in a delicate gesture of reconciliation. Even before he inclined his head to whisper his confidence, N knew what he was going to say. 'Your question about that marquetry table troubled me more and more this evening. After all, my reputation is at stake every time I put a piece on display. I examined it with great care, and I think you may have been right. There is a definite possibility that I was misled. I'll have to look into the matter further, but I thank you for bringing it to my attention.' The two fingers tapped N's arm.

He straightened his posture and in a conversational tone said, 'So you had dinner at my favorite auberge? Agreeable, isn't it?' Hubert took one brisk stride over the narrow road, then another, pleased to have concluded one bit of business and eager to get on to the next.

A step behind him, N drew the pistol from the case and shoved the barrel into the base of Hubert's skull. The dapper little fraud knew what was happening – he tried to dodge sideways. N rammed the muzzle into his pad of hair and pulled the trigger. With the sudden flash and a sound no louder than a cough came a sharp scent of gunpowder and burning flesh. Hubert jolted forward and flopped to the ground. N heard Martine screaming at him even before she got out of the Mercedes.

He pushed the gun into the satchel, clamped the satchel beneath his elbow, bent down to grasp Hubert's ankles, and began dragging him to the edge of the road. Martine stood up on the far side of the Mercedes, still screaming. When her voice sailed into outraged hysteria, he glanced up from his task and saw a nice little automatic, a sibling to the one in his bedside drawer at home, pointed at his chest. Martine was panting, but she held the gun steady, both arms extended across the top of the Mercedes. He stopped moving and looked at her with an unruffled calm curiosity. 'Put that thing down,' he said. He dragged M. Hubert's body another six inches backward.

'Stop!' she screeched.

He stopped and looked back up at her. 'Yes?'

Martine stood up, keeping her arms extended. 'Don't do anything, just listen.' She took a moment to work out what she would say. 'We work for the same people. You don't know who I am, but you are using the name Cash. You weren't supposed to show up until the deal was set, so what's going on?' Her voice was steadier than he would have expected.

Hubert's ankles in his hands, N said, 'First of all, I do know who you are, Martine. And it should be obvious that what's going on is a sudden revision of our plans for the evening. Our people found out your friend was planning to cheat his customers. Don't you think we ought to get him off the road before the customers turn up?'

She glanced downhill without moving the pistol. 'They didn't tell me about any change.'

'Maybe they couldn't. I'm sorry I startled you.' N walked backward until he reached the edge of the road. He dropped Hubert's feet and moved forward to grab the collar of his jacket and pull the rest of his body onto the narrow verge. He set the satchel beside his feet.

She lowered the gun. 'How do you know my name?'

'Our contact. What's he called now? Our divisional region controller. He said you'd be handling all the paperwork. Interesting guy. He's an Indian, did you know that? Lives in Fontainebleau. His daughter has a rabbit named

Custer.' N bent at the knees and planted his hands on either side of Hubert's waist. When he pulled up, the body folded in half and released a gassy moan.

'He's still alive,' Martine said.

'No, he isn't.' N looked over the edge of the narrow strip of grass and down into the same abyss he had seen from the edge of the parking lot. The road followed the top of the gorge as it rose to the plateau.

'It didn't look to me like he was planning to cheat anybody.' She had not left the side of the Mercedes. 'He was going to make a lot of money. So were we.'

'Cheating is how this weasel made money.' N hauled the folded corpse an inch nearer the edge, and Hubert's bowels emptied with a string of wet popping sounds and a strong smell of excrement. N swung his body over the edge and let go. Hubert instantly disappeared. Five or six seconds later came a soft sound of impact and a rattle of scree, and then nothing until an almost inaudible thud.

'He even cheated his customers,' N said. 'Half the stuff in that shop is no good.' He brushed off his hands and looked down at his clothes for stains before tucking the satchel back under his left arm.

'I wish someone had told me this was going to happen.' She put the pistol in her handbag and came slowly around the trunk of the Mercedes. 'I could always call for confirmation, couldn't I?'

'You'd better,' N said. In English, he added, 'If you know what's good for you.'

She nodded and licked her lips. Her hair gleamed in the light from the Mercedes. The skimpy black thing was a shift, and her black sheer nylons ended in low-heeled pumps. She had dressed for the Arabs, not the auberge. She flattened a hand on the top of her head and gave him a straight look. 'All right, Monsieur Cash, what do I do now?'

'About what you were supposed to do before. I'll drive

up to the restaurant, and you go back to town for your car. The mule who's driving it down from Paris takes this one to Russia. Call in as soon as you get to your – what is it? – your LUD.'

'What about . . . ?' She waved in the direction of the auberge.

'I'll express our profound regrets and assure our friends that their needs will soon be answered.'

'They said fieldwork was full of surprises.' Martine smiled at him uncertainly before walking back to the Mercedes.

Through the side window N saw a flat black briefcase on the back seat. He got behind the wheel, put his satchel on his lap, and examined the controls. Depressing a button in the door made the driver's seat glide back to give him more room. 'I almost hate to turn this beautiful car over to some Russian mobster.' He fiddled with the button, tilting the seat forward and lowering it. 'What do we call our armament-deprived friends, anyway? Tonto calls them ragheads, but even ragheads have names.'

'Monsieur Temple and Monsieur Law. Daniel didn't know their real names. Shouldn't we be going?'

Finally, N located the emergency brake and eased it in. He depressed the brake pedal and moved the automatic shift from park to its lowest gear. 'Get me the briefcase from the back seat. Doing it now will save time.' The Mercedes swam forward as he released the brake pedal. Martine glanced at him, then shifted around to put one knee on her seat. She bent sideways and stretched toward the briefcase. N dipped into the satchel, raised the tip of the silencer to the wall of her chest, and fired. He heard the bullet splat against something like bone and then realized that it had passed through her body and struck a metal armature within the leather upholstery. Martine slumped into the gap between the seats. Before him, a long leg jerked out, struck the dash, and cracked the heel off a black pump. The cartridge came pinging off the windshield and ricocheted straight to his ribs.

He shoved the pistol back home and tapped the accelerator. Martine slipped deeper into the well between the seats. N thrust open his door and cranked the wheel to the left. Her hip slid onto the handle of the gearshift. He touched the accelerator again. The Mercedes grumbled and hopped forward. Alarmingly near the edge, he jumped off the seat and turned into the spin his body took when his feet met the ground.

He was close enough to the sleek, recessed handle on the back door to caress it. Inch by inch, the car stuttered toward the side of the road. Martine uttered an indecipherable dream-word. The Mercedes lurched to the precipice, nosed over, tilted forward and down, advanced, hesitated, stopped. The roof light illuminated Martine's half-conscious struggle to pull herself back into her seat. The Mercedes trembled forward, dipped its nose, and with exquisite reluctance slid off the earth into the huge darkness. Somersaulting in midair, it cast wheels of yellow light, which extinguished when it smashed into whatever was down there.

Visited by the blazing image of a long feminine leg unfurling before his eyes like a lightning bolt, N loped uphill. That lineament running from the molded thigh to the tender back of the knee, the leap of the calf muscle. The whole perfect thing, like a sculpture of the ideal leg, filling the space in front of him. When would she have made her move, he wondered. She had been too uncertain to act when she should have, and she could not have done it while he was driving, so it would have happened in the parking lot. She'd had that .25-caliber Beretta, a smart gun, in N's opinion. Martine's extended leg flashed before him again, and he suppressed a giddy, enchanted swell of elation.

Ghostly church bells pealed, and a black-haired young

priest shone glimmering from the chiaroscuro of a rearing boulder.

He came up past the retaining wall into the mild haze of light from the windows of the auberge. His feet crunched on the pebbles of the parking lot. After a hundred-foot uphill run he was not even breathing hard, pretty good for a man of his age. He came to the far end of the lot, put his hands on the fence, and inhaled air of surpassing sweetness and purity. Distant ridges and peaks hung beneath fast-moving clouds. This was a gorgeous part of the world. It was unfortunate that he would have to leave it behind. But he was leaving almost everything behind. The books were the worst of it. Well, there were book dealers in Switzerland, too. And he still had *Kim*.

N moved down the fence toward the auberge. Big windows displayed the usual elderly men in berets playing cards, a local family dining with the grandparents, one young couple flirting, flames jittering and weaving over the hearth. A solid old woman carried a steaming platter to the family's table. The Japanese golfers had not returned, and all the other tables were empty. On her way back to the kitchen, the old woman sat down with the card players and laughed at a remark from an old boy missing most of his teeth. No one in the dining room would be leaving for at least an hour. N's stomach audibly complained of being so close to food without being fed, and he moved back into the relative darkness to wait for the second half of his night's work.

And then he stepped forward again, for headlights had come beaming upward from below the lot. N moved into the gauzy light and once again experienced the true old excitement, that of opening himself to unpredictability, of standing at the intersection of infinite variables. A Peugeot identical to his in year, model, and color followed its own headlights into the wide parking lot. N walked toward the car, and the two men in the front seats took him in with wary, expressionless faces. The Peugeot moved alongside him, and the window cranked down. A lifeless, pockmarked face regarded him with a cold, threatening neutrality. N liked that – it told him everything he needed to know.

'Monsieur Temple? Monsieur Law?'

Without any actual change in expression, the driver's face *deepened*, intensified into itself in a way that made the man seem both more brutal and more human, almost pitiable. N saw an entire history of rage, disappointment, and meager satisfactions in his response. The driver hesitated, looked into N's eyes, then slowly nodded.

'There's been a problem,' N said. 'Please, do not be alarmed, but Monsieur Hubert cannot join you tonight. He has been in a serious automobile accident.'

The man in the passenger seat spoke a couple of sentences in Arabic. His hands were curled around the grip of a fat black attaché case. The driver answered in monosyllables before turning back to N. 'We have heard nothing of an accident.' His French was stiff but correct, and his accent was barbaric. 'Who are you supposed to be?'

'Marc-Antoine Labouret. I work for Monsieur Hubert. The accident happened late this afternoon. I think he spoke to you before that?'

The man nodded, and another joyous flare of adrenaline flooded into N's bloodstream.

'A tour bus went out of control near Montory and ran into his Mercedes. Fortunately, he suffered no more than a broken leg and a severe concussion, but his companion, a young woman, was killed. He goes in and out of consciousness, and of course he is very distressed about his friend, but when I left him at the hospital Monsieur Hubert emphasized his regrets at this inconvenience.' N drew in another liter of transcendent air. 'He insisted that I communicate in person his profound apologies and continuing respect. He also wishes you to know that after no more than a small delay matters will go forward as arranged.'

'Hubert never mentioned an assistant,' the driver said. The other man said something in Arabic. 'Monsieur Law and I wonder what is meant by this term, "a small delay".'

'A matter of days,' N said. 'I have the details in my computer.'

Their laughter sounded like branches snapping, like an automobile landing on trees and rocks. 'Our friend Hubert adores the computer,' said the driver.

M. Law leaned forward to look at N. He had a thick mustache and a high, intelligent forehead, and his dark eyes were clear and penetrating. 'What was the name of the dead woman?' His accent was much worse than the driver's.

'Martine is all I know,' N said. 'The bitch turned up out of nowhere.'

M. Law's eyes creased in a smile. 'We will continue our discussion inside.'

'I wish I could join you, but I have to get back to the hospital.' He waved the satchel at the far side of the lot. 'Why don't we go over there? It'll take five minutes to show you what I have on the computer, and you could talk about it over dinner.'

M. Temple glanced at M. Law. M. Law raised and lowered an index finger and settled back. The Peugeot ground over pebbles and pulled up at the fence. The taillights died, and the two men got out. M. Law was about six feet tall and lean, M. Temple a few inches shorter and thick in the chest and waist. Both men wore nice-looking dark suits and gleaming white shirts. Walking toward them, N watched them straighten their clothes. M. Temple carried a large weapon in a shoulder holster, M. Law something smaller in a holster clipped to his belt. They felt superior, even a bit contemptuous toward M. Labouret – the antiques dealer's flunky, as wed to his computer as an infant to the breast. N came up beside M. Temple, smiled, and ducked through the fence. 'Better if they don't see the screen,' he told their scowling faces. 'The people in the restaurant.'

Already impatient with this folly, M. Law nodded at M. Temple. 'Go on, do it.' He added something in Arabic.

M. Temple grinned, yanked down the front of his suit jacket, bent down, clamped his right arm across his chest, and steadied himself with the other as he thrust his trunk through the three-foot gap. N moved sideways and held the satchel upright on the top of the fence. M. Temple swung one leg over the white board and hesitated, deciding between raising his right leg before or behind. Leaning left, he bent his right knee and swiveled. A tasseled loafer rapped against the board. N took another step along the fence, pulling the satchel to his chest as if protecting it. M. Temple skipped sideways and pulled his leg through. Embarrassed, he frowned and yanked again at his jacket.

N knelt down with the satchel before him. M. Law gripped the board and passed his head through the gap. When he stepped over the board, N eased out the pistol and fired upward into the center of his intelligent forehead. The bullet tore through the back of M. Law's skull and, guided by the laws of physics and sheer good luck, smacked into M. Temple's chest as blood and gray pulp spattered his shirt. M. Temple staggered back and hit the ground, groaning. N felt like a golfer scoring a hole in one during a farewell tournament. He bounced up and moved alongside M. Temple. Grimacing and blowing red froth from his lips, the Arab was still gamely trying to yank his gun from the shoulder holster. The bullet had passed through a lung, or maybe just roamed around inside it before stopping. N settled the muzzle of the silencer behind a fleshy ear, and M. Temple's right eye, large as a cow's, swiveled toward him.

Light spilled from the auberge's windows onto the row of cars and spread across the gravel. M. Law lay sprawled out on the board, his arms and legs dangling on either side. Blood dripped onto the grass beneath his head.

'A thing of beauty is a joy forever,' N said. Whatever unpleasantness M. Temple offered in return was cut short by the fall of the nine millimeter's hammer.

N grabbed M. Law's collar and belt and slid him off the board. Then he grasped his wrists and pulled him through the grass to the edge of the gorge and went back for M. Temple. He took their wallets from their hip pockets and removed the money, altogether about a thousand dollars in francs. He folded the bills into his jacket pocket and threw the wallets into the gorge. Taking care to avoid getting blood on his hands or clothes, N shoved M. Temple closer to the edge and rolled him over the precipice. The body dropped out of view almost instantly. He pushed M. Law after him, and this time thought he heard a faint sound of impact from far down in the darkness. Smiling, he walked back to the fence and ducked through it.

N opened the driver's door of the Arabs' Peugeot, took the keys from the ignition, and pushed the seat forward to lean in for the attaché case. From its weight, it might have been filled with books. He closed the door softly and tossed the keys over the fence. So buoyant he could not keep from breaking into quiet laughter, he moved across the gravel and walked down the hill to his car with the satchel beneath his left elbow, the case swinging from his right hand.

When he got behind the wheel, he shoved the case onto the passenger seat and turned on the roof light. For a couple of seconds he could do nothing but look at the smooth black leather, the stitching, the brass catches. His breath caught in his throat. N leaned toward the case and brought his hands to the catches and their sliding releases. He closed his eyes and thumbed the releases sideways.

There came a substantial, almost resonant sound as the catches flew open. He pushed the top of the case a few inches up and opened his eyes upon banded rows of thousand-dollar bills lined edge to edge and stacked three deep. 'One for the Gipper,' he whispered. For a couple of seconds, he was content to breathe in and out, feeling all the muscles in his body relax and breathe with him. Then he started the car and sailed down the mountain.

When he turned into the walled lot, the bright windows framed what appeared to be a celebration. Candles glowed on the lively tables, and people dodged up and down the aisles, turning this way and that in the buzz and hum of conversation floating toward him. This happy crowd seemed to have claimed every parking spot not preempted by the Comet truck, parked in front of the kitchen at an angle that eliminated three spaces. N trolled past the dirty Renault belonging to the drunken Basques, the Japanese tourists' tall red van, the Germans' Saab, and other vehicles familiar and unfamiliar. There was a narrow space in front of the trellis beside the entrance. He slid into the opening, gathered his cases, and, holding his breath and sucking in his waist, managed to squeeze out of the car. Beyond the kitchen doors, the Comet man in the blue work suit occupied a chair with the bored patience of a museum guard while the women bustled back and forth with laden trays and stacks of dishes. N wondered what was so important that it was delivered after dark on Sunday and then saw a bright flash of blue that was Albertine, facing a sink with her back to him. Only a few inches from her hip, the innkeeper was leaning against the sink, arms crossed over his chest and speaking from the side of his mouth with an almost conspiratorial air. The intimacy of their communication, her close attention to his words, informed N that they were father and daughter. What Daddy doesn't know won't hurt him, he thought. The man's gaze shifted outside and met N's eyes. N smiled at his host and pushed the glass door open with his shoulder.

On his way to the counter he saw that his own elation had imbued an ordinary Sunday dinner with the atmosphere of a party. The Japanese men, the German family, French tourists, and groups of local Basques ate and drank at their separate tables. Albertine would not be free for hours. He had enough time to arrange the flights, pack his things, enjoy a long bath, even take a nap. As his adrenaline subsided, he could feel his body demand rest. The hunger he had experienced earlier had disappeared, another sign that he should get some sleep. N took his key from the board and lugged the increasingly heavy attaché case up the stairs, turning on the lights as he went.

He locked his door and sat on the bed to open the case. Twenty-five bills in each packet, six rows across, three stacks high. Four hundred and fifty thousand dollars: no million, but a pretty decent golden handshake. He closed the case, slid it onto the closet shelf, and picked up the telephone. In twenty minutes he had secured for a fictitious gentleman named Kimball O'Hara a four a.m. charter from Pau to Toulouse and a five o'clock connecting flight to Marseilles. His employers' concern would not reach the stage of serious worry until he was on his way to Toulouse, and he would be on a plane to Italy before they had completely advanced into outright panic. The bodies could go undiscovered for days. N folded and packed his clothes into his carry-on bag and set it beside the door, leaving out what he would wear later that night. *Kim* went on the bedside table. He would push the satchel down a drain somewhere in Oloron.

Hot water pounded into the fiberglass tub while he shaved for the second time that day. The bath lulled him into drowsiness. He wrapped a towel around his waist and stretched out on the bed. Before he dropped into sleep, the last image in his mind was that of a rigid, magnificent female leg encased in sheer black nylon.

Soft but insistent raps at the door awakened him. N looked at his watch: eleven-thirty, earlier than he had expected. 'I'll be right there.' He stood up, stretched, re-fastened the towel around his waist. A mist of sickeningly floral perfume enveloped him when he unlocked the door. Wearing a raincoat over her nightgown, Albertine slipped into the room. N kissed her neck and grazed at her avid mouth, smiling as she moved him toward the bed.

She closed the door behind her, and the three men in the corridor stepped forward in unison, like soldiers. The one on the right jerked open a refuse bag and extended it toward her. She shoved the bloody cleaver and the ruined nightgown into the depths of the bag. The man quizzed her with a look. 'You can go in,' she said, grateful he had not exercised his abominable French. All three of them bowed. Despite her promises to herself, she was unable to keep from bowing back. Humiliated, she straightened up again, feeling their eyes moving over her face, hands, feet, ankles, hair, and whatever they detected of her body through the raincoat. Albertine moved aside, and they filed through the door to begin their work.

Her father stood up from his desk behind the counter when she descended into the darkened lobby. Beneath the long table, Gaston, the black-and-white dog, stirred in his sleep. 'Did it go well?' her father asked. He, too, inspected her for bloodstains.

'How do you think it went?' she said. 'He was almost asleep. By the time he knew what was happening, his chest was wide open.'

The lock on the front door responded to the keypad and clicked open. The two permanent Americans eyed her as they came through the arch. Gaston raised his head, sighed, and went back to sleep. She said, 'Those idiots in the berets are up there now. How long have you been using Japanese, anyhow?'

'Maybe six months.' The one in the tweed jacket spoke in English because he knew English annoyed her, and annoyance was how he flirted. 'Hey, we love those wild and crazy guys, they're our little samurai brothers.'

'Don't let your stupid brothers miss the briefcase in the closet,' she said. The ugly one in the running suit leered at her. 'That man had good clothes. You could try wearing some nice clothes, for a change.'

'His stuff goes straight into the fire,' the ugly one said. 'We don't even look at it. You know, we're talking about a real character. Kind of a legend. I heard lots of amazing stories about him.'

'Thank you, Albertine,' said her father. He did not want her to hear the amazing stories.

'You ought to thank me,' she said. 'The old rooster made me take a bath. On top of that, I wasted my perfume because he wanted me to smell like a girl in Bora Bora.'

Both of the Americans stared at the floor.

'What does it mean to say,' she asked, and in her heavily accented English said, 'I wish I had that swing in my backyard?'

The permanent Americans glanced at each other. The one in the tweed jacket clapped his hands over his eyes. The ugly one said, 'Albertine, you're the ideal woman. Everybody worships you.'

'Good, then I should get more money.' She wheeled around to go downstairs, and the ugly one sang out, 'Izz-unt it roman-tic?' Beneath his sweet false tremulous tenor came the rumble of the disposal truck as it backed toward the entrance.

The Ghost Village

1

In Vietnam I knew a man who went quietly and purpose-fully crazy because his wife wrote him that his son had been sexually abused – 'messed with' – by the leader of their church choir. This man was a black six-foot-six grunt named Leonard Hamnet, from a small town in Tennessee named Archibald. Before writing, his wife had waited until she had endured the entire business of going to the police, talking to other parents, returning to the police with another accusation, and finally succeeding in having the man charged. He was up for trial in two months. Leonard Hamnet was no happier about that than he was about the original injury.

'I got to murder him, you know, but I'm seriously thinking on murdering her too,' he said. He still held the letter in his hands, and he was speaking to Spanky Burrage, Michael Poole, Conor Linklater, SP4 Cotton, Calvin Hill, Tina Pumo, the magnificent M. O. Dengler, and myself. 'All this is going on, my boy needs help, this here Mr Brewster needs to be dismantled, needs to be *racked* and *stacked*, and she don't tell me! Makes me want to put her *down*, man. Take her damn head off and put it up on a stake in the yard, man. With a sign saying: *Here is one stupid woman.*'

We were in the unofficial part of Camp Crandall known as No Man's Land, located between the wire perimeter and a shack, also unofficial, where a cunning little weasel named Wilson Manly sold contraband beer and liquor. No

Man's Land, so called because the CO pretended it did not exist, contained a mound of old tires, a piss tube, and a lot of dusty red ground. Leonard Hamnet gave the letter in his hand a dispirited look, folded it into the pocket of his fatigues, and began to roam around the heap of tires, aiming kicks at the ones that stuck out farthest. 'One stupid woman,' he repeated. Dust exploded up from a burst, worn-down wheel of rubber.

I wanted to make sure Hamnet knew he was angry with Mr Brewster, not his wife, and said, 'She was trying –'

Hamnet's great glistening bull's head turned toward me.

'Look at what the woman did. She nailed that bastard. She got other people to admit that he messed with their kids too. That must be almost impossible. And she had the guy arrested. He's going to be put away for a long time.'

'I'll put that bitch away, too,' Hamnet said, and kicked an old gray tire hard enough to push it nearly a foot back into the heap. All the other tires shuddered and moved. For a second it seemed that the entire mound might collapse.

'This is my *boy* I'm talking about here,' Hamnet said. 'This shit has gone far enough.'

'The important thing,' Dengler said, 'is to take care of your boy. You have to see he gets help.'

'How'm I gonna do that from here?' Hamnet shouted.

'Write him a letter,' Dengler said. 'Tell him you love him. Tell him he did right to go to his mother. Tell him you think about him all the time.'

Hamnet took the letter from his pocket and stared at it. It was already stained and wrinkled. I did not think it could survive many more of Hamnet's readings. His face seemed to get heavier, no easy trick with a face like Hamnet's. 'I got to get home,' he said. 'I got to get back home and take *care* of these people.'

Hamnet began putting in requests for compassionate leave relentlessly – one request a day. When we were out on patrol, sometimes I saw him unfold the tattered sheet of notepaper from his shirt pocket and read it two or three times, concentrating intensely. When the letter began to shred along the folds, Hamnet taped it together.

We were going out on four- and five-day patrols during that period, taking a lot of casualties. Hamnet performed well in the field, but he had retreated so far within himself that he spoke in monosyllables. He wore a dull, glazed look, and moved like a man who had just eaten a heavy dinner. I thought he looked like a man who had given up, and when people gave up they did not last long – they were already very close to death, and other people avoided them.

We were camped in a stand of trees at the edge of a paddy. That day we had lost two men so new that I had already forgotten their names. We had to eat cold C rations because heating them with C-4 would have been like putting up billboards and arc lights. We couldn't smoke, and we were not supposed to talk. Hamnet's C rations consisted of an old can of Spam that dated from an earlier war and a can of peaches. He saw Spanky staring at the peaches and tossed him the can. Then he dropped the Spam between his legs. Death was almost visible around him. He fingered the note out of his pocket and tried to read it in the damp gray twilight.

At that moment someone started shooting at us, and the Lieutenant yelled '*Shit!*' and we dropped our food and returned fire at the invisible people trying to kill us. When they kept shooting back, we had to go through the paddy.

The warm water came up to our chests. At the dikes, we scrambled over and splashed down into the muck on the other side. A boy from Santa Cruz, California, named Thomas Blevins got a round in the back of his neck and dropped dead into the water just short of the first dike, and another boy named Tyrell Budd coughed and dropped down right beside him. The FO called in an artillery strike. We leaned against the backs of the last two dikes when the big shells came thudding in. The ground shook and the water rippled, and the edge of the forest went up in a series of fireballs. We could hear the monkeys screaming.

One by one we crawled over the last dike onto the damp but solid ground on the other side of the paddy. Here the trees were much sparser, and a little group of thatched huts was visible through them.

Then two things I did not understand happened, one after the other. Someone off in the forest fired a mortar round at us – just one. One mortar, one round. That was the first thing. I fell down and shoved my face in the muck, and everybody around me did the same. I considered that this might be my last second on earth, and greedily inhaled whatever life might be left to me. Whoever fired the mortar should have had an excellent idea of our location, and I experienced that endless moment of pure, terrifying helplessness – a moment in which the soul simultaneously clings to the body and readies itself to let go of it – until the shell landed on top of the last dike and blew it to bits. Dirt, mud, and water slopped down around us, and shell fragments whizzed through the air. One of the fragments sailed over us, sliced a hamburger-size wad of bark and wood from a tree, and clanged into Spanky Burrage's helmet with a sound like a brick hitting a garbage can. The fragment fell to the ground, and a little smoke drifted up from it.

We picked ourselves up. Spanky looked dead, except that he was breathing. Hamnet shouldered his pack and picked up Spanky and slung him over his shoulder. He saw me looking at him.

'I gotta take *care* of these people,' he said.

The other thing I did not understand – apart from why there had been only one mortar round – came when we entered the village.

Lieutenant Harry Beevers had yet to join us, and we

were nearly a year away from the events at Ia Thuc, when everything, the world and ourselves within the world, went crazy. I have to explain what happened. Lieutenant Harry Beevers killed thirty children in a cave at Ia Thuc and their bodies disappeared, but Michael Poole and I went into that cave and knew that something obscene had happened in there. We smelled evil, we touched its wings with our hands. A pitiful character named Victor Spitalny ran into the cave when he heard gunfire, and came pinwheeling out right away, screaming, covered with welts or hives that vanished almost as soon as he came out into the air. Poor Spitalny had touched it too. Because I was twenty and already writing books in my head, I thought that the cave was the place where the other *Tom Sawyer* ended, where Injun Joe raped Becky Thatcher and slit Tom's throat.

When we walked into the little village in the woods on the other side of the rice paddy, I experienced a kind of foretaste of Ia Thuc. If I can say this without setting off all the Gothic bells, the place seemed intrinsically, inherently wrong – it was too quiet, too still, completely without noise or movement. There were no chickens, dogs, or pigs; no old women came out to look us over, no old men offered conciliatory smiles. The little huts, still inhabitable, were empty – something I had never seen before in Vietnam, and never saw again. It was a ghost village, in a country where people thought the earth was sanctified by their ancestors' bodies.

Poole's map said that the place was named Bong To.

Hamnet lowered Spanky into the long grass as soon as we reached the center of the empty village. I bawled out a few words in my poor Vietnamese.

Spanky groaned. He gently touched the sides of his helmet. 'I caught a head wound,' he said.

'You wouldn't have a head at all, you was only wearing your liner,' Hamnet said.

Spanky bit his lips and pushed the helmet up off his head. He groaned. A finger of blood ran down beside his ear. Finally the helmet passed over a lump the size of an apple that rose up from under his hair. Wincing, Spanky fingered this enormous knot. 'I see double,' he said. 'I'll never get that helmet back on.'

The medic said, 'Take it easy, we'll get you out of here.'

'Out of *here*?' Spanky brightened up.

'Back to Crandall,' the medic said.

Spitalny sidled up, and Spanky frowned at him. 'There ain't nobody here,' Spitalny said. 'What the fuck is going on?' He took the emptiness of the village as a personal affront.

Leonard Hamnet turned his back and spat.

'Spitalny, Tiano,' the Lieutenant said. 'Go into the paddy and get Tyrell and Blevins. Now.'

Tattoo Tiano, who was due to die six and a half months later and was Spitalny's only friend, said, 'You do it this time, Lieutenant.'

Hamnet turned around and began moving toward Tiano and Spitalny. He looked as if he had grown two sizes larger, as if his hands could pick up boulders. I had forgotten how big he was. His head was lowered, and a rim of clear white showed above the irises. I wouldn't have been surprised if he had blown smoke from his nostrils.

'Hey, I'm gone, I'm already there,' Tiano said. He and Spitalny began moving quickly through the sparse trees. Whoever had fired the mortar had packed up and gone. By now it was nearly dark, and the mosquitoes had found us.

'So?' Poole said.

Hamnet sat down heavily enough for me to feel the shock in my boots. He said, 'I have to go home, Lieutenant. I don't mean no disrespect, but I cannot take this shit much longer.'

The Lieutenant said he was working on it.

Poole, Hamnet, and I looked around at the village.

Spanky Burrage said, 'Good quiet place for Ham to catch up on his reading.'

'Maybe I better take a look,' the Lieutenant said. He flicked the lighter a couple of times and walked off toward the nearest hut. The rest of us stood around like fools, listening to the mosquitoes and the sounds of Tiano and Spitalny pulling the dead men up over the dikes. Every now and then Spanky groaned and shook his head. Too much time passed.

The Lieutenant said something almost inaudible from inside the hut. He came back outside in a hurry, looking disturbed and puzzled even in the darkness.

'Underhill, Poole,' he said, 'I want you to see this.'

Poole and I glanced at each other. I wondered if I looked as bad as he did. Poole seemed to be a couple of psychic inches from either taking a poke at the Lieutenant or exploding altogether. In his muddy face his eyes were the size of hen's eggs. He was wound up like a cheap watch. I thought that I probably looked pretty much the same.

'What is it, Lieutenant?' he asked.

The Lieutenant gestured for us to come to the hut, then turned around and went back inside. There was no reason for us not to follow him. The Lieutenant was a jerk, but Harry Beevers, our next lieutenant, was a baron, an earl among jerks, and we nearly always did whatever dumb thing he told us to do. Poole was so ragged and edgy that he looked as if he felt like shooting the Lieutenant in the back. *I* felt like shooting the Lieutenant in the back, I realized a second later. I didn't have an idea in the world what was going on in Poole's mind. I grumbled something and moved toward the hut. Poole followed.

The Lieutenant was standing in the doorway, looking over his shoulder and fingering his sidearm. He frowned at us to let us know we had been slow to obey him, then flicked on the lighter. The sudden hollows and shadows in his face made him resemble one of the corpses I had opened up when I was in graves registration at Camp White Star.

'You want to know what it is, Poole? Okay, you tell me what it is.'

He held the lighter before him like a torch and marched into the hut. I imagined the entire dry, flimsy structure bursting into heat and flame. This Lieutenant was not destined to get home walking and breathing, and I pitied and hated him about equally, but I did not want to turn into toast because he had found an American body inside a hut and didn't know what to do about it. I'd heard of platoons finding the mutilated corpses of American prisoners, and hoped that this was not our turn.

And then, in the instant before I smelled blood and saw the Lieutenant stoop to lift a panel on the floor, I thought that what had spooked him was not the body of an American POW but of a child who had been murdered and left behind in this empty place. The Lieutenant had probably not seen any dead children yet. Some part of the Lieutenant was still worrying about what a girl named Becky Roddenburger was getting up to back at Idaho State, and a dead child would be too much reality for him.

He pulled up the wooden panel in the floor, and I caught the smell of blood. The Zippo died, and darkness closed down on us. The Lieutenant yanked the panel back on its hinges. The smell of blood floated up from whatever was beneath the floor. The Lieutenant flicked the Zippo, and his face jumped out of the darkness. 'Now. Tell me what this is.'

'It's where they hide the kids when people like us show up,' I said. 'Smells like something went wrong. Did you take a look?'

I saw in his tight cheeks and almost lipless mouth that he had not. He wasn't about to go down there and get killed by the Minotaur while his platoon stood around outside.

'Taking a look is your job, Underhill,' he said.

For a second we both looked at the ladder, made of peeled branches lashed together with rags, that led down into the pit.

'Give me the lighter,' Poole said, and grabbed it away from the Lieutenant. He sat on the edge of the hole and leaned over, bringing the flame beneath the level of the floor. He grunted at whatever he saw, and surprised both the Lieutenant and myself by pushing himself off the ledge into the opening. The light went out. The Lieutenant and I looked down into the dark open rectangle in the floor.

The lighter flared again. I could see Poole's extended arm, the jittering little fire, a packed-earth floor. The top of the concealed room was less than an inch above the top of Poole's head. He moved away from the opening.

'What is it? Are there any –' The Lieutenant's voice made a creaky sound. 'Any bodies?'

'Come down here, Tim,' Poole called up.

I sat on the floor and swung my legs into the pit. Then I jumped down.

Beneath the floor, the smell of blood was almost sickeningly strong.

'What do you see?' the Lieutenant shouted. He was trying to sound like a leader, and his voice squeaked on the last word.

I saw an empty room shaped like a giant grave. The walls were covered by some kind of thick paper held in place by wooden struts sunk into the earth. Both the thick brown paper and two of the struts showed old bloodstains.

'Hot,' Poole said, and closed the lighter.

'Come *on*, damn it,' came the Lieutenant's voice. 'Get out of there.'

'Yes, sir,' Poole said. He flicked the lighter back on. Many layers of thick paper formed an absorbent pad between the earth and the room, and the topmost, thinnest layer had been covered with vertical lines of Vietnamese writing. The writing looked like poetry, like the left-hand pages of Kenneth Rexroth's translations of Tu Fu and Li Po.

'Well, well,' Poole said, and I turned to see him pointing at what first looked like intricately woven strands of rope fixed to the bloodstained wooden uprights. Poole stepped forward and the weave jumped into sharp relief. About four feet off the ground, iron chains had been screwed to the uprights. The thick pad between the two lengths of chain had been soaked with blood. The three feet of ground between the posts looked rusty. Poole moved the lighter closer to the chains, and we saw dried blood on the metal links.

'I want you guys out of there, and I mean *now*,' whined the Lieutenant.

Poole snapped the lighter shut.

'I just changed my mind,' I said softly. 'I'm putting twenty bucks into the Elijah fund. For two weeks from today. That's what, June twentieth?'

'Tell it to Spanky,' he said. Spanky Burrage had invented the pool we called the Elijah fund, and he held the money. Michael had not put any money into the pool. He thought that a new lieutenant might be even worse than the one we had. Of course he was right. Harry Beevers was our next lieutenant. Elijah Joys, Lieutenant Elijah Joys of New Utrecht, Idaho, a graduate of the University of Idaho and basic training at Fort Benning, Georgia, was an inept, weak lieutenant, not a disastrous one. If Spanky could have seen what was coming, he would have given back the money and prayed for the safety of Lieutenant Joys.

Poole and I moved back toward the opening. I felt as if I had seen a shrine to an obscene deity. The Lieutenant leaned over and stuck out his hand – uselessly, because he did not bend down far enough for us to reach him. We levered ourselves up out of the hole stiff-armed, as if we were leaving a swimming pool. The Lieutenant stepped back. He had a thin face and thick, fleshy nose, and his Adam's apple danced around in his neck like a jumping bean. He might not have been Harry Beevers, but he was no prize. 'Well, how many?'

'How many what?' I asked.

'How many are there?' He wanted to go back to Camp Crandall with a good body count.

'There weren't exactly any bodies, Lieutenant,' said Poole, trying to let him down easily. He described what we had seen.

'Well, what's that good for?' He meant, *How is that going to help me?*

'Interrogations, probably,' Poole said. 'If you questioned someone down there, no one outside the hut would hear anything. At night, you could just drag the body into the woods.'

Lieutenant Joys nodded. 'Field Interrogation Post,' he said, trying out the phrase. 'Torture, Use of, Highly Indicated.' He nodded again. 'Right?'

'Highly,' Poole said.

'Shows you what kind of enemy we're dealing with in this conflict.'

I could no longer stand being in the same three square feet of space with Elijah Joys, and I took a step toward the door of the hut. I did not know what Poole and I had seen, but I knew it was not a Field Interrogation Post, Torture, Use of, Highly Indicated, unless the Vietnamese had begun to interrogate monkeys. It occurred to me that the writing on the wall might have been names instead of poetry – I thought that we had stumbled into a mystery that had nothing to do with the war, a Vietnamese mystery.

For a second, music from my old life, music too beautiful to be endurable, started playing in my head. Finally I recognized it: 'The Walk to the Paradise Garden', from *A Village Romeo and Juliet* by Frederick Delius. Back in Berkeley, I had listened to it hundreds of times.

If nothing else had happened, I think I could have replayed the whole piece in my head. Tears filled my eyes, and I stepped toward the door of the hut. Then I froze. A ragged Vietnamese boy of seven or eight was regarding me with great seriousness from the far corner of the hut. I knew he was not there – I knew he was a spirit. I had no belief in spirits, but that's what he was. Some part of my mind as detached as a crime reporter reminded me that 'The Walk to the Paradise Garden' was about two children who were about to die, and that in a sense the music *was* their death. I wiped my eyes with my hand, and when I lowered my arm, the boy was still there. He was beautiful, beautiful in the ordinary way, as Vietnamese children nearly always seemed beautiful to me. Then he vanished all at once, like the flickering light of the Zippo. I nearly groaned aloud. That child had been murdered in the hut: he had not just died, he had been murdered.

I said something to the other two men and went through the door into the growing darkness. I was very dimly aware of the Lieutenant asking Poole to repeat his description of the uprights and the bloody chain. Hamnet and Burrage and Calvin Hill were sitting down and leaning against a tree. Victor Spitalny was wiping his hands on his filthy shirt. White smoke curled up from Hill's cigarette, and Tina Pumo exhaled a long white stream of vapor. The unhinged thought came to me with an absolute conviction that *this* was the Paradise Garden. The men lounging in the darkness; the pattern of the cigarette smoke, and the patterns they made, sitting or standing; the in-drawing darkness, as physical as a blanket; the frame of the trees and the flat gray-green background of the paddy.

My soul had come back to life.

Then I became aware that there was something wrong about the men arranged before me, and again it took a moment for my intelligence to catch up to my intuition. Every member of a combat unit makes unconscious adjustments as members of the unit go down in the field; survival sometimes depends on the number of people you know are with you, and you keep count without being quite aware of doing it. I had registered that two men too many were in front of me. Instead of seven, there were nine, and the two men that made up the nine of us left were still behind me in the hut. M. O. Dengler was looking at me with growing curiosity, and I thought he knew exactly what I was thinking. A sick chill went through me. I saw Tom Blevins and Tyrell Budd standing together at the far right of the platoon, a little muddier than the others but otherwise different from the rest only in that, like Dengler, they were looking directly at me.

Hill tossed his cigarette away in an arc of light. Poole and Lieutenant Joys came out of the hut behind me. Leonard Hamnet patted his pocket to reassure himself that he still had his letter. I looked back at the right of the group, and the two dead men were gone.

'Let's saddle up,' the Lieutenant said. 'We aren't doing any good around here.'

'Tim?' Dengler asked. He had not taken his eyes off me since I had come out of the hut. I shook my head.

'Well, what was it?' asked Tina Pumo. 'Was it juicy?'

Spanky and Calvin Hill laughed and slapped hands.

'Aren't we gonna torch this place?' asked Spitalny.

The Lieutenant ignored him. 'Juicy enough, Pumo. Interrogation Post. Field Interrogation Post.'

'No shit,' said Pumo.

'These people are into torture, Pumo. It's just another indication.'

'Gotcha.' Pumo glanced at me and his eyes grew curious. Dengler moved closer.

'I was just remembering something,' I said. 'Something from the world.'

'You better forget about the world while you're over here, Underhill,' the Lieutenant told me. 'I'm trying to keep you alive, in case you hadn't noticed, but you have to cooperate with me.' His Adam's apple jumped like a begging puppy.

As soon as he went ahead to lead us out of the village, I gave twenty dollars to Spanky and said, 'Two weeks from today.'

'My man,' Spanky said.

The rest of the patrol was uneventful.

The next night we had showers, real food, alcohol, cots to sleep in. Sheets and pillows. Two new guys replaced Tyrell Budd and Thomas Blevins, whose names were never mentioned again, at least by me, until long after the war was over and Poole, Linklater, Pumo, and I looked them up, along with the rest of our dead, on the Wall in Washington. I wanted to forget the patrol, especially what I had seen and experienced inside the hut. I wanted the oblivion that came in powdered form.

I remember that it was raining. I remember the steam lifting off the ground, and the condensation dripping down the metal poles in the tents. Moisture shone on the faces around me. I was sitting in the brothers' tent, listening to the music Spanky Burrage played on the big reel-to-reel recorder he had bought on R&R in Taipei. Spanky Burrage never played Delius, but what he played was paradisal: great jazz from Armstrong to Coltrane, on reels recorded for him by his friends back in Little Rock and that he knew so well he could find individual tracks and performances without bothering to look at the counter. Spanky liked to play disc jockey during these long sessions, changing reels and speeding past thousands of feet of tape to play the same songs by different musicians, even the same song hiding under different names – 'Cherokee' and 'KoKo', 'Indiana' and 'Donna Lee' – or long series of songs connected by titles that used the same words – 'I Thought About You' (Art Tatum), 'You and the Night and the Music' (Sonny Rollins), 'I Love

You' (Bill Evans), 'If I Could Be with You' (Ike Quebec), 'You Leave Me Breathless' (Milt Jackson), even, for the sake of the joke, 'Thou Swell', by Glenroy Breakstone. In his single-artist mode on this day, Spanky was ranging through the work of a great trumpet player named Clifford Brown.

On this sweltering, rainy day, Clifford Brown's music sounded regal and unearthly. Clifford Brown was walking to the Paradise Garden. Listening to him was like watching a smiling man shouldering open an enormous door to let in great dazzling rays of light. We were out of the war. The world we were in transcended pain and loss, and imagination had banished fear. Even SP4 Cotton and Calvin Hill, who preferred James Brown to Clifford Brown, lay on their bunks listening as Spanky followed his instincts from one track to another.

After he had played disc jockey for something like two hours, Spanky rewound the long tape and said, 'Enough.' The end of the tape slapped against the reel. I looked at Dengler, who seemed dazed, as if awakening from a long sleep. The memory of the music was still all around us: light still poured in through the crack in the great door.

'I'm gonna have a smoke *and* a drink,' Hill announced, and pushed himself up off his cot. He walked to the door of the tent and pulled the flap aside to expose the green wet drizzle. That dazzling light, the light from another world, began to fade. Hill sighed, plopped a wide-brimmed hat on his head, and slipped outside. Before the stiff flap fell shut, I saw him jumping through the puddles on the way to Wilson Manly's shack. I felt as though I had returned from a long journey.

Spanky finished putting the Clifford Brown reel back into its cardboard box. Someone in the rear of the tent switched on Armed Forces' Radio. Spanky looked at me and shrugged. Leonard Hamnet took his letter out of his pocket, unfolded it, and read it through very slowly.

'Leonard,' I said, and he swung his big buffalo's head

toward me. 'You still putting in for compassionate leave?'

He nodded. 'You know what I gotta do.'

'Yes,' Dengler said, in a slow, quiet voice.

'They gonna let me take care of my people. They gonna send me back.'

He spoke with a complete absence of nuance, like a man who had learned to get what he wanted by parroting words without knowing what they meant.

Dengler looked at me and smiled. For a second he seemed as alien as Hamnet. 'What do you think is going to happen? To us, I mean. Do you think it'll just go on like this day after day until some of us get killed and the rest of us go home, or do you think it's going to get stranger and stranger?' He did not wait for me to answer. 'I think it'll always sort of look the same, but it won't be – I think the edges are starting to melt. I think that's what happens when you're out here long enough. The edges melt.'

'Your edges melted a long time ago, Dengler,' Spanky said, and applauded his own joke.

Dengler was still staring at me. He always resembled a serious, dark-haired child, and never looked as though he belonged in uniform. 'Here's what I mean, kind of,' he said. 'When we were listening to that trumpet player –'

'*Brownie,* Clifford *Brown,*' Spanky whispered.

'– I could see the notes in the air. Like they were written out on a long scroll. And after he played them, they stayed in the air for a long time.'

'Sweetie-*pie,*' Spanky said softly. 'You pretty hip, for a little ofay square.'

'When we were back in that village, last week,' Dengler said. 'Tell me about that.'

I said that he had been there too.

'But something happened to you. Something special.'

'I put twenty bucks in the Elijah fund,' I said.

'Only twenty?' Cotton asked.

'What was in that hut?' Dengler asked.

I shook my head.

'All right,' Dengler said. 'But it's happening, isn't it? Things are changing.'

I could not speak. I could not tell Dengler in front of Cotton and Spanky Burrage that I had imagined seeing the ghosts of Blevins, Budd, and a murdered child. I smiled and shook my head.

'Fine,' Dengler said.

'What the fuck you sayin' is *fine*?' Cotton said. 'I don't mind listening to that music, but I do draw the line at this bullshit.' He flipped himself off his bunk and pointed a finger at me. 'What date you give Spanky?'

'Twentieth.'

'He last longer than that.' Cotton tilted his head as the song on the radio ended. Armed Forces' Radio began playing a song by Moby Grape. Disgusted, he turned back to me. 'Check it out. End of August. He be so tired, he be *sleepwalkin'*. Be halfway through his tour. The fool will go to pieces, and that's when he'll get it.'

Cotton had put thirty dollars on August thirty-first, exactly the midpoint of Lieutenant Joys's tour of duty. He had a long time to adjust to the loss of the money, because he himself stayed alive until a sniper killed him at the beginning of February. Then he became a member of the ghost platoon that followed us wherever we went. I think this ghost platoon, filled with men I had loved and detested, whose names I could or could not remember, disbanded only when I went to the Wall in Washington, DC, and by then I felt that I was a member of it myself.

2

I left the tent with a vague notion of getting outside and enjoying the slight coolness that followed the rain. The packet of Si Van Vo's white powder rested at the bottom of my right front pocket, which was so deep that my fingers just brushed its top. I decided that what I needed was a beer.

Wilson Manly's shack was all the way on the other side of camp. I never liked going to the enlisted men's club, where they were rumored to serve cheap Vietnamese beer in American bottles. Certainly the bottles had often been stripped of their labels, and to a suspicious eye the caps looked dented; also, the beer there never quite tasted like the stuff Manly sold.

One other place remained, farther away than the enlisted men's club but closer than Manly's shack and somewhere between them in official status. About twenty minutes' walk from where I stood, just at the curve in the steeply descending road to the airfield and the motor pool, stood an isolated wooden structure called Billy's. Billy himself, supposedly a Green Beret captain who had installed a handful of bar girls in an old French command post, had gone home long ago, but his club had endured. There were no more girls, if there ever had been, and the brand-name liquor was about as reliable as the enlisted men's club's beer. When it was open, a succession of slender Montagnard boys who slept in the nearly empty upstairs rooms served drinks. I visited these rooms two or three times, but I never learned where the boys went when Billy's was closed. They spoke almost no English. Billy's did not look anything like a French command post, even one that had been transformed into a bordello: it looked like a roadhouse.

A long time ago, the building had been painted brown. The wood was soft with rot. Someone had once boarded up the two front windows on the lower floor, and someone else had torn off a narrow band of boards across each of the windows, so that light entered in two flat white bands that traveled across the floor during the day. Around six-thirty the light bounced off the long foxed mirror that stood behind the row of bottles. After five minutes of blinding light, the sun disappeared beneath the pine boards, and for ten or fifteen minutes a shadowy pink glow filled the barroom. There was no electricity and no ice. Fingerprints covered the glasses. When you needed a toilet, you went to a cubicle with inverted metal boot prints on either side of a hole in the floor.

The building stood in a little grove of trees in the curve of the descending road, and as I walked toward it in the diffuse reddish light of the sunset, a mud-spattered jeep painted in the colors of camouflage gradually came into view to the right of the bar, emerging from invisibility like an optical illusion. The jeep seemed to have floated out of the trees behind it, to be a part of them.

I heard low male voices, which stopped when I stepped onto the soft boards of the front porch. I glanced at the jeep, looking for insignia or identification, but the mud covered the door panels. Something white gleamed dully from the back seat. When I looked more closely, I saw in a coil of rope an oval of bone that it took me a moment to recognize as the top of a painstakingly cleaned and bleached human skull.

Before I could reach the handle, the door opened. A boy named Mike stood before me, in loose khaki shorts and a dirty white shirt much too large for him. Then he saw who I was. 'Oh,' he said. 'Yes. Tim. Okay. You come in.' His real name was not Mike, but Mike was what it sounded like. He carried himself with an odd defensive alertness, and he shot me a tight, uncomfortable smile. 'Far table, right side.'

'It's okay?' I asked, because everything about him told me that it wasn't.

'*Yesss.*' He stepped back to let me in.

I smelled cordite before I saw the other men. The bar looked empty, and the band of light coming in through the opening over the windows had already reached the long mirror, creating a bright dazzle, a white fire. I took a couple of steps inside, and Mike moved around me to return to his post.

'Oh, hell,' someone said from off to my left. 'We have to put up with *this*?'

I turned my head to look into the murk of that side of the bar, and saw three men sitting against the wall at a round table. None of the kerosene lamps had been lighted yet, and the dazzle from the mirror made the far reaches of the bar even less distinct.

'Is okay, is okay,' said Mike. 'Old customer. Old friend.'

'I bet he is,' the voice said. 'Just don't let any women in here.'

'No women,' Mike said. 'No problem.'

I went through the tables to the farthest one on the right.

'You want whiskey, Tim?' Mike asked.

'Tim?' the man said. '*Tim?*'

'Beer,' I said, and sat down.

A nearly empty bottle of Johnnie Walker Black, three glasses, and about a dozen cans of beer covered the table before them. The soldier with his back against the wall shoved aside some of the beer cans so that I could see the .45 next to the Johnnie Walker bottle. He leaned forward with a drunk's guarded coordination. The sleeves had been ripped off his shirt, and dirt darkened his skin as if he had not bathed in years. His hair had been cut with a knife, and had once been blond.

'I just want to make sure about this,' he said. 'You're not a woman, right? You swear to that?'

'Anything you say,' I said.

'No woman walks into this place.' He put his hand on the gun. 'No nurse. No wife. No *anything*. You got that?'

'Got it,' I said. Mike hurried around the bar with my beer.

'Tim. Funny name. Tom, now – that's a name. Tim

97

sounds like a little guy – like him.' He pointed at Mike with his left hand, the whole hand and not merely the index finger, while his right still rested on the .45. 'Little fucker ought to be wearing a dress. Hell, he practically *is* wearing a dress.'

'Don't you like women?' I asked. Mike put a can of Budweiser on my table and shook his head rapidly, twice. He had wanted me in the club because he was afraid the drunken soldier was going to shoot him, and now I was just making things worse.

I looked at the two men with the drunken officer. They were dirty and exhausted – whatever had happened to the drunk had also happened to them. The difference was that they were not drunk yet.

'That is a complicated question,' the drunk said. 'There are questions of responsibility. You can be responsible for yourself. You can be responsible for your children and your tribe. You are responsible for anyone you want to protect. But can you be responsible for women? If so, how responsible?'

Mike quietly moved behind the bar and sat on a stool with his hands out of sight. I knew he had a shotgun under there.

'You don't have any idea what I'm talking about, do you, Tim, you rear-echelon dipshit?'

'You're afraid you'll shoot any women who come in here, so you told the bartender to keep them out.'

'This wise-ass sergeant is personally interfering with my state of mind,' the drunk said to the burly man on his right. 'Tell him to get out of here, or a certain degree of unpleasantness will ensue.'

'Leave him alone,' the other man said. Stripes of dried mud lay across his lean, haggard face.

The drunken officer startled me by leaning toward the other man and speaking in a clear, carrying Vietnamese. It was an old-fashioned, almost literary Vietnamese, and he must have thought and dreamed in it to speak it so well. He assumed that neither I nor the Montagnard boy would understand him.

This is serious, he said, *and I am serious. If you wish to see how serious, just sit in your chair and do nothing. Do you not know of what I am capable by now? Have you learned nothing? You know what I know. I know what you know. A great heaviness is between us. Of all the people in the world at this moment, the only ones I do not despise are already dead, or should be. At this moment, murder is weightless.*

There was more, and I cannot swear that this was exactly what he said, but it's pretty close. He may have said that murder was *empty*.

Then he said, in that same flowing Vietnamese that even to my ears sounded as stilted as the language of a third-rate Victorian novel: *Recall what is in our vehicle* [carriage]; *you should remember what we have brought with us, because I shall never forget it. Is it so easy for you to forget?*

It takes a long time and a lot of patience to clean and bleach bone. A skull would be more difficult than most of a skeleton.

Your leader requires more of this nectar, he said, and rolled back in his chair, looking at me with his hand on his gun.

'Whiskey,' said the burly soldier. Mike was already pulling the bottle off the shelf. He understood that the officer was trying to knock himself out before he would find it necessary to shoot someone.

For a moment I thought that the burly soldier to his right looked familiar. His head had been shaved so close he looked bald, and his eyes were enormous above the streaks of dirt. A stainless-steel watch hung from a slot in his collar. He extended a muscular arm for the bottle Mike passed him while keeping as far from the table as he could. The soldier twisted off the cap and poured into all three glasses. The man in the center immediately drank all the whiskey in his glass and banged the glass down on the table for a refill.

The haggard soldier who had been silent until now said, 'Something is gonna happen here.' He looked straight at me. 'Pal?'

'That man is nobody's pal,' the drunk said. Before anyone could stop him, he snatched up the gun, pointed it across the room, and fired. There was a flash of fire, a huge explosion, and the reek of cordite. The bullet went straight through the soft wooden wall, about eight feet to my left. A stray bit of light slanted through the hole it made.

For a moment I was deaf. I swallowed the last of my beer and stood up. My head was ringing.

'Is it clear that I hate the necessity for this kind of shit?' said the drunk. 'Is that much understood?'

The soldier who had called me *pal* laughed, and the burly soldier poured more whiskey into the drunk's glass. Then he stood up and started coming toward me. Beneath the exhaustion and the stripes of dirt, his face was taut with anxiety. He put himself between me and the man with the gun.

'I am not a rear-echelon dipshit,' I said. 'I don't want any trouble, but people like him do not own this war.'

'Will you maybe let me save your ass, Sergeant?' he whispered. 'Major Bachelor hasn't been anywhere near white men in three years, and he's having a little trouble readjusting. Compared to him, we're all rear-echelon dipshits.'

I looked at his tattered shirt. 'Are you his baby-sitter, Captain?'

He gave me an exasperated look and glanced over his shoulder at the major. 'Major, put down your damn weapon. The sergeant is a combat soldier. He is on his way back to camp.'

I don't care what he is, the major said in Vietnamese.

The captain began pulling me toward the door, keeping his body between me and the other table. I motioned for Mike to come out with me.

'Don't worry, the major won't shoot him. Major Bachelor loves the Yards,' the captain said. He gave me an impatient glance because I had refused to move at his pace. Then I saw him notice my pupils. 'God damn,' he said, and then he stopped moving altogether and said 'God damn' again, but in a different tone of voice.

I started laughing.

'Oh, this is –' He shook his head. 'This is really –'

'Where have you *been*?' I asked him.

John Ransom turned to the table. 'Hey, I know this guy. He's an old football friend of mine.'

Major Bachelor shrugged and put the .45 back on the table. His eyelids had nearly closed. 'I don't care about football,' he said, but he kept his hand off the weapon.

'Buy the sergeant a drink,' said the haggard officer.

'Buy the fucking sergeant a drink,' the major chimed in.

John Ransom quickly moved to the bar and reached for a glass, which the confused Mike put into his hand. Ransom went through the tables, filled his glass and mine, and carried both back to join me.

We watched the major's head slip down by notches toward his chest. When his chin finally reached the unbuttoned top of his ruined shirt, Ransom said, 'All right, Bob,' and the other man slid the .45 out from under the major's hand. He pushed it beneath his belt.

'The man is out,' Bob said.

Ransom turned back to me. 'He was up three days straight with us, God knows how long before that.' Ransom did not have to specify who *he* was. 'Bob and I got some sleep, trading off, but he just kept on talking.' He fell into one of the chairs at my table and tilted his glass to his mouth. I sat down beside him.

For a moment no one in the bar spoke. The line of light from the open space across the windows had already left the mirror, and was now approaching the place on the wall that meant it would soon disappear. Mike lifted the cover from one of the lamps and began trimming the wick.

'How come you're always fucked up when I see you?'

'You have to ask?'

He smiled. He looked very different from when I had seen him preparing to give a sales pitch to Senator Burrman at Camp White Star. His body had thickened and hardened, and his eyes had retreated far back into his head. He seemed to me to have moved a long step nearer the goal I had always seen in him than when he had given me the zealot's word about stopping the spread of communism. This man had taken in more of the war, and that much more of the war was inside him now.

'I got you off graves registration at White Star, didn't I?'

I agreed that he had.

'What did you call it, the body squad? It wasn't even a real graves registration unit, was it?' He smiled and shook his head. 'I took care of your Captain McCue, too – he was using it as a kind of dumping ground. I don't know how he got away with it as long as he did. The only one with any training was that sergeant, what's-his-name. Italian.'

'DiMaestro.'

Ransom nodded. 'The whole operation was going off the rails.' Mike lit a big kitchen match and touched it to the wick of the kerosene lamp. 'I heard some things –' He slumped against the wall and swallowed whiskey. He closed his eyes. 'Some crazy stuff went on back there.'

I asked if he was still stationed in the highlands up around the Laotian border. He almost sighed when he shook his head.

'You're not with the tribesmen anymore? What were they, Khatu?'

He opened his eyes. 'You have a good memory. No, I'm not there anymore.' He considered saying more, but decided not to. He had failed himself. 'I'm kind of on hold until they send me up around Khe Sahn. It'll be better up there – the Bru are tremendous. But right now, all I want to do is take a bath and get into bed. Any bed. Actually, I'd settle for a dry level place on the ground.'

'Where did you come from now?'

'In-country.' His face creased and he showed his teeth. The effect was so unsettling that I did not immediately realize that he was smiling. 'Way in-country. We had to get the major out.'

'Looks more like you had to pull him out, like a tooth.'

My ignorance made him sit up straight. 'You mean you never heard of him? Franklin Bachelor?'

And then I thought I had, that someone had mentioned him to me a long time ago.

'In the bush for years. Bachelor did stuff that ordinary people don't even *dream* of – he's a legend.'

A legend, I thought. Like the Green Berets Ransom had mentioned a lifetime ago at White Star.

'Ran what amounted to a private army, did a lot of good work in Darlac Province. He was out there on his own. The man was a hero. That's straight. Bachelor got to places we couldn't even get close to – he got *inside* an NVA encampment, you hear me, *inside* the encampment and *silently* killed about an entire division.'

Of all the people in the world at this minute, I remembered, the only ones he did not detest were already dead. I thought I must have heard it wrong.

'He was absorbed right into Rhade life,' Ransom said. I could hear the awe in his voice. 'The man even got married. Rhade ceremony. His wife went with him on missions. I hear she was beautiful.'

103

Then I knew where I had heard of Franklin Bachelor before. He had been a captain when Ratman and his platoon had run into him after a private named Bobby Swett had been blown to pieces on a trail in Darlac Province. Ratman had thought his wife was a black-haired angel.

And then I knew whose skull lay wound in rope in the back seat of the jeep.

'I did hear of him,' I said. 'I knew someone who met him. The Rhade woman, too.'

'His *wife*,' Ransom said.

I asked him where they were taking Bachelor.

'We're stopping overnight at Crandall for some rest. Then we hop to Tan Son Nhut and bring him back to the States – Langley. I thought we might have to strap him down, but I guess we'll just keep pouring whiskey into him.'

'He's going to want his gun back.'

'Maybe I'll give it to him.' His look told me what he thought Major Bachelor would do with his .45, if he was left alone with it long enough. 'He's in for a rough time at Langley. There'll be some heat.'

'Why Langley?'

'Don't ask. But don't be naive, either. Don't you think they're . . .' He would not finish that sentence. 'Why do you think we had to bring him out in the first place?'

'Because something went wrong.'

'Oh, everything went wrong. Bachelor went totally out of control. He had his own war. Ran a lot of sidelines, some of which were supposed to be under, shall we say, tighter controls?'

He had lost me.

'Ventures into Laos. Business trips to Cambodia. Sometimes he wound up in control of airfields Air America was using, and that meant he was in control of the cargo.'

When I shook my head, he said, 'Don't you have a little something in your pocket? A little package?'

A secret world – inside this world, another, secret world.

'You understand, I don't care what he did any more than I care about what *you* do. I think Langley can go fuck itself. Bachelor wrote the book. In spite of his sidelines. In spite of whatever *trouble* he got into. The man was effective. He stepped over a boundary, maybe a lot of boundaries – but tell me that you can do what we're supposed to do without stepping over boundaries.'

I wondered why he seemed to be defending himself, and asked if he would have to testify at Langley.

'It's not a trial.'

'A debriefing.'

'Sure, a debriefing. They can ask me anything they want. All I can tell them is what I saw. That's *my* evidence, right? What I saw? They don't have any evidence, except maybe this, uh, these human remains the major insisted on bringing out.'

For a second, I wished that I could see the sober shadowy gentlemen of Langley, Virginia, the gentlemen with slicked-back hair and pin-striped suits, question Major Bachelor. They thought *they* were serious men.

'It was like Bong To, in a funny way.' Ransom waited for me to ask. When I did not, he said, 'A ghost town, I mean. I don't suppose you've ever heard of Bong To.'

'My unit was just there.' His head jerked up. 'A mortar round scared us into the village.'

'You saw the place?'

I nodded.

'Funny story.' Now he was sorry he had ever mentioned it. 'Well, think about Bachelor, now. I think he must have been in Cambodia or someplace, doing what he does, when his village was overrun. He comes back and finds everybody dead, his wife included. I mean, I don't think *Bachelor* killed those people – they weren't just dead, they'd been made to beg for it. So Bachelor wasn't there, and his assistant, a Captain Bennington, must have just run off – we never did find him. Officially, Bennington's MIA. It's simple. You can't find the main guy, so you make sure he can see how mad you are when he gets back. You do a little grievous bodily harm on his people. They were not nice to his wife, Tim, to her they were especially not nice. What does he do? He buries all the bodies in the village graveyard, because that's a sacred responsibility. Don't ask me what else he does, because you don't have to know this, okay? But the bodies are buried. Generally speaking. Captain Bennington never does show up. We arrive and take Bachelor away. But sooner or later, some of the people who escaped are going to come back to that village. They're going to go on living there. The worst thing in the world happened to them in that place, but they won't leave. Eventually, other people in their family will join them, if they're still alive, and the terrible thing will be a part of their lives. Because it is not thinkable to leave your dead.'

'But they did in Bong To,' I said.

'In Bong To, they did.'

I saw the look of regret on his face again, and said that I wasn't asking him to tell me any secrets.

'It's not a secret. It's not even military.'

'It's just a ghost town.'

Ransom was still uncomfortable. He turned his glass around and around in his hands before he drank. 'I have to get the major into camp.'

'A real ghost town,' I said. 'Complete with ghosts.'

'I honestly wouldn't be surprised.' He drank what was left in his glass and stood up. He had decided not to say any more about it. 'Let's take care of Major Bachelor, Bob,' he said.

'Right.'

Ransom carried our bottle to the bar and paid Mike. I stepped toward him to do the same, and Ransom said, 'Taken care of.'

There was that phrase again – it seemed I had been hearing it all day, and that its meaning would not stay still.

Ransom and Bob picked up the major between them. They were strong enough to lift him easily. Bachelor's greasy head rolled forward. Bob put the .45 into his pocket, and Ransom put the bottle into his own pocket. Together they carried the major to the door.

I followed them outside. Artillery pounded hills a long way off. It was dark now, and light from the lanterns spilled out through the gaps in the windows.

All of us went down the rotting steps, the major bobbing between the other two.

Ransom opened the jeep, and they took a while to maneuver the major into the back seat. Bob squeezed in beside him and pulled him upright.

John Ransom got in behind the wheel and sighed. He had no taste for the next part of his job.

'I'll give you a ride back to camp,' he said. 'We don't want an MP to get a close look at you.'

I took the seat beside him. Ransom started the engine and turned on the lights. He jerked the gearshift into reverse and rolled backward. 'You know why that mortar round came in, don't you?' he asked me. He grinned at me, and we bounced onto the road back to the main part of camp. 'He was trying to chase you away from Bong To, and your fool of a lieutenant went straight for the place instead.' He was still grinning. 'It must have steamed him, seeing a bunch of round-eyes going in there.'

'He didn't send in any more fire.'

'No. He didn't want to damage the place. It's supposed to stay the way it is. I don't think they'd use the word, but that village is supposed to be like a kind of monument.' He glanced at me again. 'To shame.'

For some reason, all I could think of was the drunken major in the seat behind me, who had said that you were responsible for the people you wanted to protect.

Ransom said, 'Did you go into any of the huts? Did you see anything unusual there?'

'I went into a hut. I saw something unusual.'

'A list of names?'

'I thought that's what they were.'

'Okay,' Ransom said. 'You know a little Vietnamese?'

'A little.'

'You notice anything about those names?'

I could not remember. My Vietnamese had been picked up in bars and markets, and was almost completely oral.

'Four of them were from a family named Trang. Trang was the village chief, like his father before him, and his grandfather before him. Trang had four daughters. As each one got to the age of six or seven, he took them down into that underground room and chained them to the posts and raped them. A lot of those huts have hidden storage areas, but Trang must have modified his after his first daughter was born. The funny thing is, I think everybody in the village knew what he was doing. I'm not saying they thought it was okay, but they let it happen. They could pretend they didn't know: the girls never complained, and nobody ever heard any screams. I guess Trang was a good enough chief. When the daughters got to sixteen, they left for the cities. Sent back money, too. So maybe they thought it was okay, but I don't think they did, myself, do you?'

'How would I know? But there's a man in my platoon, a guy from –'

'I think there's a difference between private and public shame. Between what's acknowledged and what is not acknowledged. That's what Bachelor has to cope with, when he gets to Langley. Some things are acceptable, as long as you don't talk about them.' He looked sideways at me as we began to approach the northern end of the camp proper. He wiped his face, and flakes of dried mud fell off his cheek. The exposed skin looked red, and so did his eyes. 'Because the way I see it, this is a whole general issue. The issue is: what is *expressible*? This goes way beyond the tendency of people to tolerate thoughts, actions, or behavior they would otherwise find unacceptable.'

I had never heard a soldier speak this way before. It was a little bit like being back in Berkeley.

'I'm talking about the difference between what is expressed and what is described,' Ransom said. 'A lot of experience is unacknowledged. Religion lets us handle some of the unacknowledged stuff in an acceptable way. But suppose – just suppose – that you were forced to confront extreme experience directly, without any mediation?'

'I have,' I said. 'You have, too.'

'More extreme than combat, more extreme than terror. Something like that happened to the major: he *encountered* God. Demands were made upon him. He had to move out of the ordinary, even as *he* defined it.'

Ransom was telling me how Major Bachelor had wound up being brought to Camp Crandall with his wife's skull, but none of it was clear to me.

'I've been learning things,' Ransom told me. He was almost whispering. 'Think about what would make all the people of a village pick up and leave, when sacred obligation ties them to that village.'

'I don't know the answer,' I said.

'An even more sacred obligation, created by a really spectacular sense of shame. When a crime is too great to live with, the memory of it becomes sacred. Becomes the crime itself –'

I remembered thinking that the arrangement in the hut's basement had been a shrine to an obscene deity.

'Here we have this village and its chief. The village knows but does not know what the chief has been doing. They are used to consulting and obeying him. Then – one day, a little boy disappears.'

My heart gave a thud.

'A little boy. Say: three. Old enough to talk and get into trouble, but too young to take care of himself. He's just gone – *poof*. Well, this is Vietnam, right? You turn your back, your kid wanders away, some animal gets him. He could get lost in the jungle and wander into a claymore. Someone like you might even shoot him. He could fall into a booby trap and never be seen again. It could happen.

'A couple of months later, it happens again. Mom turns her back, where the hell did Junior go? This time they really look, not just Mom and Grandma, all their friends. They scour the village. The *villagers* scour the village, every square foot of that place, and then they do the same to the rice paddy, and then they look through the forest.

'And guess what happens next. This is the interesting part. An old woman goes out one morning to fetch water from the well, and she sees a ghost. This old lady is part of the extended family of the first lost kid, but the ghost she sees isn't the kid's – it's the ghost of a disreputable old man from another village, a drunkard, in fact. A local no-good, in fact. He's just standing near the well with his hands together, he's hungry – that's what these people know about ghosts. The skinny old bastard wants *more*. He wants to be *fed*. The old lady gives a squawk and passes out. When she comes to again, the ghost is gone.

'Well, the old lady tells everybody what she saw, and the whole village gets in a panic. Evil forces have been set loose. Next thing you know, two thirteen-year-old girls are working in the paddy, they look up and see an old woman who died when they were ten – she's about six feet away from them. Her hair is stringy and gray and her fingernails are about a foot long. She used to be a friendly old lady, but she doesn't look too friendly now. She's hungry too, like all ghosts. They start screaming and crying, but no one else can see her, and she comes closer and closer, and they try to get away but one of them falls down, and the old woman is on her like a cat. And do you know what she does? She rubs her filthy hands over the screaming girl's face, and licks the tears and slobber off her fingers.

'The next night, another little boy disappears. Two men go looking around the village latrine behind the houses, and they see two ghosts down in the pit, shoving excrement into their mouths. They rush back into the village, and then they both see half a dozen ghosts around the chief's hut. Among them are a sister who died during the war with the French and a twenty-year-old first wife who died of dengue fever. They want to eat. One of the men screeches, because not only did he see his dead wife, who looks something like what we could call a vampire, he saw her pass into the chief's hut without the benefit of the door.

'These people believe in ghosts, Underhill, they know ghosts exist, but it is extremely rare for them to see these ghosts. And these people are like psychoanalysts, because they do not believe in accidents. Every event contains meaning.

'The dead twenty-year-old wife comes back out through the wall of the chief's hut. Her hands are empty but dripping with red, and she is licking them like a starving cat.

'The former husband stands there pointing and jabbering, and the mothers and grandmothers of the missing boys come out of their huts. They are as afraid of what they're thinking as they are of all the ghosts moving around them. The ghosts are part of what they know they know, even though most of them have never seen one until now. What is going through their minds is something new: new because it was hidden.

'The mothers and grandmothers go to the chief's door and begin howling like dogs. When the chief comes out, they push past him and they take the hut apart. And you know what they find. They find the end of Bong To.'

Ransom had parked the jeep near my battalion head-quarters five minutes before, and now he smiled as if he had explained everything.

'But what *happened*?' I asked. 'How did you hear about it?'

He shrugged. 'We learned all this in interrogation. When the women found the underground room, they knew the chief had forced the boys into sex, and then killed them. They didn't know what he had done with the bodies, but they knew he had killed the boys. The next time the VC paid one of their courtesy calls, they told the cadre leader what they knew. The VC did the rest. They were disgusted – Trang had betrayed *them*, too – betrayed everything he was supposed to represent. One of the VC we captured took the chief downstairs into his underground room and chained the man to the posts, wrote the names of the dead boys and Trang's daughters on the padding that covered the walls, and then . . . then they did what they did to him. They probably carried out the pieces and threw them into the excrement pit. And over months, bit by bit, not all at once but slowly, everybody in the village moved out. By that time, they were seeing ghosts all the time. They had crossed a kind of border.'

'Do you think they really saw ghosts?' I asked him. 'I mean, do you think they were real ghosts?'

'If you want an expert opinion, you'd have to ask Major Bachelor. He has a lot to say about ghosts.' He hesitated for a moment, and then leaned over to open my door. 'But if you ask me, sure they did.'

I got out of the jeep and closed the door.

Ransom peered at me. 'Take better care of yourself.'

'Good luck with your Bru.'

'The Bru are fantastic.' He slammed the jeep into gear and shot away, cranking the wheel to turn the jeep around in a giant circle in front of the battalion headquarters before he jammed it into second and took off to wherever he was going.

Two weeks later Leonard Hamnet managed to get the Lutheran chaplain at Crandall to write a letter to the Tin Man for him, and two days after that he was in a clean uniform, packing up his kit for an overnight flight to an air force base in California. From there he was connecting to a Memphis flight, and from there the army had booked him onto a six-passenger puddle jumper to Lookout Mountain.

When I came into Hamnet's tent he was zipping his bag shut in a zone of quiet afforded him by the other men. He did not want to talk about where he was going or the reason he was going there, and instead of answering my questions about his flights, he unzipped a pocket on the side of his bag and handed me a thick folder of airline tickets.

I looked through them and gave them back. 'Hard travel,' I said.

'From now on, everything is easy,' Hamnet said. He seemed rigid and constrained as he zipped the precious tickets back into the bag. By this time his wife's letter was a rag held together with Scotch tape. I could picture him reading and rereading it, for the thousandth or two thousandth time, on the long flight over the Pacific.

'They need your help,' I said. 'I'm glad they're going to get it.'

'That's right.' Hamnet waited for me to leave him alone.

Because his bag seemed heavy, I asked about the length of his leave. He wanted to get the tickets back out of the bag rather than answer me directly, but he forced himself to speak. 'They gave me seven days. Plus travel time.'

'Good,' I said, meaninglessly, and then there was nothing left to say, and we both knew it. Hamnet hoisted his bag off his bunk and turned to the door without any of the usual farewells and embraces. Some of the other men called to him, but he seemed to hear nothing but his own thoughts. I followed him outside and stood beside him in the heat. Hamnet was wearing a tie and his boots had a high polish. He was already sweating through his stiff khaki shirt. He would not meet my eyes. In a minute a jeep pulled up before us. The Lutheran chaplain had surpassed himself.

'Good-bye, Leonard,' I said, and Hamnet tossed his bag in back and got into the jeep. He sat up straight as a statue. The private driving the jeep said something to him as they drove off, but Hamnet did not reply. I bet he did not say a word to the stewardesses, either, or to the cabdrivers or baggage handlers or anyone else who witnessed his long journey home.

3

On the day after Leonard Hamnet was scheduled to return, Lieutenant Joys called Michael Poole and myself into his quarters to tell us what had happened back in Tennessee. He held a sheaf of papers in his hand, and he seemed both angry and embarrassed. Hamnet would not be returning to the platoon. It was a little funny. Well, of course it wasn't funny at all. The whole thing was terrible – that was what it was. Someone was to blame, too. Irresponsible decisions had been made, and we'd all be lucky if there wasn't an investigation. We were closest to the man, hadn't we seen what was likely to happen? If not, what the hell was our excuse?

Didn't we have any inkling of what the man was planning to do?

Well, yes, at the beginning, Poole and I said. But he seemed to have adjusted.

We have stupidity and incompetence all the way down the line here, said Lieutenant Elijah Joys. Here is a man who manages to carry a semiautomatic weapon through security at three different airports, bring it into a courthouse, and carry out threats he made months before, without anybody stopping him.

I remembered the bag Hamnet had tossed into the back of the jeep; I remembered the reluctance with which he had zipped it open to show me his tickets. Hamnet had not carried his weapon through airport security. He had just shipped it home in his bag and walked straight through customs in his clean uniform and shiny boots.

As soon as the foreman had announced the guilty verdict, Leonard Hamnet had gotten to his feet, pulled the semiautomatic pistol from inside his jacket, and executed Mr Brewster where he was sitting at the defense table. While people shouted and screamed and dove for cover, while the courthouse officer tried to unsnap his gun, Hamnet killed his wife and his son. By the time he raised the pistol to his own head, the security officer had shot him twice in the chest. He died on the operating table at Lookout Mountain Lutheran Hospital, and his mother had requested that his remains receive burial at Arlington National Cemetery.

His mother. Arlington. I ask you.

That was what the Lieutenant said. *His mother. Arlington. I ask you.*

A private from Indianapolis named E. W. Burroughs won the six hundred and twenty dollars in the Elijah fund when Lieutenant Joys was killed by a fragmentation bomb thirty-two days before the end of his tour. After that we were delivered unsuspecting into the hands of Harry Beevers, the Lost Boss, the worst lieutenant in the world. Private Burroughs died a week later, down in Dragon Valley along with Tiano and Calvin Hill and lots of others, when Lieutenant Beevers walked us into a mined field, where we spent forty-eight hours under fire between two companies of NVA. I suppose Burroughs's mother back in Indianapolis got the six hundred and twenty dollars.

Bunny Is Good Bread

for Stephen King

Part One

1

Fee's first memory was of a vision of fire, not an actual fire but an imagined fire leaping upward at an enormous grate upon which lay a naked man. Attached to this image was the accompanying memory of his father gripping the telephone. For a moment his father, Bob Bandolier, the one and only king of this realm, seemed rubbery, almost boneless with shock. He repeated the word, and a second time five-year-old Fielding Bandolier, little blond Fee, saw the flames jumping at the blackening figure on the grate. 'I'm fired? This has got to be a joke.'

The flames engulfed the tiny man on the slanting grate. The man opened his mouth to screech. This was hell, it was interesting. Fee was scorched, too, by those flames. His father saw the child looking up at him, and the child saw his father take in his presence. A fire of pain and anger flashed out of his father's face, and Fee's insides froze. His father waved him away with a back-paddling gesture of his left hand. In the murk of their apartment, Bob Bandolier's crisp white shirt gleamed like an apparition. The creases from the laundry jutted up from the shirt's starched surface.

'You *know* why I haven't been coming in,' he said. 'This is not a matter where I have a choice. You will never, ever find a man who is as devoted –'

He listened, bowing over as if crushing down a spring

116

in his chest. Fee crept backward across the room, hoping to make no noise at all. When he backed into the chaise against the far wall, he instinctively dropped to his knees and crawled beneath it, still looking at the way his father was bending over the telephone. Fee bumped into a dark furry lump, Jude the cat, and clamped it to his chest until it stopped struggling.

'No, sir,' his father said. 'If you think about the way I work, you will have to –'

He blew air out of his mouth, still pushing down that coiled spring in his chest. Fee knew that his father hated to be interrupted.

'I see that, sir, but a person on my salary can't hire a nurse or a housekeeper, and –'

Another loud exhalation.

'Do I have to tell you what goes on in hospitals? The infections, the sheer sloppiness, the . . . I have to keep her at home. I don't know if you're aware of this, sir, but there have been very few nights when I have not been able to spend most of my time at the hotel.'

Slowly, as if he had become aware of the oddness of his posture, Fee's father began straightening up. He pressed his hand into the small of his back. 'Sometimes we pray.'

Fee saw the air around his father darken and fill with little white sparkling swirling things that winked and dazzled before they disappeared. Jude saw them too, and moved deeper beneath the chaise.

'Well, I suppose you are entitled to your own opinion about that,' said his father, 'but you are very much mistaken if you feel that my religious beliefs did in any way –'

'I dispute that absolutely,' his father said.

'I have already explained that,' his father said. 'Almost every night since my wife fell ill, I managed to get to the hotel. I bring an attitude to work with me, sir, of absolute dedication –'

'I'm sorry you feel that way, sir,' his father said, 'but you are making a very great mistake.'

'I mean, you are making a *mistake*,' his father said. The little white dancing lines spun and winked out in the air like fireworks.

Both Fee and Jude stared raptly from beneath the chaise.

His father gently replaced the receiver, and then set the telephone down on the table. His face was set in the cement of prayer.

Fee looked at the black telephone on its little table between the big chair and the streaky window: the headset like a pair of droopy ears, the round dial. On the matching table, a porcelain fawn nuzzled a porcelain doe.

Heavy footsteps strode toward him. Jude searched warmth against his side. His father came striding in his gleaming shirt with the boxy lines from the dry cleaner's, his dark trousers, his tacked-down necktie, his shiny shoes. His mustache, two fat commas, seemed like another detachable ornament.

Bob Bandolier bent down, settled his thick white hands beneath Fee's arms, and pulled him up like a toy. He set him on his feet and frowned down at the child.

Then his father slapped his face and sent him backward against the chaise. Fee was too stunned to cry. When his father struck the other side of his face, his knees went away and he began to slip toward the rug. His cheeks burned. Bob Bandolier leaned down again. Silver light from the window painted a glowing white line on his dark hair. Fee's breath burned its way past the hot ball in his throat, and he closed his eyes and wailed.

'Do you know why I did that?'

His father's voice was still as low and reasonable as it had been when he was on the telephone.

Fee shook his head.

'Two reasons. Listen to me, son. Reason number one.'
He raised his index finger. 'You disobeyed me, and I will
always punish disobedience.'

'No,' Fee said.

'I sent you from the room, didn't I? Did you go out?'

Fee shook his head again, and his father gripped him
tightly between his two hands and waited for him to stop
sobbing. 'I will not be contradicted, is that clear?'

Fee nodded miserably. His father gave a cool kiss to his
burning cheek.

'I said there were two reasons, remember?'

Fee nodded.

'Sin is the second reason.' Bob Bandolier's face moved
hugely through the space between them, and his eyes,
deep brown with luminous eggshell whites, searched
Fee and found his crime. Fee began to cry again. His
father held him upright. 'The Lord Jesus is very, very
angry today, Fielding. He will demand payment, and we
must pay.'

When his father talked like this, Fee saw a page from
Life magazine, a torn battlefield covered with shell craters,
trees burned to charred stumps, and huddled corpses.

'We will pray together,' his father said, and hitched up
the legs of his trousers and went down on his knees. 'Then
we will go in to see your mother.' His father touched one
of his shoulders with an index finger and pressed down,
trying to push Fee all the way through the floor to the
regions of eternal flame. Fee finally realized that his father
was telling him to kneel, and he too went to his knees.

His father had closed his eyes, and his forehead was full
of vertical lines. 'Are you going to talk?' Fee said.

'Pray *silently*, Fee – say the words to yourself.'

He put his hands together before his face and began
moving his lips. Fee closed his own eyes and heard Jude
dragging her tongue over and over the same spot of
fur.

His father said, 'Let's get in there. She's our job, you know.'

Inside the bedroom, he opened the clothing press and took his suit jacket from a hanger, replaced the hanger, and closed the door of the press. He shoved his arms into the jacket's sleeves and transformed himself into the more formal and forbidding man Fee knew best. He dipped his knees in front of the bedroom mirror to check the knot in his tie. He swept his hands over the smooth hair at the sides of his head. His eyes in the mirror found Fee's. 'Go to your mother, Fee.'

Until two weeks ago, the double bed had stood on the far end of the rag rug, his mother's perfume and lotion bottles had stood on the left side of what she called her 'vanity table', her blond wooden chair in front of it. His father now stood there, watching him in the mirror. Up until two weeks ago, the curtains had been open all day, and the bedroom had always seemed full of a warm magic. Fat black Jude spent all day lying in the pool of sunlight that collected in the middle of the rug. Now the curtains stayed shut, and the room smelled of sickness – it reminded Fee of the time his father had brought him to work with him and, giddy with moral outrage, thrust him into a ruined, stinking room. *You want to see what people are really like*? Slivers of broken glass had covered the floor, and the stuffing foamed out of the slashed sofa, but the worst part had been the smell of the lumps and puddles on the floor. The walls had been streaked with brown. *This is their idea of fun*, his father had said. *Of a good time.* Now the rag rug was covered by the old mattress his father had placed on the floor beside the bed. The blond chair in front of the vanity table had disappeared, as had the row of little bottles his mother had cherished. Two weeks ago, when everything had changed, Fee had heard his father smashing these bottles, roaring, smashing the chair against the wall. It was as if a monster had burst from his father's

120

skin to rage back and forth in the bedroom. The next morning, his father said that Mom was sick. Pieces of the chair lay all over the room, and the walls were covered with explosions. The whole room smelled overpoweringly sweet, like heaven with its flowers. *Your mother needs to rest. She needs to get better.* Fee had dared one glance at her tumbled hair and open mouth. A tiny curl of blood crept from her nose. *She's sick, but we'll take care of her.*

She had not gotten any better. As the perfume explosions had dried on the wall, his father's shirts and socks and underwear had gradually covered the floor between the old mattress and the bare vanity table, and Fee now walked over the litter of clothing to step on the mattress and approach the bed. The sickroom smell intensified as he came closer to his mother. He was not sure that he could look at his mother's face – the bruised, puffy mask he had seen the last time his father had let him into the bedroom. He stood on the thin mattress beside the bed, looking at the wisps of brown hair that hung down over the side of the bed. They reached all the way to the black letters stamped on the sheet that read *St Alwyn Hotel*. Maybe her hair was still growing. Maybe she was waiting for him to look at her. Maybe she was better – the way she used to be. Fee touched the letters, and let his fingers drift upward so that his mother's hair brushed his hand. He could hear breath moving almost soundlessly in his mother's throat.

'See how good she looks now? She's looking real good, aren't you, honey?'

Fee moved his eyes upward. It felt as though his chest and his stomach, everything inside him, swung out of his body and swayed in the air a moment before coming back inside him. Except for a fading yellow bruise that extended from her eye to her hairline, she looked like his mother again. Flecks of dried oatmeal clung to her chin and the sides of her mouth. The fine lines in her cheeks looked like pencil marks. Her mouth hung a little bit open, as if to sip the air, or to beg for more oatmeal.

Fee is five, and he is looking at his mother for the first time since he saw her covered with bruises. His conscious life – the extraordinary life of Fee's consciousness – has just begun.

He thought for a second that his mother was going to answer. Then he realized that his father had spoken to her as he would speak to Jude, or to a dog in the street. He let his fingertips touch her skin. Unlike her face, his mother's hands were rough, with enlarged knuckles like knots and callused fingertips that widened out at their ends. The skin on the back of her hand felt cool and peculiarly coarse.

'Sure you are, honey,' said his father behind him. 'You're looking better every day.'

Fee clutched her hand and tried to squeeze some of his own life into her. His mother lay on her bed like a princess frozen by a curse in a fairy tale. A blue vein pulsed in her eyelid. All she could see was black night.

For a second Fee saw night too, a deep swooning blackness that called to him.

Yes, he thought. *Okay. That's okay.*

'We're here, honey,' his father said.

Fee wondered if he had ever before heard his father call his mother *honey*.

'That's your little Fee holding your hand, honey, can't you feel his love?'

A startling sense of negation – of revulsion – caused Fee to pull back his hands. If his father saw, he did not mind, for he said nothing. Fee saw his mother floating away into the immense sea of blackness inside her.

For a second he forgot to breathe through his mouth, and the stench that rose from the bed assaulted him.

'Didn't have time to clean her up yet today. I'll get to it before long – but you know, she could be lying on a bed of silk, it'd be all the same to her.'

Fee wanted to lean forward and put his arms around his mother, but he stepped back.

'We're none of us doctors and nurses here, Fee.'

For a moment Fee thought there must be more people in the room. Then he realized that his father meant the two of them, and that put into his head an idea of great simplicity and truth.

'Mommy ought to have a doctor,' he said, and risked looking up at his father.

His father leaned over and pulled him by the shoulders, making him move awkwardly backward over the mattress on the floor. Fee braced himself to be struck again, but his father turned him around and faced him with neither the deepening of feeling nor the sparkling of violence that usually preceded a blow.

'If I was three nurses instead of just one man, I could give her a change of sheets twice a day – hell, I could probably wash her hair and brush her teeth for her. But, Fee –' His father's grip tightened, and the wedges of his fingers drove into Fee's skin. 'Do you think your mother would be happy, away from us?'

The person lying on the bed no longer had anything to do with happiness and unhappiness.

'She could only be happy being here with us, that's right, Fee, you're *right*. She knew you were holding her hand – that's why she's going to get better.' He looked up. 'Pretty soon, you're going to be sitting up and sassing back, isn't that right?'

He wouldn't allow anybody to sass him back, not ever.

'Let's pray for her now.'

His father pushed him down to his knees again, then

joined him on the blanket. 'Our Father who art in heaven,' he said. 'Your servant, Anna Bandolier, my wife and this boy's mother, needs Your help. And so do we. Help us to care for her in her weakness, and we ask You to help her to overcome this weakness. Not a single person on earth is perfect, this poor sick woman included, and maybe we all have strayed in thought and deed from Your ways. Mercy is the best we can hope for, and we sinners know we do not deserve it, amen.'

He lowered his hands and got to his feet. 'Now leave the room, Fee.' He removed his jacket and hung it on one of the bedposts and rolled up his sleeves. He tucked his necktie into his shirt. He stopped to give his son a disturbingly concentrated look. 'We're going to take care of her by ourselves, and we don't want anybody else knowing our business.'

'Yes, sir,' Fee said.

His father jerked his head toward the bedroom door. 'You remember what I said.'

2

His father never asked if he wanted to kiss his mom, and he never thought to ask if he could – the pale woman lying on the bed with her eyes closed was not someone you could kiss. She was sailing out into the vast darkness within her a little more every day. She was like a radio station growing fainter and fainter as you drove into the country.

The yellow bruise faded away, and one morning Fee realized that it had vanished altogether. Her cheeks sank inward toward her teeth, drawing a new set of faint pencil lines across her face. One day, five or six days after the bruise had disappeared, Fee saw that the round blue shadows of her temples had collapsed some fraction of an inch inward, like soft ground sinking after rain.

Fee's father kept saying that she was getting better, and Fee knew that this was true in a way that his father could not understand and he himself could only barely see. She was getting better because her little boat had sailed a long way into the darkness.

Sometimes Fee held a half-filled glass of water to her lips and let teaspoon-sized sips slide, one after another, into the dry cavern of her mouth. His mother never seemed to swallow these tiny drinks, for the moisture slipped down her throat by itself. He could see it move, quick as a living thing, shining and shivering as it darted into her throat.

Sometimes when his father prayed, Fee found himself examining the nails on his mother's hand, which grew longer by themselves. At first her fingernails were pink, but in a week, they turned an odd yellowish-white. The moons disappeared. Oddest of all, her long fingernails grew a yellow-brown rind of dirt.

He watched the colors alter in her face. Her lips darkened to brown, and a white fur appeared in the corner of her mouth.

Lord, this woman needs Your mercy. We're counting on You here, Lord.

When Fee left the bedroom each evening, he could hear his father go about the business of cleaning her up. When his father came out of the room, he carried the reeking ball of dirty sheets downstairs into the basement, his face frozen with distaste.

Mrs Sunchana from the upstairs apartment washed her family's things twice a week, on Monday and Wednesday mornings, and never came downstairs at night. Fee's father put the clean sheets through the wringer and then took the heavy sheets outside to hang them on the two washing lines that were the Bandoliers'.

One night, his father slapped him awake and leaned over him in the dark. Fee, too startled to cry, saw his father's enormous eyes and the glossy commas of the mustache glaring down at him. His teeth shone. Heat and the odor of alcohol poured from him.

– You think I was put on earth to be your servant. I was not put on earth to be your servant. I could close the door and walk out of here tomorrow and never look back. Don't kid yourself – I'd be a lot happier if I did.

3

One day Bob Bandolier got a temporary job as desk man at the Hotel Hepton. Fee buffed his father's black shoes and got the onyx cuff links from the top of the dresser. He pulled on his own clothes and watched his father pop the dry cleaner's band from around a beautiful stiff white shirt, settle the shirt like armor around his body and squeeze the buttons through the holes, coax the cuff links into place, tug his sleeves, knot a lustrous and silvery tie, button his dark suit. His father dipped his knees before the bedroom mirror, brushed back the smooth hair at the sides of his head, used his little finger to rub wax into his perfect mustache, a comb no larger than a thumbnail to coax it through the whiskers.

His father pulled his neat dark topcoat on over the suit, patted his pockets, and gave Fee a dollar. He was to sit on the steps until noon, when he could walk to the Beldame Oriental Theater. A quarter bought him admission, and fifty cents would get him a hot dog, popcorn, and a soft drink; he could see *From Dangerous Depths*, starring Robert Ryan and Ida Lupino, along with a second feature, the travelogue, previews, and a cartoon; then he was to walk back down Livermore without talking to anybody and wait on the steps until his father came back home to let him in. The movies ended at twenty-five minutes past five, and his father said he would be home before six, so it would not be a long wait.

'We have to make it snappy,' his father said. 'You can't be late for the Hepton, you know.'

Fee went dutifully to the closet just inside the front door, where his jacket and his winter coat hung from hooks screwed in halfway down the door. He reached up dreamily, and his father ripped the jacket off the hook and pushed it into his chest.

Before Fee could figure out the jacket, his father had opened the front door and shoved him out onto the landing. Fee got an arm into a sleeve while his father locked the door. Then he pulled at the jacket, but his other arm would not go into its sleeve.

'Fee, you're deliberately trying to louse me up,' his father said. He ripped the jacket off his arm, turned it around, and jammed his arms into the sleeves. Then he fought the zipper for a couple of seconds. 'You zip it. I have to go. You got your money?'

He was going down the steps and past the rosebushes to the path that went to the sidewalk.

Fee nodded.

Bob Bandolier walked away without looking back. He was tall and almost slim in his tight black coat. Nobody else on the street looked like him – all the other men wore plaid caps and old army jackets.

In a little while, smiling Mrs Sunchana came up the walk carrying a bag of groceries. 'Fee, you are enjoying the sunshine? You don't feel the cold today?' Her slight foreign accent made her speech sound musical, and her creamy round face, with its dark eyes and black eyebrows beneath her black bangs, could seem either witchlike or guilelessly pretty. Mrs Sunchana looked nothing at all like Fee's mother – short, compact, and energetic where his mother was tall, thin, and weary; dark and cheerful where she was sorrowing and fair.

'I'm not cold,' he said, though the chill licked in under the collar of his jacket, and his ears had begun to tingle.

Mrs Sunchana smiled at him again, said, 'Hold this for me, Fee,' and thrust the grocery bag onto his lap. He gripped the heavy bag as she opened her purse and searched for her key. There were no lines in her face at all. Both her cheeks and her lips were plump with health and life – for a second, bending over her black plastic purse and frowning with concentration, she seemed almost volcanic to Fee, and he wondered what it would be like to have this woman for his mother. He thought of her plump strong arms closing around him. Her face expanded above him. A rapture that was half terror filled his body.

For a second he was her child.

Mrs Sunchana unlocked the door and held it open with one hip while she bent to take the groceries from Fee's lap. Fee looked down into the bag and saw a cardboard carton of brown eggs and a box of sugar-covered doughnuts. Mrs Sunchana's live black hair brushed his forehead. The world wavered before him, and a trembling electricity filled his head. She drew the bag out of his arms, then quizzed him with a look.

'Coming in?'

'I'm going to the movies pretty soon.'

'You don't want to wait inside, where it is warm?'

He shook his head. Mrs Sunchana tightened her grip on the grocery bag. The expression on her face frightened him, and he turned away to look at the empty sidewalk.

'Is your mother all right, Fee?'

'She's sleeping.'

'Oh.' Mrs Sunchana nodded.

'We're letting her sleep until my dad gets home.'

Mrs Sunchana kept nodding as she backed through the door. Fee remembered the eggs and the sugary doughnuts, and turned around again before she could see how hungry he was. 'Do you know what time it is?'

She leaned over the bag to look at her watch. 'About ten-thirty. Why, Fee?'

A black car moved down the street, its tires swishing through the fallen elm leaves. The front door clicked shut behind him.

A minute later, a window slid upward in its frame. A painful self-consciousness brought him to his feet. He put his hands in his pockets.

Fee walked stiffly and slowly down the path to the sidewalk and turned left toward Livermore Avenue. He remembered the moment when Mrs Sunchana's electrically alive hair had moved against his forehead, and an extraordinary internal pain sent him gliding over the pavement.

The elms of Livermore Avenue interlocked their branches far overhead. Preoccupied men and women in coats moved up and down past the shop fronts. Fee was away from his block, and no one was going to ask him questions. Fee glanced to his right and experienced a sharp flame of anger and disgrace that somehow seemed connected to Mrs Sunchana's questions about his mother.

But of course what was across the street had nothing to do with his mother. Beyond the slowly moving vehicles, the high boxy automobiles and the slat-sided trucks, a dark, arched passage led into a narrow alley. In front of the brick passage was a tall gray building with what to Fee looked like a hundred windows, and behind it was the blank facade of a smaller, brown brick building. The gray building was the St Alwyn Hotel, the smaller building its annex. Fee felt that he was no longer supposed to *look* at the St Alwyn. The St Alwyn had done something bad, grievously bad – it had opened a most terrible hole in the world, and from that hole had issued hellish screams and groans.

A pure, terrible ache occurred in the middle of his body. From across the street, the St Alwyn leered at him. Cold gray air sifted through his clothing. Brilliant leaves packed the gutters; water more transparent than the air streamed over and through the leaves. The ache within

Fee threatened to blow him apart. He wanted to lower his face into the water – to dissolve into the transparent stream.

A man in a dark coat had appeared at the end of the tunnel behind the St Alwyn, and Fee's heart moved with an involuntary constriction of pain and love before he consciously took in that the man was his father.

His father staring at a spot on the tunnel wall.

Why was his father behind the hated St Alwyn, when he was supposed to be working at the Hotel Hepton?

His father looked from side to side, then moved into the darkness of the tunnel.

Bob Bandolier began fleeing down the alley. A confusion of feelings like voices raised in Fee's chest.

Now the alley was empty. Fee walked a few yards along the sidewalk, looking down at the clear water moving through the brilliant leaves. The sorrow and misery within him threatened to overflow. Without thinking, Fee dropped to his knees and thrust both of his hands into the water. A shock of cold bit into him. His small white hands sank farther than he had expected into the transparent water, and handcuffs made of burning ice formed around his wrists. The leaves drifted apart when he touched them. A brown stain oozed out and drifted, obscuring the leaves. Gasping, Fee pulled his hands from the water and wiped them on his jacket. He leaned over the gutter to watch the brown stain pour from the hole he had made in the leaves. Whatever it was, he had turned it loose, set it free.

4

The box of popcorn warmed Fee's hands. The Beldame Oriental Theater's luxurious space, with its floating cherubs and robed women raising lamps, its gilded arabesques and swooping curves of plaster, lay all about him. Empty rows of seats extended forward and back, and high up in the darkness hung the huge raft of the balcony. An old woman in a flowerpot hat sat far down in the second row; off to his left a congregation of shapeless men drank from pint bottles in paper bags.

This happened every day, Fee realized.

MOVIETONE NEWS blared from the screen, and a voice like a descending fist spoke over film of soldiers pointing rifles into dark skies, of a black boxer with a knotted forehead knocking down a white boxer in a brilliant spray of sweat. Women in bathing suits and sashes stood in a row and smiled at the camera; a woman in a long gown raised a crown from her head and placed it on the glowing black hair of a woman who looked like Mrs Sunchana. It *was* Mrs Sunchana, Fee thought, but then saw that her face was thinner than Mrs Sunchana's, and his panic calmed.

The grinning heads of a gray cat and a small brown mouse popped onto the screen. Fee laughed in delight. In cartoons the music was loud and relentless, and the animals behaved like bad children. Characters were turned to smoking ruins, pressed flat, dismembered, broken like twigs, consumed by fires, and in seconds were whole again. Cartoons were about not being hurt.

Abruptly, he was running through a cartoon house, alongside a cartoon mouse. The mouse ran upright on his legs, like a human being. Behind him, also on whirling back legs, ran the cat. The mouse scorched a track through the carpet and zoomed into a neat mouse hole seconds before the cat's huge paw filled the hole. Fee brought salty popcorn to his mouth. Jerry Mouse sat at a little table and ate a mouse-sized steak with a knife and a fork. Fee drank in the enormity of his pleasure, the self-delight and swagger of the mouse, and the jealous rage of Tom Cat, rolling his giant bloodshot eye at the mouse hole.

After the cartoon, Fee walked up the aisle to buy a hot

dog. Two or three people had taken seats in the vast space behind him. An old woman wrapped in a hairy brown coat mumbled to herself; a teenage boy cutting school cocked his feet on the seat in front of him. Fee saw the outline of a big man's head and shoulders on the other side of the theater, looked away, felt an odd sense of recognition, and looked back at an empty seat. He had been seen, but who had seen him?

Fee pushed through the wide doors into the lobby. A skinny man in a red jacket stood behind the candy counter, and an usher exhaled smoke from a velvet bench. The door to the men's room was just now swinging shut.

Fee bought a steaming hot dog and squirted ketchup onto it, wrapped it in a flimsy paper napkin, and hurried back into the theater. He heard the door of the men's room sliding across the lobby carpet. He rushed down the aisle and took his seat as the titles came up on the screen.

The stars of *From Dangerous Depths* were Robert Ryan and Ida Lupino. It was directed by Robert Siodmak. Fee had never heard of any of these people, nor of any of the supporting actors, and he was disappointed that the movie was not in color.

Charlie Carpenter (Robert Ryan) was a tall, well-dressed accountant who lived alone in a hotel room like those at the St Alwyn. Charlie Carpenter put a wide-brimmed hat on the floor and flipped cards into it. He wore a necktie at home and, like Bob Bandolier, he peered into the mirror to scowl at his handsome, embittered face. At work he snubbed his office mates, and after work he drank in a bar. On Sundays he attended mass. One day, Charlie Carpenter noticed a discrepancy in the accounts, but when he asked about it, his angry supervisor (William Bendix) said that he had come upon traces of the Elijah Fund – this fund was used for certain investments, it was none of Charlie's business, he should never have discovered it in the first place, a junior clerk had made a mistake, Charlie must forget he'd ever heard of it. When Charlie wondered about the corporate officers in control of the fund, his supervisor reluctantly gave him two names, Fenton Welles and Lily Sheehan, but warned him to leave the matter alone.

Fenton Welles (Ralph Meeker) and Lily Sheehan (Ida Lupino) owned comfortable houses in the wealthy part of town. Charlie Carpenter scanned their lawn parties through field glasses; he followed them to their country houses on opposite sides of Random Lake, fifty miles north of the city.

Lily Sheehan summoned Charlie to her office. He feared that she knew he had been following her, but Lily gave Charlie a cigarette and sat on the edge of her desk and said she had noticed that his reports were unusually perceptive. Charlie was a smart loner, just the sort of man whose help she needed.

Lily had suspicions about Fenton Welles. Charlie didn't have to know more than he *should* know, but Lily thought that Welles had been stealing from the company by manipulating a confidential fund. Was Charlie willing to work for her?

Charlie broke the lock on Fenton Welles's back door and groped through the dark house. Using a flashlight, he found the staircase and worked his way upstairs. He found the master bedroom and went to the desk. Just as he opened the center drawer and found a folder marked ELIJAH, the front door opened downstairs. Holding his breath, he looked in the file and saw photographs of various men, alone and in groups, in military uniform. He put the file back in the drawer, climbed out the window, and scrambled down the roof until he could jump onto the lawn. A dog charged him out of the darkness, and Charlie picked up a heavy stick beneath a tree and battered the dog to death.

Lily Sheehan told Charlie to take a room at the Random Lake Motel, rent a motorboat, and break into Welles's house when he was at a country club dance. Charlie and Lily were both smoking, and Lily prowled around him. She sat on the arm of his chair. Her dress seemed tighter.

In the dark behind him, somebody whistled.

Charlie and Lily kissed.

The music behind Charlie Carpenter announced *doom, ruin, death*. He pulled a carton from a closet in Fenton Welles's lake house and dumped its contents onto the floor. Stacks of bills held together with rubber bands fell out of the carton, along with a big envelope marked ELIJAH. Charlie opened the envelope and pulled out photographs of Fenton Welles and Lily Sheehan shot through the window of a restaurant, Fenton Welles and Lily walking down a street arm in arm, Fenton Welles and Lily in the back seat of a taxi, driving away.

'Aha,' said a voice from the back of the theater.

An angry, betrayed Charlie shouted at Lily Sheehan, waved a fist in the air, kicked at furniture. These sounds, Fee knew, were those that came before the screams and the sobs.

But the beatings did not come. Lily Sheehan began to cry, and Charlie took her in his arms.

He's evil, Lily said.

A stunned look bloomed in Charlie's dark eyes.

It's the only way I'll ever be free.

'Watch out,' the man called, and Fee turned around and squinted into the back of the theater.

In the second row from the back, far under the beam of light from the projectionist's booth, a big man with light hair leaned forward with his hands held up like binoculars. 'Peekaboo,' he said. Fee whirled around, his face burning.

'I know who you are,' the man said.

I'm all the soul you need, Lily said from the screen.

Fenton Welles walked in from a round of golf at the

Random Lake Country Club, and Charlie Carpenter came sneering out from behind the staircase with a fireplace poker raised in his right hand. He smashed it down onto Welles's head.

Lily wiped the last trace of blood from Charlie's face with a tiny handkerchief, and for a second Fee *had* it, he knew the name of the man behind him, but this knowledge disappeared into the dread taking place on the screen, where Lily and Charlie lay in a shadowy bed talking about the next thing Charlie must do.

Death death death sang the soundtrack.

Charlie hid in the shadowy corner of William Bendix's office. Slanting shadows of the blinds fell across his suit, his face, his broad-brimmed hat.

A sweet pressure built in Fee's chest.

William Bendix walked into his office, and suddenly Fee knew the identity of the man behind him. Charlie Carpenter stepped out of the shadow-stripes with a knife in his hands. William Bendix smiled and waggled his fat hands – what's going on here, Miss Sheehan told him there wouldn't be any trouble – and Charlie rammed the knife into his chest.

Fee remembered the odor of raw meat, the heavy smell of blood in Mr Stenmitz's shop.

Charlie Carpenter scrubbed his hands and face in the company bathroom until the basin was black with blood. Charlie ripped towel after towel from the dispenser, blotted his face, and threw the damp towels on the floor. Impatient Charlie Carpenter rode a train out of the city, and two girls across the aisle peeked at him, wondering *Who's that handsome guy?* and *Why is he so nervous?* The train pulled past the front of an immense Catholic church with stained-glass windows blazing with light.

Fee turned around to see the big head and wide shoulders of Heinz Stenmitz. In the darkness, he could just make out white teeth shining in a smile. Joking, Mr

Stenmitz put his hands to his eyes again and pretended to peer at Fee through binoculars.

Fee giggled.

Mr Stenmitz motioned for Fee to join him, and Fee got out of his seat and walked up the long aisle toward the back of the theater. Mr Stenmitz wound his hand in the air, reeling him in. He patted the seat beside him and leaned over and whispered, 'Sit here next to your old friend Heinz.' Fee sat down. Mr Stenmitz's hand swallowed his. 'I'm very very glad you're here,' he whispered. 'This movie is too scary for me to see alone.'

Charlie Carpenter piloted a motorboat across Random Lake. It was early morning. Drops of foam spattered across his lapels. Charlie was smiling a dark, funny smile.

'Do you know what?' Mr Stenmitz asked.

'What?'

'Do you know what?'

Fee giggled. 'No, what?'

'You have to guess.'

There was blood everywhere on the screen but it was invisible blood, it was the blood scrubbed from the office floor and washed away in the sink.

The boat slid into the reeds, and Charlie jumped out onto marshy ground – the boat will drift away, Charlie doesn't care about the boat, it's nothing but a stolen boat, let it go, let it be gone . . .

An unimaginable time later Fee found himself standing in the dark outside the Beldame Oriental Theater. The last thing he could remember was Lily Sheehan turning from her stove and saying *Decided to stop off on your way to work, Charlie?* She wore a long white robe, and her hair looked loose and full. *You're full of surprises. I thought you'd be here last night.* His face burned, and his heart was pounding. Smoke and oil filled his stomach.

He felt appallingly, astoundingly dirty.

The world turned spangly and gray. The headlights on Livermore Avenue swung toward him. The smoke in his stomach spilled upward into his throat.

Fee moved a step deeper into the comparative darkness of the street and bent over the curb. Something that looked and tasted like smoke drifted from his mouth. He gagged and wiped his mouth and his eyes. It seemed to him that an enormous arm lay across his shoulders, that a deep low voice was saying – was saying –

No.

Fee fled down Livermore Avenue.

Part Two

1

He turned into his street and saw the neat row of cement blocks bisecting the dead lawn and the concrete steps leading up to the rosebushes and the front door.

Nothing around him was real. The moon had been painted, and the houses had no backs, and everything he saw was a fraction of an inch thick, like paint.

He watched himself sit down on the front steps. The night darkened. Footsteps came down the stairs from the Sunchanas' apartment, and the relief of dread focused his attention. The lock turned, and the door opened.

'Fee, poor child,' said Mrs Sunchana. 'I thought I heard you crying.'

'I wasn't crying,' Fee said in a wobbly voice, but he felt cold tears on his cheeks.

'Won't your mother let you in?' Mrs Sunchana stepped around him, and he scooted aside to let her pass.

He wiped his face on his sleeve. She was still waiting

for an answer. 'My mother's sick,' he said. 'I'm waiting for my daddy to come back.'

Pretty, dark-haired Mrs Sunchana wrapped her arms about herself. 'It's almost seven,' she said. 'Why don't you come upstairs? Have some hot chocolate. Maybe you want a bowl of soup? Vegetables, chicken, good thick soup for you. Delicious. I know, I made it myself.'

Fee's reason began to slip away beneath the barrage of these seductive words. He saw himself at the Sunchanas' table, raising a spoon of intoxicating soup to his mouth. Saliva poured into his mouth, and his stomach growled.

By itself, a sob flexed wide black wings in his throat and flew from his mouth.

And then, like salvation, came his father's voice. 'Leave my son alone! Get away from him!' Fee opened his eyes.

Mrs Sunchana pressed her hands together so tightly her fingers looked flat. Fee saw that she was frightened, and understood that he was safe again – back in the movie of his life.

And here came Bob Bandolier up the walk, his face glowing, his eyes glowing, his mustache riding confidently above his mouth, his coat billowing out behind him.

'Fee was sitting here alone in the cold,' Mrs Sunchana said.

'You will go upstairs, please, Mrs Sunchana.'

'I was just trying to help,' persisted Mrs Sunchana. Only her flattened-out hands betrayed her.

'Well, we don't need your help,' bellowed Fee's glorious dad. 'Go away and leave us alone.'

'There is no need to give me orders.'

'*Shut up!*'

'Or to yell at me.'

'*LEAVE MY SON ALONE!*' Bob Bandolier raised his arms like a madman and stamped his foot. 'Go!' He rushed toward the front steps, and Mrs Sunchana went quickly past Fee into the building.

Bob Bandolier grasped Fee's hand, yanked him upright, and pulled him through the front door. Fee cried out in pain. Mrs Sunchana had retreated halfway up the stairs, and her husband's face hung like a balloon in the cracked-open door to their apartment. In front of their own door, Bob Bandolier let go of Fee's hand to reach for his key.

'I think you must be crazy,' said Mrs Sunchana. 'I was being nice to your little boy. He was locked out of the house in the cold.'

Bob Bandolier unlocked the door and turned sideways toward her.

'We live right above you, you know,' said Mrs Sunchana. 'We know what you do.'

Fee's father pushed him into their apartment, and the smell from the bedroom announced itself like the boom of a bass drum. Fee thought that Mrs Sunchana must have been able to smell it, too.

'And what do I do?' his father asked. His voice was dangerously calm.

Fee knew that his father was smiling.

He heard Mrs Sunchana move one step up.

'You know what you do. It is not right.'

Her husband whispered her name from the top of the stairs.

'On the contrary,' his father said. 'Everything I do, Mrs Sunchana, is precisely right. Everything I do, I do for a reason.' He moved away from the door, and Mrs Sunchana went two steps up.

Fee watched his father with absolute admiration. He had won. He had said the brave right things, and the enemy had fled.

Bob Bandolier came scowling toward him.

Fee backed into the living room. His father strode

through the doorway and pushed the door shut. He gave Fee one flat, black-eyed glare, removed his topcoat, and hung it carefully in the closet without seeming to notice the smell from the bedroom. He unbuttoned his suit jacket and the top of his shirt and pulled his necktie down a precise half inch.

'I'm going to tell you something very important. You are never to talk to them again, do you hear me? They might try to get information out of you, but if you say one word to those snoops, I'll whale the stuffing out of you.' He patted Fee's cheek. 'You won't say anything to them, I know.'

Fee shook his head.

'They think they know things – ten generations of keyhole listeners.'

His father gave his cheek another astounding pat. He snapped his fingers. At the code for cat food, Jude stalked out from beneath the chaise. Fee followed both of them into the kitchen. His father spooned half a can of cat food into Jude's dish and put the remainder of the can into the refrigerator.

Bob Bandolier was an amazing man, for now he went whirling and dancing across the kitchen floor, startling even Jude. Amazing Bob spun through the living room, not forgetting to smile up at the ceiling and toss a cheery wave to the Sunchanas, clicked open the bedroom door with his hip, and called *Hello, honeybunch* to his wife. Fee followed, wondering at him. His father supped from a brown bottle of Pforzheimer beer, Millhaven's own, winked at Sleeping Beauty, and said, *Darling, don't give up yet.*

'Here she is, Fee,' his father said. 'She knows, she knows, you know she knows.'

Fee nodded: that was right. His mother knew exactly what it was that he himself had forgotten.

'This lady right here, *she* never doubted.' He kissed

her yellow cheek. 'Let's rustle up some grub, what do you say?'

Fee was in the presence of a miracle.

2

After dinner his father washed the dishes, now and then taking a soapy hand from the foam to pick up his beer bottle. Fee marveled at the speed with which his father drank – three long swallows, and the bottle was empty, like a magic trick.

Bob Bandolier filled a plastic bucket with warm tap water, put some dishwashing powder in the bucket, swirled it around with his hand, and dropped in a sponge.

'Well, here goes.' He winked at Fee. 'The dirty part of the day. Your mother is one of the decent people in this world, and that's why we take care of her.' He was swirling the water around in the bucket again, raising a white lather. 'Let me tell you something. There's a guy who is not one of the decent people of the world, who thinks all he has to do is sit behind a desk all day and count his money. He even thinks he knows the hotel business.' Bob Bandolier laughed out loud. 'I have a little plan, and we'll see how fine and dandy Mr Fine and Dandy really is, when he starts to sweat.' His face was red as an apple.

Fee understood – his father was talking about the St Alwyn.

He squeezed the sponge twice, and water drizzled into the bucket. 'Tonight I'm going to tell you about the blue rose of Dachau. Which was the bottom of the world. That was where you saw the things that are real in this world. You come along while I wash your mother.'

*   *   *

'Not all the way in,' his father said. 'You don't have to see the whole thing, just stay in the door. I just want you to be able to hear me.'

Bob Bandolier put a hand on Fee's shoulder and showed him where to stand.

'This one's going to be messy,' he said.

The smell in the bedroom took root in Fee's nose and invaded the back of his throat. Bob Bandolier set down the bucket, grasped the blanket near his wife's chin, and flipped it down to the end of the bed.

As the blanket moved, his mother's arms jerked up and snapped back into place, elbows bent and the hands curled toward the wrists. Beneath the blanket lay a sheet molded around his mother's body. Watery brown stains covered the parts of the sheet clinging to her waist and hips.

'Anyway,' Bob said, and grabbed the sheet with one hand and walked down the length of the bed, pulling it away from his wife's body. At the bottom of the bed, he yanked the end of the sheet from under the mattress and carefully wadded it up.

From his place in the doorway, Fee saw the yellow soles of his mother's feet, from which her long toenails twisted away; the starved undersides of her legs, peaking at her slightly raised knees; her bony thighs, which disappeared like sticks into the big St Alwyn towel his father had folded around her groin. Once white, this towel was now stained the same watery brown that had leaked through to the sheet. Above the towel was her small swollen belly; two distinct, high-arched rows of ribs; her small flat breasts and brown nipples; shoulders with sunken flesh, from which thin straight bones seemed to want to escape; a lined, deeply hollowed neck; and above all these, propped on a pillow in the limp nest of her hair, his mother's familiar and untroubled face.

'How does stuff still come out, hey, when so damn little goes in? Hold on, honey, we gotta get this *thing* off of you.'

Dedicated Bob Bandolier tugged at the folds of the wet towel, managing with the use of only two fingers to pull it free, exposing Anna Bandolier's knifelike hipbones and her astonishingly thick pubic bush – astonishingly, that is, to Fee, who had expected only a smooth pink passage of flesh, like the region between the legs of a doll. Where all the rest of his mother's skin was the color of yellowing milk, the area uncovered by the towel was a riot of color: milk chocolate flecks and smears distributed over the blazing red of the thighs, and the actual crumbling or shredding of blue and green flesh disappearing into the wound where her buttocks should have been. From this wound surrounded by evaporating flesh came the smell that flooded their apartment.

Fee's heart froze, and the breath in his lungs turned to ice.

Deep within the hole of ragged flesh that was his mother's bottom was a stripe of white bone.

His father slid the dripping sponge beneath her arms, over the pubic tangle and the reddish-gray drooping flesh between her legs. After every few passes he squeezed the sponge into the bucket. He dabbed at the enormous bedsores. 'This started happening a while ago – figured it would take care of itself long as I kept her clean, but . . . well, I just do what I can do.' He touched the oddly stiff bottom sheet. 'See this? Rubber. Sponge it off, it's good as new. Weren't for this baby, we'd have gone through a lot of mattresses by now. Right, honey?'

His father knew he was in a movie.

'Get me another sheet and towel from the linen cabinet.'

His father was wiping the rubber sheet with a clean section of the old towel when Fee came back into the bedroom. He dropped the towel on top of the wadded sheet and took the new linen out of Fee's arms.

'Teamwork, that's what we got.'

He set the linen on the end of the bed and bent to squeeze out the sponge before lightly, quickly passing it over the rubber sheet.

'I don't know if I ever told you much about my war,' he said. 'You're old enough now to begin to understand things.'

It seemed to Fee that he had no heartbeat all. His mouth was a desert. Everything around him, even the dust in the air, saw what he himself was seeing.

'This war was no damn picnic.' Bob Bandolier tilted his wife's body up to wipe beneath her, and Fee raised his eyes to the top of the bedstead.

Bob wiped the fresh towel over the damp sheet, straightened it out, and turned his wife over onto the towel. Her toenails clicked together.

'But I want to tell you about this one thing I did, and it has to do with roses.' He gave Fee a humorous look. 'You know how I feel about roses.'

Fee knew how he felt about roses.

From the bottom of the bed, his father snapped open the clean sheet and sent it sailing over Anna Bandolier's body. 'I was crazy about roses even way back then. But the kind of guy I am, I didn't just grow them, I got interested in them. I did research.' He tucked the sheet beneath the mattress.

Bob Bandolier smoothed the sheet over his wife's body, and Fee saw him taking a mental picture of the tunnel behind the St Alwyn hotel.

'There's one kind, one color, of rose no one has ever managed to grow. There has never been a true blue rose. You could call it a Holy Grail.'

He lifted first one arm, then the other, to slide the sheet beneath them.

He moved back to appraise the sheet. He gave it a sharp tug, snapping it into alignment. Then he stepped back again, with the air of a painter stepping back from a finished canvas.

'What it is, is an enzyme. An enzyme controls the color of a rose. Over the years, I've managed to teach myself a little bit about enzymes. Basically, an enzyme is a biological catalyst. It speeds up chemical changes without going through any changes itself. Believe it or not, Millhaven, this city right here, is one of the enzyme centers of the world – because of the breweries. You need enzymes to get fermentation, and without fermentation you don't get beer. When they managed to crystallize an enzyme, they discovered that it was protein.' He pointed at Fee. 'Okay so far, but here's your big problem. Enzymes are picky. They react with only a tiny little group of molecules. Some of them only work with one molecule!'

He pointed the forefinger at the ceiling. 'Now, what does that say about roses? It says that you have to be a pretty damn good chemist to create your blue rose. Which is the reason that no one has ever done it.' He paused for effect.

'Except for one man. I met him in Germany in 1945, and I saw his rose garden. He had four blue rosebushes in that garden. The ones on the first bush were deep, dark blue, the color of the ink in fountain pens. On the second bush the roses grew a rich navy blue; on the third bush, they were the most beautiful pale blue – the color of a nigger's Cadillac. All of these roses were beautiful, but the most beautiful roses grew on the fourth bush. They were all the other shades in stripes and feathers, dark blue against that heaven-sky blue, little brush strokes of heaven-sky blue against that velvety black-blue. The man who grew them was the greatest gardener in the history of rose cultivation. And there are two other things you should know about him. He grew these roses in ten square empty feet of ground in a concentration camp during the war. He was a guard there. And the second thing is, I shot him dead.'

He put his hands on his hips. 'Let's go get this lady her dinner, okay? Now that she's had her bath, my baby's hungry.'

3

Fee's father busied himself measuring out dry oatmeal into a saucepan, poured in milk, lit a match, and snapped the gas flame into life. He stood beside the stove, holding a long wooden spoon and another bottle of beer, looking as though a spotlight were trained on him.

'We get this job.' He gave the oatmeal another twirl of the spoon. 'It could have been any company, any unit. It didn't have to be mine, but it was mine. We were going to be the first people into what they called the death camp. I didn't even know what it meant, death camp, I didn't know what it was.

'There were some English soldiers that met us there, sort of a share-the-glory, Allied effort. Let the English grab their share. The officers of the camp will surrender to a joint Anglo-American force, and the prisoners will be identified and assisted in their eventual relocation. Meaning, we ship them off after somebody else decides what to do with them. We liberate them. We're the liberators. What does that mean? Women, music, champagne, right?'

He stirred the oatmeal again, looking down into the saucepan and frowning.

'So we get lined up on the road to the camp. We're outside this little town on some river. From where we're standing, I can see a castle, a real castle on a hill over the river, like something out of a movie. There's us, and there's the British. There's photographers, too, from the newsreels and the papers. This is a big deal, because nobody really knows what we're going to find once we get in. The brass is in front. We start moving in columns toward the camp, and all of a sudden everything looks ugly – even the ground looks ugly. We're going toward barbed wire and guardhouses, and you *know* it's some kind of prison.

'I was wrong about everything, I see that right away. The place is like a factory. Once we go through the gates, we're on a long straight road, everything right angles, with little wooden buildings in rows. Okay, we're ready.'

He upturned the pot and spooned oatmeal into a bowl. He added butter, brown sugar, and a dollop of milk. 'Perfect. Let's feed your mother, Fee.'

In radiant humor, he stood beside the bed and raised a spoonful of oatmeal to his wife's lips. 'You have to help me out now, honey, I know you have to be hungry. Here comes some delicious oatmeal – open your mouth.' He pushed the spoon into her mouth and slid it back and forth to dislodge the oatmeal. 'Attaway. Getting a little better every day, aren't we? Pretty soon we're going to be up on our feet.'

Fee remembered what his mother's feet looked like. It was as though a vast dark light surrounded them, a light full of darkness with a greater, deeper darkness all around it, the three of them all alone at its center.

His father slid the spoon from his mother's mouth. A trace of oatmeal remained in the bottom of the spoon. He filled it again and pushed it between her lips. Fee had not seen his mother swallow. He wondered if she could swallow. His father withdrew the spoon again, and a wad of oatmeal the size of a housefly stuck to his mother's top lip.

'Right away I noticed this terrible smell. You couldn't imagine working in a place that smelled that bad. Like a fire in a garbage dump.

'Anyhow, we go marching up this street without seeing anybody, and when we pass this courtyard I see something I can't figure out at all. At first, I don't even know what it is. You know what it was? A giant pile of glasses. Eyeglasses! Must be a thousand of them. Creepy. I mean, that's when I begin to get the idea. They were saving the metal, you did that during the war, but there used to be people that went with those glasses.

'We can see those smokestacks up ahead, big smoke-stacks on top of the furnaces. We go past buildings that seem like they're full of old clothes, piles and piles of shirts and jackets . . .'

The spoon went in full and came out half full. Flecks of oatmeal coated his mother's lips.

'Then we get to the main part of the camp, the barracks, and we see what the people are like. We're not even marching in step anymore, we're not marching at all, we're just moving along, because these are *people* out in front of these barracks, but you never saw people like this in your life. They're walking skeletons. Bones and eyes, like monkeys. Big heads and tiny little bodies. You wonder how smart is it to liberate these zombies in the first place. The ones that can talk are whining, whining, whining – man! These people are watching every move we make, and what you think is: they want to eat us alive.

'So I'm walking along with my company. Half of us want to throw up. These things, these zombies are watch-ing us go by, most of them too weak to do anything but prop themselves up, and I actually realize what is going on. This is the earth we live on, I say to myself. This is what we call earth. There was no *pretending* about what was going on in this place. This was it. This was the last stop.'

Bob Bandolier absentmindedly ate a spoonful of oatmeal. His eyes shone. He licked the spoon.

'And why do I say that? Even the Nazis, the most efficient organization on earth, couldn't move all these people through the gas chambers and into the ovens. Besides the zombies, they had all these dead bodies left over. You can't imagine. Nobody could. This place, the most horrible place the world has ever seen – it was holy.'

Bob Bandolier noticed he was still holding a spoon and a bowl of oatmeal. He smiled at himself, and began again to feed his wife. Oatmeal bubbled out past her lips.

'Finished, honey? Looks like you had enough for today. Good baby.'

He ran the edges of the spoon over her mouth and scraped off most of the visible oatmeal. He set the bowl down on the bed and turned to Fee, still smiling.

'And then I knew I was exactly right, because we turned into this square where the Germans were waiting for us, and here was this ordinary little house, a fence, a walk to the front door, and in this little lot beside it was the rose garden. With those four bushes full of blue roses.

'I stepped out of the column and went up to the garden. Nobody said anything. I sort of heard what was going on – the captain was taking over from the commandant, and the two of them and some other brass went to the back of the square and into the commandant's office. What did I care? I was looking at a miracle. In this miserable hell, someone had managed to grow blue roses. It was a sign. I knew one thing, Fee. I was in the only place on earth where a blue rose could grow.

'I wanted to grab people and say, *For God's sake, look at that garden over there*, but why waste my time? They were just staring at the zombies or the guards.

'But everybody felt *something*, Fee.

'I looked each one of those guards in the face. They just stared straight ahead, no expression, nothing in their eyes, no fear . . . These guys were just doing their jobs like good little cops, they had no more imagination than they were allowed. Except for one man, the one I wanted to find.

'Of course, it was easy. He was the only one who actually looked back at me. He had the moral courage of knowing who he was. Besides that, he saw me standing in front of his roses. Maybe the commandant thought they were *his* roses, maybe some of the zombies even thought they were *their* roses, but they belonged to one man only, their gardener. The goddamned genius who was the right man in the right place at the right time. He knew what he had done, and he knew that *I* knew. He looked straight into my eyes when I stood in front of him.

'You'd never pick him out of a crowd. He was a big bullet-headed guy with a wide nose and little eyes. Big, fat hands and a huge chest. Sort of – sort of like an overgrown dwarf. I would have gone right past him, I almost did go right past him, but then I caught his eye and he caught mine, and I saw that *light* . . . he was the one. He didn't give a damn about anything else on earth.

'I stood in front of him and I said, *How did you do it?* The guys who heard me thought I was asking how he could have treated people that way, but he knew what I meant.

'Our captain and the commandant come out of the office and the captain gets everybody back into formation and tells my platoon to keep watch on the guards. The captain goes away to take care of business. The guys are loading prisoners on trucks, they're setting up desks and taking down names, *I* don't know, my job is to keep an eye on the guards until someone else shows up to take them away.

'Pretty soon it's just us and the guards in the square. Ten of us; about fifteen, twenty of them. There are Americans running all over the camp by now, the place is organized chaos. I decide to try again, and I go up to the guy, the gardener, and boy oh boy I know I'm right all over again because his eyes light up as soon as I come up to him.

'I ask him again. *How did you do it?* This time he almost smiles. He shakes his head.

'*I want to know about the roses*, I say. I point at them, as if he didn't know what I was talking about.

'*Do any of you people speak English?*

'A guy off to the left, a tall gray-haired character with a scar on his forehead, sort of looks at me, and I tell him to help me or I'll blow his head off. He comes up. I say, I want to know about the roses. He can hardly believe that *this* is what I'm interested in, but he gets the idea, and I hear him say something about *blaue rose*.

'My guard, the genius, the one man on earth who ever managed to create a blue rose, finally starts talking. He's bored – he knows this stuff backwards and forwards, he worked it all out by himself and I'm some American private, I don't deserve to know it. But he's under arrest, he'll tell me, all right? He starts spouting this scientific gobbledygook German full of chemical formulas, and not only do I not have any chance of understanding it, neither does the *other* guy, the other Nazi. The gardener knows we don't get it.

'When he's done talking he shuts up, he came to the end and he stopped, like he read the whole thing off a card. Nobody has the faintest idea what he said. Some of the other guys are giving me funny looks, because the zombies get all worked up, they can't hear what the guard is saying but they're excited anyhow.

'Picture this. There's us and them, and then there's the freak show behind us. On the other side of the guards are the camp offices, two wooden buildings about ten feet apart. Between the offices, you can see walls of barbed wire and an empty guardhouse, maybe fifty yards away. Way off to the left are those chimneys. There's just a muddy field between the offices and the fence.

'So the gardener spits on the ground and starts walking away. He just walks right through the other guards. Now the zombies are going crazy. The guard is going toward the space between the buildings. The other guards sort of watch him out of the corners of their eyes. I figure he's going to take a leak, come back.

'One of our guys says, *Hey, that Kraut's getting away.*

'I tell him to shut up.

'But he doesn't stop when he gets to the offices, he just keeps walking on through.

'The rabble is screaming the place down. Some guy says, *What do we do, what are we supposed to do?*

'The gardener just keeps on walking until he's in the field. Then he turns around and looks at me. He's one ugly fucker. He doesn't smile, he doesn't blink, he just gives me a look. Then he starts running for the fence.

'You know what he thinks? He thinks I'll let him get away, on account of I know how great he is. This is what I know – this bastard is taking advantage of me, and I do know how great he is, but nobody takes advantage of me, Fee.

'I raise my rifle and take aim. I pull the trigger, and I shoot him right in the back. Down he goes, boom. One shot. That's all she wrote. We left him where he dropped. None of the rest of those assholes made a move until the truck came for them, you can bet on that.'

His father picked up the bowl of oatmeal and smiled. 'I never even knew his name. For two weeks, me and my platoon, all we did was identify corpses. I mean, that's what we tried to do. The survivors who could still get around made the identifications and we wrote them down. In the end, the Corps of Engineers dug these big trenches and we just plowed 'em in there. Men, women, and children. Poured lime over them and covered them up with dirt. When I went back to see those roses again, the bushes were all pulled up and chopped to pieces. The colonel came in, and he thought they were the ugliest things he'd ever seen in his life. The colonel said: Rip these ugly goddamned blue nightmares out of the ground and chop 'em up, pronto. The guy who cut them down told me that. You know what else he said? He said they gave him the creeps, too.

We're in a concentration camp, and *roses* gave him the creeps.'

Bob Bandolier shook his head. He leaned over and kissed his wife's waxy forehead.

'We'll let her get some rest.'

They returned the bowl and spoon to the kitchen. 'I have to go back to the Hepton tomorrow. So you'll get another day at the movies.' He was mellow and slow; tonight Bob Bandolier was a satisfied man.

Fee could not remember having seen a movie.

'You know what you are? You're a little blue rose, that's what you are.'

Fee brushed his teeth and put himself to bed while his father leaned against the wall with an impatient hand on the light switch. Fee's breathing lengthened; his body seemed to grow mysteriously heavy. The noises of the house, the creaking of boards, the wind moving past his window, the slow chugging of the washing machine carried him to a boat with a prow like an eagle's head before the similarly proud and upright head of his mother, whose silken hair stirred in the sea air. They sailed far and away for many a day, and he found himself bobbing and blooming in a garden. Bob Bandolier moved his hand toward the pocket of his gray suit and took out a pair of shears.

4

Fee came awake with no memory of what had happened in the night. His father was leaning against the wall, flipping the light on and off and saying, 'Come on, come on.' His face was blotchy and white. 'If you make me one minute late for work at the Hepton, you are going to be one sorry little boy, is that understood?'

He walked out of the room. Fee's body seemed to be made of ice, of lead, of a substance impossible to move.

'Don't you understand?' His father leaned back into the room. 'This is the Hepton. You get out of bed, little boy.'

His father's breath still smelled like beer. Fee pushed back his covers and swung his legs over the side of the bed.

'You want oatmeal?'

He nearly threw up on Bob Bandolier's perfect black shoes.

'No? Then that's it, I'm not your personal short-order cook. You can go hungry until you get to the show.'

Fee struggled into underpants, socks, yesterday's shirt and pants. His father stood over him, snapping his fingers like a metronome.

'Get in the bathroom and wash up, for God's sake.'

Fee scampered down the hall.

'You made a lot of noise last night. What the hell was the matter?'

He looked up from the sink and saw, behind his own dripping face, his father's powerful, scowling face. Pouches of dark flesh hung beneath his eyes.

Into his yellow towel, Fee mumbled that he did not remember. His father batted the side of his head.

'What was wrong with you?'

'I don't know,' Fee cried. 'I don't *remember*.'

'There will be no more screaming and shouting in the middle of the night. You will make no noise at all from the time you enter your bedroom until the time you leave it in the morning. Is that understood?' His father was pointing at him. 'Or else there will be punishment.'

'Yes, sir.'

His father straightened up. 'Okay, we understand each other. Get set to go, and I'll get you a glass of milk or something. You have to have something in your stomach.'

When Fee had dried his face and pulled on his coat and zipped it up, when he went down the hall and into

154

the kitchen with Jude winding in and out of his feet, his father, also enclosed in his coat, held out a tall white glass of milk.

'Drink up, drink up.'

Fee took the glass from his hand.

'I'll say good-bye to your mother.'

His father hurried out of the kitchen, and Fee looked at the glass in his hand. He raised it to his mouth. An image blazed in his mind and was banished before he had even a glimpse of it. His hand started shaking. In order to keep from spilling the milk, Fee swung the glass toward the counter with both hands and set it down. He moaned to see a pattern of little white drops on the counter.

'God damn, *God damn, GOD DAMN,*' his father shouted.

Fee wiped the dots of milk with his hand. They turned to white streaks, then smears, then nothing. He was panting, and his face was hot.

Bob Bandolier raged back into the kitchen, and Fee quailed back against the cabinets. His father seemed hardly to notice him as he turned on the water and passed a dish towel back and forth beneath the stream. His face was tight with impatience and disgust.

'Go outside and wait for me.'

He hurried back toward the bedroom. Fee poured the milk into the sink, his heart beating as if he had committed a crime.

Jude followed him to the front door, crying for food. He bent over to stroke the cat, and Jude arched her back and made a noise like fat sizzling in a pan. Still hissing, she moved back several steps. Her huge eyes gleamed, but not at Fee.

Fee groped for the doorknob. Through the open bedroom door, he saw his father's back, bent over the bed. He turned around and pulled the door open.

Standing before him were the Sunchanas, he in a suit,

she two steps behind him in a checked robe. Both of them looked startled.

'Oh!' said Mr Sunchana. His wife clasped both hands in front of her chest. 'Fee,' she said, and then looked past her husband into the apartment. The cat sizzled and spat.

'David,' said Mrs Sunchana.

David took his eyes from Fee and looked over his head toward whatever his wife had seen. His eyes changed.

Slowly, Fee turned around.

Bob Bandolier was stepping away from the bed, holding stretched out between his hands a dish towel blotched with brilliant red. The usual odor floated from the bedroom.

Something black and wet covered his mother's chin.

Bob Bandolier dropped one end of the cloth and began moving toward the bedroom door. He did not shout, although he looked as though he wanted to yell the house down. He slammed the door.

'Last night –' said Mr Sunchana.

'We heard you last night,' said Mrs Sunchana.

'You were making a lot of noise.'

'And we were worried for you. Are you all right, Fee?'

Fee swallowed and nodded.

'Really?'

'Yes,' he said. 'Really.'

The bedroom door burst open, and Bob Bandolier stepped out and immediately closed the door behind him. He was not holding the dish towel. 'Haven't we had enough violations of our privacy from you two? Get away from our apartment or I'll throw you out of this house. I mean it.'

Mr Sunchana backed away and bumped into his wife.

'Out, out, out.'

'What is wrong with your wife?' asked Mrs Sunchana.

Fee's father stopped moving a few feet from the door. 'My wife had a nosebleed. She has been unwell. I am in danger of being late for work, and I cannot allow you to delay me any longer.'

'You call that a nosebleed?' Mrs Sunchana's wide face had grown pale. Her hands were shaking.

Bob Bandolier shut the door and waited for them to retreat up the stairs.

Outside, white breath steamed from his father's mouth. 'You'll need money.' He gave Fee a dollar bill. 'This is for today and tomorrow. I hope I don't have to tell you not to talk to the Sunchanas. If they won't leave you alone, just tell them to go away.'

Fee put the bill in his jacket pocket.

His father patted his head before striding down South Seventh Street to Livermore Avenue and the bus to the Hotel Hepton.

5

Fee paused again on his way to the Beldame Oriental, feeling dazed, as if caught between two worlds, and stared down into the moving water.

A huge man with warm hands was waiting to pull him into a movie.

6

Most of the seats are empty. The big man with kind eyes and a flaring mustache looms beside you. He puts his arm around your shoulders. A Negro boxer knits his forehead and batters another man. Mrs Sunchana accepts her crown. She looks at him, and he whispers *nosebleed*. God's arm tightens around his shoulders and

157

God whispers *nice boy*. The cat chased the mouse on whirling legs. I know you're glad to see me. God's hand is huge and hot, and the gray slab of his face weighs a thousand pounds. You came back to see me. With Robert Ryan, Ida Lupino, and William Bendix. You could hear Jerry's ghost sobbing in the black-and-white shadows. Charlie Carpenter sat in a long quiet church and turned his attention to God, who chuckled and took your hand. Candles flared and sputtered. Mrs Sunchana bowed her head at the edge of the frame. You don't remember what we did? You liked it, and I liked it. Why did God make lonely people? Answer: He was lonely, too. Some of my special friends come to visit and we go into my basement. You're the special friend I go to visit, so you're the most special of all the special friends. There is a toy you have to play with now. Lily Sheehan takes Charlie Carpenter's hand. Here it is, here's the toy. Lily smiles and places Charlie's hand on her toy. Unzip it, God says. Come on. Lucky Strike Means Fine Tobacco. I'd Walk a Mile for a Camel. You see it, here it is, it's all yours. You know what to do with it. Little dear one. God is so stern and tender. Have a cigarette, Charlie. It likes you, can't you see how much it likes you? Random Lake is a pretty nice lake. I need you to help me. Here we are, on Fenton Welles's long lawn. If you stop now, I'll kill you. Hah hah. That's a joke. I'll cut you up and turn you into lamb chops, sweetie-pie, I know how to do that. But here is the envelope marked ELIJAH, here are the photographs. Every one of those soldiers has one like mine, a big thick one that likes to come out and play. The dog jumps up from Fenton Welles's lawn and you smash its head in with a stick. You are kissing a long kiss. Smoke from his mouth fills the air. God placed both hands on the sides of your head and pushed your head down toward the other little mouth. Hello, Duffy's Tavern, Duffy speaking. Jack Armstrong, the all-American boy. Welcome to the Adventures of. The roaring in his ears. He pushed the big thing into his cheek so he would not gag, but God's hands raised his head and lowered it again. Charlie and Lily kissed and Lily's penis threshed out like a snake. A woman should put your mouth on her breast, and milk should flow. I'm all the soul you need. The second you take it in your mouth, it moves – it twitches and shoves itself upward. God's pleasure makes Him sigh. His hand around yours. Now kiss. They are burning photographs, the smell is harsh. The taste is sour burning. Wait for it, the music says. Mrs Sunchana covers her face. The world bursts into flame. From up out of that long thing, all the way up from its bottom, from the deep bottom of the well, it rushes. God presses His hands against your head. You open your mouth and smoke and drool leak out. If he wanted, God could drown the world. Maxwell House Coffee Is Good to the Very Last Drop. The tiny Arab man on the lip of the huge tilted cup. What is in your mouth is the taste of bread. The taste of bread is warm and silky. To be loved. Charlie in his good suit rides the train, and the girls stare. Bunny is good bread. A normal girl is attracted by a handsome man. Invisible blood, God's blood, washes through the world. Charlie Carpenter rides across the lake and water mists his lapels. You can lean back against God's giant chest. His hand strokes your cheek. Jack Armstrong eats Wheaties every day. The boat slides into the reeds. Water-music, death-music. God rubs your chest, and His hand is rough. Make big money selling Christmas cards to all your neighbors. The hotel business is America's business. Don't you think that they all take towels, the big guys? The best hamburgers come with the works. Charlie shoved the boat into the reeds, and now he strides across the lawn to Lily's house. Oh the face of Charlie Carpenter, oh the anger in his stride. You could be crushed to death. This man is holding on. The little Arab clings to his giant cup. What grows out of him is not human, that thing is not human. His arms surrounding you, blue rose, little blue rose.

7

The Story of the Leaves

His mother had a nosebleed from her mouth. The boy put his hand in the water to stop her from going, and a cloud swarmed out of the leaves and darkened all the water like a stain.

The Story of the Movie

Charlie Carpenter and Lily Sheehan held hands and looked out of the screen. Kiss me, Lily said, and the dead boy leaned over and kissed it by taking it into his mouth. Every day the same thing happened in the seats of the Beldame Oriental. The end of the movie was so terrible that you could never remember it, not even if you tried.

The Story of the Nosebleed

When Mrs Sunchana saw it, she said, 'Do you call that a nosebleed?' His father said, 'What else could you call it?'

The Story of the Movie

Lily Sheehan wrapped her arms around Charlie Carpenter the way Someone wrapped his arms around the dead boy. Something grew between her legs and from that Something Charlie Carpenter did take suck. We remember folds of gray flesh. Whenever the warm silky fluid shuddered out, it tasted like bread.

The Story of the Blue Rose

Charlie Carpenter rang Lily Sheehan's bell, and when she opened the door he gave her a blue rose. This stands for dying, for death. My daddy met the man who grew them, and when the man tried to run away my daddy shot him in the back.

The Story of the Movie

After a long time, the movie ended. Robert Ryan lay in a pool of blood, and a rank, feral odor filled the air. Lily Sheehan closed her front door and a little boat drifted away across Random Lake. A few people left their seats and walked up the aisle and swung open the doors to the lobby. My entire body is buzzing, with what feelings I do not know. In my hands I can feel the weight of plums in a coarse sack, my fingers retain the heat of – my hands tingle. No other world exists but this, with its empty seats and the enormous body beside mine. I am doubly dead, I am buried beneath the carpet, strewn with flecks of popcorn, of the Beldame Oriental. My heart buzzes when the enormous man pulls me tight into his chest. The story of the movie was too terrible to remember. I say, yes, I will be back tomorrow. I have forgotten everything. Words from the radio gong through my mind. Jack Armstrong, Lucky Strikes, the Irish songs on Saint Patrick's Day when I was sick and stayed in bed all day and heard my mother humming and talking to herself while she cleaned the rooms we lived in.

The Story of my First Victim

The first person I ever killed was a six-year-old boy named Lance Torkelson. I was thirteen. We were in a quarry in Tangent, Ohio, and I made Lance hold my erection in his hand and put the tip against his face. Amazed by sensation, I cried out, and the semen shot out like ropes and clung to his face. If I had kept my mouth shut he would have been all right, but my yelling frightened him and he began to wail. I was still shooting and pumping – some of it hit Lance's throat and slid down inside his collar. He screamed. I picked up a rock and hit Lance as hard as I could on the side of his head. He fell right down. Then I hit him until something broke and his head felt soft. My cock was still hard, but there was nothing left inside me. I tossed aside the rock and watched myself stay so stiff and alive, so ready. I could hardly believe what had happened. I never knew that was how it worked.

8

A sudden change in air pressure brought him groaning out of the movie. His entire body felt taut with misery. *She's dead*, he thought, *she just died*. Into his bedroom floated the odors of beer and garbage. The darkness above his bed whirled itself into a pattern as meaningless as an oil slick. He tossed back his covers and swung his feet over the edge of the bed. The shape in the darkness above him shifted and rolled.

Everything in his room, his bed and dresser, the toys and clothes on the floor, had been thrown into unfamiliarity by the white light that filtered in through the gauze curtains. His room seemed larger than in the daytime. A deep sound had been reaching him since he had thrown off his blankets, a deep mechanical rasp that poured up from the floor and through the walls. This sound flowed up from the earth – it was the earth itself at work, the great machine at the heart of the earth.

He came into the living room. Pale moonlight covered the carpet and chaise. Sleeping Jude had curled into a dark knot, from which only the points of her ears protruded. All the furniture looked as if it would float away if he touched it. The bedroom door had been closed. The earth's great chugging machinelike noise went on.

The sound grew louder as he approached the bedroom door. A great confusion went through him like a fog.

He stood in the moonlight-flooded room with his hand frozen to the knob and gulped down fire. A certain terrible knowledge had come to him: the rasping sound that had awakened him was the sound of his mother's breathing, a relentless struggle to draw in air and then force it out again. Fee nearly passed out on the spot – the cloud of confusion had left him so swiftly that it was as if he had been stripped. He had thought his mother was dead, but now she was going to have to die all over again.

He turned the knob and opened the door, and the rattling sounds not only became louder but *increased in size and mass*. Inside the Beldame Oriental, you paused while your eyes adjusted to the darkness. Lightly counterpointing the noises of his mother's body attempting to keep itself alive came the milder sounds of his father's snores.

He stepped into the bedroom, and the shapes before him gradually coalesced and solidified. His mother lay with her hands on her chest, her face pointed to the ceiling. It sounded as if, length by length, something long and rough and reluctantly surrendered were being torn out of her. Faceup on the mattress to the right of the bed, clad only in white boxer shorts, lay his father's pale, muscular body, an arm curved over the top of his head, a leg bent at the knee. A constellation of beer bottles fanned out beside his mattress.

Fee wiped his hands over his eyes and finally saw that his mother's hands shook up and down with the rapid regular quiver of a small animal's heartbeat. He reached out and laid his fingers on her forearm. It moved with the same quick pulse as her hands. Another ragged inhalation negotiated air into his mother, and when he tightened his hold on her arm, invisible hands tore the breath out of her. The little boat his mother rowed was now only the tiniest speck on the black water.

His mother's body seemed as long as a city block. How could he do anything to affect what was happening to that body? The hands curling into her chest were as big as his head. The nails that sprouted from those hands were longer than his fingers. Her chin separated volumes of darkness. His mother's face was as wide as a map. All of this size and power shrank him – her struggle erased him, breath by breath.

The hands on her breasts jittered on. The sounds of taking in and releasing air no longer seemed to have anything to do with breathing. They were the sounds of combat, of scores of men dying at either hand, of heavy feet thudding into the earth, of shells destroying ancient trees, of aircraft moving through the sky. Men groaned on a battlefield. The air was pink with shellburst. Garish yellow tracers ripped across it.

Fee opened his eyes. His mother's body *was* a battlefield. Her feet trembled beneath the sheet; her breathing settled into a raspy, inhuman chug. He reached out to touch her arm again, and the arm danced away from his fingers. He wailed in loneliness and terror, but the sounds coming from her mouth obliterated his cry. Her arms shot up three or four inches and slammed down onto her body. Two fingernails cracked off with sharp popping sounds like the snapping of chicken bones. The long yellow fingernails rolled down the sheet and clicked together at the side of the bed. Fee felt that whatever was happening inside his mother was also happening to him. He could feel the great hands reaching down inside him, grasping his essence and tearing it out.

For an instant, she stopped moving. Her hands hung in the air with their fingernails intertwined; her feet were planted flat on the mattress; her hips floated up. Her feet skidded out, and her hips collapsed back to the bed. The sheet drifted down to her waist. The smell of blood filled the room. His mother's hands fell back on her breasts, and the rumpled sheet turned a deep red which soaked down to her knees. At her waist, blood darkened and rose through the gathered sheet.

Something inside his mother made a soft ripping sound. Her breathing began again in midbeat, softer than before. Fee could feel the enormous hands within him pulling harder at some limp, exhausted thing. Groans rose from the ruined earth. Her breathing moved in and out like a freight train. His own breath pounded in and out with hers.

Her hands settled into the sides of her chest. The long nails clicked. He looked for, but did not see, the broken fingernails that had rolled toward him – he was afraid to look down and see them curling beside his naked feet. If he had stepped on them, he would have screeched like an owl.

He pulled in a searing rush of air. Blood and death dragged themselves far into his body and snagged on his flesh so that they stayed behind when he exhaled in time with his mother. Somehow blood had coated his hands, and he left dark prints on the bed.

The rhythm of their breathing halted. His heart halted, too. The giant hands clamped down inside his mother's body. A breath caught in her thoat and pushed itself out with a sharp exclamation. He and his mother drew in a ragged lungful of blood and death and released a mouthful of steam.

The little rower on the black lake trembled on the horizon.

Sips of air entered her mouth, paused, and got lost. She took in two, waited, waited, and released one. A long time passed. Amazed, he noticed feeble daylight leaking into the room. Her mouth was furry with labor and dehydration. His mother took another sip of air and lost it inside herself. She did not take another.

Fee observed that he had left his body and could see himself standing by the bed.

He waited, not breathing, for what would happen next. He saw that he was smaller than he had imagined, and that beneath the streaks of blood on his face, he looked blank with fear. Bruises covered his chest, arms, and back. He saw himself gripping his mother's arm – he had not known he was doing that.

A ripple moved through his mother's body, beginning near her ankles and passing up her legs and into her hips. It rolled through her belly and entered her chest. Those powerful hands had found what they wanted, and now they would never let go of it.

Her face tightened as if around a bad taste. Both of them, his body and himself standing beside his body, leaned over the bed. The movement made its way into her throat, then moved like a current up into her head. Something inside him grabbed his essential substance and squeezed. His feet left the ground. A silent explosion transformed the shape and pressure of the air, transformed color, transformed everything. A final twitch cleared her forehead of lines, her head came to rest on the pillow, and it was over. For a moment he saw or thought he saw some small white thing move rapidly toward the ceiling. Fee was back in his body. He reeled back from the bed.

His father said, 'Hey? Huh?'

Fee screamed – he had forgotten that his father was on the other side of the bed.

Bob Bandolier's puffy face appeared above the midpoint of the body on the bed. He rubbed his eyes, then took in the bloody sheet. He staggered to his feet. 'Get out of here, Fee. This is no place for you.'

'Mom is dead,' Fee said.

His father moved around the bed so quickly that Fee did not see him move at all – he simply appeared beside him and pushed him toward the door. 'Do what I say, right now.'

Fee walked out of the bedroom.

His father yelled, 'She's going to be okay!'

Fee moved on damp, cold feet to the chaise and lay down.

'Close your eyes,' his father said.

Obediently, Fee closed his eyes. When he heard the bedroom door close, he opened them again. The sheet made a wet, sloppy sound when it hit the floor. Fee let himself revisit what had happened. He heard the inhuman, chugging noise come out of his throat. He drummed his feet against the back of the chaise. Something in his stomach flipped into the back of his throat and filled his mouth with the taste of vomit. In his mind, he leaned over and smoothed the wrinkles from his mother's forehead.

The bedroom door banged open, and he closed his eyes.

Bob Bandolier came walking fast through the living room. 'You ought to be in bed,' he said, but without heat. Fee kept his eyes shut. His father went into the kitchen. Water gushed from the tap: a drawer opened, an object rustled against other objects, the drawer closed. All this had happened before, therefore it was comforting. In Fee's mind Charlie Carpenter stood at the wheel of his motorboat and sped across the glossy lake. A bearded man in Arab dress lifted his head and took into his mouth the last drop from an enormous cup. The warm liquid fell on his tongue like bread, but burned as he swallowed it. His father carried a sloshing pail past him, and the pail exuded the surpassing sweetness and cleanliness of the dishwashing soap. The bedroom door slammed shut, and Fee opened his eyes again.

They were still open when Bob Bandolier walked out

with the bucket and sponge in one hand, a huge red wad wrapped in the dripping rubber sheet under the other arm. 'I have to talk to you,' he said to Fee. 'After I get this stuff downstairs.'

Fee nodded. His father walked toward the kitchen and the basement stairs.

Downstairs, the washing machine gurgled and hummed. Footsteps came up the stairs, the door closed. There came the sound of cupboard doors, of liquid gurgling from a bottle. Bob Bandolier came back into the living room. He was wearing a stretched-out T-shirt and striped boxer shorts, and he was carrying a glass half full of whiskey. His hair stood up on the crown of his head, and his face was still puffy.

'This isn't easy, kid.' He looked around for somewhere to sit, and moved backward three or four feet to lower himself into a chair. He swung his eyes up at Fee and sipped from the glass. 'We did our best, we did everything we could, but it just didn't pan out. This is going to be hard on both of us, but we can help each other out. We can be buddies.' He drank without taking his eyes from Fee.

'Okay?'

'Okay.'

'All that help and love we gave your mother – it didn't do the job.' He took a swallow of his drink, and this time lowered his eyes before raising them again to Fee's. 'She passed away last night. It was very peaceful. She did not suffer, Fee.'

'Oh,' Fee said.

'When you were trying to get her attention in there, before I chased you out, she was already gone. She was already in heaven.'

'Uh-huh,' Fee said.

Bob Bandolier dropped his head and looked down for a little time. He scratched his head. He swallowed more whiskey. 'It's hard to believe.' He shook his head. 'That it could end like this. That woman.' He looked away, then turned back to Fee with tears in his eyes. 'That woman, she loved me. She was the best. Lots of people think they know me, but your mother knew what I was really capable of – for good and bad.' Another shake of the head. He wiped his eyes. 'Anna, Anna was what a wife should be. She was what *people* should be. She was *obedient*. She knew the meaning of *duty*. She didn't question my decisions more than three, four times in all the years we spent together, she was *clean*, she could *cook* . . .' He raised his wet eyes. 'And she was one hell of a mother to you, Fee. Never forget that. There was never a dirty floor in this house.'

He put down his glass and covered his face with his hands. Suffocated sobs leaked through his fingers.

'This isn't over,' his father said. 'This isn't over by a long shot.'

Fee sighed.

'I know who's to blame,' his father said to the floor. Then he raised his head. 'How do you think this all started?'

Fee said nothing.

'A hotshot at the St Alwyn Hotel decided that he didn't need me anymore. *That* is when the trouble started. And why did I miss some time at the job? Because I had to take care of my wife.'

He grinned at nothing. 'They didn't have the simple decency to understand that a man has to take care of his wife.' His ghastly smile was like a convulsion. 'But my campaign has started, sonny boy. I have fired the first shot. Let them pay heed.' He leaned forward. 'And the next time *I won't be interrupted*.

'She didn't only die,' Bob Bandolier said. 'The St Alwyn killed her.' He finished his whiskey, and his face convulsed again. 'They didn't *get* it. In sickness as in health, you

169

know? And they think someone else can do Bob Bandolier's job. You think they asked the guests? They did not. They could have asked that nigger saxophone player – even *him*. Glenroy Breakstone. Every night that man said, "Good evening, Mr Bandolier," when he wouldn't waste two words on anyone else – thought he was too important. But he paid his respects to me, he did. Did they want to know? Well, now they're going to find out. Things are going to happen.' He composed his face. 'It's my whole life – like that woman in there.'

He stood up. 'Now there's things to do. Your mom is dead, but the world goes on.'

All of a sudden the truth came to Fee. He was one-half dead himself; half of him belonged to his dead mother. His father went to the telephone. 'We're going to be all right. Everybody else, watch out.' He peered at the telephone for a second, trying to remember a number, then dialed.

The Sunchanas began walking around their bedroom.

'Dr Hudson, this is Bob Bandolier.' His imitation of a smile appeared and disappeared. 'I know it's early, Hudson. I'm not calling to pass the time of day. Do you know where I live? . . . Because . . . Yes, I'm serious. You better believe I'm serious.'

Fee got off the chaise. He bent down and picked up fat black Jude, who began purring. His hands and arms were still covered with drying blood, and his fingers showed red against the black fur.

'Because I need you here right now, old pal. My wife died during the night, and I need a death certificate so I can take care of her.'

Long individual cat hairs adhered to the backs of Fee's fingers.

'Hudson.'

Overhead, a toilet flushed.

Fee carried Jude to the window.

'Hudson, listen to me. Remember how I covered your ass? I was the *night manager*, I know what goes on.'

Fee wiped his eyes and looked out the window. Some invisible person was out there, looking in.

'I'd say you were a busy boy, that's what was going on.'

'Call it heart disease,' his father said.

Jude could see the invisible person. Jude had always seen the invisible people – they were nothing new to her. The Sunchanas moved around in their bedroom, getting dressed.

'We'll cremate,' his father said.

For some reason, Fee blushed.

'Hello, give me Mr Ledwell,' his father said. 'I'm Bob Bandolier. Mr Ledwell? Bob Bandolier. I'm sorry to have to say that my wife passed away during the night and unless I am *absolutely* required, I'd like to stay home today. There are many arrangements to make, and I have a young son . . . She'd been ill, yes, sir, gravely ill, but it's still a great tragedy for the two of us . . .'

Fee's eyes filled, and a tear slipped down his cheek. Held too tightly, Jude uttered a high-pitched cry of irritation and sank a claw into Fee's forearm.

'That is much appreciated, sir,' said Bob Bandolier. He put down the phone and in a different voice said, 'That old lush of a doctor will be here as soon as he can find a whole suit from the clothes on the floor. We have work to do, so stop crying and get dressed. Hear me?'

9

Bob Bandolier opened the door as Mr Sunchana was leaving for work, and Fee saw their upstairs neighbors take in their undistinguished-looking visitor: the black bag, the wrinkled suit, the cigarette burned down to his lips. Dr Hudson was shown to the bedroom and escorted in.

When Dr Hudson came back out of the bedroom, he looked at his watch and began filling out a printed form at the dining room table. Bob Bandolier supplied his wife's maiden name (Dymczeck), date of birth (August 16, 1928), place of birth (Azure, Ohio). The cause of death was respiratory failure.

Half an hour after the doctor left, two men in dark suits arrived to wrap Fee's mother in the sheet that covered her and carry her away on a stretcher.

Bob Bandolier shaved twice, giving his face a military glaze. He dressed in a dark blue suit. He took a shot of whiskey while he looked through the knife drawer. Finally he slipped a black-handled paring knife into the pocket of his suit jacket. He put on his dark overcoat and told Fee that he would be home soon. He let himself out of the apartment and locked the door behind him.

An hour later, he returned in a mood so foul that when he struck Fee, his son could tell that he was being beaten simply because he was within reach. It had nothing to do with him. To keep the Sunchanas from hearing, he tried to keep silent. Anger made Bob Bandolier so clumsy that he cut himself taking the paring knife out of his pocket. Bob Bandolier raged and stamped his feet and wrapped his finger in tissue paper – another outburst when he could not find bandages, I can't find any bandages, don't we even have any goddamned *bandages*? He opened a fresh bottle and poured drink after drink after drink.

In the morning, Bob Bandolier dressed in the same blue suit and returned to the Hotel Hepton. Fee, who had said he was too sick to go to the movies, spent the day waiting to see the invisible people.

Some nights later, Bob remembered to cook dinner, and long after the moon had risen and his son lay in a semiconscious stupor on the living room rug, sucking on his pain as if on a piece of candy, he returned to the knife drawer in ruminating, well-fed, well-exercised fashion, and selected a six-inch blade with a carved wooden handle. Many hours later, Fee came awake long enough to register that his father was actually carrying him to bed, and knew at once from the exultant triumph he saw in his father's handsome face that late at night, when no one had seen him, Bob Bandolier had gone back to the St Alwyn Hotel.

Their life became regular again. Bob Bandolier left sandwiches on the table and locked the door behind him – he seemed to have forgotten about the Beldame Oriental, or to have decided that going to and from the theater exposed his son to unwelcome attention from the neighbors: better to lock him up and leave him alone.

One night Fee awakened when his father picked him up from the chaise, and when he saw the gleeful face burning over his, he knew again that his father had been to the hotel he hated: that his father hated the St Alwyn because he loved it, and that this time at least he had managed to get inside it.

Sometimes it was as if Fee had never had a mother at all. Now and then he saw the cat staring at empty air, and knew that Jude could see one of the people from the invisible world. *From Dangerous Depths* returned to him, and alone in the empty room he played at being Charlie Carpenter – Charlie killing the big dog, Charlie stepping away from the wall to batter William Bendix to death, Charlie dying while Lily Sheehan smiled.

After his father gave him a box of crayons and a pad of paper left behind by a guest at the Hepton, Fee spent days drawing pictures of enormous feet smashing houses, feet crushing men and women, crushing whole cities, of people sprawled dead in bomb craters and encampments as a pair of giant feet walked away. He hid these drawings beneath his bed. Once he lowered a drawing of a naked foot onto his exposed penis and nearly fainted from a combination of bliss and terror. He was Charlie Carpenter, living out Charlie Carpenter's secret history.

Whenever he saw the Sunchanas, either alone or with his father, they fled behind their front door. Bob Bandolier said: 'Never uttered a word about your mother, never dropped a card or paid her the honor of making a telephone call. People like that are no better than animals.'

On the night of October twenty-fifth, Bob Bandolier came home from work restless and impatient despite the two steaks and the bottle of whiskey he had in a big brown bag, and he slapped his son almost as soon as he took off his coat. He fried the steaks and drank the whiskey from the bottle. Every ten minutes he left the table to check on the state of his collar, the perfection of the knot in his necktie, the gloss of his mustache. The Hotel Hepton, once second only to the Pforzheimer, was a 'sewer', a 'sty'. He could see it now. They thought they knew what it was all about, but the penny-pinching assholes didn't have the first idea. They get a first-class hotel man, and what do they do to him? Give him lectures. Suggest he say less to the guests. Even the St Alwyn, even the *St Alwyn*, the hotel that had done the greatest damage to him, the hotel that had *insulted and injured* him, had *actually managed to kill his wife*, hadn't been so stupid. Maybe he ought to 'switch operations', 'change the battlefield', 'carry the fight into another theater'. You give and give, and *this* – this humiliation – was how they repaid you.

Staring through the window the next morning, Fee finally glimpsed one of the invisible people. He nearly fainted. She was a pale, unhappy-looking blond woman, a woman who had seemed ghostly even when she had been alive. She had come to see him, Fee knew. She was looking for him – as if his lost mother were trying to find him. The second that the tears came into his eyes, the woman on the sidewalk vanished. Hurriedly, almost guiltily, he wiped the tears off his face. If he could, he would have gone through the door and followed her – straight to the St Alwyn Hotel, for that was where she was going.

The next great change in Fee's life began after his father discovered his drawings. In the midst of the whirlwind caused by this next change, for the second time an inhabitant of the invisible world appeared before Fee, in a form and manner suggesting that he had caused a death.

It began as a calm dinner. There was the 'hypocritical lowlife' who gave orders to Bob Bandolier, there was an 'untrustworthy and corrupt' colleague, there were mentions of the fine Christian woman Anna Bandolier had been – Fee warmed his hands at the fire of his father's loves and hates. In the midst of the pleasure he took from this warmth, he realized that his father had asked him a question. He asked to hear it again.

'Whatever happened to the drawing paper and those crayons I gave you? That stuff costs money, you know.'

It had not cost Bob Bandolier any money, but that was secondary: the loss or waste of the precious materials would be a crime. You did not have to want to be bad to succeed in being as bad as possible.

'I don't know,' Fee said, but his eyes shifted sideways.

'Oh, you don't know,' said Bob Bandolier, his manner transformed in an instant. Fee was very close now to being beaten, but a beating was preferable to having his father see his drawings.

'You expect me to believe that?'

Again Fee glanced toward the hallway and his bedroom. His father jumped out of his chair, leaned across the table, and pushed him over in his chair.

Bob Bandolier rushed around the table and pulled him

up by his collar. 'Are you so goddamned stupid you think you can get away with lying to me?'

Fee blubbered and whined, and his father pulled him into the hallway.

'You could have made it easy for yourself, but you made it hard. What did you do? Break the crayons? Tear up the paper?'

Fee shook his head, trying to work out how much truth he could give his father without showing him the drawings.

'Then show me.' His father pulled him into his room and pushed him toward the bed. 'Where are they?'

Again Fee could not avoid self-betrayal: he looked beneath his bed.

'I see.'

Fee wailed *nooo*, and scrambled under the bed in a crazy attempt to protect the drawings with his own body.

Swearing, his father got down on the floor, reached beneath the bed, grabbed Fee's arm, and pulled him out. Sweating, struggling Fee threw his armful of drawings into the room and feebly struck his father. He tried to charge out of his arms to destroy the drawings – he wanted to cram them into his mouth, rip them to confetti, escape through the front door and run down the block.

For a time they were both roaring and screaming. Fee ran out of breath, but he continued to writhe.

His father hit him on the ear and said, 'I should rip your heart out.'

Fee went limp – the drawings lay all about them, waiting to be seen. Bob Bandolier's attention went out to the images on the big pieces of paper. Then he put Fee down and bent to pick up the two drawings closest to him.

Fee hid his face in his arms.

'Feet,' his father said. 'What the hell? I don't get it.'

He moved around the room, turning over the pictures. He flipped one over and displayed it to Fee:

the giant's feet striding away from a flattened movie theater.

'You are going to tell me what this is about, right now.'

An absolutely unprecedented thing happened to Fee Bandolier: he opened his mouth and spoke words over which he had no control at all. Someone else inside him spoke these words. Fee heard them as they proceeded from his mouth, but forgot them as soon as they were uttered.

Finally he had said it all, though he could not have repeated a single word if he had been held over a fire. His father's face had turned red. Troubled in some absolutely new way, Bob Bandolier seemed uncertain whether to comfort Fee or to beat him up. He could no longer meet Fee's eyes. He wandered around the room, picking up scattered drawings. After a few seconds he dropped them back onto the floor.

'Pick these up. Then get rid of them. I never want to see any of this ever again.'

The first sign of the change was in Bob Bandolier's new attitude toward his son. For Fee, the new attitude suggested that he had simultaneously become both much better and much worse. His father never struck him anymore, but Fee felt that his father did not want to touch him in any way. Days and nights passed almost wordlessly. Fee began to feel that he too had become invisible, at least to his father. Bob Bandolier drank, but instead of talking he read and reread that morning's copy of the *Ledger*.

On the night of November seventh, the closing of the front door awakened Fee. From the perfect quiet in the apartment, he knew his father had just gone out. He was sleeping again when his father returned.

The following morning, Fee turned toward his bedroom window as he zipped up his pants, and all the breath seemed to leave his body. A dark-haired boy roughly his own age stood looking in from the little front lawn. He had been waiting for Fee to notice him, but made no effort to communicate. He did not have to. The boy's plaid shirt was too large for him, as if he had stolen or scrounged it. His dirty tan trousers ended above his ankles. On a cold November morning in Millhaven, his feet were bare. The dark eyes beneath the scrappy black hair burned angrily, and the sallow face was frozen with rage. He seemed to quiver with feeling, but Fee had the oddest conviction that all this feeling was not about him – it concerned someone else. The boy had come because of a complicity, an understanding, between them. Dirty, battered-looking, he stared in to find his emotions matched by Fielding Bandolier. But Fielding Bandolier could not match the feelings that came streaming from the boy: he could only remember the sensation of speaking without willing to speak. Something inside him was weeping and gnashing its teeth, but Fee could scarcely hear it.

If you forgot you were in a movie, your own feelings would tear you into bloody rags.

Fee looked down to fasten the button on his waistband. When he looked back through the window, he saw the boy growing fainter and fainter, like a drawing being erased. Traces of the lawn and sidewalk shone through him. All at once it seemed to Fee that something vastly important, an absolutely precious quantity, was fading from his world. Once this quantity was gone, it would be lost forever. Fee moved toward the window, but by now he could not see the blazing dark eyes, and when he touched the glass the boy had disappeared.

That was all right, he told himself: really, he had lost nothing.

Bob Bandolier spent another evening poring over the

Ledger, which had a large photograph of Heinz Stenmitz on its front page. He ordered Fee to bed early, and Fee felt that he was being dismissed because his father did not want to have a witness to his anxiety.

For he was anxious – he was nervous. His leg jittered when he sat at the table, and he jumped whenever the telephone rang. The calls that came were never the call that his father feared, but their innocence did not quiet his anxiety. For something like a week, Fee's few attempts to talk to his father met either angry silence or a command to shut up, and Fee knew that only his father's reluctance to touch him saved him from a blow.

Over the following days, Bob Bandolier relaxed. He would forget who was in the room with him, and lapse back into the old talk of the 'hypocritical lowlife' and the 'corrupt gang' that worked with him. Then he would look up from his plate or his newspaper, see his son, and blush with a feeling for which he refused to find words. Fee witnessed the old anger only once, when he walked into Bob Bandolier's bedroom and found him sitting on the bed, leafing through a small stack of papers from the shoe box beside him. His father's face darkened, and his eyes darkened, and for a second Fee knew the sick, familiar thrill of knowing he was to be beaten. The beating did not happen. His father slipped the papers into the shoe box and told him to find something to do in the other room, fast.

Bob Bandolier came home with the news that the Hepton had let him go – the hypocritical lowlife had finally managed to catch him in the meat locker, and the bastard would not listen to any explanations. It was okay, though. The St Alwyn was taking him back. After everything he had been through, he wouldn't mind going back to the old St Alwyn. He had settled his score, and now they could go forward.

He and Fee could not go forward together, however,

at least not for a while. It wasn't working. He needed quiet, he had to work things out. Fee needed to have a woman around, he needed play with other kids. Anna's sister Judy in Azure had written, saying that she and her husband, Arnold, would be willing to take the boy in, if Bob was finding it difficult to raise the boy by himself.

His father stared at his hands as he said all this to Fee, and looked up only when he had reached this point.

'It's all arranged.'

Bob Bandolier turned his head to look at the window, the porcelain figures, the sleeping cat, anything but his son. Bob Bandolier detested Judy and Arnold, exactly as he detested Anna's brother, Hank, and his wife, Wilda. Fee understood that his father detested him, too.

Bob Bandolier took Fee to the train station in downtown Millhaven, and in a confusion of color and noise passed him and his cardboard suitcase, along with a five-dollar bill, into the hands of a conductor. Fee rode all the way from Millhaven to Chicago by himself, and in Chicago the pitying conductor made sure he boarded the train to Cleveland. He followed his father's orders and talked to no one during the long journey through Illinois and Ohio, though several people, chiefly elderly women, spoke to him. At Cleveland, Judy and Arnold Leatherwood were waiting for him, and drove the sleeping boy the remaining two hundred miles to Azure.

10

The rest can be told quickly. Though nothing frightening or truly upsetting ever happened – nothing *overt* – the Leatherwoods, who had expected to love their nephew unreservedly and had been overjoyed to claim him from the peculiar and unpleasant man who had married Judy Leatherwood's sister, found that Fee Bandolier made them more uncomfortable with every month he lived in their house. He screamed himself awake two or three nights a week, but could not describe what frightened him. The boy refused to talk about his mother. Not long after Christmas, Judy Leatherwood found a pile of disturbing drawings beneath Fee's bed, but the boy denied having drawn them. He insisted that *someone had sneaked them into his room,* and he became so wild-eyed and terrified that Judy dropped the subject. In February, a neighbor's dog was found stabbed to death in an empty lot down the street. A month later, a neighborhood cat was discovered with its throat slashed open in a ditch two blocks away. Fee spent most of his time sitting quietly in a chair in a corner of the living room, looking into space. At night, sometimes the Leatherwoods could hear him breathing in a loud, desperate way that made them want to put the pillows over their heads. When Judy discovered that she was pregnant that April, she and Arnold came to a silent agreement and asked Hank and Wilda in Tangent if they could take Fee in for a while.

Fee moved to Tangent and lived in Hank and Wilda Dymczeck's drafty old house with their fifteen-year-old son, Hank Junior, who regularly beat him up but otherwise paid little attention to him. Hank was the vice principal of Tangent's Lawrence B. Freeman High School and Wilda was a nurse, so they spent less time with Fee than the Leatherwoods had. If he was a little quiet, a little reserved, he was still 'getting over' his mother's death. Because he had nowhere else to go, Fee made an effort to behave in ways other people expected and understood. In time, his nightmares went away. He found a safe secret place for the things he wrote and drew. Whenever anyone asked him what he wanted to be when he grew up, he said he wanted to be a policeman.

Fee passed through grade school and his uncle's high school with average grades. A few animals were found killed (and a few more were not), but Fee Bandolier was so inconspicuous that no one imagined that he might be responsible for their deaths. Lance Torkelson's murder horrified the community, but Tangent decided that an outsider had killed the boy. At the end of Fee's senior year, a young woman named Margaret Loewy disappeared after dropping her two children off at a public swimming pool. Six months later, her mutilated body was discovered buried in the woods beside a remote section of farmland. By that time, Fielding Bandolier had enlisted in the army under another name. Margaret Loewy's breasts, vagina, and cheeks had been sliced off, along with sections of her thighs and buttocks; her womb and ovaries had been removed; traces of semen could still be found in her throat, anus, and abdominal wounds.

Far more successful in basic training than he had ever been in high school, Fee applied for Special Forces training. He dialed his father's telephone number when he learned of his acceptance, and when Bob Bandolier answered by saying 'Yes?' Fee held on to the telephone without speaking, without even breathing, until his father cursed and hung up.

Porkpie Hat

Part One

1

If you know jazz, you know about him, and the title of this memoir tells you who he is. If you don't know the music, his name doesn't matter. I'll call him Hat. What does matter is what he meant. I don't mean what he meant to people who were touched by what he said through his horn. (His horn was an old Selmer Balanced Action tenor saxophone, most of its lacquer worn off.) I'm talking about the whole long curve of his life, and the way that what appeared to be a long slide from joyous mastery to outright exhaustion can be seen in another way altogether.

Hat did slide into alcoholism and depression. The last ten years of his life amounted to suicide by malnutrition, and he was almost transparent by the time he died. Yet he was able to play until nearly the end. When he was working, he would wake up around seven in the evening, listen to Frank Sinatra or Billie Holiday records while he dressed, get to the club by nine, play three sets, come back to his room sometime after three, drink and listen to more records (he was on a lot of those records), and finally go back to bed around the time of day most people begin thinking about lunch. When he wasn't working, he got into bed about an hour earlier, woke up about five or six, and listened to records and drank through his long upside-down day.

It sounds like a miserable life, but it was just an unhappy one. The unhappiness came from a deep, irreversible sadness. Sadness is different from misery, at least Hat's was. His sadness seemed impersonal – it did not disfigure him, as misery can do. Hat's sadness seemed to be for the universe, or to be a larger-than-usual personal share of a sadness already existing in the universe. Inside it, Hat was unfailingly gentle, kind, even funny. His sadness seemed merely the opposite face of the equally impersonal happiness that shone through his earlier work.

In Hat's later years, his music thickened, and sorrow spoke through the phrases. In his last years, what he played often sounded like heartbreak itself. He was like someone who had passed through a great mystery, who *was passing* through a great mystery, and had to speak of what he had seen, what he was seeing.

2

I brought two boxes of records with me when I first came to New York from Evanston, Illinois, where I'd earned a BA in English at Northwestern, and the first thing I set up in my shoe box at the top of John Jay Hall in Columbia University was my portable record player. I did everything to music in those days, and I supplied the rest of my unpacking with a soundtrack provided by Hat's disciples. The kind of music I most liked when I was twenty-one was called 'cool' jazz, but my respect for Hat, the progenitor of this movement, was almost entirely abstract. I didn't know his earliest records, and all I'd heard of his later style was one track on a Verve sampler album. I thought he must almost certainly be dead, and I imagined that if by some miracle he was still alive, he would have been in his early seventies, like Louis Armstrong. In fact, the man who seemed a virtual ancient to me was a few months short of his fiftieth birthday.

In my first weeks at Columbia I almost never left the

campus. I was taking five courses, as well as a seminar that was intended to lead me to a master's thesis, and when I was not in lecture halls or my room, I was in the library. But by the end of September, feeling less overwhelmed, I began to go downtown to Greenwich Village. The IRT, the only subway line I actually understood, described a straight north-south axis that allowed you to get on at 116th Street and get off at Sheridan Square. From Sheridan Square radiated out an unimaginable wealth (unimaginable if you'd spent the previous four years in Evanston, Illinois) of cafés, bars, restaurants, record shops, bookstores, and jazz clubs. I'd come to New York to get an MA in English, but I'd also come for this.

I learned that Hat was still alive about seven o'clock in the evening on the first Saturday in October, when I saw a poster bearing his name on the window of a storefront jazz club near St Mark's Place. My conviction that Hat was dead was so strong that I first saw the poster as an advertisement of past glory. I stopped to gaze longer at this relic of a historical period. Hat had been playing with a quartet including a bassist and drummer of his own era, musicians long associated with him. But the piano player had been John Hawes, one of *my* musicians – John Hawes was on half a dozen of the records back in John Jay Hall. He must have been about twenty at the time, I thought, convinced that the poster had been preserved as memorabilia. Maybe Hawes's first job had been with Hat – anyhow, Hat's quartet must have been one of Hawes's first stops on the way to fame. John Hawes was a great figure to me, and the thought of him playing with a back number like Hat was a disturbance in the texture of reality. I looked down at the date on the poster, and my snobbish and rule-bound version of reality shuddered under another assault of the unthinkable. Hat's engagement had begun on the Tuesday of this week – the first Tuesday in October – and its last night took place on the second Sunday after next – the Sunday before Halloween. Hat was still alive, and John Hawes was playing with him. I couldn't have told you which half of this proposition was the more surprising.

I went inside and asked the short, impassive man behind the bar if John Hawes were really playing there tonight. 'He'd better be, if he wants to get paid,' the man said.

'So Hat is still alive,' I said.

'Put it this way,' he said. 'If it was you, you probably wouldn't be.'

3

Two hours and twenty minutes later, Hat came through the front door, and I saw what he meant. Maybe a third of the tables between the door and the bandstand were filled with people listening to the piano trio. This was what I'd come for, and I thought that the evening was perfect. I hoped that Hat would stay away. All he could accomplish by showing up would be to steal soloing time from Hawes, who, apart from seeming a bit disengaged, was playing wonderfully. Maybe Hawes always seemed a bit disengaged. That was fine with me. Hawes was *supposed* to be cool. Then the bass player looked toward the door and smiled, and the drummer grinned and knocked one stick against the side of his snare drum in a rhythmic figure that managed both to suit what the trio was playing and serve as a half-comic, half-respectful greeting. I turned away from the trio and looked back toward the door. The bent figure of a light-skinned black man in a long, drooping, dark coat was carrying a tenor saxophone case into the club. Layers of airline stickers covered the case, and a black porkpie hat concealed most of the man's face. As soon as he got past the door, he fell into a chair next to an empty table – really fell, as if he would need a wheelchair to get any farther.

Most of the people who had watched him enter turned

back to John Hawes and the trio, who were beginning the last few choruses of 'Love Walked In'. The old man laboriously unbuttoned his coat and let it fall off his shoulders onto the back of the chair. Then, with the same painful slowness, he lifted the hat off his head and lowered it to the table beside him. A brimming shot glass had appeared between himself and the hat, though I hadn't seen any of the waiters or waitresses put it there. Hat picked up the glass and poured its entire contents into his mouth. Before he swallowed, he let himself take in the room, moving his eyes without changing the position of his head. He was wearing a dark gray suit, a blue shirt with a tight tab collar, and a black knit tie. His face looked soft and worn with drink, and his eyes were of no real color at all, as if not merely washed out but washed clean. He bent over, unlocked the case, and began assembling his horn. As soon as 'Love Walked In' ended, he was on his feet, clipping the horn to his strap and walking toward the bandstand. There was some quiet applause.

Hat stepped neatly up onto the bandstand, acknowledged us with a nod, and whispered something to John Hawes, who raised his hands to the keyboard. The drummer was still grinning, and the bassist had closed his eyes. Hat tilted his horn to one side, examined the mouthpiece, and slid it a tiny distance down the cork. He licked the reed, tapped his foot twice, and put his lips around the mouthpiece.

What happened next changed my life – changed me, anyhow. It was like discovering that some vital, even necessary substance had all along been missing from my life. Anyone who hears a great musician for the first time knows the feeling that the universe has just expanded. In fact, all that happened was that Hat had started playing 'Too Marvelous for Words', one of the twenty-odd songs that were his entire repertoire at the time. Actually, he was playing some oblique, one-time-only melody of his own that floated above 'Too Marvelous for Words', and this spontaneous melody seemed to me to comment affectionately on the song while utterly transcending it – to turn a nice little song into something profound. I forgot to breathe for a little while, and goosebumps came up on my arms. Halfway through Hat's solo, I saw John Hawes watching him and realized that Hawes, whom I all but revered, revered *him*. But by that time, I did, too.

I stayed for all three sets, and after my seminar the next day, I went down to Sam Goody's and bought five of Hat's records, all I could afford. That night, I went back to the club and took a table right in front of the bandstand. For the next two weeks, I occupied the same table every night I could persuade myself that I did not have to study – eight or nine, out of the twelve nights Hat worked. Every night was like the first: the same things, in the same order, happened. Halfway through the first set, Hat turned up and collapsed into the nearest chair. Unobtrusively, a waiter put a drink beside him. Off went the porkpie and the long coat, and out from its case came the horn. The waiter carried the case, porkpie, and coat into a back room while Hat drifted toward the bandstand, often still fitting the pieces of his saxophone together. He stood straighter, seemed almost to grow taller, as he got on the stand. A nod to his audience, an inaudible word to John Hawes. And then that sense of passing over the border between very good, even excellent music and majestic, mysterious art. Between songs, Hat sipped from a glass placed beside his left foot. Three forty-five-minute sets. Two half-hour breaks, during which Hat disappeared through a door behind the bandstand. The same twenty or so songs, recycled again and again. Ecstasy, as if I were hearing *Mozart* play Mozart.

One afternoon toward the end of the second week, I stood up from a library book I was trying to stuff whole into my brain – *Modern Approaches to Milton* – and walked out of my carrel to find whatever I could that had been written about Hat. I'd been hearing the sound of Hat's tenor in my head ever since I'd gotten out of bed. And in those days, I was a sort of apprentice scholar: I thought that real answers in the form of interpretations could be found in the pages of scholarly journals. If there were at least a thousand, maybe two thousand, articles concerning John Milton in Low Library, shouldn't there be at least a hundred about Hat? And out of the hundred shouldn't a dozen or so at least begin to explain what happened to me when I heard him play? I was looking for *close readings* of his solos, for analyses that would explain Hat's effects in terms of subdivided rhythms, alternate chords, and note choices, in the way that poetry critics parsed diction levels, inversions of meter, and permutations of imagery.

Of course I did not find a dozen articles that applied a musicological version of the New Criticism to Hat's recorded solos. I found six old concert write-ups in *The New York Times*, maybe as many record reviews in jazz magazines, and a couple of chapters in jazz histories. Hat had been born in Mississippi, played in his family band, left after a mysterious disagreement at the time they were becoming a successful 'territory' band, then joined a famous jazz band in its infancy and quit, again mysteriously, just after its breakthrough into nationwide success. After that, he went out on his own. It seemed that if you wanted to know about him, you had to go straight to the music: there was virtually nowhere else to go.

I wandered back from the catalogs to my carrel, closed the door on the outer world, and went back to stuffing *Modern Approaches to Milton* into my brain. Around six o'clock, I opened the carrel door and realized that *I* could write about Hat. Given the paucity of criticism of his work – given the absence of information about the man himself – I virtually had to write something. The only drawback to this inspiration was that I knew

189

nothing about music. I could not write the sort of article I had wished to read. What I could do, however, would be to interview Hat. Potentially, an interview would be more valuable than analysis. I could fill in the dark places, answer the unanswered questions: Why had he left both bands just as they began to do well? I wondered if he'd had problems with his father and then transferred these problems to his next bandleader. There had to be some kind of story. Any band within smelling distance of its first success would be more than reluctant to lose its star soloist – wouldn't they beg him, bribe him, to stay? I could think of other questions no one had ever asked: What did he think of all those tenor players whom he had influenced? Was he friendly with any of his artistic children? Did they come to his house and talk about music?

Above all, I was curious about the texture of his life – I wondered what his life, the life of a genius, tasted like. If I could have put my half-formed fantasies into words, I would have described my naive, uninformed conceptions of Leonard Bernstein's surroundings. Mentally, I equipped Hat with a big apartment, handsome furniture, advanced stereo equipment, a good but not flashy car, paintings . . . the surroundings of a famous American artist, at least by the standards of John Jay Hall and Evanston, Illinois. The difference between Bernstein and Hat was that the conductor probably lived on Fifth Avenue, and the tenor player in the Village.

I walked out of the library humming 'Love Walked In'.

4

The dictionary-sized Manhattan telephone directory chained to the shelf beneath the pay telephone on the ground floor of John Jay Hall failed to provide Hat's number. Moments later, I met similar failure back in the library after having consulted the equally impressive directories for Brooklyn, Queens, and the Bronx, as well as the much smaller volume for Staten Island. But of course Hat lived in New York – where else would he live? Like other celebrities, he avoided the unwelcome intrusions of strangers by going unlisted. I could not explain his absence from the city's five telephone books in any other way. Of course Hat lived in the Village – that was what the Village was *for*.

Yet even then, remembering the unhealthy-looking man who each night entered the club to drop into the nearest chair, I experienced a wobble of doubt. Maybe the great man's life was nothing like my imaginings. Hat wore decent clothes but did not seem rich – he seemed to exist at the same oblique angle to worldly success that his nightly variations on 'Too Marvelous for Words' bore to the original melody. For a moment, I pictured my genius in a slum apartment where roaches scuttled across a bare floor and water dripped from the ceiling. I had no idea of how jazz musicians actually lived. Hollywood, unafraid of cliché, surrounded them with squalor. On the rare moments when literature stooped to consider jazz people, it, too, served up an ambience of broken bedsprings and peeling walls. And literature's bohemians – Rimbaud, Jack London, Kerouac, Hart Crane, William Burroughs – had often inhabited mean, unhappy rooms. It was possible that the great man was not listed in the city's directories because he could not afford a telephone.

This notion was unacceptable. There had to be another explanation – Hat could not live in a tenement room without a telephone. The man possessed the elegance of his generation of jazz musicians, the generation that wore good suits and polished shoes, played in big bands, and lived on buses and in hotel rooms.

And there, I thought, was my answer. It was a come-down from the apartment in the Village with which I had supplied him, but a room in some 'artistic' hotel like the

Chelsea would suit him just as well, and probably cost a lot less in rent. Feeling inspired, I looked up the Chelsea's number on the spot, dialed, and asked for Hat's room. The clerk told me that he wasn't registered in the hotel. 'But you know who he is,' I said. 'Sure,' said the clerk. 'Guitar, right? I know he was in one of those San Francisco bands, but I can't remember which one.'

I hung up without replying, realizing that the only way I was going to discover Hat's telephone number, short of calling every hotel in New York, was by asking him for it.

5

This was on a Monday, and the jazz clubs were closed. On Tuesday, Professor Marcus told us to read all of *Vanity Fair* by Friday; on Wednesday, after I'd spent a nearly sleepless night with Thackeray, my seminar leader asked me to prepare a paper on James Joyce's 'Two Gallants' for the Friday class. Wednesday and Thursday nights I spent in the library. On Friday I listened to Professor Marcus being brilliant about *Vanity Fair* and read my laborious and dim-witted Joyce paper, on each of the five pages of which the word *epiphany* appeared at least twice, to my fellow scholars. The seminar leader smiled and nodded throughout my performance and when I sat down metaphorically picked up my little paper between thumb and forefinger and slit its throat. 'Some of you kiddies are so *certain* about things,' he said. The rest of his remarks disappeared into a vast, horrifying sense of shame. I returned to my room, intending to lie down for an hour or two, and woke up ravenous ten hours later, when even the West End Bar, even the local Chock Full o' Nuts, were shut for the night.

On Saturday night, I took my usual table in front of the

bandstand and sat expectantly through the piano trio's usual three numbers. In the middle of 'Love Walked In' I looked around with an insider's foreknowledge to enjoy Hat's dramatic entrance, but he did not appear, and the number ended without him. John Hawes and the other two musicians seemed untroubled by this break in the routine and went on to play 'Too Marvelous for Words' without their leader. During the next three songs, I kept turning around to look for Hat, but the set ended without him. Hawes announced a short break, and the musicians stood up and moved toward the bar. I fidgeted at my table, nursing my second beer of the night and checking the door. The minutes trudged by. I feared he would never show up. He had passed out in his room. He'd been hit by a cab, he'd had a stroke, he was already lying dead in a hospital room – just when I was going to write the article that would finally do him justice!

Half an hour later, still without their leader, John Hawes and the other sidemen went back on the stand. No one but me seemed to have noticed that Hat was not present. The other customers talked and smoked – this was in the days when people still smoked – and gave the music the intermittent and sometimes ostentatious attention they allowed it even when Hat was on the stand. By now, Hat was an hour and a half late, and I could see the gangsterish man behind the bar, the owner of the club, scowling as he checked his wristwatch. Hawes played two originals I particularly liked, favorites of mine from his Contemporary records, but in my mingled anxiety and irritation I scarcely heard them.

Toward the end of the second of these songs, Hat entered the club and fell into his seat a little more heavily than usual. The owner motioned away the waiter, who had begun moving toward him with the customary shot glass. Hat dropped the porkpie on the table and struggled with his coat buttons. When he heard what Hawes was playing, he sat listening with his hands still on a coat button, and I listened, too – the music had a tighter, harder, more modern feel, like Hawes's records. Hat nodded to himself, got his coat off, and struggled with the snaps on his saxophone case. The audience gave Hawes unusually appreciative applause. It took Hat longer than usual to fit the horn together, and by the time he was on his feet, Hawes and the other two musicians had turned around to watch his progress as if they feared he would not make it all the way to the bandstand. Hat wound through the tables with his head tilted back, smiling to himself. When he got close to the stand, I saw that he was walking on his toes like a small child. The owner crossed his arms over his chest and glared. Hat seemed almost to float onto the stand. He licked his reed. Then he lowered his horn and, with his mouth open, stared out at us for a moment. 'Ladies, ladies,' he said in a soft, high voice. These were the first words I had ever heard him speak. 'Thank you for your appreciation of our pianist, Mr Hawes. And now I must explain my absence during the first set. My son passed away this afternoon, and I have been . . . busy . . . with details. Thank you.'

With that, he spoke a single word to Hawes, put his horn back in his mouth, and began to play a blues called 'Hat Jumped Up', one of his twenty songs. The audience sat motionless with shock. Hawes, the bassist, and the drummer played on as if nothing unusual had happened – they must have known about his son, I thought. Or maybe they knew that he had no son, and had invented a grotesque excuse for turning up ninety minutes late. The club owner bit his lower lip and looked unusually introspective. Hat played familiar, uncomplicated figures, his tone rough, almost coarse. At the end of his solo, he repeated one note for an entire chorus, fingering the key while staring toward the back of the club. Maybe he was watching the customers leave – three couples and a couple of single people walked out while he was playing. But I don't think he saw anything at all. When the song was over, Hat leaned over to whisper to Hawes, and the piano player announced a short break. The second set was over.

Hat put his tenor on top of the piano and stepped down off the bandstand, pursing his mouth with concentration. The owner had come out from behind the bar and moved in front of him as Hat tiptoed around the stand. The owner spoke a few quiet words. Hat answered. From behind, he looked slumped and tired, and his hair curled far over the back of his collar. Whatever he had said only partially satisfied the owner, who spoke again before leaving him. Hat stood in place for a moment, perhaps not noticing that the owner had gone, and resumed his tiptoe glide toward the door. Looking at his back, I think I took in for the first time how genuinely *strange* he was. Floating through the door in his gray flannel suit, hair dangling in ringletlike strands past his collar, leaving in the air behind him the announcement about a dead son, he seemed absolutely separate from the rest of humankind, a species of one.

I turned as if for guidance to the musicians at the bar. Talking, smiling, greeting a few fans and friends, they behaved just as they did every other night. Could Hat really have lost a son earlier today? Maybe this was the jazz way of facing grief – to come back to work, to carry on. Still, it seemed the worst of all times to approach Hat with my offer. His playing was a drunken parody of itself. He would forget anything he said to me; I was wasting my time.

On that thought, I stood up and walked past the bandstand and opened the door – if I was wasting my time, it didn't matter what I did.

He was leaning against a brick wall about ten feet up the alleyway from the club's back door. The door clicked shut behind me, but Hat did not open his eyes. His face tilted up, and a sweetness that might have been sleep lay over his features. He looked exhausted and insubstantial, too frail to move. I would have gone back inside the club if he had not produced a cigarette from a pack in his shirt pocket, lit it with a match, and then flicked the match away, all without opening his eyes. At least he was awake. I stepped toward him, and his eyes opened. He glanced at me and blew out white smoke. 'Taste?' he said.

I had no idea what he meant. 'Can I talk to you for a minute, sir?' I asked.

He put his hand into one of his jacket pockets and pulled out a half-pint bottle. 'Have a taste.' Hat broke the seal on the cap, tilted it into his mouth, and drank. Then he held the bottle out toward me.

I took it. 'I've been coming here as often as I can.'

'Me, too,' he said. 'Go on, do it.'

I took a sip from the bottle – gin. 'I'm sorry about your son.'

'Son?' He looked upward, as if trying to work out my meaning. 'I got a son – out on Long Island. With his momma.' He drank again and checked the level of the bottle.

'He's not dead, then.'

He spoke the next words slowly, almost wonderingly. 'Nobody . . . told . . . me . . . if . . . he . . . is.' He shook his head and drank another mouthful of gin. 'Damn. Wouldn't that be something, boy dies and nobody tells me? I'd have to think about that, you know, have to really *think* about that one.'

'I'm talking about what you said on stage.'

He cocked his head and examined an empty place in the dark air about three feet from his face. 'Uh-huh. That's right. I did say that. Son of mine passed.'

It was like dealing with a sphinx. All I could do was plunge in. 'Well, sir, actually there's a reason I came out here,' I said. 'I'd like to interview you. Do you think that might be possible? You're a great artist, and there's very little about you in print. Do you think we could set up a time when I could talk to you?'

He looked at me with his bleary, colorless eyes, and I wondered if he could see me at all. And then I felt that, despite his drunkenness, he saw everything – that he saw things about me that I couldn't see.

'You a jazz writer?' he asked.

'No, I'm a graduate student. I'd just like to do it. I think it would be important.'

'Important.' He took another swallow from the half-pint and slid the bottle back into his pocket. 'Be nice, doing an *important* interview.'

He stood leaning against the wall, moving farther into outer space with every word. Only because I had started, I pressed on: I was already losing faith in this project. The reason Hat had never been interviewed was that ordinary American English was a foreign language to him. 'Could we do the interview after you finish up at this club? I could meet you anywhere you like.' Even as I said these words, I despaired. Hat was in no shape to know what he had to do after this engagement finished. I was surprised he could make it back to Long Island every night.

Hat rubbed his face, sighed, and restored my faith in him. 'It'll have to wait a little while. Night after I finish here, I go to Toronto for two nights. Then I got something in Hartford on the thirtieth. You come see me after that.'

'On the thirty-first?' I asked.

'Around nine, ten, something like that. Be nice if you brought some refreshments.'

'Fine, great,' I said, wondering if I would be able to take a late train back from wherever he lived. 'But where on Long Island should I go?'

His eyes widened in mock horror. 'Don't go nowhere

on Long Island. You come see me. In the Albert Hotel, Forty-ninth and Eighth. Room 821.'

I smiled at him – I had guessed right about one thing, anyhow. Hat did not live in the Village, but he did live in a Manhattan hotel. I asked him for his phone number, and wrote it down, along with the other information, on a napkin from the club. After I folded the napkin into my jacket pocket, I thanked him and turned toward the door.

'Important as a motherfucker,' he said in his soft, slurry voice.

I turned around in alarm, but he had tilted his head toward the sky again, and his eyes were closed.

'"Indiana,"' he said. His voice made the word seem sung. '"Moonlight in Vermont." "I Thought About You." "Flamingo."'

He was deciding what to play during his next set. I went back inside, where twenty or thirty new arrivals, more people than I had ever seen in the club, waited for the music to start. Hat soon reappeared through the door, the other musicians left the bar, and the third set began. Hat played all four of the songs he had named, interspersing them through his standard repertoire during the course of an unusually long set. He was playing as well as I'd ever heard him, maybe better than I'd heard on all the other nights I had come to the club. The Saturday-night crowd applauded explosively after every solo. I didn't know if what I was seeing was genius or desperation.

An obituary in the Sunday *New York Times*, which I read over breakfast the next morning in the John Jay cafeteria, explained some of what had happened. Early Saturday morning, a thirty-eight-year-old tenor saxophone player named Grant Kilbert had been killed in an automobile accident. One of the most successful jazz musicians in the world, one of the few jazz musicians known outside of the immediate circle of fans, Kilbert had probably been Hat's most prominent disciple. He had certainly been one of my favorite musicians. More important, from his first record, *Cool Breeze*, Kilbert had excited respect and admiration. I looked at the photograph of the handsome young man beaming out over the neck of his saxophone and realized that the first four songs on *Cool Breeze* were 'Indiana', 'Moonlight in Vermont', 'I Thought About You', and 'Flamingo'. Sometime late Saturday afternoon, someone had called up Hat to tell him about Kilbert. What I had seen had not merely been alcoholic eccentricity; it had been grief for a lost son. And when I thought about it, I was sure that the lost son, not himself, had been the important motherfucker he'd addressed. What I had taken for spaciness and disconnection had all along been irony.

Part Two

1

On the thirty-first of October, after calling to make sure he remembered our appointment, I did go to the Albert Hotel, room 821, and interview Hat. That is, I asked him questions and listened to the long, rambling, often obscene responses he gave them. During the long night I spent in his room, he drank the fifth of Gordon's gin, the 'refreshments' I brought with me – all of it, an entire bottle of gin, without tonic, ice, or other dilutents. He just poured it into a tumbler and drank, as if it were water. (I refused his single offer of a 'taste'.) I frequently checked to make sure that the tape recorder I'd borrowed from a business student down the hall from me was still working, I changed tapes until they ran out, I made detailed backup notes with a ballpoint pen in a stenographic notebook. A couple of times, he played me sections of records that he wanted me to hear, and now and then he sang a couple of bars to make sure that I understood what he was telling me. He sat me in his only chair, and during the entire night stationed himself, dressed in his porkpie hat, a dark blue chalk-stripe suit, and a white button-down shirt with a black knit tie, on the edge of his bed. This was a formal occasion. When I arrived at nine o'clock, he addressed me as 'Mr Leonard Feather' (the name of a well-known jazz critic), and when he opened his door at six-thirty the next morning, he called me 'Miss Rosemary'. By then, I knew that this was an allusion to Rosemary Clooney, whose singing I had learned that he liked, and that the nickname meant he liked me, too. It was not at all certain, however, that he remembered my name.

I had three sixty-minute tapes and a notebook filled with handwriting that gradually degenerated from my usual scrawl into loops and wiggles that resembled Arabic more than English. Over the next month, I spent whatever spare time I had transcribing the tapes and trying to decipher my handwriting. I wasn't sure that what I had was an interview. My carefully prepared questions had been met either with evasions or blank, silent refusals to answer – he had simply started talking about something else. After about an hour, I realized that this was his interview, not mine, and let him roll.

After my notes had been typed up and the tapes transcribed, I put everything in a drawer and went back to work on my MA. What I had was even more puzzling than I'd thought, and straightening it out would have taken more time than I could afford. The rest of that academic year was a long grind of studying for the comprehensive exam and getting a thesis ready. Until I picked up an old *Time* magazine in the John Jay lounge and saw his name in the 'Milestones' columns, I didn't even know that Hat had died.

Two months after I'd interviewed him, he had begun to hemorrhage on a flight back from France; an ambulance had taken him directly from the airport to a hospital. Five days after his release from the hospital, he had died in his bed at the Albert.

After I earned my degree, I was determined to wrestle something usable from my long night with Hat – I owed it to him. During the first weeks of that summer, I wrote out a version of what Hat had said to me and sent it to the only publication I thought would be interested in it. *Downbeat* accepted the interview, and it appeared there about six months later. Eventually, it acquired some fame as the last of his rare public statements. I still see lines from the interview quoted in the sort of pieces about Hat never printed during his life. Sometimes they are lines he really did say to me; sometimes they are stitched together from remarks he made at different times; sometimes, they are quotations I invented in order to be able to use other things he did say.

But one section of that interview has never been quoted, because it was never printed. I never figured out what to make of it. Certainly I could not believe all he had said. He had been putting me on, silently laughing at my credulity, for he could not possibly believe that what he was telling me was literal truth. I was a white boy with a tape recorder, it was Halloween, and Hat was having fun with me. He was *jiving* me.

Now I feel different about his story, and about him, too. He was a great man, and I was an unworldly kid. He was drunk, and I was priggishly sober, but in every important way, he was functioning far above my level. Hat had lived forty-nine years as a black man in America, and I'd spent all of my twenty-one years in white suburbs. He was an immensely talented musician, a man who virtually thought in music, and I can't even hum in tune. That I expected to understand anything at all about him staggers me now. Back then, I didn't know anything about grief, and Hat wore grief about him daily, like a cloak. Now that I am the age he was then, I see that most of what is called information is interpretation, and interpretation is always partial.

Probably Hat was putting me on, jiving me, though not maliciously. He certainly was not telling me the literal truth, though I have never been able to learn what was the literal truth of this case. It's all so unreliable. A woman named Mary Randolph lived first in one place, then she lived in another. It's possible that even Hat never knew what was the literal truth behind the story he told me – possible, I mean, that he was still trying to work out what the truth was, nearly forty years after the fact.

2

He started telling me the story after we heard what I thought were gunshots from the street. I jumped from the chair and rushed to the windows, which looked out onto Eighth Avenue. 'Kids,' Hat said. In the hard yellow light of the streetlamps, four or five teenage boys trotted up the avenue. Three of them carried paper bags. 'Kids shooting?' I asked. My amazement tells you how long ago this was.

'Fireworks,' Hat said. 'Every Halloween in New York, fool kids run around with bags full of fireworks, trying to blow their hands off.'

Here and in what follows, I am not going to try to represent the way Hat actually spoke. I cannot indicate the way his voice glided over certain words and turned others into mushy growls, though he expressed more than half of his meaning by sound; and I don't want to reproduce his constant, reflexive obscenity. Hat couldn't utter four

words in a row without throwing in a 'motherfucker'.
Mostly, I have replaced his obscenities with other words,
and the reader can imagine what was really said. Also, if I
tried to imitate his grammar, I'd sound racist and he would
sound stupid. Hat left school in the fourth grade, and his
language, though precise, was casual. To add to these
difficulties, Hat employed a private language of his own,
a code to ensure that he would be understood only by the
people he wished to understand him. I have replaced most
of his code words with their equivalents.

It must have been around one in the morning, which
means that I had been in his room about four hours. Until
Hat explained the 'gunshots', I had forgotten that it was
Halloween night, and I told him this as I turned away from
the window.

'I never forget about Halloween,' Hat said. 'If I can, I
stay home on Halloween. Don't want to be out on the
street, that night.'

He had already given me proof that he was superstitious,
and as he spoke he glanced almost nervously around the
room, as if looking for sinister presences.

'You'd feel in danger?' I asked.

He rolled gin around in his mouth and looked at me
as he had in the alley behind the club, taking note of
qualities I myself did not yet perceive. This did not feel
at all judgmental. The nervousness I thought I had seen
had disappeared, and his manner seemed marginally more
concentrated than earlier in the evening. He swallowed
the gin and looked at me without speaking for a couple
of seconds.

'No,' he said. 'Not exactly. But I wouldn't feel safe,
either.'

I sat with my pen half an inch from the page of my
notebook, uncertain whether or not to write this down.

'I'm from Mississippi, you know.'

I nodded.

'Funny things happen down there. Back when I was a little kid, it was a whole different world. Know what I mean?'

'I can guess,' I said.

He nodded. 'Sometimes people disappeared. They'd be *gone*. All kinds of stuff used to happen, stuff you wouldn't even believe in now. I met a witch-lady once who could put curses on you, make you go blind and crazy. Another time, I saw a mean, murdering son of a bitch named Eddie Grimes die and come back to life – he got shot to death at a dance we were playing, he was *dead*, and a woman bent down and whispered to him, and Eddie Grimes stood right back up on his feet. The man who shot him took off double-quick, and he must have kept on going, because we never saw him after that.'

'Did you start playing again?' I asked, taking notes as fast as I could.

'We never stopped,' Hat said. 'You let the people deal with what's going on, but you gotta keep on playing.'

'Did you live in the country?' I asked, thinking that all of this sounded like Dogpatch – witches and walking dead men.

He shook his head. 'I was brought up in town, Woodland, Mississippi. On the river. Where we lived was called Darktown, you know, but most of Woodland was white, with nice houses and all. Lots of our people did the cooking and washing in the big houses on Miller's Hill, that kind of work. In fact, we lived in a pretty nice house, for Darktown – the band always did well, and my father had a couple of other jobs on top of that. He was a good piano player, mainly, but he could play any kind of instrument. And he was a big, strong guy, nice-looking, real light-complected, so he was called Red, which was what that meant in those days. People respected him.'

Another long, rattling burst of explosions came from Eighth Avenue. I wanted to ask him again about leaving his father's band, but Hat once more gave his little room a quick inspection, swallowed another mouthful of gin, and went on talking.

'We even went out trick-or-treating on Halloween, you know, like the white kids. I guess our people didn't do that everywhere, but we did. Naturally, we stuck to our neighborhood, and probably we got a lot less than the kids from Miller's Hill, but they didn't have anything up there that tasted as good as the apples and candy we brought home in our bags. Around us, folks made instead of bought, and that's the difference.' He smiled at either the memory or the unexpected sentimentality he had just revealed – for a moment, he looked both lost in time and uneasy with himself for having said too much. 'Or maybe I just remember it that way, you know? Anyhow, we used to raise some hell, too. You were *supposed* to raise hell, on Halloween.'

'You went out with your brothers?' I asked.

'No, no, they were –' He flipped his hand in the air, dismissing whatever it was that his brothers had been. 'I was always apart, you dig? Me, I was always into my own little things. I was that way right from the beginning. I play like that – never play like anyone else, don't even play like myself. You gotta find new places for yourself, or else nothing's happening, isn't that right? Don't want to be a repeater pencil.' He saluted this declaration with another swallow of gin. 'Back in those days, I used to go out with a boy named Rodney Sparks – we called him Dee, short for Demon, 'cause Dee Sparks would do anything that came into his head. That boy was the bravest little bastard I ever knew. He'd wrassle a mad dog. And the reason was, Dee was the preacher's boy. If you happen to be the preacher's boy, seems like you gotta prove every way you can that you're no Buster Brown, you know? So I hung with Dee, because I wasn't any Buster Brown, either. This is when we were eleven, around then – the time when you talk about girls, you know, but you still aren't too sure what that's about. You don't know what *anything's* about, to tell the truth. You along for the ride, you trying to pack in as much fun as possible. So Dee was my right hand, and when I went out on Halloween in Woodland, I went out with *him*.'

He rolled his eyes toward the window and said, 'Yeah.' An expression I could not at all read took over his face. By the standards of ordinary people, Hat almost always looked detached, even impassive, tuned to some private wavelength, and this sense of detachment had intensified. I thought he was changing mental gears, dismissing his childhood, and opened my mouth to ask him about Grant Kilbert. But he raised his glass to his mouth again and rolled his eyes back to me, and the quality of his gaze told me to keep quiet.

'I didn't know it,' he said, 'but I was getting ready to stop being a little boy. To stop believing in little-boy things and start seeing like a grown-up. I guess that's part of what I liked about Dee Sparks – he seemed like he was a lot more grown-up than I was, shows you what my head was like. The age we were, this would have been the last time we went out on Halloween to get apples and candy. From then on, we would have gone out mainly to raise hell. Scare the shit out of little kids. But the way it turned out, it was the last time we ever went out on Halloween.'

He finished off the gin in his glass and reached down to pick the bottle up off the floor and pour another few inches into the tumbler. 'Here I am, sitting in this room. There's my horn over there. Here's this bottle. You know what I'm saying?'

I didn't. I had no idea what he was saying. The hint of fatality clung to his earlier statement, and for a second I thought he was going to say that he was here but Dee Sparks was nowhere because Dee Sparks had died in Woodland, Mississippi, at the age of eleven on Halloween night. Hat was looking at me with a steady curiosity that compelled a response. 'What happened?' I asked.

Now I know that he was saying, *It has come down to just this, my room, my horn, my bottle*. My question was as good as any other response.

'If I was to tell you everything that happened, we'd have to stay in this room for a month.' He smiled and straightened up on the bed. His ankles were crossed, and for the first time I noticed that his feet, shod in dark suede shoes with crepe soles, did not quite touch the floor. 'And, you know, I never tell anybody everything, I always have to keep something back for myself. Things turned out all right. Only thing I mind is, I should have earned more money. Grant Kilbert, he earned a lot of money, and some of that was mine, you know.'

'Were you friends?' I asked.

'I knew the man.' He tilted his head and stared at the ceiling for so long that eventually I looked up at it, too. It was not a remarkable ceiling. A circular section near the center had been replastered not long before.

'No matter where you live, there are places you're not supposed to go,' he said, still gazing up. 'And sooner or later, you're gonna wind up there.' He smiled at me again. 'Where we lived, the place you weren't supposed to go was called The Backs. Out of town, stuck in the woods off one little path. In Darktown, we had all kinds from preachers on down. We had washerwomen and blacksmiths and carpenters, and we had some no-good thieving trash, too, like Eddie Grimes, that man who came back from being dead. In The Backs, they started with trash like Eddie Grimes, and went down from there. Sometimes, our people went out there to buy a jug, and sometimes they went there to get a woman, but they never talked about it. The Backs was *rough*. What they had was *rough*.' He rolled his eyes at me and said, 'That witch-lady I told you about, she lived in The Backs.' He snickered. 'Man, they were a mean bunch of people. They'd cut you, you looked at 'em bad. But one thing funny about the place, white and colored lived there just the same – it was *integrated*: Backs people were so evil, color didn't make no difference to them. They hated everybody anyhow, on principle.' Hat pointed his glass at me, tilted his head, and narrowed his eyes. 'At least, that was what everybody *said*. So this particular Halloween, Dee Sparks says to me after we finish with Darktown, we ought to head out to The Backs and see what the place is really like. Maybe we can have some fun.

'The idea of going out to The Backs kind of scared me, but being scared was part of the fun – Halloween, right? And if anyplace in Woodland was perfect for all that Halloween shit, you know, someplace where you might really see a ghost or a goblin, The Backs was better than the graveyard.' Hat shook his head, holding the glass out at a right angle to his body. A silvery amusement momentarily transformed him, and it struck me that his innate elegance, the product of his character and bearing much more than of the handsome suit and the suede shoes, had been paid for by the surviving of a thousand unimaginable difficulties, each painful to a varying degree. Then I realized that what I meant by elegance was really dignity, that for the first time I had recognized actual dignity in another human being, and that dignity was nothing like the self-congratulatory superiority people usually mistook for it.

'We were just little babies, and we wanted some of those good old Halloween scares. Like those dumbbells out on the street, tossing firecrackers at each other.' Hat wiped his free hand down over his face and made sure that I was prepared to write down everything he said. (The tapes had already been used up.) 'When I'm done, tell me if we found it, okay?'

'Okay,' I said.

3

'Dee showed up at my house just after dinner, dressed in an old sheet with two eyeholes cut in it and carrying a paper bag. His big old shoes stuck out underneath the sheet. I had the same costume, but it was the one my brother used the year before, and it dragged along the ground and my feet got caught in it. The eyeholes kept sliding away from my eyes. My mother gave me a bag and told me to behave myself and get home before eight. It didn't take but half an hour to cover all the likely houses in Darktown, but she knew I'd want to fool around with Dee for an hour or so afterwards.

'Then up and down the streets we go, knocking on the doors where they'd give us stuff and making a little mischief where we knew they wouldn't. Nothing real bad, just banging on the door and running like hell, throwing rocks on the roof, little stuff. A few places, we plain and simple stayed away from – the places where people like Eddie Grimes lived. I always thought that was funny. We knew enough to steer clear of those houses, but we were still crazy to get out to The Backs.

'Only way I can figure it is, The Backs was *forbidden*. Nobody had to tell us to stay away from Eddie Grimes's house at night. You wouldn't even go there in the daylight, 'cause Eddie Grimes would get you and that would be that.

'Anyhow, Dee kept us moving along real quick, and when folks asked us questions or said they wouldn't give us stuff unless we sang a song, he moaned like a ghost and shook his bag in their faces, so we could get away faster. He was so excited, I think he was almost shaking.

'Me, I was excited, too. Not like Dee – sort of sick-excited, the way people must feel the first time they use a parachute. Scared-excited.

'As soon as we got away from the last house, Dee crossed the street and started running down the side of the little general store we all used. I knew where he was going. Out behind the store was a field, and on the other side of the field was Meridian Road, which took you out into the woods and to the path up to The Backs. When he realized that I wasn't next to him, he turned around and yelled at me to hurry up. *No*, I said inside myself, *I ain't gonna jump outa this here airplane, I'm not dumb enough to do that*. And then I pulled up my sheet and scrunched up my eye to look through the one hole close enough to see through, and I took off after him.

'It was beginning to get dark when Dee and I left my house, and now it was dark. The Backs was about a mile and a half away, or at least the path was. We didn't know how far along that path you had to go before you got there. Hell, we didn't even know what it was – I was still thinking the place was a collection of little houses, like a sort of shadow-Woodland. And then, while we were crossing the field, I stepped on my costume and fell down flat on my face. Enough of this stuff, I said, and yanked the damned thing off. Dee started cussing me out, I wasn't doing this the right way, we had to keep our costumes on in case anybody saw us, did I forget that this is Halloween, on Halloween a costume *protected* you. So I told him I'd put it back on when we got there. If I kept on falling down, it'd take us twice as long. That shut him up.

'As soon as I got that blasted sheet over my head, I discovered that I could see at least a little ways ahead of me. The moon was up, and a lot of stars were out. Under his sheet, Dee Sparks looked a little bit like a real ghost. It kind of glimmered. You couldn't really make out its edges, so the darn thing like *floated*. But I could see his legs and those big old shoes sticking out.

'We got out of the field and started up Meridian Road, and pretty soon the trees came up right to the ditches alongside the road, and I couldn't see too well anymore. The road seemed like it went smack into the woods and disappeared. The trees looked taller and thicker than in the daytime, and now and then something right at the edge of the woods shone round and white, like an eye – reflecting the moonlight, I guess. Spooked me. I didn't think we'd ever be able to find the path up to The Backs, and that was fine with me. I thought we might go along the road another ten, fifteen minutes, and then turn around and go home. Dee was swooping around up in front of me, flapping his sheet and acting bughouse. *He* sure wasn't trying too hard to find that path.

'After we walked about a mile down Meridian Road, I saw headlights like yellow dots coming toward us fast – Dee didn't see anything at all, running around in circles the way he was. I shouted at him to get off the road, and he took off like a rabbit – disappeared into the woods before I did. I jumped the ditch and hunkered down behind a pine about ten feet off the road to see who was coming. There weren't many cars in Woodland in those days, and I knew every one of them. When the car came by, it was Dr Garland's old red Cord – Dr Garland was a white man, but he had two waiting rooms and took colored patients, so colored patients was mostly what he had. And the man was a heavy drinker, *heavy* drinker. He zipped by, goin' at least fifty, which was mighty fast for those days, probably as fast as that old Cord would go. For about a second, I saw Dr Garland's face under his white hair, and his mouth was wide open, stretched like he was screaming. After he passed, I waited a long time before I came out of the woods. Turning around and going home would have been fine with me. Dr Garland changed everything. Normally, he was kind of slow and quiet, you know, and I could still see that black screaming hole opened up in his face – he looked like he was being tortured, like he was in hell. I sure as hell didn't want to see whatever *he* had seen.

'I could hear the Cord's engine after the taillights disappeared, I turned around and saw that I was all alone on the road. Dee Sparks was nowhere in sight. A couple of times, real soft, I called out his name. Then I called his name a little louder. Away off in the woods, I heard Dee giggle. I said he could run around all night if he liked but I was going home, and then I saw that pale silver sheet moving through the trees, and I started back down Meridian Road. After about twenty paces, I looked back, and there he was, standing in the middle of the road in that silly sheet, watching me go. Come on, I said, let's get back. He paid me no mind. Wasn't that Dr Garland? Where was he going, as fast as that? What was happening? When I said the doctor was probably out on some emergency, Dee said the man was going *home* – he lived in Woodland, didn't he?

'Then I thought maybe Dr Garland had been up in The Backs. And Dee thought the same thing, which made him want to go there all the more. Now he was determined. Maybe we'd see some dead guy. We stood there until I understood that he was going to go by himself if I didn't go with him. That meant that I *had* to go. Wild as he was, Dee'd get himself into some kind of mess for sure if I wasn't there to hold him down. So I said okay, I was coming along, and Dee started swooping along like before, saying crazy stuff. There was no way we were going to be able to find some little old path that went up into the woods. It was so dark, you couldn't see the separate trees, only giant black walls on both sides of the road.

'We went so far along Meridian Road I was sure we must have passed it. Dee was running around in circles about ten feet ahead of me. I told him that we'd missed the path, and now it was time to get back home. He laughed at me and ran across to the right side of the road and disappeared into the darkness.

'I told him to get back, damn it, and he laughed some more and said I should come to *him*. Why? I said, and he said, Because this here is the path, dummy. I didn't believe him – came right up to where he disappeared. All I could see was a black wall that could have been trees or just plain night. Moron, Dee said, look down. And I did. Sure enough, one of those white things like an eye shone up from where the ditch should have been. I bent down and touched cold little stones, and the shining dot of white went off like a light – a pebble that caught the moonlight just right. Bending down like that, I could see the hump of grass growing up between the tire tracks that led out onto Meridian Road. He'd found the path, all right.

'At night, Dee Sparks could see one hell of a lot better than me. He spotted the break in the ditch from across the road. He was already walking up the path in those big old shoes, turning around every other step to look back at me, make sure I was coming along behind him. When I started following him, Dee told me to get my sheet back on, and I pulled the thing over my head even though I'd rather have sucked the water out of a hollow stump. But I knew he was right – on Halloween, especially in a place like where we were, you were safer in a costume.

'From then on in, we were in No Man's Land. Neither one of us had any idea how far we had to go to get to The Backs, or what it would look like once we got there. Once I set foot on that wagon track I knew for sure The Backs wasn't anything like the way I thought. It was a lot more primitive than a bunch of houses in the woods. Maybe they didn't even have houses! Maybe they lived in caves!

'Naturally, after I got that blamed costume over my head, I couldn't see for a while. Dee kept hissing at me to hurry up, and I kept cussing him out. Finally I bunched up a couple handfuls of the sheet right under my chin and held it against my neck, and that way I could see pretty well and walk without tripping all over myself. All I had to do was follow Dee, and that was easy. He was only a couple of inches in front of me, and even through one eyehole, I could see that silvery sheet moving along.

'Things moved in the woods, and once in a while an owl hooted. To tell you the truth, I never did like being out in the woods at night. Even back then, give me a nice warm barroom instead, and I'd be happy. Only animal I ever liked was a cat, because a cat is soft to the touch, and it'll fall asleep on your lap. But this was even worse than usual, because of Halloween, and even before we got to The Backs, I wasn't sure if what I heard moving around in the woods was just a possum or a fox or something a lot worse, something with funny eyes and long teeth that liked the taste of little boys. Maybe Eddie Grimes was out there, looking for whatever kind of treat Eddie Grimes liked on Halloween night. Once I thought of that, I got so close to Dee Sparks I could smell him right through his sheet.

'You know what Dee Sparks smelled like? Like sweat, and a little bit like the soap the preacher made him use on his hands and face before dinner, but really like a fire in a junction box. A sharp kind of bitter smell. That's how excited he was.

'After a while we were going uphill, and then we got to the top of the rise, and a breeze pressed my sheet against my face. We started going downhill, and over Dee's electrical fire, I could smell wood smoke. And something else I couldn't name. Dee stopped moving so sudden, I bumped into him. I asked him what he could see. Nothing but the woods, he said, but we're getting there. People are up ahead somewhere. And they got a still. We got to be real quiet from here on out, he told me, as if he had to, and to let him know I understood I pulled him off the path into the woods.

'Well, I thought, at least I know what Dr Garland was after.

'Dee and I went snaking through the trees – me holding

214

that blamed sheet under my chin so I could see out of one eye, at least, and walk without falling down. I was glad for that big fat pad of pine needles on the ground. An elephant could have walked over that stuff as quiet as a beetle. We went along a little farther, and it got so I could smell all kinds of stuff – burned sugar, crushed juniper berries, tobacco juice, grease. And after Dee and I moved a little bit along, I heard voices, and that was enough for me. Those voices sounded angry.

'I yanked at Dee's sheet and squatted down – I wasn't going any farther without taking a good look. He slipped down beside me. I pushed the wad of material under my chin up over my face, grabbed another handful, and yanked that up, too, to look out under the bottom of the sheet. Once I could actually *see* where we were, I almost passed out. Twenty feet away through the trees, a kerosene lantern lit up the grease-paper window cut into the back of a little wooden shack, and a big raggedy guy carrying another kerosene lantern came stepping out of a door we couldn't see and stumbled toward a shed. On the other side of the building I could see the yellow square of a window in another shack, and past that, another one, a silver of yellow shining out through the trees. Dee was crouched next to me, and when I turned to look at him, I could see another chink of yellow light from somewhere off in the woods over that way. Whether he knew it or not, he'd just about walked us straight into the middle of The Backs.

'He whispered for me to cover my face. I shook my head. Both of us watched the big guy stagger toward the shed. Somewhere in front of us, a woman screeched, and I almost dumped a load in my pants. Dee stuck his hand out from under his sheet and held it out, as if I needed *him* to tell me to be quiet. The woman screeched again, and the big guy sort of swayed back and forth. The light from the lantern swung around in big circles. I saw that

215

the woods were full of little paths that ran between the shacks. The light hit the shack, and it wasn't even wood, but tar paper. The woman laughed or maybe sobbed. Whoever was inside the shack shouted, and the raggedy guy wobbled toward the shed again. He was so drunk he couldn't even walk straight. When he got to the shed, he set down the lantern and bent to get in.

'Dee put his mouth up to my ear and whispered, Cover up – you don't want these people to see who you are. Rip the eyeholes, if you can't see good enough.

'I didn't want anyone in The Backs to see my face. I let the costume drop down over me again, and stuck my fingers in the nearest eyehole and pulled. Every living thing for about a mile around must have heard that cloth ripping. The big guy came out of the shed like someone pulled him out on a string, yanked the lantern up off the ground, and held it in our direction. Then we could see his face, and it was Eddie Grimes. You wouldn't want to run into Eddie Grimes anywhere, but The Backs was the last place you'd want to come across him. I was afraid he was going to start looking for us, but that woman started making stuck-pig noises, and the man in the shack yelled something, and Grimes ducked back into the shed and came out with a jug. He lumbered back toward the shack and disappeared around the front of it. Dee and I could hear him arguing with the man inside.

'I jerked my thumb toward Meridian Road, but Dee shook his head. I whispered, Didn't you already see Eddie Grimes, and isn't that enough for you? He shook his head again. His eyes were gleaming behind that sheet. So what do you want, I asked, and he said, I want to see that girl. We don't even know where she is, I whispered, and Dee said, All we got to do is follow her sound.

'Dee and I sat and listened for a while. Every now and then, she let out a sort of whoop, and then she'd sort of cry, and after that she might say a word or two that

sounded almost ordinary before she got going again or crying or laughing, the two all mixed up together. Sometimes
we could hear other noises coming from the shacks, and
none of them sounded happy. People were grumbling and
arguing or just plain talking to themselves, but at least they
sounded normal. That lady, she sounded like *Halloween* –
like something that came up out of a grave.

'Probably you're thinking what I was hearing was sex
– that I was too young to know how much noise ladies
make when they're having fun. Well, maybe I was only
eleven, but I grew up in Darktown, not Miller's Hill, and
our walls were none too thick. What was going on with
this lady didn't have anything to do with fun. The strange
thing is, Dee didn't know that – he thought just what you
were thinking. He wanted to see this lady getting humped.
Maybe he even thought he could sneak in and get some
for himself, I don't know. The main thing is, he thought
he was listening to some wild sex, and he wanted to get
close enough to see it. Well, I thought, his daddy was
a preacher, and maybe preachers didn't do it once they
got kids. And Dee didn't have an older brother like mine,
who sneaked girls into the house whenever he thought
he wouldn't get caught.

'He started sliding sideways through the woods, and I
had to follow him. I'd seen enough of The Backs to last
me the rest of my life, but I couldn't run off and leave
Dee behind. And at least he was going at it the right way,
circling around the shacks sideways, instead of trying to
sneak straight through them. I started off after him. I could
see a little better ever since I ripped at my eyehole, but I
still had to hold my blasted costume bunched up under
my chin, and if I moved my head or my hand the wrong
way, the hole moved away from my eye and I couldn't
see anything at all.

'So naturally, the first thing that happened was that I
lost sight of Dee Sparks. My foot came down in a hole and I

stumbled ahead for a few steps, completely blind, and then I hit a tree. I just came to a halt, sure that Eddie Grimes and a few other murderers were about to jump on me. For a couple of seconds I stood as still as a wooden Indian, too scared to move. When I didn't hear anything, I hauled at my costume until I could see out of it. No murderers were coming toward me from the shack beside the still. Eddie Grimes was saying *You don't understand* over and over, like he was so drunk that one phrase got stuck in his head, and he couldn't say or hear anything else. That woman yipped, like an animal noise, not a human one – like a fox barking. I sidled up next to the tree I'd run into and looked around for Dee. All I could see was dark trees and that one yellow window I'd seen before. To hell with Dee Sparks, I said to myself, and pulled the costume off over my head. I could see better, but there wasn't any glimmer of white over that way. He'd gone so far ahead of me I couldn't even see him.

'So I had to catch up with him, didn't I? I knew where he was going – the woman's noises were coming from the shack way up there in the woods – and I knew he was going to sneak around the outside of the shacks. In a couple of seconds, after he noticed I wasn't there, he was going to stop and wait for me. Makes sense, doesn't it? All I had to do was keep going toward that shack off to the side until I ran into him. I shoved my costume inside my shirt, and then I did something else – set my bag of candy down next to the tree. I'd clean forgotten about it ever since I saw Eddie Grimes's face, and if I had to run, I'd go faster without holding on to a lot of apples and chunks of taffy.

'About a minute later, I came out into the open between two big old chinaberry trees. There was a patch of grass between me and the next stand of trees. The woman made a gargling sound that ended in one of those fox-yips, and I looked up in that direction and saw that the clearing extended in a straight line up and down, like a path. Stars shone out of the patch of darkness between the two parts of the woods. And when I started to walk across it, I felt a grassy hump between two beaten tracks. The path into The Backs off Meridian Road curved around somewhere up ahead and wound back down through the shacks before it came to a dead end. It had to come to a dead end, because it sure didn't join back up with Meridian Road.

'And this was how I'd managed to lose sight of Dee Sparks. Instead of avoiding the path and working his way north through the woods, he'd just taken the easiest way toward the woman's shack. Hell, I'd had to pull him off the path in the first place! By the time I got out of my sheet, he was probably way up there, out in the open for anyone to see and too excited to notice that he was all by himself. What I had to do was what I'd been trying to do all along, save his ass from anybody who might see him.

'As soon as I started going as soft as I could up the path, I saw that saving Dee Sparks's ass might be a tougher job than I thought – maybe I couldn't even save my own. When I first took off my costume, I'd seen lights from three or four shacks. I thought that's what The Backs was – three or four shacks. But after I started up the path, I saw a low square shape standing between two trees at the edge of the woods and realized that it was another shack. Whoever was inside had extinguished his kerosene lamp, or maybe wasn't home. About twenty, thirty feet on, there was another shack, all dark, and the only reason I noticed that one was I heard voices coming from it, a man and a woman, both of them sounding drunk and slowed down. Deeper in the woods past that one, another grease-paper window gleamed through the trees like a firefly. There were shacks all over the woods. As soon as I realized that Dee and I might not be the only people walking through The Backs on Halloween night, I bent down low to the ground and damn near slowed to a standstill. The only thing Dee had going for him, I thought, was good night vision – at least he might spot someone before they spotted him.

'A noise came from one of those shacks, and I stopped cold, with my heart pounding away like a bass drum. Then a big voice yelled out, *Who's that?* and I just lay down in the track and tried to disappear. *Who's there?* Here I was calling Dee a fool, and I was making more noise than he did. I heard that man walk outside his door, and my heart pretty near exploded. Then the woman moaned up ahead, and the man who'd heard me swore to himself and went back inside. I just lay there in the dirt for a while. The woman moaned again, and this time it sounded scarier than ever, because it had a kind of a chuckle in it. She was crazy. Or she was a witch, and if she was having sex, it was with the devil. That was enough to make me start crawling along, and I kept on crawling until I was long past the shack where the man had heard me. Finally I got up on my feet again, thinking that if I didn't see Dee Sparks real soon, I was going to sneak back to Meridian Road by myself. If Dee Sparks wanted to see a witch in bed with the devil, he could do it without me.

'And then I thought I was a fool not to ditch Dee, because hadn't he ditched me? After all this time, he must have noticed that I wasn't with him anymore. Did he come back and look for me? The hell he did.

'And right then I would have gone back home, but for two things. The first was that I heard that woman make another sound – a sound that was hardly human, but wasn't made by any animal. It wasn't even loud. And it sure as hell wasn't any witch in bed with the devil. It made me want to throw up. That woman was being *hurt*. She wasn't just getting beat up – I knew what that sounded like – she was being hurt bad enough to drive her crazy, bad enough to kill her. Because you couldn't live through being hurt bad enough to make that sound. I was in The

Backs, sure enough, and the place was even worse than it was supposed to be. Someone was killing a woman, everybody could hear it, and all that happened was that Eddie Grimes fetched another jug back from the still. I froze. When I could move, I pulled my ghost costume out from inside my shirt, because Dee was right, and for certain I didn't want anybody seeing my face out there on *this* night. And then the second thing happened. While I was pulling the sheet over my head, I saw something pale lying in the grass a couple of feet back toward the woods I'd come out of, and when I looked at it, it turned into Dee Sparks's Halloween bag.

'I went up to the bag and touched it to make sure about what it was. I'd found Dee's bag, all right. And it was empty. Flat. He had stuffed the contents into his pockets and left the bag behind. What that meant was, I couldn't turn around and leave him – because he hadn't left me after all. He'd waited for me until he couldn't stand it anymore, and then he'd emptied his bag and left it behind as a sign. He was counting on me to see in the dark as well as he could. But I wouldn't have seen it all if that woman hadn't stopped me cold.

'The top of the bag was pointing north, so Dee was still heading toward the woman's shack. I looked up that way, and all I could see was a solid wall of darkness underneath a lighter darkness filled with stars. For about a second, I realized, I had felt pure relief. Dee had ditched me, so I could ditch him and go home. Now I was stuck with Dee all over again.

'About twenty feet ahead, another surprise jumped up at me out of the darkness. Something that looked like a little tiny shack began to take shape, and I got down on my hands and knees to crawl toward the path when I saw a long silver gleam along the top of the thing. That meant it had to be metal – tar paper might have a lot of uses, but it never yet reflected starlight. Once I realized that the thing in front of me was metal, I remembered its shape and realized it was a car. You wouldn't think you'd come across a car in a down-and-out rathole like The Backs, would you? People like that, they don't even own two shirts, so how do they come by cars? Then I remembered Dr Garland speeding away down Meridian Road, and I thought, *You don't have to live in The Backs to drive there.* Someone could turn up onto the path, drive around the loop, pull his car off onto the grass, and no one would ever see it or know that he was there.

'And this made me feel funny. The car probably belonged to someone I knew. Our band played dances and parties all over the county and everywhere in Woodland, and I'd probably seen every single person in town, and they'd seen me, too, and knew me by name. I walked closer to the car to see if I recognized it, but it was just an old black Model T. There must have been twenty cars just like it in Woodland. Whites and coloreds, the few coloreds that owned cars, both had them. And when I got right up beside the Model T, I saw what Dee had left for me on the hood – an apple.

'About twenty feet farther along, there was an apple on top of a big old stone. He was putting those apples where I couldn't help but see them. The third one was on top of a post at the edge of the woods, and it was so pale it looked almost white. Next to the post one of those paths led back into the woods. If it hadn't been for that apple, I would have gone right past it.

'At least I didn't have to worry so much about making noise once I got back into the woods. Must have been six inches of pine needles and fallen leaves underfoot, and I walked so quiet I could have been floating – I've worn crepe soles ever since then, and for the same reason. You walk *soft*. But I was still plenty scared – back in the woods there was a lot less light, and I'd have to step on an apple to see it. All I wanted was to find Dee and persuade him to get out of there.

'For a while, all I did was keep moving between the trees and try to make sure I wasn't coming up on a shack. Every now and then, a faint, slurry voice came from somewhere off in the woods, but I didn't let it spook me. Then, way up ahead, I saw Dee Sparks. The path didn't go in a straight line, it kind of angled back and forth, so I didn't have a good clear look at him, but I got a flash of that silvery-looking sheet way off through the trees. If I sped up I could get to him before he did anything stupid. I pulled my costume up a little farther toward my neck and started to jog.

'The path started dipping *downhill*. I couldn't figure it out. Dee was in a straight line ahead of me, and as soon as I followed the path downhill a little bit, I lost sight of him. After a couple more steps, I stopped. The path got a lot steeper. If I kept running, I'd go ass over teakettle. The woman made another terrible sound, and it seemed to come from everywhere at once. Like everything around me had been *hurt*. I damn near came unglued. Seemed like everything was *dying*. That Halloween stuff about horrible creatures wasn't any story, man, it was the way things really were – you couldn't know anything, you couldn't trust anything, and you were surrounded by *death*. I almost fell down and cried like a baby boy. I was lost. I didn't think I'd ever get back home.

'Then the worst thing of all happened.

'I heard her die. It was just a little noise, more like a sigh than anything, but that sigh came from everywhere and went straight into my ear. A soft sound can be loud, too, you know, be the loudest thing you ever heard. That sigh about lifted me up off the ground, about blew my head apart.

'I stumbled down the path, trying to wipe my eyes with my costume, and all of a sudden I heard men's voices from off to my left. Someone was saying a word I couldn't understand over and over, and someone else was telling him to shut up. Then, behind me, I heard running – heavy running, a man. I took off, and right away my feet got tangled up in the sheet and I was rolling downhill, hitting my head on rocks and bouncing off trees and smashing into stuff I didn't have any idea what it was. Biff bop bang slam smash clang crash ding dong. I hit something big and solid and wound up half-covered in water. Took me a long time to get upright, twisted up in the sheet the way I was. My ears buzzed, and I saw stars – yellow and blue and red stars, not real ones. When I tried to sit up, the blasted sheet pulled me back down, so I got a faceful of cold water. I scrambled around like a fox in a trap, and when I finally got so I was at least sitting up, I saw a slash of real sky out the corner of one eye, and I got my hands free and ripped that hole in the sheet wide enough for my whole head to fit through it.

'I was sitting in a little stream next to a fallen tree. The tree was what had stopped me. My whole body hurt like the dickens. No idea where I was. Wasn't even sure I could stand up. Got my hands on the top of the fallen tree and pushed myself up with my legs – blasted sheet ripped in half, and my knees almost bent back the wrong way, but I got up on my feet. And there was Dee Sparks, coming toward me through the woods on the other side of the stream.

'He looked like he didn't feel any better than I did, like he couldn't move in a straight line. His silvery sheet was smearing through the trees. *Dee got hurt, too*, I thought – he looked like he was in some total panic. The next time I saw the white smear between the trees it was twisting about ten feet off the ground. *No*, I said to myself, and closed my eyes. Whatever that thing was, it wasn't Dee. An unbearable feeling, an absolute despair, flowed out from it. I fought against this wave of despair with every weapon

I had. I didn't want to know that feeling. I couldn't know that feeling – I was eleven years old. If that feeling reached me when I was eleven years old, my entire life would be changed, I'd be in a different universe altogether.

'But it did reach me, didn't it? I could say *no* all I liked, but I couldn't change what had happened. I opened my eyes, and the white smear was gone.

'That was almost worse – I wanted it to be Dee after all, doing something crazy and reckless, climbing trees, running around like a wild man, trying to give me a big whopping scare. But it wasn't Dee Sparks, and it meant that the worst things I'd ever imagined were true. Everything was dying. You couldn't know anything, you couldn't trust anything, we were all lost in the midst of the death that surrounded us.

'Most people will tell you growing up means you stop believing in Halloween things – I'm telling you the reverse. You start to grow up when you understand that the stuff that scares you is part of the air you breathe.

'I stared at the spot where I'd seen that twist of whiteness, I guess trying to go back in time to before I saw Dr Garland fleeing down Meridian Road. My face looked like his, I thought – because now I knew that you really *could* see a ghost. The heavy footsteps I'd heard before suddenly cut through the buzzing in my head, and after I turned around and saw who was coming at me down the hill, I thought it was probably my own ghost I'd seen.

'Eddie Grimes looked as big as an oak tree, and he had a long knife in one hand. His feet slipped out from under him, and he skidded the last few yards down to the creek, but I didn't even try to run away. Drunk as he was, I'd never get away from him. All I did was back up alongside the fallen tree and watch him slide downhill toward the water. I was so scared I couldn't even talk. Eddie Grimes's shirt was flapping open, and big long scars ran all across his chest and belly. He'd been raised from the dead at least a couple of times since I'd seen him get killed at the dance. He jumped back up on his feet and started coming for me. I opened my mouth, but nothing came out.

'Eddie Grimes took another step toward me, and then he stopped and looked straight at my face. He lowered the knife. A stink of sweat and alcohol came off him. All he could do was stare at me. Eddie Grimes knew my face all right, he knew my name, he knew my whole family – even at night, he couldn't mistake me for anyone else. I finally saw that Eddie was actually afraid, like he was the one who'd seen a ghost. The two of just stood there in the shallow water for a couple more seconds, and then Eddie Grimes pointed his knife at the other side of the creek.

'That was all I needed, baby. My legs unfroze, and I forgot all my aches and pains. Eddie watched me roll over the fallen tree and lowered his knife. I splashed through the water and started moving up the hill, grabbing at weeds and branches to pull me along. My feet were frozen, and my clothes were soaked and muddy, and I was trembling all over. About halfway up the hill, I looked back over my shoulder, but Eddie Grimes was gone. It was like he'd never been there at all, like he was nothing but the product of a couple of good raps to the noggin.

'Finally, I pulled myself shaking up over the top of the rise, and what did I see about ten feet away through a lot of skinny birch trees but a kid in a sheet facing away from me into the woods, and hopping from foot to foot in a pair of big clumsy shoes? And what was in front of him but a path I could make out from even ten feet away? Obviously, this was where I was supposed to turn up, only in the dark and all I must have missed an apple stuck onto a branch or some blasted thing, and I took that little side trip downhill on my head and wound up throwing a spook into Eddie Grimes.

'As soon as I saw him, I realized I hated Dee Sparks. I wouldn't have tossed him a rope if he was drowning.

Without even thinking about it, I bent down and picked up a stone and flung it at him. The stone bounced off a tree, so I bent down and got another one. Dee turned around to find out what made the noise, and the second stone hit him right in the chest, even though it was his head I was aiming at.

'He pulled his sheet up over his face like an Arab and stared at me with his mouth wide open. Then he looked back over his shoulder at the path, as if the real me might come along at any second. I felt like pegging another rock at his stupid face, but instead I marched up to him. He was shaking his head from side to side. *Jim Dawg*, he whispered, *what happened to you?* By way of answer, I hit him a good hard knock on the breastbone. *What's the matter?* he wanted to know. *After you left me*, I say, *I fell down a hill and ran into Eddie Grimes*.

'That gave him something to think about, all right. Was Grimes coming after me, he wanted to know? Did he see which way I went? Did Grimes see who I was? He was pulling me into the woods while he asked me these dumb-ass questions, and I shoved him away. His sheet flopped back down over his front, and he looked like a little boy. He couldn't figure out why I was mad at him. From his point of view, he'd been pretty clever, and if I got lost, it was my fault. But I wasn't mad at him because I got lost. I wasn't even mad at him because I'd run into Eddie Grimes. It was everything else. Maybe it wasn't even him I was mad at.

'*I want to get home without getting killed*, I whispered. *Eddie ain't gonna let me go twice*. Then I pretended he wasn't there anymore and tried to figure out how to get back to Meridian Road. It seemed to me that I was still going north when I took that tumble downhill, so when I climbed up the hill on the other side of the creek I was still going north. The wagon track that Dee and I took into The Backs had to be off to my right. I turned away from Dee and started moving through the woods. I didn't care if he followed me or not. He had nothing to do with me anymore, he was on his own. When I heard him coming along after me, I was sorry. I wanted to get away from Dee Sparks. I wanted to get away from everybody.

'I didn't want to be around anybody who was supposed to be my friend. I'd rather have had Eddie Grimes following me than Dee Sparks.

'Then I stopped moving, because through the trees I could see one of those grease-paper windows glowing up ahead of me. That yellow light looked evil as the devil's eye – everything in The Backs was evil, poisoned, even the trees, even the air. The terrible expression on Dr Garland's face and the white smudge in the air seemed like the same thing – they were what I didn't want to know.

'Dee shoved me from behind, and if I hadn't felt so sick inside I would have turned around and punched him. Instead, I looked over my shoulder and saw him nodding toward where the side of the shack would be. He wanted to get closer! For a second, he seemed as crazy as everything else out there, and then I got it: I was all turned around, and instead of heading back to the main path, I'd been taking us toward the woman's shack. That was why Dee was following me.

'I shook my head. No, I wasn't going to sneak up to that place. Whatever was inside there was something I didn't have to know about. It had too much power – it turned Eddie Grimes around, and that was enough for me. Dee knew I wasn't fooling. He went around me and started creeping toward the shack.

'And damnedest thing, I watched him slipping through the trees for a second, and started following him. If he could go up there, so could I. If I didn't exactly look at whatever was in there myself, I could watch Dee look at it. That would tell me most of what I had to know. And anyways, probably Dee wouldn't see anything anyhow, unless the front door was hanging open, and that didn't seem too likely to me. He wouldn't see anything, and I wouldn't either, and we could both go home.

'The door of the shack opened up, and a man walked outside. Dee and I freeze, and I mean *freeze*. We're about twenty feet away, on the side of this shack, and if the man looked sideways, he'd see our sheets. There were a lot of trees between us and him, and I couldn't get a very good look at him, but one thing about him made the whole situation a lot more serious. This man was white, and he was wearing good clothes – I couldn't see his face, but I could see his rolled-up sleeves, and his suit jacket slung over one arm, and some kind of wrapped-up bundle he was holding in his hands. All this took about a second. The white man started carrying his bundle straight through the woods, and in another two seconds he was out of sight.

'Dee was a little closer than I was, and his sight line was clearer than mine. On top of that, he saw better at night than I did. Dee didn't get around like me, but he might have recognized the man we'd seen, and that would be pure trouble. Some rich white man, killing a girl out in The Backs? And us two boys close enough to see him? Do you know what would have happened to us? There wouldn't be enough left of either one of us to make a decent smudge.

'Dee turned around to face me, and I could see his eyes behind his costume, but I couldn't tell what he was thinking. He just stood there, looking at me. In a little bit, just when I was about to explode, we heard a car starting up off to our left. I whispered at Dee if he saw who that was. *Nobody*, Dee said. Now, what the hell did that mean? Nobody? You could say Santa Claus, you could say J. Edgar *Hoover*, it'd be a better answer than Nobody. The Model T's headlights shone through the trees when the car swung around the top of the path and started going toward Meridian Road. *Nobody I ever saw before*, Dee said. When the headlights cut through the trees, both of us ducked out of sight. Actually, we were so far from the path, we had nothing to worry about. I could barely see the car when it went past, and I couldn't see the driver at all.

'We stood up. Over Dee's shoulder I could see the side of the shack where the white man had been. Lamplight flickered on the ground in front of the open door. The last thing in the world I wanted to do was to go inside that place – I didn't even want to walk around to the front and look in the door. Dee stepped back from me and jerked his head toward the shack. I knew it was going to be just like before. I'd say no, he'd say yes, and then I'd follow him wherever he thought he had to go. I felt the same way I did when I saw that white smear in the woods – hopeless, lost in the midst of death. *You go, if you have to*, I whispered to him, *it's what you wanted to do all along*. He didn't move, and I saw that he wasn't too sure about what he wanted anymore.

'Everything was different now, because the white man made it different. Once a white man walked out that door, it was like raising the stakes in a poker game. But Dee had been working toward that one shack ever since we got into The Backs, and he was still curious as a cat about it. He turned away from me and started moving sideways in a straight line, so he'd be able to peek inside the door from a safe distance.

'After he got about halfway to the front, he looked back and waved me on, like this was still some great adventure he wanted me to share. He was afraid to be on his own, that was all. When he realized I was going to stay put, he bent down and moved real slow past the side. He still couldn't see more than a sliver of the inside of the shack, and he moved ahead another little ways. By then, I figured, he should have been able to see about half of the inside of the shack. He hunkered down inside his sheet, staring in the direction of the open door. And there he stayed.

'I took it for about half a minute, and then I couldn't anymore. I was sick enough to die and angry enough to explode, both at the same time. How long could Dee Sparks look at a dead whore? Wouldn't a couple of seconds be enough? Dee was acting like he was watching a goddamn Hopalong Cassidy movie. An owl screeched, and some man in another shack said, *Now that's over*, and someone else shushed him. If Dee heard, he paid it no mind. I started along toward him, and I don't think he noticed me, either. He didn't look up until I was past the front of the shack, and had already seen the door hanging open, and the lamplight spilling over the plank floor and onto the grass outside.

'I took another step, and Dee's head snapped around. He tried to stop me by holding out his hand. All that did was make me mad. Who was Dee Sparks to tell me what I couldn't see? All he did was leave me alone in the woods with a trail of apples, and he didn't even do that right. When I kept on coming, Dee started waving both hands at me, looking back and forth between me and the inside of the shack. Like something was happening in there that I couldn't be allowed to see. I didn't stop, and Dee got up on his feet and skittered toward me.

'*We gotta get out of here*, he whispered. He was close enough so I could smell that electrical stink. I stepped to his side, and he grabbed my arm. I yanked my arm out of his grip and went forward a little ways and looked through the door of the shack.

'A bed was shoved up against the far wall, and a woman lay naked on the bed. There was blood all over her legs, and blood all over the sheets, and big puddles of blood on the floor. A woman in a raggedy robe, hair stuck out all over her head, squatted beside the bed, holding the other woman's hand. She was a colored woman – a Backs woman – but the other one, the one on the bed, was white. Probably she was pretty, when she was alive. All I could see was white skin and blood, and I near fainted.

'This wasn't some white-trash woman who lived out in The Backs – she was brought there, and the man who brought her had killed her. More trouble was coming down than I could imagine, trouble enough to kill lots of our people. And if Dee and I said a word about the white man we'd seen, the trouble would come right straight down on us.

'I must have made some kind of noise, because the woman next to the bed turned halfways around and looked at me. There wasn't any doubt about it – she saw me. All she saw of Dee was a dirty white sheet, but she saw my face, and she knew who I was. I knew her, too, and she wasn't any Backs woman. She lived down the street from us. Her name was Mary Randolph, and she was the one who came up to Eddie Grimes after he got shot to death and brought him back to life. Mary Randolph followed my dad's band, and when we played roadhouses or colored dance halls, she'd be likely to turn up. A couple of times she told me I played good drums – I was a drummer back then, you know, switched to saxophone when I turned twelve. Mary Randolph just looked at me, her hair stuck out straight all over her head like she was already inside a whirlwind of trouble. No expression on her face except that look you get when your mind is going a mile a minute and your body can't move at all. She didn't even look surprised. She almost looked like she *wasn't* surprised, like she was expecting to see me. As bad as I'd felt that night, this was the worst of all. I liked to have died. I'd have disappeared down an anthill, if I could. I didn't know what I had done – just be there, I guess – but I'd never be able to undo it.

'I pulled at Dee's sheet, and he tore off down the side of the shack like he'd been waiting for a signal. Mary

Randolph stared into my eyes, and it felt like I had to pull myself away – I couldn't just turn my head, I had to *disconnect*. And when I did, I could still feel her staring at me. Somehow I made myself go down past the side of the shack, but I could still see Mary Randolph inside there, looking out at the place where I'd been.

'If Dee had said anything at all when I caught up with him, I'd have knocked his teeth down his throat, but he just moved fast and quiet through the trees, seeing the best way to go, and I followed after. I felt like I'd been kicked by a horse. When we got on the path, we didn't bother trying to sneak down through the woods on the other side, we lit out and ran as hard as we could – like wild dogs were after us. And after we got onto Meridian Road, we ran toward town until we couldn't run anymore.

'Dee clamped his hand over his side and staggered forward a little bit. Then he stopped and ripped off his costume and lay down by the side of the road, breathing hard. I was leaning forward with my hands on my knees, as winded as he was. When I could breathe again, I started walking down the road. Dee picked himself up and got next to me and walked along, looking at my face and then looking away, and then looking back at my face again.

'*So?* I said.

'*I know that lady*, Dee said.

'Hell, that was no news. Of course he knew Mary Randolph – she was his neighbor, too. I didn't bother to answer, I just grunted at him. Then I reminded him that Mary hadn't seen his face, only mine.

'*Not Mary*, he said. *The other one.*

'He knew the dead white woman's name? That made everything worse. A lady like that shouldn't be in Dee Sparks's world, especially if she's going to wind up dead in The Backs. I wondered who was going to get lynched, and how many.

'Then Dee said that I knew her, too. I stopped walking and looked him straight in the face.

'*Miss Abbey Montgomery*, he said. *She brings clothes and food down to our church, Thanksgiving and Christmas.*

'He was right – I wasn't sure if I'd ever heard her name, but I'd seen her once or twice, bringing baskets of ham and chicken and boxes of clothes to Dee's father's church. She was about twenty years old, I guess, so pretty she made you smile just to look at. From a rich family in a big house right at the top of Miller's Hill. Some man didn't think a girl like that should have any associations with colored people, I guess, and decided to express his opinion about as strong as possible. Which meant that we were going to take the blame for what happened to her, and the next time we saw white sheets, they wouldn't be Halloween costumes.

'*He sure took a long time to kill her*, I said.

'And Dee said, *She ain't dead.*

'So I asked him, What the hell did he mean by that? I saw the girl. I saw the blood. Did he think she was going to get up and walk around? Or maybe Mary Randolph was going to tell her that magic word and bring her back to life?

'*You can think that if you want to*, Dee said. *But Abbey Montgomery ain't dead.*

'I almost told him I'd seen her ghost, but he didn't deserve to hear about it. The fool couldn't even see what was right in front of his eyes. I couldn't expect him to understand what happened to me when I saw that miserable . . . that *thing*. He was rushing on ahead of me anyhow, like I'd suddenly embarrassed him or something. That was fine with me. I felt the exact same way. I said, *I guess you know neither one of us can ever talk about this*, and he said, *I guess you know it, too*, and that was the last thing we said to each other that night. All the way down Meridian Road Dee Sparks kept his eyes straight ahead and his mouth shut. When we got to the field, he turned toward me like he had something to say, and I waited for it, but he faced forward again and ran away. Just ran. I watched him disappear past the general store, and then I walked home by myself.

'My mom gave me hell for getting my clothes all wet and dirty, and my brothers laughed at me and wanted to know who beat me up and stole my candy. As soon as I could, I went to bed, pulled the covers up over my head, and closed my eyes. A little while later, my mom came in and asked if I was all right. Did I get into a fight with that Dee Sparks? Dee Sparks was born to hang, that was what she thought, and I ought to have a better class of friends. *I'm tired of playing those drums, Momma*, I said. *I want to play the saxophone instead*. She looked at me surprised, but said she'd talk about it with Daddy, and that it might work out.

'For the next couple days, I waited for the bomb to go off. On that Friday, I went to school, but couldn't concentrate for beans. Dee Sparks and I didn't even nod at each other in the hallways – just walked by like the other guy was invisible. On the weekend I said I felt sick and stayed in bed, wondering when that whirlwind of trouble would come down. I wondered if Eddie Grimes would talk about seeing me – once they found the body, they'd get around to Eddie Grimes real quick.

'But nothing happened that weekend, and nothing happened all the next week. I thought Mary Randolph must have hid the white girl in a grave out in The Backs. But how long could a girl from one of those rich families go missing without investigations and search parties? And, on top of that, what was Mary Randolph doing there in the first place? She liked to have a good time, but she wasn't one of those wild girls with a razor under her skirt – she went to church every Sunday, was good to people, nice to kids. Maybe she went out to comfort that poor girl, but how did she know she'd be there in the first place? Misses Abbey Montgomerys from the hill didn't share their plans with Mary Randolphs from Darktown. I couldn't forget the way she looked at me, but I couldn't understand it, either. The more I thought about that look, the more it was like Mary Randolph was saying something to me, but what? *Are you ready for this? Do you understand this? Do you know how careful you must be?*

'My father said I could start learning the C-melody sax, and when I was ready to play it in public, my little brother wanted to take over the drums. Seems he always wanted to play drums, and in fact, he's been a drummer ever since, a good one. So I worked out how to play my little sax, I went to school and came straight home after, and everything went on like normal, except Dee Sparks and I weren't friends anymore. If the police were searching for a missing rich girl, I didn't hear anything about it.

'Then one Saturday I was walking down our street to go to the general store, and Mary Randolph came through her front door just as I got to her house. When she saw me, she stopped moving real sudden, with one hand still on the side of the door. I was so surprised to see her that I was in a kind of slow motion, and I must have stared at her. She gave me a look like an X-ray, a look that searched around down inside me. I don't know what she saw, but her face relaxed, and she took her hand off the door and let it close behind her, and she wasn't looking inside me anymore. *Miss Randolph*, I said, and she told me she was looking forward to hearing our band play at a Beergarden dance in a couple of weeks. I told her I was going to be playing the saxophone at that dance, and she said something about that, and all the time it was like we were having two conversations, the top one about me and the band, and the one underneath about her and the murdered white girl in The Backs. It made me so nervous, my words got all mixed up. Finally she said, *You make sure you say hello to your daddy from me, now*, and I got away.

'After I passed her house, Mary Randolph started walking down the street behind me. I could feel her watching me, and I started to sweat. Mary Randolph was a total mystery to me. She was a nice lady, but probably she buried that girl's body. I didn't know but that she was going to come and kill *me*, one day. And then I remembered her kneeling down beside Eddie Grimes at the roadhouse. She had been *dancing* with Eddie Grimes, who was in jail more often than he was out. I wondered if you could be a respectable lady and still know Eddie Grimes well enough to dance with him. And how did she bring him back to life? Or was that what happened at all? Hearing that lady walk along behind me made me so uptight, I crossed to the other side of the street.

'A couple days after that, when I was beginning to think that the trouble was never going to happen after all, it came down. We heard police cars speeding down the street right when we were finishing dinner. I thought they were coming for me, and I almost lost my chicken and rice. The sirens went right past our house, and then more sirens came toward us from other directions – the old klaxons they had in those days. It sounded like every cop in the state was rushing into Darktown. This was bad, bad news. Someone was going to wind up dead, that was certain. No way all those police were going to come into our part of town, make all that commotion, and leave without killing at least one man. That's the truth. You just had to pray that the man they killed wasn't you or anyone in your family. My daddy turned off the lamps, and we went to the window to watch the cars go by. Two of them were state police. When it was safe, Daddy went outside to see where all the trouble was headed. After he came back in, he said it looked like the police were going toward Eddie Grimes's place. We wanted to go out and look, but they wouldn't let us, so we went to the back windows that faced toward Grimes's house. Couldn't see anything but a lot of cars and police standing all over the road back there. Sounded like they were knocking down Grimes's house with sledgehammers. Then a whole bunch of cops took off running, and all I could see was the cars spread out across the road. About ten minutes later, we heard lots of gunfire coming from a couple of streets farther back. It like to have lasted forever. Like hearing the Battle of the Bulge. My momma started to cry, and so did my little brother. The shooting stopped. The police shouted to each other, and then they came back and got in their cars and went away.

'On the radio the next morning, they said that a known criminal, a Negro man named Edward Grimes, had been killed while trying to escape arrest for the murder of a white woman. The body of Eleanore Monday, missing for three days, had been found in a shallow grave by Woodland police searching near an illegal distillery in the region called The Backs. Miss Monday, the daughter of grocer Albert Monday, had been in poor mental and physical health, and Grimes had apparently taken advantage of her weakness to either abduct or lure her to The Backs, where she had been savagely murdered. That's what it said on the radio – I still remember the words. *In poor mental and physical health. Savagely murdered.*

'When the paper finally came, there on the front page was a picture of Eleanore Monday, a girl with dark hair and a big nose. She didn't look anything like the dead woman in the shack. She hadn't even disappeared on the right day. Eddie Grimes was never going to be able to explain things, because the police had finally cornered him in the old jute warehouse just off Meridian Road next to the general store. I don't suppose they even bothered trying to arrest him – they weren't interested in *arresting* him. He killed a white girl. They wanted revenge, and they got it.

'After I looked at the paper, I got out of the house and ran between the houses to get a look at the jute warehouse. Turned out a lot of folks had the same idea. A big crowd strung out in a long line in front of the warehouse, and cars were parked all along Meridian Road. Right up in front of the warehouse door was a police car, and a big cop stood in the middle of the big doorway, watching people file by. They were walking past the doorway one by one, acting like they were at some kind of exhibit. Nobody was talking. It was a sight I never saw before in that town, whites and colored all lined up together. On the other side of the warehouse, two groups of men stood alongside the road, one colored and one white, talking so quietly you couldn't hear a word.

'Now I was never one who liked standing in lines, so I figured I'd just dart up there, peek in, and save myself some time. I came around the end of the line and ambled toward the two bunches of men, like I'd already had my look and was just hanging around to enjoy the scene. After I got a little past the warehouse door, I sort of drifted up alongside it. I looked down the row of people, and there was Dee Sparks, just a few yards away from being able to see in. Dee was leaning forward, and when he saw me he almost jumped out of his skin. He looked away as fast as he could. His eyes turned as dead as stones. The cop at the door yelled at me to go to the end of the line. He never would have noticed me at all if Dee hadn't jumped like someone just shot off a firecracker behind him.

'About halfway down the line, Mary Randolph was standing behind some of the ladies from the neighborhood. She looked terrible. Her hair stuck out in raggedy clumps, and her skin was ashy, like she hadn't slept in a long time. I sped up a little, hoping she wouldn't notice me, but after I took one more step, Mary Randolph looked down and her eyes hooked into mine. I swear, what was in her eyes almost knocked me down. I couldn't even tell what it was, unless it was pure hate. Hate and pain. With her eyes hooked into mine like that, I couldn't look away. It was like I was seeing that miserable, terrible white smear twisting up between the trees on that night in The Backs. Mary let me go, and I almost fell down all over again.

'I got to the end of the line and started moving along regular and slow with everybody else. Mary Randolph stayed in my mind and blanked out everything else. When I got up to the door, I barely took in what was inside the warehouse – a wall full of bullet holes and bloodstains all over the place, big slick ones and little drizzly ones. All I could think of was the shack and Mary Randolph sitting next to the dead girl, and I was back there all over again.

'Mary Randolph didn't show up at the Beergarden dance, so she didn't hear me play saxophone in public for the first time. I didn't expect her, either, not after the way she looked out at the warehouse. There'd been a lot of news about Eddie Grimes, who they made out to be less civilized than a gorilla, a crazy man who'd murder anyone as long as he could kill all the white women first. The paper had a picture of what they called Grimes's 'lair', with busted furniture all over the place and holes in the walls, but they never explained that it was the police tore it up and made it look that way.

'The other thing people got suddenly all hot about was The Backs. Seems the place was even worse than everybody thought. Seems white girls besides Eleanore Monday had been taken out there – according to some, there was even white girls living out there, along with a lot of bad coloreds. The place was a nest of vice, Sodom and Gomorrah. Two days before the town council was supposed to discuss the problem, a gang of white men went out there with guns and clubs and torches and burned every shack in The Backs clear down to the ground. While they were there, they didn't see a single soul, white, colored, male, female, damned or saved. Everybody who lived in The Backs had skedaddled. And the funny thing was, long as The Backs had existed right outside of Woodland, no one in Woodland could recollect the name of anyone who had ever lived there. They couldn't even recall the name of anyone who had ever gone there, except for Eddie Grimes. In fact, after the place got burned down, it appeared that it must have been a sin just to say its name, because no one ever mentioned it. You'd think men so fine and moral as to burn down The Backs would be willing to take the credit, but none ever did.

'You could think they must have wanted to get rid of some things out there. Or wanted real bad to forget about things out there. One thing I thought, Dr Garland and the man I saw leaving that shack had been out there with torches.

'But maybe I didn't know anything at all. Two weeks later, a couple things happened that shook me good.

'The first one happened three nights before Thanksgiving. I was hurrying home, a little bit late. Nobody else on the street, everybody inside either sitting down to dinner or getting ready for it. When I got to Mary Randolph's house, some kind of noise coming from inside stopped me. What I thought was, it sounded exactly like somebody trying to scream while someone else was holding a hand over their mouth. Well, that was plain foolish, wasn't it? How did I know what that would sound like? I moved along a step or two, and then I heard it again. Could be anything, I told myself. Mary Randolph didn't like me too much, anyway. She wouldn't be partial to my knocking on her door. Best thing I could do was get out. Which was what I did. Just went home to supper and forgot about it.

'Until the next day, anyhow, when a friend of Mary's walked in her front door and found her lying dead with her throat cut and a knife in her hand. A cut of fatback, we heard, had boiled away to cinders on her stove. I didn't tell anybody about what I heard the night before. Too scared. I couldn't do anything but wait to see what the police did.

'To the police, it was all real clear. Mary killed herself, plain and simple.

'When our minister went across town to ask why a lady who intended to commit suicide had bothered to start cooking her supper, the chief told him that a female bent on killing herself probably didn't care *what* happened to the food on her stove. Then I suppose Mary Randolph nearly managed to cut her own head off, said the minister. A female in despair possesses a god-awful strength, said the chief. And asked, wouldn't she have screamed if she'd been attacked? And added, couldn't it be that maybe this female here had secrets in her life connected to the late savage murderer named Eddie Grimes? We might all be better off it these secrets get buried with your Mary Randolph, said the chief. I'm sure you understand me, Reverend. And yes, the reverend did understand, he surely did. So Mary Randolph got laid away in the cemetery, and nobody ever said her name again. She was put away out of mind, like The Backs.

'The second thing that shook me up and proved to me that I didn't know anything, that I was no better than a blind dog, happened on Thanksgiving Day. My daddy played piano in church, and on special days, we played our instruments along with the gospel songs. I got to church early with the rest of my family, and we practiced with the choir. Afterwards, I went to fooling around outside until the people came, and saw a big car come into the church parking lot. Must have been the biggest, fanciest car I'd ever seen. Miller's Hill was written all over that vehicle. I couldn't have told you why, but the sight of it made my heart stop. The front door opened, and out stepped a colored man in a fancy gray uniform with a cap. He didn't so much as dirty his eyes by looking at me, or at the church, or at anything around him. He stepped around the front of the car and opened the rear door on my side. A young woman was in the passenger seat, and when she got out of the car, the sun fell on her blond hair and the little fur jacket she was wearing. I couldn't see more than the top of her head, her shoulders under the jacket, and her legs. Then she straightened up, and her eyes lighted right on me. She smiled, but I couldn't smile back. I couldn't even begin to move.

'It was Abbey Montgomery, delivering baskets of food to our church, the way she did every Thanksgiving and Christmas. She looked older and thinner than the last time I'd seen her alive – older and thinner, but more than that, like there was no fun at all in her life anymore. She walked to the trunk of the car, and the driver opened it up, leaned in, and brought out a great big basket of food. He took it into the church by the back way and came back for another one. Abbey Montgomery just stood still and watched him carry the baskets. She looked – she looked like she was just going through the motions, like going through the motions was all she was ever going to do from now on, and she knew it. Once she smiled at the driver, but the smile was so sad that the driver didn't even try to smile back. When he was done, he closed the trunk and let her into the passenger seat, got behind the wheel, and drove away.

'I was thinking, *Dee Sparks was right, she was alive all the time*. Then I thought, *No, Mary Randolph brought her back, too, like she did Eddie Grimes. But it didn't work right, and only part of her came back*.

'And that's the whole thing, except that Abbey Montgomery didn't deliver food to our church that Christmas – she was traveling out of the country, with her aunt.

And she didn't bring food the next Thanksgiving, either, just sent her driver with the baskets. By that time, we didn't expect her, because we'd already heard that, soon as she got back to town, Abbey Montgomery stopped leaving her house. That girl shut herself up and never came out. I heard from somebody who probably didn't know any more than I did that she eventually got so she wouldn't even leave her room. Five years later, she passed away. Twenty-six years old, and they said she looked to be fifty.'

4

Hat fell silent, and I sat with my pen ready over the notebook, waiting for more. When I realized that he had finished, I asked, 'What did she die of?'

'Nobody ever told me.'

'And nobody ever found who had killed Mary Randolph.'

The limpid, colorless eyes momentarily rested on me. 'Was she killed?'

'Did you ever become friends with Dee Sparks again? Did you at least talk about it with him?'

'Surely did not. Nothing to talk about.'

This was a remarkable statement, considering that for an hour he had done nothing but talk about what had happened to the two of them, but I let it go. Hat was still looking at me with his unreadable eyes. His face had become particularly bland, almost immobile. It was not possible to imagine this man as an active eleven-year-old boy. 'Now you heard me out, answer my question,' he said.

I couldn't remember the question.

'Did we find what we were looking for?'

Scares – that was what they had been looking for. 'I think you found a lot more than that,' I said.

He nodded slowly. 'That's right. It was more.'

Then I asked him some question about his family's band, he lubricated himself with another swallow of gin, and the interview returned to more typical matters. But the experience of listening to him had changed. After I had heard the long, unresolved tale of his Halloween night, everything Hat said was like his conversation with Mary Randolph. It seemed to have two separate meanings, the daylight meaning created by sequences of ordinary English words and another, nighttime meaning, far less determined and knowable. He was like a man discoursing with eerie rationality in the midst of a surreal dream – like a man carrying on an ordinary conversation with one foot placed on solid ground and the other suspended above a bottomless abyss. I focused on the rationality, on the foot placed in the context I understood; the rest was unsettling to the point of being frightening. By six-thirty, when he kindly called me 'Miss Rosemary' and opened his door, I felt as if I'd spent several weeks, if not whole months, in his room.

Part Three

1

Although I did get my MA at Columbia, I didn't have enough money to stay on for a Ph.D., so I never became a college professor. I never became a jazz critic, either, or anything else very interesting. For a couple of years after Columbia, I taught English in a high school, until I quit to take the job I have now, which involves a lot of traveling and pays a little bit better than teaching. Maybe even quite a bit better, but that's not saying much, especially when you consider my expenses. I own a nice little house in the Chicago suburbs, my marriage has held up against everything life did to it, and my twenty-two-year-old son, a young man who never once in his life for the purpose of pleasure read a novel, looked at a painting, visited a museum, or listened to anything but the most readily available music, recently announced to his mother and myself that he has decided to become an artist, actual type of art to be determined later, but probably to include aspects of photography, videotape, and the creation of 'installations'. I take this as proof that he was raised in a manner that left his self-esteem intact.

I no longer provide my life with a perpetual sound-track (though my son, who has moved back in with us, does), in part because my income does not permit the purchase of a great many compact discs. (A friend presented me with a CD player on my forty-fifth birthday.) And these days, I'm as interested in classical music as in jazz. Of course, I never go to jazz clubs when I am home. Are there still people, apart from New Yorkers, who patronize jazz nightclubs in their own hometowns? The concept seems faintly retrograde, even somehow illicit. But when I am out on the road, living in air-planes and hotel rooms, I often check the jazz listings in the local papers to see if I can find some way to fill my evenings. Many of the legends of my youth are still out there, in most cases playing at least as well as before. Some months ago, while I was San Francisco, I came across John Hawes's name in this fashion. He was working in a club so close to my hotel that I could walk to it.

His appearance in any club at all was surprising. Hawes had ceased performing jazz in public years before. He had earned a great deal of fame (and undoubtedly, a great deal of money) writing film scores, and in the past decade he had begun to appear in swallowtail coat and white tie as a conductor of the standard classical repertoire. I believe he had a permanent post in some city like Seattle, or perhaps Salt Lake City. If he was spending a week playing jazz with a trio in San Francisco, it must have been for the sheer pleasure of it.

I turned up just before the beginning of the first set, and got a table toward the back of the club. Most of the tables were filled – Hawes's celebrity had guaranteed him a good house. Only a few minutes after the announced time of the first set, Hawes emerged through a door at the front of the club and moved toward the piano, followed by his bassist and drummer. He looked like a more successful version of the younger man I had seen in New York, and the only indications of the extra years were his silver-gray hair, still abundant, and a little paunch. His playing, too, seemed essentially unchanged, but I could not hear it in the way I once had. He was still a good pianist – no doubt about that – but he seemed to be skating over the surface of the songs he played, using his wonderful technique and good time merely to decorate their melodies. It was the sort of playing that becomes less impressive the more attention you give it – if you were listening with half an ear, it probably sounded like Art Tatum. I wondered if John Hawes had always had this superficial streak in him, or if he had lost a certain necessary passion during his years away from jazz. Certainly he had not sounded superficial when I had heard him play with Hat.

Hawes, too, might have been thinking about his old employer, because in the first set he played 'Love Walked In,' 'Too Marvelous for Words', and 'Up Jumped Hat'. In the last of these, inner gears seemed to mesh, the rhythm simultaneously relaxed and intensified, and the music turned into real, not imitation, jazz. Hawes looked pleased with himself when he stood up from the piano bench, and half a dozen fans moved to greet him as he stepped off the bandstand. Most of them were carrying old records they wished him to sign.

A few minutes later, I saw Hawes standing by himself at the end of the bar, drinking what appeared to be club soda, in proximity to his musicians but not actually speaking with them. Wondering if his allusions to Hat had been deliberate, I left my table and walked toward the bar. Hawes watched me approach out of the side of his eye, neither encouraging nor discouraging me. When I introduced myself, he smiled nicely and shook my hand and waited for whatever I wanted to say to him.

At first, I made some inane comment about the difference between playing in clubs and conducting in concert halls, and he replied with the noncommital and equally banal agreement that yes, the two experiences were very different.

Then I told him that I had seen him play with Hat all those years ago in New York, and he turned to me with genuine pleasure in his face. 'Did you? At that little club on St Mark's Place? That sure was fun. I guess I must have been thinking about it, because I played some of those songs we used to do.'

'That was why I came over,' I said. 'I guess that was one of the best musical experiences I ever had.'

'You and me both.' Hawes smiled to himself. 'Sometimes, I just couldn't believe what he was doing.'

'It showed,' I said.

'Well.' His eyes slid away from mine. 'Great character. Completely otherwordly.'

'I saw some of that,' I said. 'I did that interview with him that turns up now and then, the one in *Downbeat*.'

'Oh!' Hawes gave me his first genuinely interested look so far. 'Well, that was him, all right.'

'Most of it was, anyhow.'

'You cheated?' Now he was looking even more interested.

'I had to make it understandable.'

'Oh, sure. You couldn't put in all those ding-dings and bells and Bob Crosbys.' These had been elements of Hat's private code. Hawes laughed at the memory. 'When he

248

wanted to play a blues in G, he'd lean over and say, "G's, please."'

'Did you get to know him at all well, personally?' I asked, thinking that the answer must be that he had not – I didn't think that anyone had ever really known Hat very well.

'Pretty well,' Hawes said. 'A couple of times, around '54 and '55, he invited me home with him, to his parents' house, I mean. We got to be friends on a Jazz at the Phil tour, and twice when we were in the South, he asked me if I wanted to eat some good home cooking.'

'You went to his hometown?'

He nodded. 'His parents put me up. They were interesting people. Hat's father, Red, was about the lightest black man I ever saw, and he could have passed for white anywhere, but I don't suppose the thought ever occurred to him.'

'Was the family band still going?'

'No, to tell you the truth, I don't think they were getting much work up toward the end of the forties. At the end, they were using a tenor player and a drummer from the high school band. And the church work got more and more demanding for Hat's father.'

'His father was a deacon, or something like that?'

He raised his eyebrows. 'No, Red was the Baptist minister. The reverend. He ran that church. I think he even started it.'

'Hat told me his father played piano in church, but . . .'

'The reverend would have made a hell of a blues piano player, if he'd ever left his day job.'

'There must have been another Baptist church in the neighborhood,' I said, thinking this the only explanation for the presence of two Baptist ministers. But why had Hat not mentioned that his own father, like Dee Sparks's, had been a clergyman?

'Are you kidding? There was barely enough money in

that place to keep one of them going.' He looked at his watch, nodded at me, and began to move closer to his sidemen.

'Could I ask you one more question?'

'I suppose so,' he said, almost impatiently.

'Did Hat strike you as superstitious?'

Hawes grinned. 'Oh, he was superstitious, all right. He told me he never worked on Halloween – he didn't even want to go out of his room on Halloween. That's why he left the big band, you know. They were starting a tour on Halloween, and Hat refused to do it. He just quit.' He leaned toward me. 'I'll tell you another funny thing. I always had the feeling that Hat was terrified of his father – I thought he invited me to Hatchville with him so I could be some kind of buffer between him and his father. Never made any sense to me. Red was a big strong old guy, and I'm pretty sure a long time ago he used to mess around with the ladies, reverend or not, but I couldn't ever figure out why Hat should be afraid of him. But whenever Red came into the room, Hat shut up. Funny, isn't it?'

I must have looked very perplexed. 'Hatchville?'

'Where they lived. Hatchville, Mississippi – not too far from Biloxi.'

'But he told me –'

'Hat never gave too many straight answers,' Hawes said. 'And he didn't let the facts get in the way of a good story. When you come to think of it, why should he? He was *Hat*.'

After the next set, I walked back uphill to my hotel, wondering again about the long story Hat had told me. Had there been any truth in it at all?

2

Three weeks later I found myself released from a meeting at our midwestern headquarters in downtown Chicago earlier than I had expected, and instead of going to a bar with the other wandering corporate ghosts like myself, I made up a story about dinner with visiting relatives. I didn't want to admit to my fellow employees, committed like all male businesspeople to aggressive endeavors such as raquetball, drinking, and the pursuit of women, that I intended to visit the library. Short of a trip to Mississippi, a good periodical room offered the most likely means of finding out once and for all how much truth had been in what Hat had told me.

I hadn't forgotten everything I had learned at Columbia – I still knew how to look things up.

In the main library, a boy set me up with a monitor and spools of microfilm representing the complete contents of the daily newspapers from Biloxi and Hatchville, Mississippi, for Hat's tenth and eleventh years. That made three papers, two for Biloxi and one for Hatchville, but all I had to examine were the issues dating from the end of October through the middle of November – I was looking for references to Eddie Grimes, Eleanore Monday, Mary Randolph, Abbey Montgomery, Hat's family, The Backs, and anyone named Sparks.

The Hatchville *Blade*, a gossipy daily, offered plenty of references to each of these names and places, and the papers from Biloxi contained nearly as many – Biloxi could not conceal the delight, disguised as horror, aroused in its collective soul by the unimaginable events taking place in the smaller, supposedly respectable town ten miles west. Biloxi was riveted, Biloxi was superior, Biloxi was virtually intoxicated with dread and outrage. In Hatchville, the press maintained a persistent optimistic dignity: when wickedness had appeared, justice official and unofficial had dealt with it. Hatchville was shocked but proud (or at least pretended to be proud), and Biloxi all but preened. The *Blade* printed detailed news stories, but the Biloxi papers suggested implications not allowed by Hatchville's version of events. I needed Hatchville to confirm or question Hat's story, but Biloxi gave me at least the beginning of a way to understand it.

A black ex-convict named Edward Grimes had in some fashion persuaded or coerced Eleanore Monday, a retarded young white woman, to accompany him to an area variously described as 'a long-standing local disgrace' (the *Blade*) and 'a haunt of deepest vice' (Biloxi) and, after 'the perpetration of the most offensive and brutal deeds upon her person' (the *Blade*) or 'acts that the judicious commentator must decline to imagine, much less describe' (Biloxi), murdered her, presumably to ensure her silence, and then buried the body near the 'squalid dwelling' where he made and sold illegal liquor. State and local police departments acting in concert had located the body, identified Grimes as the fiend, and, after a search of his house, had tracked him to a warehouse, where the murderer was killed in a gun battle. The *Blade* covered half its front page with a photograph of a gaping double door and a blood-stained wall. All Mississippi, both Hatchville and Biloxi declared, could now breathe more easily.

The *Blade* gave the death of Mary Randolph a single paragraph on its back page, the Biloxi papers nothing.

In Hatchville, the raid on The Backs was described as a heroic assault on a dangerous criminal encampment that had somehow come to flourish in a little-noticed section of the countryside. At great risk to themselves, anonymous citizens of Hatchville had descended like the army of the righteous and driven forth the hidden sinners from their dens. Troublemakers, beware! The Biloxi papers, while seeming to endorse the action in Hatchville, took another tone altogether. Can it be, they asked, that the Hatchville police had never before noticed the existence of a Sodom and Gomorrah so close to the town line? Did it take the savage murder of a helpless woman to bring it to their attention? Of course Biloxi celebrated the destruction of

The Backs – such vileness must be eradicated – but it wondered what else had been destroyed along with the stills and the mean buildings where loose women had plied their trade. Men ever are men, and those who have succumbed to temptation may wish to remove from the face of the earth any evidence of their lapses. Had not the police of Hatchville ever heard the rumor, vague and doubtless baseless, that operations of an illegal nature had been performed in the selfsame Backs? That in an atmosphere of drugs, intoxication, and gambling, the races had mingled there and that 'fast' young women had risked life and honor in search of illicit thrills? Hatchville may have rid itself of a few buildings, but Biloxi was willing to suggest that the problems of its smaller neighbor might not have disappeared with them.

As this campaign of innuendo went on in Biloxi, the *Blade* blandly reported the ongoing events of any smaller American city. Miss Abigail Montgomery sailed with her aunt, Miss Lucinda Bright, from New Orleans to France for an eight-week tour of the Continent. The Reverend Jasper Sparks of the Miller's Hill Presbyterian Church delivered a sermon on the subject of 'Christian forgiveness'. (Just after Thanksgiving, the Reverend Sparks's son, Rodney, was sent off with the blessings and congratulations of all Hatchville to a private academy in Charleston, South Carolina.) There were bake sales, church socials, and costume parties. A saxophone virtuoso named Albert Woodland demonstrated his astonishing wizardy at a well-attended recital presented in Temperance Hall.

Well, I knew the name of at least one person who had attended the recital. If Hat had chosen to disguise the name of his hometown, he had done so by substituting for it a name that represented another sort of home.

But, although I had more ideas about this than before, I still did not know exactly what Hat had seen or done on Halloween night in The Backs. It seemed possible

that he had gone there with a white boy of his age, a
preacher's son like himself, and had the wits scared out
of him by whatever had happened to Abbey Montgomery
– and after that night, Abbey herself had been sent out
of town, as had Dee Sparks. I couldn't think that a man
had murdered the young woman, leaving Mary Randolph
to bring her back to life. Surely whatever had happened
to Abbey Montgomery had brought Dr Garland out to The
Backs, and what he had witnessed or done there had sent
him away screaming. And this event – what had befallen
a rich young white woman in the shadiest, most criminal
section of a Mississippi county – had led to the slaying of
Eddie Grimes and the murder of Mary Randolph. Because
they knew what had happened, they had to die.

I understood all this, and Hat had understood it, too. Yet
he had introduced needless puzzles, as if embedded in the
midst of this unresolved story were something he either
wished to conceal or not to know. And concealed it would
remain; if Hat did not know it, I never would. Whatever
had really happened in The Backs on Halloween night was
lost for good.

On the *Blade*'s entertainment page for a Saturday in the
middle of November I had come across a photograph of
Hat's family's band, and when I had reached this hopeless
point in my thinking, I spooled back across the pages to
look at it again. Hat, his two brothers, his sister, and
his parents stood in a straight line, tallest to smallest,
in front of what must have been the family car. Hat
held a C-melody saxophone, his brothers a trumpet and
drumsticks, his sister a clarinet. As the piano player, the
reverend carried nothing at all – nothing except for what
came through even a grainy, sixty-year-old photograph
as a powerful sense of self. Hat's father had been a tall,
impressive man, and in the photograph he looked as
white as I did. But what was impressive was not the
lightness of his skin, or even his striking handsomeness:

what impressed was the sense of authority implicit in his posture, his straightforward gaze, even the dictatorial set of his chin. In retrospect, I was not surprised by what John Hawes had told me, for this man could easily be frightening. You would not wish to oppose him, you would not elect to get in his way. Beside him, Hat's mother seemed vague and distracted, as if her husband had robbed her of all certainty. Then I noticed the car, and for the first time realized why it had been included in the photograph. It was a sign of their prosperity, the respectable status they had achieved – the car was as much an advertisement as the photograph. It was, I thought, an old Model T Ford, but I didn't waste any time speculating that it might have been the Model T Hat had seen in The Backs.

And that would be that – the hint of an absurd supposition – except for something I read a few days ago in a book called *Cool Breeze: The Life of Grant Kilbert*.

There are few biographies of any jazz musicians apart from Louis Armstrong and Duke Ellington (though one does now exist of Hat, the title of which was drawn from my interview with him), and I was surprised to see *Cool Breeze* at the B. Dalton in our local mall. Biographies have not yet been written of Art Blakey, Clifford Brown, Ben Webster, or many others of more musical and historical importance than Kilbert. Yet I should not have been surprised. Kilbert was one of those musicians who attract and maintain a large personal following, and twenty years after his death, almost all of his records have been released on CD, many of them in multidisc boxed sets. He had been a great, great player, the closest to Hat of all his disciples. Because Kilbert had been one of my early heroes, I bought the book (for thirty-five dollars!) and brought it home.

Like the lives of many jazz musicians, I suppose of artists in general, Kilbert's had been an odd mixture of public fame and private misery. He had committed burglaries, even armed robberies, to feed his persistent heroin addiction; he had spent years in jail; his two marriages had ended in outright hatred; he had managed to betray most of his friends. That this weak, narcissistic louse had found it in himself to create music of real tenderness and beauty was one of art's enigmas, but not actually a surprise. I'd heard and read enough stories about Grant Kilbert to know what kind of man he'd been.

But what I had not known was that Kilbert, to all appearances an American of conventional northern European, perhaps Scandinavian or Anglo-Saxon, stock, had occasionally claimed to be black. (This claim had always been dismissed, apparently, as another indication of Kilbert's mental aberrancy.) At other times, being Kilbert, he had denied ever making this claim.

Neither had I known that the received versions of his birth and upbringing were in question. Unlike Hat, Kilbert had been interviewed dozens of times both in *Downbeat* and in mass-market weekly newsmagazines, invariably to offer the same story of having been born in Hattiesburg, Mississippi, to an unmusical, working-class family (a plumber's family), of knowing virtually from infancy that he was born to make music, of begging for and finally being given a saxophone, of early mastery and the dazzled admiration of his teachers, then of dropping out of school at sixteen and joining the Woody Herman band. After that, almost immediate fame.

Most of this, the Grant Kilbert myth, was undisputed. He had been raised in Hattiesburg by a plumber named Kilbert, he had been a prodigy and high school dropout, he'd become famous with Woody Herman before he was twenty. Yet he told a few friends, not necessarily those to whom he said he was black, that he'd been adopted by the Kilberts, and that once or twice, in great anger, either the plumber or his wife had told him that he had been born into poverty and disgrace and that he'd better by God be grateful for the opportunities he'd been given. The source of this story was John Hawes, who'd met Kilbert on another long JATP tour, the last he made before leaving the road for film scoring.

'Grant didn't have a lot of friends on that tour,' Hawes told the biographer. 'Even though he was such a great player, you never knew what he was going to say, and if he was in a bad mood, he was liable to put down some of the older players. He was always respectful around Hat, his whole style was based on Hat's, but Hat could go days without saying anything, and by that time he certainly wasn't making any new friends. Still, he'd let Grant sit next to him on the bus, and nod his head while Grant talked to him, so he must have felt some affection for him. Anyhow, eventually I was about the only guy on the tour that was willing to have a conversation with Grant, and we'd sit up in the bar late at night after the concerts. The way he played, I could forgive him a lot of failings. One of those nights, he said that he'd been adopted, and that not knowing who his real parents were was driving him crazy. He didn't even have a birth certificate. From a hint his mother once gave him, he thought one of his birth parents was black, but when he asked them directly, they always denied it. These were white Mississippians, after all, and if they had wanted a baby so bad that they had taken in a child who looked completely white but maybe had a drop or two of black blood in his veins, they weren't going to admit it, even to themselves.'

In the midst of so much supposition, here is a fact. Grant Kilbert was exactly eleven years younger than Hat. The jazz encyclopedias give his birth date as November first, which instead of his actual birthday may have been the day he was delivered to the couple in Hattiesburg.

I wonder if Hat saw more than he admitted to me of the man leaving the shack where Abbey Montgomery lay on bloody sheets; I wonder if he had reason to fear his father. I don't know if what I am thinking is correct – I'll never know that – but now, finally, I think I know why Hat never wanted to go out of his room on Halloween nights. The story he told me never left him, but it must have been most fully present on those nights. I think he heard the screams, saw the bleeding girl, and saw Mary Randolph staring at him with displaced pain and rage. I think that in some small closed corner deep within himself, he knew who had been the real object of these feelings, and therefore had to lock himself inside his hotel room and gulp gin until he obliterated the horror of his thoughts.

Hunger, an Introduction

I have a sturdy first sentence all prepared, and as soon as I settle down and get used to the reversal of our usual roles I'll give you the pleasure. Okay. Here goes. *Considering that everyone dies sooner or later, people know surprisingly little about ghosts.* Is my point clear? Every person on earth, whether saint or turd, is going to wind up as a ghost, but not one of them, I mean, of *you* people, knows the first thing about them. Almost everything written, spoken, or imagined about the subject is, I'm sorry, absolute junk. It's disgusting. I'm speaking from the heart here, I'm laying it on the line – disgusting. All it would take to get this business right is some common, everyday, sensible thinking, but sensible thinking is easier to ask for than to get, believe you me.

I see that I have already jumped my own gun, because the second sentence I intended to deliver was: *In fact, when it comes to the subject of ghosts, human beings are completely clueless.* And the third sentence, after which I am going to scrap my prepared text and speak from the heart, is: *A lot of us are kind of steamed about that.*

For! The most common notion about ghosts, the granddaddy, is the one that parades as grown-up reason, shakes its head, grins, fixes you with a steely glint that asks if you're kidding, and says: Ghosts don't exist.

Wrong.

Sorry, wrong.

Sorry, I know, you'd feel better if you could persuade yourself that accounts of encounters with beings previously but not presently alive are fictional. Doesn't matter how many people say they have seen a woman in black moving back and forth behind the window from which in 1892 the chambermaid Ethel Carroway defenestrated a newborn infant fathered by a seagoing rogue named Captain Starbuck, thousands of fools might swear to having seen Ethel's shade drag itself past that window, it don't, sorry, it doesn't matter, they're all deluded. They saw a breeze twitch the curtain and imagined the rest. *They want you to think they're interesting.* You're too clever for that one. You know what happens to people after they chuck it, and one thing that's sure is, they don't turn into ghosts. At the moment of death, people either (1) depart this and all other possible spheres, leaving their bodies to fade out in a messier, more time-consuming fashion; or (2) leave behind the poor old skinbag as their immortal part soars heavenward, rejoicing, or plummets wailing to eternal torment; or (3) shuffle out of one skinbag, take a few turns around the celestial block, and reincarnate in a different, fresher skinbag, thereupon starting all over again. Isn't that more or less the menu? Extinction, moral payback, or rebirth. During my own life, for example, I favored (1), a good clean departure.

Now we come to one of my personal bugaboos or, I could say, anathemas, in memory of someone I have to bring in sooner or later anyhow, my former employer, Mr Harold McNair, a gentleman with an autodidact's fondness for big words. Mr McNair once said to me, *Dishonesty is my particular anathema*. One other time, he used the word *peculation*. Peculation was his anathema, too. Mr Harold McNair was confident of his personal relationship to his savior, and as a result he was also pretty confident that what lay ahead of him, after a dignified leave-taking in the big bed on the third floor, was a one-way excursion to paradise. As I say, he was pretty sure about that. Maybe now and then the thought came to him that a depraved, greedy, mean-spirited weasel like himself might have some trouble squeaking through the pearly gates, no matter how many Sundays he strutted over to the church on Abercrombie Road to lip-synch to the hymns and nod over the sermon – yes, maybe Harold McNair had more doubts than he let on. When it came down to what we have to call the crunch, he did not go peacefully. How he went was screeching and sweating and cursing, trying to shield his head from the hammer and struggling to get back on his feet, for all the world as though he feared spending eternity as a rasher of bacon. And if asked his opinion on the existence of ghosts, this big-shot retail magnate would probably have nodded slowly, sucked his lower lip, pondered mightily, and opined –

All right, I never actually heard the position of my former employer in re ghostly beings despite our many, ofttimes tediously lengthy colloquies. Harold McNair spoke to me of many things, of the anathemas dishonesty and peculation, of yet more anathemas, including the fair sex, any human being under the age of twenty, folk of the Hebraic, Afric, or Papist persuasions, customers who demand twenty minutes of a salesman's attention and then sashay out without making a purchase, customers – *female* customers – who return undergarments soiled by use, residents of California or New York, all Europeans, especially bogtrotters and greaseballs, eggheads, per-fessers, pinkos, idiots who hold hands in public, all music but the operettas of Gilbert and Sullivan, all literature not of the 'improving' variety, tight shoes, small print, lumpy potatoes, dogs of any description, and much else. He delivered himself so thoroughly on the topics that excited his indignation that he never got around to describing his vision of the afterlife, even while sputtering and screeching as the hammer sought out the tender spots on his tough little noggin. Yet I know what Mr McNair would have said.

Though ghosts may fail to be nonexistent, they are at least comfortingly small in number.

Wrong. This way of thinking disregards the difference between Ghosts Visible, like poor Ethel Carroway, who dropped that baby from the fourth-floor window of the Oliphant Hotel, and Invisible, which is exactly like pretending there is no difference between living Visibles, like Mr Harold McNair, and Living Invisibles, which, in spite of everything, is what I was back then, not to mention most everyone else, when you get down to it. Most people are about as visible to others as the headlines on a week-old newspaper.

I desire with my entire heart to tell you what I am looking at, I yearn to describe the visible world as seen from my vantage point beside the great azalea bush on my old enemy's front lawn on Tulip Lane, the spot I head for every day at this time. That would clear up this whole *numbers* confusion right away. But before I can get into describing what I can see, I must at last get around to introducing myself, since that's the point of my being here today.

Francis T. Wardwell is my handle, Frank Wardwell as I was known, and old Frank can already feel himself getting heated up over the third numbskull idea the run of people have about ghosts, so he better take care of that one before going any further. The third idea is: Ghosts are ghosts because they are unhappy. Far too many of you out there believe that every wandering spirit is atoning for some old heart-stuffed misery, which is why they suppose Ethel drifts past that window now and again.

Ask yourself, now. Is anything that simple, even in what *you* call experience? Are all the criminals in jail? Are all the innocent free? And if the price of misery is misery, what is the price of joy? In what coin do you pay for that, laddy: shekels, sweat, or sleepless nights?

*   *   *

Though in every moment of my youthful existence I was sustained by a most glorious secret that was mine alone, I too was acquainted with shekels, sweat, and what the poets call white nights. No child of luxury, I. Francis Wardwell, Frank to his chums, born to parents on the ragged-most fringe of the lower middle class, was catapulted into corporeality a great distance from the nearest silver spoon. We were urban poor (lower-middle-class poor, that is), not rural poor, and I feel deeply within myself that a country landscape such as that of which I was deprived would have yielded to my infant self a fund of riches sorely needed. (Mark the first sounding of the hunger theme, to which we will return betimes.) Is not Nature a friend and tutor to the observant child? Does it not offer a steady flow of stuff like psychic nutrient to the developing boy? Experts say it does, or so I hear, and also that much do I recall from my reading, which was always far, far in advance of my grade level. (I was reading on the *college level* before I was out of short pants.) Old-time poets all said Nature is a better teacher than any other. In my case, blocked off by city walls from the wise friend Nature, I was forced to feed my infant mind on the harsher realities of brick, barbed wire, and peacock-feather oil slicks. That I went as far as I did is testimony to my resilient soul-strength. Forbidden was I to wander 'mongst the heather and cowslips, the foxgloves, purple vetch, tiger lilies, loosestrife, and hawkweed on country lanes; no larks or thrushes had I for company, and we never even heard of nightingales where I came from. I wandered, when I had that luxury – that is, when I wasn't running my guts out to get away from a long-nosed, red-eyed, smirking Boy Teuteburg – through unclean city streets past taverns and boardinghouses, and for streaky gold-red sunsets I had neon signs. The air was not, to put it good and plain, fresh. The animals, when not domestic, were rodentine. And from the seventh grade on, at a time when I suffered under the tyranny of a termaganty black-haired witch-thing named Missus Barksdale, who hated me because I knew more than she did, I was forced to endure the further injustice of after-school employment. Daily had I to trudge from the humiliations delivered upon my head by the witch-thing, Missus Barfsbottom, humiliations earned only through an inability to conceal entirely the mirth her errors caused in me, from sadistic, unwarranted humiliations delivered upon the head of one of the topmost scholars ever seen at that crummy school, then to trudge through sordiosities to the place of my employment, Dockweder's Hardware, where I took up my broom and swept, swept, swept.

For shekels! In the sense of measly, greasy coins of low denomination in little number! Earned by my childish sweat, the honest sorrowful perspiration, each salty drop nonaccidentally just exactly like a tear (and that, Miss Doggybreath, is what you call a metaphor, not a methapor, as your warty mustachy cakehole misinformed the massed seventh grade of the Daniel Webster State Graded School in the winter of 1928), of a promising, I mean really and truly *promising* lad, an intelligent lad, a lad deserving of the finest this world had to offer in the way of breaks and opportunities, what you might want to call and I looking back am virtually forced to call a Shining Boy!

Who day and night had to check over his shoulder for the approach of, who had to strain his innocent ears in case he could hear the footfalls of, who was made to quench his glorious shining spirit because he had to live in total awful fear of the subhuman, soulless, snakelike figure of Boy Teuteburg. Who would crouch behind garbage cans and conceal himself in doorways, was a lurker in alleys, would drag at his narrow cigarette with his narrow shoulders against the bricks and squint out from under the narrow brim of the cap on his narrow head, was a low being of no conscience or intelligence or any other merits altogether. A Boy Teuteburg is not a fellow for your flowery fields and rending sunsets. And such as this, a lowly brutal creature with no promise to him at all save the promise to wind up in jail, became yet another, perhaps the most severe, bane of the Shining Boy's existence.

Between Daniel Webster State Graded School and Dockweder's Hardware Emporium would this young terrorist lurk of an afternoon, stealing some worthless titbit there, hawking on the sidewalk there, blowing his nose by pressing two fingers against one nostril, leaning over and firing, then repeating the gesture on the opposite side, all the while skulking along, flicking his puny red eyes over the passing throng (as *Dickens* had it) in search of children younger than he, any children in actual fact, but in most especial one certain child. This, you may have divined, was yours truly. I knew myself the object of Boy Teuteburg's special hatred because of what befell the child-me on those occasions when I managed to set sail from one place to another in convoy with other kidlings of my generation – other sparrows of the street (as *Blake* might put it) – to subsume myself within the shelter of a nattering throng of classmates. We all feared Boy, having suffered under his psychotic despotism through year after year of grade-school. Our collective relief at his eventual graduation (he was sixteen!) chilled to dread when we discovered that his release from the eighth grade meant only that Boy had been freed to prowl eternally about Daniel Webster, a shark awaiting shoals of smaller fishes. (A *simile*, Missus Doggybark, a *simile*.) There he was, smirking as he tightened his skinny lips to draw on his skinny cigarette – circling. Let us say our convoy of joking lads rounds the corner of Erie Street by the Oliphant Hotel and spreads across the sidewalk as we carry on toward

Third Street, home for some, Dockweder's and the broom for me. Then a stoaty shadow separates from the entrance of Candies & Newsagent, a thrill of fear passes through us, red eyes ignite and blaze, some dreary brat begins to weep, and the rest of us scatter as Boy charges, already raising his sharp and pointy fists. And of all these larking children, which particular boy was his intended target? That child least like himself – the one he hated most – myself – and I knew why. Scatter though I would 'mongst my peers, rushing first to this one then to that, my friends, their morality stunted by the same brutal landscape which had shaped our tormentor, would'st thrust me away, abandon me, sacrifice me for their own ends. It was me, I mean I, he searched out, and we all knew it. Soon the others refused to leave the school in my presence, and I walked alone once more. Oft were the days when the body that wielded the broom ached with bruises, when the eyes within the body were dimmed with tears of pain and sorrow, and the nose of the body contained screws of tissue paper within each nostril, purpose of, to staunch the flow of blood.

Oft, too, were the nights when from a multiplicity of causes young Frank Wardwell lay sleepless abed. His concave boyish tummy begged for sustenance, for the evening repast may have been but bread and sop, and the day's beating meant that certain much-favored positions were out of the question. Yet hunger and pain were as nothing when compared to the primary reason sleep refused to grant its healing balm. This was terror. Day came when night bowed out, and day brought Boy Teuteburg. So fearsome was my tormentor that I lay paralyzed 'neath my blankets, hoping without hope that I might the next day evade my nemesis. Desperate hours I spent mapping devious alternate routes from school to store while still knowing well that however mazy the streets I took, they would in the end but deliver me unto Boy. And many times I sensed that he had glided into our yard and stood smoking beneath our tree, staring red-eyed at my unlighted window. Other times, I heard him open our back door and float through the kitchen to hover motionless outside my door. What good now was my intellectual and spiritual superiority to Boy Teuteburg? Of what use my yearnings? Ice-cold fear was all I knew. Mornings, I dragged myself from bed, quaking, opened my door to find Boy of course nowhere in sight, fed my ice-cold stomach a slice of bread and a glass of water, and dragged myself to school, hopeless as the junkman's nag.

Had I but known of the thousand eyes upon me . . .

Why does Ethel Carroway report to her window on the fourth floor of the Oliphant Hotel at the full of the moon? Guilt? Grief? Remorse?

In life, this was a thoughtless girl, vibrant but shallow, the epitome of a Visible, who felt no more of guilt than does a cast-iron pump. For months, Ethel had gone about her duties in loose overblouses to conceal her condition, of which even her slatternly friends were ignorant. The infant signified no more than a threat to her employment. She never gave it a name or fantasized about it or thought of it with aught but distaste. Captain Starbuck had departed the day following conception, in any case a hasty, rather *scuffling* matter, no doubt to sow his seed in foreign ports. Delivery took place behind the locked door of Ethel's basement room and lasted approximately twelve hours, during which she had twice to shout from her bed that she was violently ill and could not work. During the process, she consumed much of a bottle of bourbon whiskey given her by another priapic guest of the Oliphant. When at last the child bullied its way out between her legs, Ethel bit the umbilicus in two and observed that she had delivered a boy. Its swollen purple genitals were a vivid reminder of Captain Starbuck. Then she passed out. An hour later, consciousness returned on a tide of pain. Despite all, Ethel felt a curious new pride in herself – in what she had done. Her baby lay on her chest, uttering little kittenish mewls. It resembled a monkey, or a bald old man. She found herself regretting that she had to dispose of this creature who had brought her so much pain. They had shared an experience that now seemed almost hallucinatory in its intensity. She wished the baby were the kitten it sounded like, that she might keep it. She and the baby were companions of a sort. And she realized that it was hers – she had made this little being.

Yet her unanticipated affection for the infant did not alter the facts. Ethel needed her job, and that was that. The baby had to die. She moved her legs to the side of the bed, and a fresh wave of pain made her gasp. Her legs, her middle, the bed, all were soaked in blood. The baby mewed again, and more to comfort herself than it, she slid the squeaking child upward toward her right breast and bumped the nipple against his lips until he opened his mouth and tried to suck. Like Ethel, the baby was covered with blood, as well as with something that resembled grease. At that moment she wanted more than anything else to wash herself off – she wanted to wash the baby, too. At least he could die clean. She transferred him to her other breast, which gave no more milk than the first. When she stroked his body, some of the blood and grease came off on her hand, and she wiped his back with a clean part of the sheet.

Some time later, Ethel swung her feet off the bed, ignored the bolts of pain, and stood up with the baby clamped to her bosom. Grimacing, she limped to the sink and filled it with tepid water. Then she lowered the baby into the sink. As soon as his skin met the water, his eyes flew open and appeared to search her face. For the first time, she noticed that their color was a violent purple-blue, like no other eyes she had ever seen.

The infant was frowning magisterially. His legs contracted under him like a frog's. His violent eyes glowered up at her, as if he knew what she was ultimately going to do, did not at all like what she was going to do, but accepted it. As she swabbed him with the washcloth, he kept frowning up at her, scanning her face with his astonishing eyes.

Ethel considered drowning him, but if she did so, she would have to carry his body out of the hotel, and she didn't even have a suitcase. Besides, she did not enjoy the idea of holding him under the water while he looked up at her with that funny old-king frown. She let the water drain from the sink, wrapped the baby in a towel, and gave herself a rudimentary sponge bath. When she picked the baby off the floor, his eyes flew open again, then closed as his mouth gaped in an enormous yawn. She limped back to bed, tore the sheets off one-handed, cast a blanket over the mattress, and fell asleep with the baby limp on her chest.

It was still dark when Ethel awakened, but the quality of the darkness told her that it would soon be morning. The baby stirred. Its arms, which had worked free of the towel, jerked upward, paused in the air, and drifted down again. This was the hour when the hotel was still, but for the furnaceman. The hallways were empty; a single sleepy clerk manned the desk. In another hour, the bootboys would be setting out the night's polished shoes, and a few early-bird guests would be calling down their room-service orders. In two hours, a uniformed Ethel Carroway was supposed to report for duty. She intended to do this. When it became noticed that she was in pain, she would be allowed another day's sick leave, but report she must. She had approximately forty-five minutes in which to determine what to do with the baby and then to do it.

A flawless plan came to her. If she carried the baby to the service stairs, she would avoid the furnaceman's realm, and once on the service stairs, she could go anywhere without being seen. The hallways would remain empty. She could reach one of the upper floors, open a window, and – let the baby fall. Her part in his death would be over in an instant, and the death itself would be a matter of a second, less than a second, a moment too brief for pain. Afterward, no one would be able to connect Ethel Carroway with the little corpse on the Erie Street pavement. It would seem as though a guest had dropped the baby, or as though an outsider had entered the hotel to rid herself of an unwanted child. It would be a mystery: a baby from nowhere, fallen from the Oliphant Hotel. Police Are Baffled.

She pulled on a nightdress and wrapped herself in an old hotel bathrobe. Then she swaddled her child in the towel and silently left her room. On the other side of the basement, the furnaceman snored on his pallet. Gritting her teeth, Ethel limped to the stairs.

The second floor was too low, and the third seemed uncertain. To be safe, she would have to get to the fourth floor. her legs trembled, and spears of pain shot through the center of her body. She was weeping and groaning when she reached the third floor, but for the sake of the baby forced herself to keep mounting the stairs. At the fourth floor, she opened the door to the empty, gas-lit hallway and leaned panting against the frame. Sweat stung her eyes. Ethel staggered into the corridor and moved past numbered doors until she reached the elevator alcove. Opposite the closed bronze doors, two large casement windows looked out onto Erie Street. She hugged the baby to her chest, struggled with a catch, and pushed the window open.

Cold air streamed in, and the baby tugged his brows together and scowled. Impulsively, Ethel kissed the top of his lolling head, then settled her waist against the ridge at the bottom of the casement. She gripped the baby beneath his armpits, and the towel dropped onto her feet. The baby drew up his legs and kicked, as if rejecting the cold. A bright, mottled pink covered his face like a rash. His mouth was a tiny red beak. One of his eyes squeezed shut. The other slid sideways in a gaze of unfocused reproach.

Gripping his sides, Ethel extended her arms and moved his kicking body through the casement. She could feel the ribs beneath his skin. The bottom of the frame dug into her belly. Ethel took a sharp inhalation and prepared to let go by loosening her grip. Instantly, unexpectedly, he slipped through her hands and dropped into the darkness. For a moment briefer than a second, she leaned forward, open-mouthed.

What happened to her in the moment she watched her baby fall away toward the Erie Street sidewalk is the reason Ethel Carroway returns to the window on the fourth floor of the Oliphant Hotel.

A doorman found the dead infant half an hour later. By the start of the morning shift, the entire staff knew that someone had thrown a baby from an upper window. Policemen went from room to room and in a maid's basement chamber came upon an exhausted young woman stuffing bloody sheets into a pillowcase. Despite her denials of having recently given birth, she was arrested and given a medical examination. At her trial, she was condemned to death, and in April 1893, Ethel Carroway departed from her earthly state at the end of a hangman's rope. During the next two decades, several fourth-floor guests at the Oliphant remarked a peculiar atmosphere in the area of the elevators: some found it unpleasantly chilly even in the dog days, others said it was overheated in winter, and Nelly Tetrazelli, the 'Golden Thrush', an

271

Italian mezzo-soprano touring the northern states with a program of songs related to faerie legend, complained that a 'nasty, nasty porridge' in the elevator alcove had constricted her voice. In 1916, the Oliphant went out of business. For three years, the hotel steadily deteriorated, until new owners took it over; they ran it until 1930, when they went broke and sold the building for use as a boarding school for young women. The first sightings of a ghostly figure on the fourth floor were made by students of the Erie Academy for Girls; by 1948, when the academy closed its doors, local lore had supplied the name of the spectral figure, and a year later, when the Oliphant opened yet again, Ethel Carroway began putting in regular appearances, not unlike Nelly Tetrazelli, the 'Golden Thrush'. Over the decades, Ethel acquired a modest notoriety. The Oliphant devotes a long paragraph of its brochure to the legend, an undoubtedly idealized portrait of the revenant hangs above the lobby fireplace, and a bronze plaque memorializes the site of the crime. Guests with amateur or professional interests in the paranormal have often spent weeks in residence, hoping for a glimpse, a blurry photograph, a sonic, tape-recorded rustle. (None have ever been granted their wish.)

Ethel Carroway does not reappear before her window to increase her fame. She does it for another reason altogether. She's hungry.

I have told you of bad Boy and the thousand eyes fixed upon the Shining Boy, and alluded to a secret. In the same forthright manner with which I introduced myself, I shall now introduce the matter of the wondrous secret, by laying it out upon the methaporical table. All throughout my life I possessed a crystalline but painful awareness of my superiority to the common man. To put it squarely: I understood that I was better than the others. Just about *all* the others.

A fool may say this and be ridiculed. A madman may say it and be bedlamized. What befalls the ordinary-seeming mortal whose great gifts, not displayed by any outward show, he dares proclaim? He risks the disbelief and growing ire of his peers – in humbler words, spitballs, furtive kicks and knocks, whispered obscenities, and shoves into muddy ditches, that's what. Yet – and this must be allowed – *that the mortal in question is superior has already aroused ire and even hatred amongst those who have so perceived him.* Why was I the focus of Boy Teuteburg's psychopathic rage? And why did my fellow kidlings not defend me from our common enemy? *What inflamed our enemy, Boy, chilled them.* It would have been the same had I never generously taken pains to illuminate their little errors, had I never pressed home the point by adding, *and I know this because I'm a lot smarter than you are.* They already knew the deal. They had observed my struggle to suppress my smiles as I instructed our teachers in their numerous errors, and surely they had likewise noted the inner soul-light within the precocious classmate.

Now I know better than to speak of these matters (save in privileged conditions such as these). In my mid-twenties I gave all of that up, recognizing that my life had become a catastrophe, and that the gifts which so elevated me above the run of mankind (as the protagonists of the great *Poe* know themselves raised up) had not as it were elevated my outward circumstances accordingly. The inward soul-light had dimmed and guttered, would no longer draw the attacks of the envious. Life had circled 'round and stolen what was most essentially mine.

Not all ghosts are dead, but only the dead can be counted on for twenty-twenty vision. You only get to see what's in front of your nose when it's too late to do you any good.

At that point, enter hunger.

My life had already lost its luster before I understood that the process of diminishment had begun. Grade school went by in the manner described. My high school career, which should have been a four-year span of ever-increasing glories culminating in a 4.0 average and a full scholarship to a Harvard or even a College of William and Mary, ground into a weary pattern of C's and D's hurled at me by fools incapable of distinguishing the creative spirit from the glib, mendacious copycat. In his freshman year, young Frank Wardwell submitted to the school literary magazine under the pen name Orion three meritorious poems, all of which were summarily rejected on the grounds that several of their nobler phrases had been copied down from poets of the Romantic movement. Did the poets own these phrases, then? And would then a young chap like Frank Wardwell be forbidden to so much as *utter* these phrases in the course of literary conversations such as he never had, due to the absence of like-minded souls? Yes, one gathers, to the editors of a high school literary magazine.

I turned to the creation of a private journal in which to inscribe my exalted thoughts and far-flung imaginings. But the poison had already begun its deadly work. Brutal surroundings and moral isolation had robbed my pen of freshness, and much of what I committed to the page was mere lamentation for my misunderstood and friendless state. In coming from the depths to reach expression, the gleaming heroes with cascading blond hair of my high-arching thoughts met the stultifying ignorance about me and promptly shriveled into gat-toothed dwarves. The tales with which I had vowed to storm this world's castles and four-star hotels refused to take wing. I blush to remember how, when stalled in the midst of what was to be a furious vision of awe and terror, my talent turned not to Great Imagination for its forms but to popular serials broadcast at the time over the radio waves. *The Green Hornet* and *Jack Armstrong, the All-American Boy*, my personal favorites among these, supplied many of my plots and even, I grant, some of my less pungent dialogue.

A young person suffering the gradual erosion of his spirit cannot be fully aware of the ongoing damage to his being. Some vestige of the inborn wonder will beat its wings and hope for flight, and I saw with weary regularity the evidence that I was as far superior to my fellow students at Edna Ferber High as I had been at Daniel Webster State Graded School. As before, my well-intentioned exposures of intellectual errors earned me no gratitude. (Did you really imagine, Tubby Shanks, you of the quill-like red hair and carbuncled neck who sat before me in sophomore English, that Joyce Kilmer, immortal author of 'Trees', was necessarily of the female gender for the sole reason that your mother and sister shared his Christian name? My rapierlike witticism that Irish scribe James Joyce must then be a sideshow morphadite did not deserve the blow you addressed to my sternum, nor the wad of phlegm deposited atop my desk at close of day.) True, I had no more to fear the raids of Boy Teuteburg, who had metamorphosed into a sleek ratty fellow in a tight black overcoat and pearl gray snapbrim hat and who, by reason of constant appointments in pool halls, the back rooms of taverns, and the basements of garages, had no time for childish pursuits. Dare I say I almost missed the attentions of Boy Teuteburg? Almost longed for the old terror he had aroused in me? That his indifference, what might even have been his lack of recognition, awakened nameless but unhappy emotions on the few occasions when we ancient enemies caught sight of one another, me, sorry, I mean I dragging through our native byways at the end of another hopeless day at Edna Ferber, he emerging from an Erie Street establishment known as Jerry's *Hotcha!* Lounge, his narrow still-red eye falling on mine but failing to blaze (though the old terror did leap within me, that time), then my immemorial foe sliding past without a word or gesture to mark the momentous event? At such times even the dull being I had become felt the passing of a never-to-be-recovered soul-state. Then, I had known of my preeminence and nurtured myself upon it; now, knowing of it still, I knew it did not make an ounce of difference. Boy Teuteburg had become a more consequential person than Francis T. Wardwell. I had seen the shades of the prison house lowered 'til nearly all the light was blocked.

Soon after the unmarked momentousness, two other such yanked them all the way down.

After an unfortunate incident at school, admittedly not the first of its kind, involving the loss of a petty sum on the order of six or seven dollars from a handbag left hanging on a lunchroom chair, the meaningless coincidence of my having been seated adjacent to the chair from which hung the forgotten reticule somehow led to the accusation that I was the culprit. It was supposed, quite falsely and with no verification whatsoever, that I had also been responsible for the earlier incidents. I defended myself as any innocent party does, by declining to respond to the offensive accusations. I did possess a small, secret store of money, and when ordered to repay the careless slattern who had been the real source of the crime, I withdrew the wretched seven dollars from this source.

Humiliated, I chose to avoid the hostile stares and cruel taunts surely to greet me in our school's halls, so for some days I wandered the streets, squandering far too many quarters from my precious cache in diners and movie theaters when supposed to be in class, then reporting as ever to Dockweder's Hardware, where, having passed down my broom to a shifty urchin of unclean habits, I was entrusted with the stocking of shelves, the fetching of merchandise to the counter, and, during the generally inactive hour between 4:30 p.m. and 5:30 p.m., the manipulation of the cash register. After the fifth day of my self-imposed suspension from academe, Mr Dockweder kept me after work as he ostentatiously balanced the day's receipts, the first time I had ever seen him do so, found the *awesome*, the *majestic* sum of $1.65 missing from the cash tray, and immediately charged me with the theft. Not the boyish mistake of returning a surplus of change to an impatient customer or hitting a wrong button when ringing up a sale, but the theft. I protested, I denied, alas in vain. Then look to the boy, I advised, I believe he steals from the stockroom, too, fire him and the pilfering will cease. As if he had forgotten my seven years of unstinting service, Mr Dockweder informed me that sums of varying amounts had been missing from the register many nights during the period when I had been entrusted with its manipulation between the hours of 4:30 p.m. and 5:30 p.m. He demanded I turn out my pockets. When I did so, he smoothed out one of the three bills in my possession and indicated on its face the check mark he had placed upon each bill in the register before entrusting it to my charge.

In all honesty, check marks are entered upon dollar bills hundreds of times a day, and for hundreds of reasons. I have seen every possible sort of symbol used to deface our nation's currency. Mr Dockweder, however, would accept none of my sensible explanations. He insisted on bringing me home, and gripped my shoulder in an iron clamp as we took to the streets. Within our shabby dwelling, he denounced me. My denials went unheard. In fact, I was trembling and sweating and undergoing a thousand torments, for once or twice I had dipped into the register and extracted a quarter, a dime, a penny or two, coins I assumed would never be missed and with which I could sustain myself through the long day. I even *confessed* these paltry lapses, thinking to improve the situation with a show of honest remorse, but this fearless candor did nothing of the kind. After remunerating Dockweder from his own skimpy reserve of cash, my father announced that I personally would make good the (inflated) sum and learn the ways of the real world. He was sick of my airs and highfalutin' manners, sick of my books, sick of the way I talked – sick of me. From that day forth I should work. As a dumb beast works (my father, an alcoholic welder, being a prime example of the species), without hope, without education, without letup, without meaning, and with no reward save an inadequate weekly pay packet.

Reeling from the depth and swiftness of my fall, that evening after the welder and his weeping spouse had retired I let myself out of our hovel and staggered through the darkness. What I had been, I scarcely knew; what I now was, I could not bear to contemplate; what I was to become, I could not imagine. On all sides life's prison house rose up about me. In that prison house lay a grave, and within that grave lay I. The streets took me, where I knew or cared not. At intervals I looked up to behold a dirty wall, a urine stain belt-high beneath a broken warehouse window, a mound of tires in a vacant lot. These things were *emblems*. Once I glimpsed a leering moon; once I heard the shuffle of feet close by and stopped in terror, sensing mortal danger, and looked all 'round at empty Erie Street.

Bitterly, childhood's stillborn fantasies returned to me, their former glow now corpse gray. Never would I kneel in meadows and woods 'midst bird's-foot trefoil, daisy fleabane, devil's pulpit, Johnny-jump-up, jewelweed, the foxglove, and the small sundrop. Never would I bend an enchanted ear to the lowing of the kine, the tolling of bells in a country rectory, the distant call of the shepherd, the chant of the lark. Mountain lakes and mountain streams would never enfold me in their chill, breath-giving embrace. The things I was to know were but *emblems* of the death-in-life ranged 'round me now.

I lifted my all-but-unseeing eyes to the facade, six stories high, of the Oliphant Hotel, dark dark dark. Above the lobby, dimly visible through the great glass doors, the ranks of windows hung dark and empty in the darker brick. Behind those windows slept men and women endowed with college degrees and commercial or artistic skills, owners of property, sojourners in foreign lands, men and women on the inside of life. They would never know my name, nor would I ever be one of their Visible number. Radiantly Visible themselves, they would no more take note of me by daylight than at present – and if they happened to look my way, would see nothing!

A figure moved past an upper window, moved back and then reappeared behind the window. Dark dark dark. A guest, I imagined, wandering sleepless in the halls, and thought to turn away for my long journey home. Some small awareness held me, looking up. High above behind a casement window hovered a figure in black garb, that figure, I now observed, unmistakably a woman's. What was she doing, why was she there? Some trouble had sent one of the gilded travelers roaming the Oliphant, and on that trouble she brooded now, pausing at the window. Recognizing a fellow being in misery akin to my own, I brazenly stepped forward and stared up, silently demanding this woman to acknowledge that, despite all that separated and divided us, we were essentially the same. White hands twisted within her black garment. We were the same, our world the same, being dark dark dark. Perhaps the woman would beckon to me, that we each could soothe the shame of the other. For streaming from her vague figure was shame – so I thought. An oval face emerged from shadow or from beneath a hood and neared the glass.

You shall see me, you shall, I vowed, and stepped forward once again. The alabaster face gazed at a point some five feet nearer the hotel than myself. I moved to meet her gaze, and just before doing so experienced a hopeless terror far worse than anything Boy Teuteburg had ever raised in me. Yet my body had begun to move and would not stop when the mind could not command it. Two mental events had birthed this sick dread: I had seen enough of the alabaster face to know that what I had sensed streaming out was something far, far worse than shame; and I had suddenly remembered what the first sight of this figure at this window of this hotel would have recalled had I been in my normal mind – the legend of the ghost in the Oliphant. Ethel Carroway's eyes locked on mine and scorched my innards. I could not cry out, I could not weep, with throat constricted and eyes singed. For a tremendous moment I could not move at all, but stood where her infant had fallen to the pavement and met her ravishing, her *self-ravishing* gaze. When it was over – when she released me – I turned and ran like a dog whom wanton boys had set on fire.

The following day my father commanded me to go to McNair's Fine Clothing and Draperies and inquire after a full-time position. He had recently done some work for Mr Harold McNair, who had spoken of an opening available to an eager lad. Now that my circumstances had changed, I must try to claim this position and be grateful for the opportunity, if offered. I obeyed the paternal orders. Mr Harold McNair indeed had a position available, the position that of assistant stockboy, hours 7:30 a.m.– 6:00 p.m., Monday–Saturday, wages @ $0.45/hr., meals not supplied. He had thought the welder's boy might be responsive to his magnanimity, and the welder's boy, all that remained of me, was responsive, yes sir, Mr McNair, sir. And so my endless drudgery began.

At first I worked to purchase, at the employee rate, the shirts and trousers with which an assistant stockboy must be outfitted; and for the next twenty-nine years I spun long hours into dress shirts and cravats and worsted suits, as Rumpelstiltskin spun straw into gold, for a McNair's representative must advertise by wearing the very same articles of clothing offered its beloved customers. I had no friends. The only company I knew was that of my fellow employees, a half-brained lot devoted to sexual innuendo, sporting events, and the moving pictures featuring Miss Jean Harlow. Later on, Wallace Beery and James Cagney were a big hit. Even later, one heard entirely too much of John Wayne. This, not forgetting the pages of our Sunday newspaper wasted upon the 'funnies', was their culture, and it formed the whole of their conversation. Of course I held myself apart. It was the old story repeated once again, as all stories are repeated again and again, eternally, just look around you. You are myself, and I myself am you. What we did last week, last year, what we did in our infancy, shall we do again tomorrow. I could take no delight in the gulf dividing my intellect from theirs, nor could my fellow workers. Doubtless all of them, male and female alike, secretly shared the opinion expressed during our Christmas party in 1955 by Austin Hartlepoole, an accounting junior who had imbibed too freely of the fish-house punch: 'Mr Wardwell, have you always been a stuck-up jerk?'

'No,' I might have said, 'once I was a Shining Boy.' (What I did say is of no consequence.)

By then I was Mr Wardwell, note. The superior qualities that condemned me to social and intellectual isolation had seen me through a series of promotions from assistant stockboy to stockboy, then head stockboy, thence laterally to the shipping department, then upward again to counter

staff, Shirts and Neckwear, followed by a promotion literally upstairs to second floor, counter staff, Better Shirts
and Neckwear, then assistant manager, Menswear, in time
manager, Menswear, and ultimately, in 1955, the year
soon-to-be-sacked Hartlepoole called me a stuck-up jerk,
vice president and buyer, Clothing Divisions. The welder's
boy had triumphed. Just outside of town, I maintained a
large residence, never seen by my co-workers, for myself
and a companion who shall remain nameless. I dressed
in excellent clothing, as was to be expected. A gray
Bentley, which I pretended to have obtained at a 'price',
represented my single visible indulgence. Accompanied
by Nameless Companion, I regularly visited the Caribbean
on my annual two-week vacation to occupy comfortable
quarters in the same luxurious 'resort' hotel. By the
middle of the nineteen fifties, my salary had risen to
thirty thousand dollars a year, and in my regular banking
and savings accounts I had accumulated the respectable
sum of forty-two thousand dollars. In another, secret
account, I had amassed the even more respectable sum
of three hundred and sixty-eight thousand dollars, every
cent of it winkled away a little at a time from one of the
worst people, in fact by a considerable margin actually the
worst person, it has ever been my misfortune to know, my
employer, Mr Harold McNair.

All was well until my transfer to Better Shirts and
Neckwear, my 'ascension', we called it, into the vaulted
splendors of the second floor, where affluent customers
were spared contamination by the commoners examining
cheaper goods below, and where Mr McNair, my jailer-
benefactor of years ago, was wont to appear from the
depths of his walnut-paneled office, wandering between
the counters, adjusting the displays, remarking upon the
quality of a freshly purchased tweed jacket or fox stole
(Ladies' was sited across the floor), taking in the state of
his minions' fingernails and shoes. Mr McNair, a smallish,

weaselish, darkish, baldish figure in a navy suit, his solid red tie anchored to his white shirt with a visible metal bar, demanded courteous smiles, upright postures, hygenic habits. Scuffed shoes earned an errant clerk a sharply worded rebuke, unclean nails an immediate trip to the employee washroom. The dead thing I was did not object to these simple, well-intentioned codes. Neither did I object to my employer – he was but a fixed point in the universe, like his own God enthroned in His heavens. I did not take him *personally*. Not until my 'ascension', when we each fell under the other's gaze.

Living Visibles like Harold McNair do not expect merely to be seen. Though they be discreetly attired, quietly spoken, and well-mannered, within they starve, they slaver for attention and exact it however they must. In Mr McNair's case, this took the form of divisiveness, capriciousness, sanctimoniousness and, for lack of a better word, tyranny. He would favor one counter clerk, then another, thereby creating enmity and rivalry and an ardent wish in two hearts to comprehend his own heart. He would select an obscure minion for weeks of special treatment, jokes, confidences, consultations, then without explanation drop the chosen one back into obscurity, to be pecked to death by his peers. He drew certain employees aside and whispered subtle criticisms of their dearest friends. Throughout, he searched for his true, secret favorites, those whose contempt for themselves, masked behind a smooth retailer's manner, matched his own for them, masked behind the same. In time I began to think of Harold McNair as a vast architectural structure something like his great store, a building charmingly appointed with fine though not ostentatious things, where a smiling but observant guide leads you ever deeper in, deciding room by room if you have earned the right to behold the next, by stages conducting you into chambers growing successively smaller, uglier, eventually even odorous, then through foul, reeking sties, and at last opens the final door to the central, the inmost room, the room at the heart of the structure, the most terrible of all, and admits you to – the real Mr Harold McNair.

He knew I was his the first time he saw me behind the Better Shirts counter on the second floor. He may have known it on the day he hired me, long years before. In fact, he might even have regarded the alcoholic welder laboring in his basement and seen that this man's son, if he had one, would be his as if by Natural Law. His in the sense of easily flattered, thus easily dominated. Ready to be picked up by a kind word and downcast by a harsh one. Capable of attentive silences during the Great Man's monologues. Liable to be supine before power, abject before insult. A thorough and spineless subordinate. A kind of slave. Or, a slave. Long before my final promotion, I had been shown into the final room and met the true Harold McNair. I knew what he was and what I was. In many ways, I had fallen under the sway of a smoother, more corrupt Boy Teuteburg, a Boy who thought himself a noble being and wore the mask of a dignified, successful man of business.

I accepted this. But I had determined to be paid well for the role.

My thefts began with an impulsive act of revenge. I had just departed Mr McNair's office after a session in which the whip lashed out more forcefully than was customary from within the velvet bag, both before and after my employer had expressed his apocalyptic disgust for womankind, those sly scented obscenities, those temples of lust, et cetera, et cetera. Making my way granite-faced through Better Gowns, I observed an elderly temple of lust depositing her alligator bag upon the counter as she turned to scrutinize a bottle-green Better Gown with Regency sleeves. A wallet protruded slightly from the unclasped bag. Customer and saleslady conferred in re the wisdom of Regency sleeves. My legs took me past the counter, my hand closed on the wallet, the wallet flew into my pocket, and I was gone.

Heart athud, I betook myself to a stall in the male employees' washroom, opened the wallet, and discovered there sixty-eight dollars, now mine. I had been rash, I knew, but to what an electric, unharnessed surge of life force! All I regretted was that the money had been the temple's, not Mr McNair's. I left the stall and by reflex stepped up to the sinks and mirrors. Washing my spotless hands, I caught my face in the mirror and froze – a vibrant roguish Visible a decade younger than I looked back with blazing eyes, my own.

Anyone in a business that receives and disburses large amounts of cash will eventually devise a method for deflecting a portion of the moolah from its normal course. Some few will test their method, and most of those will be found out. A primitive snatch and grab like mine, unobserved, is as good as any. During my tenure in the store, many employees located the imperfections in their schemes only as the handcuffs closed around their wrists. (Mr McNair never showed mercy or granted a second chance, ever.) From the moment I met my living eyes in the washroom mirror, I was withdrawing from the cash available an amount appropriate to my degradation, or *stealing my real salary*. All that remained was to work out a method that would pass undetected.

Many such methods exist, and I will not burden you with the details of mine, save to reveal that it involved a secret set of books. It proved successful for better than two decades and yielded a sum nearly compensatory to my endless humiliation. Mr McNair knew that significant quantities of money were escaping his miserly grasp but, despite feverish plotting and the construction of elaborate rat-traps, could not discover how or where. The traps snapped down upon the necks of minor-league peculators, till tappers, short-change artists, bill padders, invoice forgers, but never upon his greatest enemy's.

On the night I placed my hundred thousandth unofficial dollar in my secret account, I celebrated with a lobster dinner and a superior bottle of champagne in our finest seafood restaurant (alone, this being prior to the Nameless Friend era) and, when filled with alcohol and rich food, remembered that the moon was full, remembered also my night of misery so long ago, and resolved to return to the Oliphant Hotel. Then, I had been a corpse within a grave within a prison; now, I was achieved, a walking secret on the inside of life, an invisible Visible. I would stand before Ethel Carroway and be witnessed – what had been written on her face now lay within me.

I walked (in those pre-Bentley days) to Erie Street and posted myself against a wall to await the appearance of the shade. By showing herself again to me, she would acknowledge that the intensity of my needs had raised me, as she was raised, above the common run. Mine was the confidence of a lover who, knowing this the night his beloved shall yield, savors each blissful, anticipated pleasure. Each moment she did not appear was made delicious by its being the moment before the moment when she would. When my neck began to ache, I lowered my chin to regard through enormous glass portals the Oliphant's lobby, once a place of unattainable luxury. Now I could take a fourth-floor suite, if I liked, and present myself to Ethel Carroway on home ground. Yet it was right to stand where I had before, the better to mark the distance I had come. An hour I waited, then another, growing cold and thirsty. My head throbbed with the champagne I had taken, and my feet complained. My faith wavered – another trial in a test more demanding with every passing minute. Determined not to fail, I turned up the collar of my coat, thrust my hands in my pockets, and kept my eyes upon the dark window.

At times I heard movement around me but saw nothing when I looked toward the sound. Mysterious footfalls came teasingly out of the darkness of Erie Street, as if Ethel Carroway had descended to present herself before me, but these footfalls were many and varied, and no pale figure in black appeared to meet my consummating gaze.

I had not understood – I knew nothing of Visibles and those not, and what I took for confidence was but its misshapen nephew, arrogance. The cynosure and focus of myriad pairs of unseen eyes, I surrendered at last after 3:00 a.m. and wandered sore-footed home through an invisible crowd that understood exactly what had happened there and why. In the morn, I rose from the rumpled bed to steal again.

Understanding, ephemeral as a transcendent insight granted in a dream, ephemeral as *dew*, came only with exposure, which is to say with loss of fortune and handsome residence, loss of Nameless Companion, of super-duper Bentley, of elegant sobersides garb, of gay Caribbean holidays on the American Plan, loss of reputation, occupation (both occupations, retailer and thief), privacy, freedom, many constitutionally guaranteed civil rights, and, ultimately, of life. As with all of you, I would have chosen these forfeited possessions, persons, states, and conditions over any mere act of understanding, yet I cannot deny the sudden startling consciousness of a certain piquant, indeterminate pleasure-state, unforeseen in the grunting violence of my last act as a free man, which surfaced hand in hand with my brief illumination. This sense of a deep but mysterious pleasure linked to my odd flash of comprehension often occupied my thoughts during the long months of trial and incarceration.

I had long since ceased to fear exposure, and the

incarnadine (see *Shakespeare*) excess of exposure's after-math would have seemed a nightmarish impossibility to the managerial Mr Wardwell, stoutly serious and seriously stout, of 1960. Weekly, a gratifying sum wafted from Mr McNair's gnarled, liver-spotted grip into my welcoming hands, and upon retirement some ten stony years hence I expected at last to float free in possession of approximately one and a quarter million dollars, maybe a million and a half. My employer's rat-traps continued to snap down on employees of the anathema stripe, of late less frequently due to widespread awareness of the Byzantinely complex modes of surveillance which universally 'kicked in' at the stage beneath the introduction of my invented figures, on account of their having been set in place by the very anathema they were designed to entrap. Had not the odious McNair decided upon a storewide renovation to mark the new decade, I should after twenty, with luck twenty-five, years of pampered existence in some tropic clime and sustained experience of every luxury from the highestly refined to basestly, piggishestly sensual, have attained upon death from corrupt old age an entire under-standing of my frustrated vigil before the Oliphant, of the walkers and shufflers I had heard but were not there, also of Ethel Carroway and her refusal to recognize one who wrongly supposed himself her spiritual equal. But McNair proceeded upon his dubious inspiration, and I induced a premature understanding by smashing the fellow's brains into porridge – 'nasty, nasty porridge' – with a workman's conveniently disposed ballpeen hammer.

The actual circumstances of my undoing were banal. Perhaps they always are. A groom neglects to shoe a horse, and a king is killed. A stranger hears a whisper in an ale-house, and – a king is killed. That sort of thing. In my case, coincidence of an otherwise harmless sort played a crucial role. The dread renovation had reached the rear of the second floor, lapping day by day nearer the accounts room, the art department, and the offices, one mine, one Mr McNair's. The tide of workers, ladders, dropcloths, yardsticks, plumb lines, sawhorses, and so forth inevitably reached our doors and then swept in. As my employer lived above the store in a velvet lair only he and his courtiers had seen, he had directed that the repaneling and recarpeting, the virtual *regilding*, of his office be done during normal working hours, he then enduring only the minor inconvenience of descending one flight to be about his normal business of oozing from customer to customer, sniffing, adjusting, prying, flattering. As I owned no such convenient bower and could not be permitted access to his, not even to one corner for business purposes, my own office received its less dramatic facelift during the hour between the closing of the store, 6:00 p.m., and the beginning of overtime, 7:00 p.m. A task that should have taken two days thus filled ten, at the close of every one of which, concurrent with my official duties, I had to manage the unofficial duties centered on the fictive set of books and the disposition of the day's harvest of cash. All this under the indifferent eyes of laborers setting up their instruments of torture.

Callous, adamantine men shifted my desk from port to starboard, from bow to stern, and on the night of my downfall informed me I had to jump ship posthaste that they might finish, our boss having lost patience with this stage of affairs. I jumped ship and bade farewells to departing employees from a position near the front doors. At 6:55 p.m. I made my way through the familiar aisles to my office door, through which I observed Harold McNair, on a busybody's journey from the sultan's quarters above, standing alone before my exposed desk and contemplating the evidence of my various anathematic peculations.

The artisans should have been packing up but had finished early and departed unseen by the rear doors; McNair should have been consulting his genius for depravity in the velvet lair but had slithered down to ensure their obedience. We were alone in the building. As Mr McNair whirled to confront me, a combination of joy and rage distorted his unpleasant features into a demonic mask. I could not save myself – he knew exactly what he had seen. He advanced toward me, spitting incoherent obscenities.

Mr McNair arrived at a point a foot from my person and continued to berate me, jabbing a knobby forefinger at my chest as he did so. Unevenly, his face turned a dangerous shade of pink, hot pink I believe it is called. The forefinger hooked my lapel, and he tugged me deskward. His color heightened as he ranted on. Finally he hurled at my bowed head a series of questions, perhaps one question repeated many times, I don't know, I could not distinguish the words. My being quailed before the onslaught; I was transported back to Dockweder's. Here again were a marked bill, an irate merchant, a shamed Frank Wardwell – the wretched boy blazed forth within the ample, settled, secretive man.

And it came to the wretched boy that the ranter before him resembled two old tormentors, Missus Barksdale and Boy Teuteburg, especially the latter, not the sleek rodent in a pearl gray hat but the red-eyed bane of childhood who came hurtling out of doorways to pummel head and body with sharp, accurate, knifelike fists. I experienced a moment of pure psychic sensation so foreign I could not at first affix a name to it. I knew only that an explosion had taken place. Then I recognized that what I felt was pain, everlasting, eternal pain long self-concealed. It was as though I had stepped outside my body. Or *into* it.

Before me on my oaken chair lay a ballpeen hammer forgotten by its owner. The instant I beheld this utilitarian object, humiliation blossomed into gleeful revenge. My hand found the hammer, the hammer found Mr McNair's head. Startled, amazed even, but not yet terrified, Mr McNair jumped back, clamoring. I moved in. He reached for the weapon, and I captured his wizened arm in my hand. The head of the hammer tapped his tough little skull, twice. A wondrous, bright red feeling bloomed in me, and the name of that wondrous feeling was Great Anger. Mr McNair wobbled to his knees. I rapped his forehead and set him on his back. He squirmed and shouted, and I tattooed his bonce another half-dozen times. Blood began to drizzle from his ears, also from the abrasions to his knotty head. I struck him well and truly above the right eye. At that, his frame twitched and jittered, and I leaned into my work and now delivered blow after blow while the head became a shapeless, bloody, brain-spattered . . . *mess*. As the blows landed, it seemed that each released a new explosion of blessed pain and anger within Frank Wardwell; it seemed too that these blessings took place in a realm, once known but long forgotten, in which emotion stood forth as a separate entity, neither without nor within, observable, breathtaking, utterly alive, like Frank Wardwell, this entranced former servant swinging a dripping hammer at the corpse of his detested and worshiped enemy. And there arose in an unsuspected chamber of my mind the remembered face of Ethel Carroway gazing down at but in fact not seeing the disgraced boy – me on Erie Street, and, like a reward, there arrived my brief, exalted moment of comprehension, with it that uprising of inexplicable, almost intellectual pleasure on which I chewed so often in the months ahead. Ethel Carroway, I thought, had known this – this shock – this *gasp* –

Into the office in search of a forgotten hammer came a burly tough in a donkey jacket and a flat cap, accompanied by an even burlier same, and whatever I had comprehended blew away in the brief cyclone that followed. Fourteen months later, approximately dogging Ethel Carroway's footsteps, I moved like a wondering cloud out of a sizzling, still-jerking body strapped into our state's electric chair.

The first thing I noticed, apart from a sudden cessation of pain and a generalized sensation of *lightness* that seemed more the product of a new relationship to gravity than actual weight loss, was the presence in the viewing room of many more people than I remembered in attendance at the great event. Surely there had been no more than a dozen witnesses, surely all of them male and Journalists by profession, save two? During the interesting period between the assumption of the greasy hood and the emergence of the wondering cloud, thirty or forty onlookers, many of them female, had somehow crowded into the sober little room. Despite the miraculous nature of my exit from my corporeal self, these new arrivals paid me no mind at all. Unlike the original twelve, they did not face the large, oblong window looking in upon the even smaller, infinitely grimmer chamber where all the action was going on.

I mean, although the obvious focus of the original twelve, one nervously caressing a shabby Bible, one locking his hands over a ponderous gabardine-swathed gut, the rest scratching 'observations' into their notebooks with chewed-looking pencils, was the hooded, enthroned corpse of the fiend Francis T. Wardwell, from which rose numerous curls and twists of white smoke as well as the mingled odors of urine and burned meat, these new people were staring at *them* – the Bible-stroker and the warden and the scribbling reporters, really *staring* at them, I mean, *lapping up* these unremarkable people with their eyes, *devouring* them.

The second thing I noticed was that except for the thirty or forty male and female shades who, it had just come to me, shared my new state, everything in the two sober chambers, including the green paint unevenly applied to the walls, including the calibrated dials and the giant switch, including the blackened leather straps and the vanishing twists of smoke, including even the bitten pencils of the scribes, but most of all including those twelve mortal beings who had gathered to witness the execution of the fiend Francis T. Wardwell, mortal beings of deep, that is to say, radiant ordinariness, expansive overflowing heartbreaking throat-catching light-shedding meaning-steeped –

The second thing I noticed was that everything –

At that moment, hunger slammed into me, stronger, more forceful, and far more enduring than the river of volts that had separated me from my former self. As avid as the others, as raptly appreciative of all you still living could not see, I moved to the glass and fastened my ravenous gaze upon the nearest mortal man.

Posted beside the blazing azalea bush on Boy Teuteburg's front lawn, I observe, mild word, what is disposed so generously to be observed. After all that has been said, there is no need to describe, as I had intended at the beginning of our journey, all I see before me. Tulip Lane is thronged with my fellow Invisibles, wandering this way and that on their self-appointed rounds; some six or seven fellow Invisibles are at this moment stretched out upon Boy Teuteburg's high-grade lawn of imported Kentucky bluegrass, enjoying the particularly lambent skies we have at this time of year while awaiting the all-important, significance-drenched arrival of a sweet human being, Tulip Lane resident or service personage. These waiting ones, myself included, resemble those eager ticket buyers who, returning to a favorite play for the umpty-umpth time, clutch their handbags or opera glasses in the dark and lean forward as the curtain rises, breath suspended, eyes wide, hearts already trilling, as the actors begin to assemble in their accustomed places, their dear, familiar words to be spoken, the old dilemmas faced once again, and the plot to spin, this time perhaps toward a conclusion equal to the intensity of our attention. Will they get it right, this time? Will they *see*? No, of course not, *they* will never see, but we lean forward in passionate concentration as their aching voices lift again and enthrall us with everything they do not know.

Boy is an old Boy now, in his eighties I believe, though it may be his nineties – distinctions of this sort no longer compel – and, wonderfully, an honored personage. He ascended, needless to say without my vote, into public life around the time of my own 'ascension' to the second floor, and continued to rise until a convenient majority elected him mayor shortly before my demise, and upon that plateau he resided through four terms, or sixteen years, after which ill health (emphysema) restrained him from further elevation. His mansion on Tulip Lane contains, I am told, many rooms – seventeen, not counting two kitchens and six bathrooms. I do not bring myself here to admire the mansion of my old adversary, now confined, I gather, to an upper floor and dependent on a wheelchair and an uninterrupted flow of oxygen. I certainly do not report to Tulip Lane at this time of the day to gloat. (Even Boy Teuteburg is a splendid presence now, a figure who plants his feet on the stage and raises his brave and frail voice.) I come here to witness a certain moment.

A little girl opens the door of the room beyond the window next to the azalea. She is Boy Teuteburg's youngest grandchild, the only offspring of the failed second marriage of his youngest child, Sherrie-Lynn, daughter of his own failed second and final marriage. Her name is Amber, Jasmine, Opal, something like that – Tiffany! Her name is Tiffany! Tiffany is five or six, a solemn, dark-haired little personage generally attired in a practical one-piece denim garment with bib and shoulder straps, like a farmer's overalls but white, and printed with a tiny, repeated pattern, flower, puppy, or kitten. Food stains, small explosions of ketchup and the like, provide a secondary layer of decoration. Beneath this winning garment Tiffany most often wears a long-sleeved cotton turtleneck, blue or white, or a white cotton T-shirt, as appropriate to the season; on her feet are clumsy but informal shoes of a sort that first appeared about a decade or two ago, somewhat resembling space boots, somewhat resembling basketball sneakers; in Tiffany's case, the sides of these swollen-looking objects sport pink check marks. Tiffany is a sallow, almost olive-skinned child in whom almost none of her grandfather's genetic inheritance is visible. Whitish-gray streaks of dust (housekeeping has slacked off considerably since Mayor Teuteburg's retirement to the upper floor) can often be observed on her round, inward-looking little face, as well as upon the wrinkled sleeves of her turtleneck and the ironic pastoral of the white overalls.

Smudgy of eye; streaky with white-gray dust; sallow of skin; dark hair depending in wisps and floaters from where it had been carelessly gathered at the back, and her wispy bangs unevenly cut; each pudgy hand dirt-crusted in a different fashion, one likely to be trailing a single footlong blond hair, formerly her mother's; introspective without notable intelligence, thus liable to fits of selfishness and brooding; round of face, arm, wrist, hand, and belly, thus liable for obesity in adulthood; yet withal surpassingly charming; yet gloriously, wholly beautiful.

This little miracle enters the room at the usual hour, marches directly to the television set located beneath our window, tucks her lower lip beneath her teeth – pearly white, straight as a Roman road – and snaps the set on. It is time for the adventures of Tom and Jerry. By now, most of those Invisibles who had been sprawled on the Kentucky blue have joined me at the window, and as matters proceed, some of those who have found themselves on Tulip Lane will wander up, too. Tiffany backpedals to a point on the floor well in advance of the nearest chair. The chairs have been positioned for adults, who do not understand television as Tiffany does and in any case do not ever watch in wondering awe the multiform adventures of Tom and Jerry. She slumps over her crossed ankles, back bent, clumsy shoes with pink check marks nearly in her lap, hands at her sides, round face beneath uneven bangs dowsing the screen. Tiffany does not laugh and only rarely smiles. She is engaged in serious business.

Generally, her none-too-clean hands flop all anyhow on her flowered denim knees, on her pink-checked feet, or in the little well between the feet and the rest of her body. At other times, Tiffany's hands go exploring unregarded on the floor about her. These forays deposit another fine, mouse-gray layer of dust or grime on whatever sectors of the probing hands come in contact with the hardwood floor.

During the forays, the small person's face maintains a soft immobility, the soft unconscious composure of a deep-diving rapture; and the conjunction of softness and immobility renders each inner delight, each moment of identification or elation, each collusion between drama and witness – in short, you people, each emotion that would cause another child to roll giggling on the floor or draw her smeary fists up to her face, each emotion is rendered *instantly visible* – written in subtle but powerful runes on the blank page that is Tiffany's face. As the eerie tube-light washes over this enchanted child's features, her lips tighten or loosen; an adult frown redraws her forehead; mysterious pouches 'neath her eyes swell with horror or with tears; a hidden smile tucks the corners of her mouth; joy leaps candlelike into her eyes; the whole face irradiates with soul-pleasure. I have not even mentioned the dreamy play brought over the wide cheeks and the area beneath the eyes by thousands of tiny muscle movements, each invoking the separate character, character as in fictional character, of a piquant, momentary shadow.

And from time to time, a probing hand returns to base and alights on a knee, a space shoe, wanders for a second through the dangling wisps, hesitates, and then, with excruciating patience, approaches the opening mouth and, finger by finger, enters to be sucked, tongued, warmed, above all cleaned of its layers of debris. Tiffany is eating. She will eat anything she finds, anything she picks up. It all goes into her mouth and is absorbed into Tiffany. Cookie crumbs; dust; loose threads from who knows what fabric; now and then a button or a coin. When she is through with her fingers, she might graze over the palm. More often, she will extend a newly washed forefinger and push it into a nostril, there to rummage until a glistening morsel is extracted, this morsel unhesitatingly to be brought to the portals of the mouth and slipped within, then munched until it too has been absorbed into the Tiffany from whence it came.

We watch so intently, we crowd so close, thrusting into the azalea, that sometimes, having heard a dim version of what twice I heard on Erie Street, she yanks her eyes from the screen and glances upward. She sees but a window, a bush. Instantly, she returns to the screen and her ceaseless meal. I have given you Ethel Carroway letting fall her child, and I have given you myself, Frank Wardwell, battering in a tyrant's brains; but no riper spectacle have I summoned to the boards than Tiffany. She embraces and encompasses living Ethel and living Frank, and exactly so, my dear ones, does Tiffany embrace and encompass you.

Mr Clubb and Mr Cuff

1

I never intended to go astray, nor did I know what that meant. My journey began in an isolated hamlet notable for the piety of its inhabitants, and when I vowed to escape New Covenant I assumed that the values instilled within me there would forever be my guide. And so, with a depth of paradox I still only begin to comprehend, they have been. My journey, so triumphant, also so excruciating, is both *from* my native village and *of* it. For all its splendor, my life has been that of a child of New Covenant.

When in my limousine I scanned *The Wall Street Journal*, when in the private elevator I ascended to the rosewood-paneled office with harbor views, when in the partners' dining room I ordered squab on a mesclun bed from a prison-rescued waiter known to me alone as Charlie-Charlie, also when I navigated for my clients the complex waters of financial planning, above all when before her seduction by my enemy Graham Leeson I returned homeward to luxuriate in the attentions of my stunning Marguerite, when transported within the embraces of my wife, even then I carried within the frame houses dropped like afterthoughts down the streets of New Covenant, the stiff faces and suspicious eyes, the stony cordialities before and after services in the grim great Temple, the blank storefronts along Harmony Street – tattooed within me was the ugly, enigmatic beauty of my birthplace. Therefore I believe that when I strayed, and stray I did, make no mistake, it was but to come home, for I claim that the two strange gentlemen who beckoned me into error were the night of its night, the dust of its dust. In the period of my life's greatest turmoil – the month of my exposure to Mr Clubb and Mr Cuff, 'Private Detectives Extraordinaire', as their business card described them – in the midst of the uproar I felt that I saw *the contradictory dimensions of . . .*

of . . .

I felt I saw . . . had seen, had at least glimpsed . . . what a wiser man might call . . . try to imagine the sheer difficulty of actually writing these words . . . the Meaning of Tragedy. You smirk; I don't blame you: in your place I'd do the same, but I assure you I saw *something*.

I must sketch in the few details necessary for you to understand my story. A day's walk from New York State's Canadian border, New Covenant was (and still is, still is) a town of just under a thousand inhabitants united by the puritanical Protestantism of the Church of the New Covenant, whose founders had broken away from the even more puritanical Saints of the Covenant. (The Saints had proscribed sexual congress in the hope of hastening the Second Coming.) The village flourished during the end of the nineteenth century and settled into its permanent form around 1920.

To wit: Temple Square, where the Temple of the New Covenant and its bell tower, flanked left and right by the Youth Bible Study Center and the Combined Boys and Girls Elementary and Middle School, dominate a modest greensward. Southerly stand the shop fronts of Harmony Street, the bank, also the modest placards indicating the locations of New Covenant's doctor, lawyer, and dentist; south of Harmony Street lie the two streets of frame houses sheltering the town's clerks and artisans, beyond these the farms of the rural faithful, beyond the farmland deep forest. North of Temple Square is Scripture Street, two blocks lined with the residences of the reverend and his Board of Brethren, the aforementioned doctor, dentist, and lawyer, the president and vice president of the bank, also the families of some few wealthy converts devoted to Temple affairs. North of Scripture Street are more farms, then the resumption of the great forest, in which our village described a sort of clearing.

My father was New Covenant's lawyer, and to Scripture Street was I born. Sundays I spent in the Youth Bible Study Center, weekdays in the Combined Boys and Girls Elementary and Middle School. New Covenant was my world, its people all I knew of the world. Three-fourths of all mankind consisted of gaunt, bony, blond-haired individuals with chiseled features and blazing blue eyes, the men six feet or taller in height, the women some inches shorter – the remaining fourth being the Racketts, Mudges, and Blunts, our farm families, who after generations of intermarriage had coalesced into a tribe of squat, black-haired, gap-toothed, moon-faced males and females seldom taller than five feet, four or five inches. Until I went to college I thought that all people were divided into the races of town and barn, fair and dark, the spotless and the mud-spattered, the reverential and the sly.

Though Racketts, Mudges, and Blunts attended our school and worshiped in our Temple, though they were at least as prosperous as we in town, we knew them tainted with an essential inferiority. Rather than intelligent they seemed *crafty*, rather than spiritual, *animal*. Both in classrooms and Temple, they sat together, watchful as dogs compelled for the nonce to be 'good', now and again tilting their heads to pass a whispered comment. Despite Sunday baths and Sunday clothes, they bore an unerasable odor redolent of the barnyard. Their public self-effacement seemed to mask a peasant amusement, and when they separated into their wagons and other vehicles, they could be heard to share a peasant laughter.

I found this mysterious race unsettling, in fact profoundly annoying. At some level they frightened me – I found them compelling. Oppressed from my earliest days by life in New Covenant, I felt an inadmissible fascination for this secretive brood. Despite their inferiority, I wished to know what they knew. Locked deep within their shabbiness and shame I sensed the presence of a freedom I did not understand but found *thrilling*.

Because town never socialized with barn, our contacts were restricted to places of education, worship, and commerce. It would have been as unthinkable for me to take a seat beside Delbert Mudge or Charlie-Charlie Rackett in our fourth-grade classroom as for Delbert or Charlie-Charlie to invite me for an overnight in their farmhouse bedrooms. Did Delbert and Charlie-Charlie actually have bedrooms, where they slept alone in their own beds? I recall mornings when the atmosphere about Delbert and Charlie-Charlie suggested nights spent in close proximity to the pigpen, others when their worn dungarees exuded a freshness redolent of sunshine, wildflowers, and raspberries.

During recess an inviolable border separated the townies at the northern end of our play area from the barnies at the southern. Our play, superficially similar, demonstrated our essential differences, for we could not cast off the unconscious stiffness resulting from constant adult measurement of our spiritual worthiness. In contrast, the barnies did not play at playing but actually *played*, plunging back and forth across the grass, chortling over victories, grinning as they muttered what must have been jokes. (We were not adept at jokes.) When school closed at end of day, I tracked the homebound progress of Delbert, Charlie-Charlie, and clan with envious eyes and a divided heart.

Why should they have seemed in possession of a liberty I desired? After graduation from Middle School, we townies progressed to Shady Glen's Consolidated High, there to monitor ourselves and our fellows while encountering the temptations of the wider world, in some cases then advancing into colleges and universities. Having concluded their educations with the seventh grade's long division and 'Hiawatha' recitations, the barnies one and all returned to their barns. Some few, some very few of *us*, among whom I had determined early on to be numbered, left for good, thereafter to be celebrated, denounced, or mourned. One of *us*, Caleb Thurlow, violated every standard of caste and morality by marrying Munna Blunt and vanishing into barnie-dom. A disgraced, disinherited pariah during my childhood, Thurlow's increasingly pronounced stoop and decreasing teeth terrifyingly mutated him into a blond, wasted barnie-parody on his furtive annual Christmas appearances at Temple. One of *them*, one only, my old classmate Charlie-Charlie Rackett, escaped his ordained destiny in our twentieth year by liberating a plow horse and Webley-Vickers pistol from the family farm to commit serial armed robbery upon Shady Glen's George Washington Inn, Town Square Feed & Grain, and Allsorts Emporium. Every witness to his crimes recognized what, if not who, he was, and Charlie-Charlie was apprehended while boarding the Albany train in the next village west. During the course of my own journey from and of New Covenant, I tracked Charlie-Charlie's gloomy progress through the way stations of the penal system until at last I could secure his release at a parole hearing with the offer of a respectable job in the financial-planning industry.

I had by then established myself as absolute monarch of three floors in a Wall Street monolith. With my two junior partners, I enjoyed the services of a fleet of paralegals, interns, analysts, investigators, and secretaries. I had chosen these partners carefully, for as well as the usual expertise, skill, and dedication, I required other, less conventional qualities.

I had sniffed out intelligent but unimaginative men of some slight moral laziness; capable of cutting corners when they thought no one would notice; controlled drinkers and secret drug takers: juniors with reason to be grateful for their positions. I wanted no *zealousness*. My employees were to be steadfastly incurious and able enough to handle their clients satisfactorily, at least with my paternal assistance.

My growing prominence had attracted the famous, the established, the notorious. Film stars and athletes, civic leaders, corporate pashas, and heirs to long-standing family fortunes regularly visited our offices, as did a number of conspicuously well-tailored gentlemen who had accumulated their wealth in a more colorful fashion. To these clients I suggested financial stratagems responsive to their labyrinthine needs. I had not schemed for their business. It simply *came to me*, willy-nilly, as our Temple held that salvation came to the elect. One May morning, a cryptic fellow in a pin-striped suit appeared in my office to pose a series of delicate questions. As soon as he opened his mouth, the cryptic fellow summoned irresistibly from memory a dour, squinting member of the Board of Brethren of New Covenant's Temple. I *knew* this man, and instantly I found the tone most acceptable to him. Tone is all to such people. After our interview he directed others of his kind to my office, and by December my business had tripled. Individually and universally these gentlemen pungently reminded me of the village I had long ago escaped, and I cherished my suspicious buccaneers even as I celebrated the distance between my moral life and theirs. While sheltering these self-justifying figures within elaborate trusts, while legitimizing subterranean floods of cash, I immersed myself within a familiar atmosphere of pious denial. Rebuking home, I *was* home.

Life had not yet taught me that revenge inexorably exacts its own revenge.

My researches eventually resulted in the hiring of the two junior partners known privately to me as Gilligan and the Skipper. The first, a short, trim fellow with a comedian's rubber face and disheveled hair, brilliant with mutual funds but an ignoramus at estate planning, each morning worked so quietly as to become invisible. To Gilligan I had referred many of our actors and musicians, and those whose schedules permitted them to attend meetings before the lunch hour met their soft-spoken adviser in a dimly lighted office with curtained windows. After lunch, Gilligan tended toward the vibrant, the effusive, the extrovert. Red-faced and sweating, he loosened his tie, turned on a powerful sound system, and ushered emaciated musicians with haystack hair into the atmosphere of a backstage party. Morning Gilligan spoke in whispers; Afternoon Gilligan batted our secretaries' shoulders as he bounced officeward down the corridors. I snapped him up as soon as one of my competitors let him go, and he proved a perfect complement to the Skipper. Tall, plump, silver-haired, this gentleman had come to me from a specialist in estates and trusts discomfited by his tendency to become pugnacious when outraged by a client's foul language, improper dress, or other offenses against good taste. Our tycoons and inheritors of family fortunes were in no danger of arousing the Skipper's ire, and I myself handled the unshaven film stars' and heavy metallists' estate planning. Neither Gilligan nor the Skipper had any contact with the cryptic gentlemen. Our office was an organism balanced in all its parts. Should any mutinous notions occur to my partners, my spy the devoted Charlie-Charlie Rackett, known to them as Charles the Perfect Waiter, every noon silently monitored their every utterance while replenishing Gilligan's wine glass. My marriage of two years seemed blissfully happy, my reputation and bank account flourished alike, and I anticipated perhaps another decade of labor followed by luxurious retirement. I could not have been less prepared for the disaster to come.

Mine, as disasters do, began at home. I admit my contribution to the difficulties. While immersed in the demands of my profession, I had married a beautiful woman twenty years my junior. It was my understanding that Marguerite had knowingly entered into a contract under which she enjoyed the fruits of income and social position while postponing a deeper marital communication until I cashed in and quit the game, at which point she and I could travel at will, occupying grand hotel suites and staterooms while acquiring every adornment that struck her eye. How could an arrangement so harmonious have failed to satisfy her? Even now I feel the old rancor. Marguerite had come into our office as a faded singer who wished to invest the remaining proceeds from a five- or six-year-old 'hit', and after an initial consultation Morning Gilligan whispered her down the corridor for my customary lecture on estate tax, trusts, so forth and so on, in her case due to the modesty of the funds in question mere show. (Since during their preliminary discussion she had casually employed the Anglo-Saxon monosyllable for excrement, Gilligan dared not subject her to the Skipper.) He escorted her into my chambers, and I glanced up with the customary show of interest. You may imagine a thick bolt of lightning slicing through a double-glazed office window, sizzling across the width of a polished teak desk, and striking me in the heart.

Already I was lost. Thirty minutes later I violated my most sacred edict by inviting a female client to a dinner date. She accepted, damn her. Six months later, Marguerite and I were married, damn us both. I had attained everything for which I had abandoned New Covenant, and for twenty-three months I inhabited the paradise of fools.

I need say only that the usual dreary signals, matters like unexplained absences, mysterious telephone calls abruptly terminated upon my appearance, and visitations of a melancholic, distracted *daemon* forced me to set one of our investigators on Marguerite's trail, resulting in the discovery that my wife had been two-backed-beasting it with my sole professional equal, the slick, the smooth Graham Leeson, to whom I, swollen with uxorious pride a year after our wedding day, had introduced her during a function at the Waldorf-Astoria hotel. I know what happened. I don't need a map. Exactly as I had decided to win her at our first meeting, Graham Leeson vowed to steal Marguerite from me the instant he set his handsome blue eyes on her between the fifty-thousand-dollar tables on the Starlight Roof.

My enemy enjoyed a number of natural advantages. Older than she by but ten years to my twenty, at six-four three inches taller than I, this reptile had been blessed with a misleadingly winning Irish countenance and a full head of crinkly red-blond hair. (In contrast, my white tonsure accentuated the severity of the all-too-Cromwellian townie face.) I assumed her immune to such obvious charms, and I was wrong. I thought Marguerite could not fail to see the meagerness of Leeson's inner life, and I was wrong again. I suppose he exploited the inevitable temporary isolation of any spouse to a man in my position. He must have played upon her grudges, spoken to her secret vanities. Cynically, I am sure, he encouraged the illusion that she was an 'artist'. He flattered, he very likely wheedled. By every shabby means at his disposal he had overwhelmed her, most crucially by screwing her brains out three times a week in a corporate suite at a Park Avenue hotel.

After I had examined the photographs and other records arrayed before me by the investigator, an attack of nausea brought my dizzied head to the edge of my desk; then rage stiffened my backbone and induced a moment of hysterical blindness. My marriage was dead, my wife a repulsive stranger. Vision returned a second or two later. The checkbook floated from the desk drawer, the Waterman pen glided into position between thumb and forefinger, and while a shadow's efficient hand inscribed a check for ten thousand dollars, a disembodied voice informed the hapless investigator that the only service required of him henceforth would be eternal silence.

For perhaps an hour I sat alone in my office, post-poning appointments and refusing telephone calls. In the moments when I had tried to envision my rival, what came to mind was some surly drummer or guitarist from her past, easily intimidated and readily bought off. In such a case, I should have inclined toward mercy. Had Marguerite offered a sufficiently self-abasing apology, I would have slashed her clothing allowance in half, restricted her public appearances to the two or three most crucial charity events of the year and perhaps as many dinners at my side in the restaurants where one is 'seen', and ensured that the resultant mood of sackcloth and ashes prohibited any reversion to bad behavior by intermittent use of another investigator.

No question of mercy, now. Staring at the photographs of my life's former partner entangled with the man I detested most in the world, I shuddered with a com-bination of horror, despair, loathing, and – appallingly – an urgent spasm of sexual arousal. I unbuttoned my trousers, groaned in ecstatic torment, and helplessly ejaculated over the images on my desk. When I had recovered, weak-kneed and trembling, I wiped away the evidence, closed the hateful folders, and picked up the telephone to request Charlie-Charlie Rackett's immediate presence in my office.

The cryptic gentlemen, experts in the nuances of re-tribution, might have seemed more obvious sources of assistance, but I could not afford obligations in that direc-tion. Nor did I wish to expose my humiliation to clients for whom the issue of respect was all-important. Devoted Charlie-Charlie's years in the jug had given him an exten-sive acquaintanceship among the dubious and irregular, and I had from time to time commandeered the services of one or another of his fellow yardbirds. My old companion sidled around my door and posted himself before me, all dignity on the outside, all curiosity within.

'I have been dealt a horrendous blow, Charlie-Charlie,' I said, 'and as soon as possible I wish to see one or two of the best.'

Charlie-Charlie glanced at the folders. 'You want serious people,' he said, speaking in code. 'Right?'

'I must have men who can be serious when seriousness is necessary,' I said, replying in the same code.

While my lone surviving link to New Covenant struggled to understand this directive, it came to me that Charlie-Charlie had now become my only true confidant, and I bit down on an upwelling of fury. I realized that I had clamped shut my eyes, and opened them upon an uneasy Charlie-Charlie.

'You're sure,' he said.

'Find them,' I said. Then, to restore some semblance of our conventional atmosphere, I asked, 'The boys still okay?'

Telling me that the juniors remained content, he said, 'Fat and happy. I'll find what you want, but it'll take a couple of days.'

I nodded, and he was gone.

For the remainder of the day I turned in an inadequate impersonation of the executive who usually sat behind my desk and, after putting off the moment as long as reasonably possible, buried the awful files in a bottom drawer and returned to the town house I had purchased for my bride-to-be and which, I remembered with an unhappy pang, she had once in an uncharacteristic moment of cuteness called 'our town home'.

Since I had been too preoccupied to telephone wife, cook, or butler with the information that I would be staying late at the office, when I walked into our dining room the table had been laid with our china and silver, flowers arranged in the centerpiece, and, in what I took to be a new dress, Marguerite glanced mildly up from her end of the table and murmured a greeting. Scarcely able to meet her eyes, I bent to bestow the usual homecoming kiss with a mixture of feelings more painful than I previously would have imagined myself capable. Some despicable portion of my being responded to her beauty with the old husbandly appreciation even as I went cold with the loathing I could not permit myself to show. I hated Marguerite for her treachery, her beauty for its falsity, myself for my susceptibility to what I knew was treacherous and false. Clumsily, my lips brushed the edge of an azure eye, and it came to me that she may well have been with Leeson while the investigator was displaying the images of her degradation. Through me coursed an involuntary tremor of revulsion with, strange to say, at its center a molten erotic core. Part of my extraordinary pain was the sense that I too had been contaminated: a layer of illusion had been peeled away, revealing monstrous blind groping slugs and maggots.

Having heard voices, Mr Moncrieff, the butler I had employed upon the abrupt decision of the Duke of Denbigh to cast off worldly ways and enter an order of Anglican monks, came through from the kitchen and awaited orders. His bland, courteous manner suggested as usual that he was making the best of having been shipwrecked on an island populated by illiterate savages. Marguerite said that she had been worried when I had not returned home at the customary time.

'I'm fine,' I said. 'No, I'm not fine. I feel unwell. Distinctly unwell. Grave difficulties at the office.' With that I managed to make my way up the table to my chair, along the way signaling to Mr Moncrieff that the Lord of the Savages wished him to bring in the predinner martini and then immediately begin serving whatever the cook had prepared. I took my seat at the head of the table, and Mr Moncrieff removed the floral centerpiece to the sideboard. Marguerite regarded me with the appearance of probing concern. This was false, false, false. Unable to meet her eyes, I raised mine to the row of Canalettos along the wall, then the intricacies of the plaster molding above the paintings, at last to the chandelier depending from the central rosette on the ceiling. More had changed than my relationship with my wife. The molding, the blossoming chandelier, even Canaletto's Venice resounded with a cold, selfish lovelessness.

Marguerite remarked that I seemed agitated.

'No, I am not,' I said. The butler placed the ice-cold drink before me, and I snatched up the glass and drained half its contents. 'Yes, I am agitated, terribly,' I said. 'The difficulties at the office are more far-reaching than I intimated.' I polished off the martini and tasted only glycerine. 'It is a matter of betrayal and treachery made all the more wounding by the closeness of my relationship with the traitor.'

I lowered my eyes to measure the effect of this thrust to the vitals on the traitor in question. She was looking back at me with a flawless imitation of wifely concern. For a moment I doubted her unfaithfulness. Then the memory of the photographs in my bottom drawer once again brought crawling into view the slugs and maggots. 'I am sickened unto rage,' I said, 'and my rage demands vengeance. Can you understand this?'

Mr Moncrieff carried into the dining room the tureens or serving dishes containing whatever it was we were to eat that night, and my wife and I honored the silence that had become conventional during the presentation of our evening meal. When we were alone again, she nodded in affirmation.

I said, 'I am grateful, for I value your opinions. I should like you to help me reach a difficult decision.'

She thanked me in the simplest of terms.

'Consider this puzzle,' I said. 'Famously, vengeance is the Lord's, and therefore it is often imagined that vengeance exacted by anyone other is immoral. Yet if vengeance is the Lord's, then a mortal being who seeks it on his own behalf has engaged in a form of worship, even an alternate version of prayer. Many good Christians regularly pray for the establishment of justice, and what lies behind an act of vengeance but a desire for justice? God tells us that eternal torment awaits the wicked. He also demonstrates a pronounced affection for those who prove unwilling to let Him do all the work.'

Marguerite expressed the opinion that justice was a fine thing indeed, and that a man such as myself would always labor in its behalf. She fell silent and regarded me with what on any night previous I would have seen as tender concern. Though I had not yet so informed her, she declared, the Benedict Arnold must have been one of my juniors, for no other employee could injure me so greatly. Which was the traitor?

'As yet I do not know,' I said. 'But once again I must be grateful for your grasp of my concerns. Soon I will put into position the bear-traps that will result in the fiend's exposure. Unfortunately, my dear, this task will demand all of my energy over at least the next several days. Until the task is accomplished, it will be necessary for me to camp out in the —— Hotel.' I named the site of her assignations with Graham Leeson.

A subtle, momentary darkening of the eyes, her first genuine response of the evening, froze my heart as I set the bear-trap into place. 'I know, the ——'s vulgarity deepens with every passing week, but Gilligan's apartment is only a few doors north, the Skipper's one block south. Once my investigators have installed their electronic devices, I shall be privy to every secret they possess. Would you enjoy spending several days at Green Chimneys? The servants have the month off, but you might enjoy the solitude there more than you would being alone in town.'

Green Chimneys, our country estate on a bluff above the Hudson River, lay two hours away. Marguerite's delight in the house had inspired me to construct in the grounds a fully equipped recording studio, where she typically spent days on end, trying out new 'songs'.

Charmingly, she thanked me for my consideration and said that she would enjoy a few days in seclusion at Green Chimneys. After I had exposed the traitor, I was to telephone her with the summons home. Accommodating on the surface, vile beneath, these words brought an anticipatory tinge of pleasure to her face, a delicate heightening of her beauty I would have, very likely *had*, misconstrued on earlier occasions. Any appetite I might have had disappeared before a visitation of nausea, and I announced myself exhausted. Marguerite intensified my discomfort by calling me her poor darling. I staggered to my bedroom, locked the door, threw off my clothes, and dropped into bed to endure a sleepless night. I would never see my wife again.

2

Sometime after first light I had attained an uneasy slumber; finding it impossible to will myself out of bed on awakening, I relapsed into the same restless sleep. By the time I appeared within the dining room, Mr Moncrieff, as well-chilled as a good Chardonnay, informed me that Madame had departed for the country some twenty minutes before. Despite the hour, did Sir wish to breakfast? I consulted, trepidatiously, my wristwatch. It was ten-thirty: my unvarying practice was to arise at six, breakfast soon after, and arrive in my office well before seven. I rushed downstairs, and as soon as I slid into the back seat of the limousine forbade awkward queries by pressing the button to raise the window between the driver and myself.

No such mechanism could shield me from Mrs Rampage, my secretary, who thrust her head around the door a moment after I had expressed my desire for a hearty breakfast of poached eggs, bacon, and whole-wheat toast from the executive dining room. All calls and appointments were to be postponed or otherwise put off until the completion of my repast. Mrs Rampage had informed me that two men without appointments had been awaiting my arrival since eight a.m. and asked if I would consent to see them immediately. I told her not to be absurd. The door to the outer world swung to admit her beseeching head. 'Please,' she said. 'I don't know who they are, but they're *frightening* everybody.'

This remark clarified all. Earlier than anticipated, Charlie-Charlie Rackett had deputized two men capable of seriousness when seriousness was called for. 'I beg your pardon,' I said. 'Send them in.'

Mrs Rampage withdrew to lead into my chambers two stout, stocky, short, dark-haired men. My spirits had taken wing the moment I beheld these fellows shouldering through the door, and I rose smiling to my feet. My secretary muttered an introduction, baffled as much by my cordiality as by her ignorance of my visitors' names.

'It is quite all right,' I said. 'All is in order, all is in train.' New Covenant had just entered the sanctum.

Barnie-slyness, barnie-freedom shone from their great, round gap-toothed faces: in precisely the manner I remembered, these two suggested mocking peasant violence scantily disguised by an equally mocking impersonation of convention. Small wonder that they had intimidated Mrs Rampage and her underlings, for their nearest exposure to a like phenomenon had been with our musicians, and when offstage they were pale, emaciated fellows of little physical vitality. Clothed in black suits, white shirts, and black neckties, holding their black derbies by their brims and turning their gappy smiles back and forth between Mrs Rampage and myself, these barnies had evidently been loose in the world for some time. They were perfect for my task. *You will be irritated by their country manners, you will be annoyed by their native insubordination*, I told myself, *but you will never find men more suitable, so grant them what latitude they need*. I directed Mrs Rampage to cancel all telephone calls and appointments for the next hour.

The door closed, and we were alone. Each of the black-suited darlings snapped a business card from his right jacket pocket and extended it to me with a twirl of the fingers. One card read:

MR CLUBB AND MR CUFF
Private Detectives Extraordinaire
MR CLUBB

and the other:

MR CLUBB AND MR CUFF
Private Detectives Extraordinaire
MR CUFF

I inserted the cards into a pocket and expressed my delight at making their acquaintance.

'Becoming aware of your situation,' said Mr Clubb, 'we preferred to report as quickly as we could.'

'Entirely commendable,' I said. 'Will you gentlemen please sit down?'

'We prefer to stand,' said Mr Clubb.

'I trust you will not object if I again take my chair,' I said, and did so. 'To be honest, I am reluctant to describe the whole of my problem. It is a personal matter, therefore painful.'

'It is a domestic matter,' said Mr Cuff.

I stared at him. He stared back with the sly imperturbability of his kind.

'Mr Cuff,' I said, 'you have made a reasonable and, as it happens, an accurate supposition, but in the future you will please refrain from speculation.'

'Pardon my plain way of speaking, sir, but I was not speculating,' he said. 'Marital disturbances are domestic by nature.'

'All too domestic, one might say,' put in Mr Clubb. 'In the sense of pertaining to the home. As we have so often observed, you find your greatest pain right smack-dab in the living room, as it were.'

'Which is a somewhat politer fashion of naming another room altogether.' Mr Cuff appeared to suppress a surge of barnie-glee.

Alarmingly, Charlie-Charlie had passed along altogether too much information, especially since the information in question should not have been in his possession. For an awful moment I imagined that the dismissed investigator had spoken to Charlie-Charlie. The man may have broadcast my disgrace to every person encountered on his final journey out of my office, inside the public elevator, thereafter even to the shoeshine 'boys' and cup-rattling vermin lining the streets. It occurred to me that I might be forced to have the man silenced. Symmetry would then demand the silencing of valuable Charlie-Charlie. The inevitable next step would resemble a full-scale massacre.

My faith in Charlie-Charlie banished these fantasies by suggesting an alternate scenario and enabled me to endure the next utterance.

Mr Clubb said, 'Which in plainer terms would be to say the bedroom.'

After speaking to my faithful spy, the Private Detectives Extraordinaire had taken the initiative by acting as if *already employed* and following Marguerite to her afternoon assignation at the —— Hotel. Here, already, was the insubordination I had forseen, but instead of the expected annoyance I felt a thoroughgoing gratitude for the two men leaning slightly toward me, their animal senses alert to every nuance of my response. That they had come to my office armed with the essential secret absolved me from embarrassing explanations; blessedly, the hideous photographs would remain concealed in the bottom drawer.

'Gentlemen,' I said, 'I applaud your initiative.'

They stood at ease. 'Then we have an understanding,' said Mr Clubb. 'At various times, various matters come to our attention. At these times we prefer to conduct ourselves according to the wishes of our employer, regardless of difficulty.'

'Agreed,' I said. 'However, from this point forward I must insist –'

A rap at the door cut short my admonition. Mrs Rampage brought in a coffeepot and cup, a plate beneath a silver cover, a rack with four slices of toast, two jam pots, silverware, a linen napkin, and a glass of water, and came to a halt some five or six feet short of the barnies. A sinfully arousing smell of butter and bacon emanated from the tray. Mrs Rampage deliberated between placing my breakfast on the table to her left or venturing into proximity to my guests by bringing the tray to my desk. I gestured her forward, and she tacked wide to port and homed in on the desk. 'All is in order, all is in train,' I said. She nodded and backed out – literally walked backward until she reached the door, groped for the knob, and vanished.

I removed the cover from the plate containing two poached eggs in a cup-sized bowl, four crisp rashers of bacon, and a mound of home fried potatoes all the more welcome for being a surprise gift from our chef.

'And now, fellows, with your leave I shall –'

For the second time my sentence was cut off in midflow. A thick barnie-hand closed upon the handle of the coffee-pot and proceeded to fill the cup. Mr Clubb transported my coffee to his lips, smacked appreciatively at the taste, then took up a toast slice and plunged it like a dagger into my egg cup, releasing a thick yellow suppuration. He crunched the dripping toast between his teeth.

At that moment, when mere annoyance passed into dumbfounded ire, I might have sent them packing despite my earlier resolution, for Mr Clubb's violation of my breakfast was as good as an announcement that he and his partner respected none of the conventional boundaries and would indulge in boorish, even disgusting behavior. I very nearly did send them packing, and both of them knew it. They awaited my reaction, whatever it should be. Then I understood that I was being tested, and half of my insight was that ordering them off would be a failure of imagination. I had asked Charlie-Charlie to send me serious men, not Boy Scouts, and in the rape of my breakfast were depths and dimensions of seriousness I had never suspected. In that instant of comprehension, I believe, I virtually knew all that was to come, down to the last detail, and gave a silent assent. My next insight was that the moment when I might have dismissed these fellows with a conviction of perfect rectitude had just passed, and with the sense of opening myself to unpredictable adventures I turned to Mr Cuff. He lifted a rasher from my plate, folded it within a slice of toast, and displayed the result.

'Here are our methods in action,' he said. 'We prefer not to go hungry while you gorge yourself, speaking freely, for the one reason that all of this stuff represents what you ate every morning when you were a kid.' Leaving me to digest this shapeless utterance, he bit into his impromptu sandwich and sent golden-brown crumbs showering to the carpet.

'For as the important, abstemious man you are now,' said Mr Clubb, 'what do you eat in the mornings?'

'Toast and coffee,' I said. 'That's about it.'

'But in childhood?'

'Eggs,' I said. 'Scrambled or fried, mainly. And bacon. Home fries, too.' Every fatty, cholesterol-crammed ounce of which, I forbore to add, had been delivered by barnie-hands directly from barnie-farms. I looked at the rigid bacon, the glistening potatoes, the mess in the egg cup. My stomach lurched.

'We prefer,' Mr Clubb said, 'that you follow your true preferences instead of muddying mind and stomach by gobbling this crap in search of an inner peace that never existed in the first place, if you can be honest with yourself.' He leaned over the desk and picked up the plate. His partner snatched a second piece of bacon and wrapped it within a second slice of toast. Mr Clubb began working on the eggs, and Mr Cuff grabbed a handful of home fried potatoes. Mr Clubb dropped the empty egg cup, finished his coffee, refilled the cup, and handed it to Mr Cuff, who had just finished licking the residue of fried potato from his free hand.

I removed the third slice of toast from the rack. Forking home fries into his mouth, Mr Clubb winked at me. I bit into the toast and considered the two little pots of jam, greengage, I think, and rosehip. Mr Clubb waggled a finger. I contented myself with the last of the toast. After a while I drank from the glass of water. All in all I felt reasonably satisfied and, but for the deprivation of my customary cup of coffee, content with my decision. I glanced in some irritation at Mr Cuff. He drained his cup, then tilted into it the third and final measure from the pot and offered it to me. 'Thank you,' I said. Mr Cuff picked up the pot of greengage jam and sucked out its contents, loudly. Mr Clubb did the same with the rosehip. They sent their tongues into the corners of the jam pots

318

and cleaned out whatever adhered to the sides. Mr Cuff burped. Overlappingly, Mr Clubb burped.

'Now, that is what I call by the name of breakfast, Mr Clubb,' said Mr Cuff. 'Are we in agreement?'

'Deeply,' said Mr Clubb. 'That is what I call by the name of breakfast now, what I have called by the name of breakfast in the past, and what I shall continue to call by that sweet name on every morning in the future.' He turned to me and took his time, sucking first one tooth, then another. 'Our morning meal, sir, consists of that simple fare with which we begin the day, except when in all good faith we wind up sitting in a waiting room with our stomachs growling because our future client has chosen to skulk in late for work.' He inhaled. 'Which was for the same exact reason that brought him to our attention in the first place and for which we went without in order to offer him our assistance. Which is, begging your pardon, sir, the other reason for which you ordered a breakfast you would ordinarily rather starve than eat, and all I ask before we get down to the business at hand is that you might begin to entertain the possibility that simple men like ourselves might possibly understand a thing or two.'

'I see that you are faithful fellows,' I began.

'Faithful as dogs,' broke in Mr Clubb.

'And that you understand my position,' I continued.

'Down to its smallest particulars,' he interrupted again. 'We are on a long journey.'

'And so it follows,' I pressed on, 'that you must also understand that no further initiatives may be taken without my express consent.'

These last words seemed to raise a disturbing echo – of what I could not say, but an echo nonetheless, and my ultimatum failed to achieve the desired effect. Mr Clubb smiled and said, 'We intend to follow your inmost desires with the faithfulness, as I have said, of trusted dogs, for one of our sacred duties is that of bringing these to fulfillment, as evidenced, begging your pardon, sir, in the matter of the breakfast our actions spared you from gobbling up and sickening yourself with. Before you protest, sir, please let me put to you the question of how you think you would be feeling right now if you had eaten that greasy stuff all by yourself?'

The straightforward truth announced itself and demanded utterance. 'Poisoned,' I said. After a second's pause, I added, 'Disgusted.'

'Yes, for you are a better man than you know. Imagine the situation. Allow yourself to picture what would have transpired had Mr Cuff and myself not acted on your behalf. As your heart throbbed and your veins groaned, you would have taken in that while you were stuffing yourself the two of us stood hungry before you. You would have remembered that good woman informing you that we had patiently awaited your arrival since eight this morning, and at that point, sir, you would have experienced a self-disgust which would forever have tainted our relationship. From that point forth, sir, you would have been incapable of receiving the full benefits of our services.'

I stared at the twinkling barnie. 'Are you saying that if I had eaten my breakfast you would have refused to work for me?'

'You did eat your breakfast. The rest was ours.'

This statement was so literally true that I burst into laughter. 'Then I must thank you for saving me from myself. Now that you may accept employment, please inform me of the rates for your services.'

'We have no rates,' said Mr Clubb.

'We prefer to leave compensation to the client,' said Mr Cuff.

This was crafty even by barnie-standards, but I knew a countermove. 'What is the greatest sum you have ever been awarded for a single job?'

'Six hundred thousand dollars,' said Mr Clubb.

'And the smallest?'

'Nothing, zero, nada, zilch,' said the same gentleman.

'And your feelings as to the disparity?'

'None,' said Mr Clubb. 'What we are given is the correct amount. When the time comes, you shall know the sum to the penny.'

To myself I said, *So I shall, and it shall be nothing*; to them, 'We must devise a method by which I may pass along suggestions as I monitor your ongoing progress. Our future consultations should take place in anonymous public places on the order of street corners, public parks, diners, and the like. I must never be seen in your office.'

'You must not, you could not,' said Mr Clubb. 'We would prefer to install ourselves here within the privacy and seclusion of your own beautiful office.'

'Here?' He had once again succeeded in dumbfounding me.

'Our installation within the client's work space proves so advantageous as to overcome all initial objections,' said Mr Cuff. 'And in this case, sir, we would occupy but the single corner behind me where the table stands against the window. We would come and go by means of your private elevator, exercise our natural functions in your private bathroom, and have our simple meals sent in from your kitchen. You would suffer no interference or awkwardness in the course of your business. So we prefer to do our job here, where we can do it best.'

'You prefer,' I said, giving equal weight to every word, 'to move in with me.'

'Prefer it to declining the offer of our help, thereby forcing you, sir, to seek the aid of less reliable individuals.'

Several factors, first among them being the combination of delay, difficulty, and risk involved in finding replacements for the pair before me, led me to give further

321

thought to this absurdity. Charlie-Charlie, a fellow of wide acquaintance among society's shadow side, had sent me his best. Any others would be inferior. It was true that Mr Clubb and Mr Cuff could enter and leave my office unseen, granting us a greater degree of security than possible in diners and public parks. There remained an insuperable problem.

'All you say may be true, but my partners and clients alike enter this office daily. How do I explain the presence of two strangers?'

'That is easily done, Mr Cuff, is it not?' said Mr Clubb.

'Indeed it is,' said his partner. 'Our experience has given us two infallible and complementary methods. The first of these is the installation of a screen to shield us from the view of those who visit this office.'

I said, 'You intend to hide behind a screen.'

'During those periods when it is necessary for us to be on-site.'

'Are you and Mr Clubb capable of perfect silence? Do you never shuffle your feet, do you never cough?'

'You could justify our presence within these sacrosanct confines by the single manner most calculated to draw over Mr Clubb and myself a blanket of respectable, anony-mous impersonality.'

'You wish to be introduced as my lawyers?' I asked.

'I invite you to consider a word,' said Mr Cuff. 'Hold it steadily in your mind. Remark the inviolability that distinguishes those it identifies, measure its effect upon those who hear it. The word of which I speak, sir, is this: Consultant.'

I opened my mouth to object and found I could not.

Every profession occasionally must draw upon the resources of impartial experts – consultants. Every insti-tution of every kind has known the visitations of per-sons answerable only to the top and given access to all departments – consultants. Consultants are *supposed* to be invisible. Again I opened my mouth, this time to say, 'Gentlemen, we are in business.' I picked up my telephone and asked Mrs Rampage to order immediate delivery from Bloomingdale's of an ornamental screen and then to remove the breakfast tray.

Eyes agleam with approval, Mr Clubb and Mr Cuff stepped forward to clasp my hand.

'We are in business,' said Mr Clubb.

'Which is by way of saying,' said Mr Cuff, 'jointly dedicated to a sacred purpose.'

Mrs Rampage entered, circled to the side of my desk, and gave my visitors a glance of deep-dyed wariness. Mr Clubb and Mr Cuff looked heavenward. 'About the screen,' she said. 'Bloomingdale's wants to know if you would prefer one six feet high in a black and red Chinese pattern or one ten feet high, Art Deco, in ochers, teals, and taupes.'

My barnies nodded together at the heavens. 'The latter, please, Mrs Rampage,' I said. 'Have it delivered this afternoon, regardless of cost, and place it beside the table for the use of these gentlemen, Mr Clubb and Mr Cuff, highly regarded consultants to the financial industry. That table shall be their command post.'

'Consultants,' she said. 'Oh.'

The barnies dipped their heads. Much relaxed, Mrs Rampage asked if I expected great changes in the future.

'We shall see,' I said. 'I wish you to extend every cooperation to these gentlemen. I need not remind you, I know, that change is the first law of life.'

She disappeared, no doubt on a beeline for her telephone.

Mr Clubb stretched his arms above his head. 'The preliminaries are out of the way, and we can move to the job at hand. You, sir, have been most *exceedingly*, most *grievously* wronged. Do I overstate?'

'You do not,' I said.

323

'Would I overstate to assert that you have been injured, that you have suffered a devastating wound?'

'No, you would not,' I responded, with some heat.

Mr Clubb settled a broad haunch upon the surface of my desk. His face had taken on a grave, sweet serenity. 'You seek redress. Redress, sir, is a *correction*, but it is nothing more. You imagine that it restores a lost balance, but it does nothing of the kind. A crack has appeared on the earth's surface, causing widespread loss of life. From all sides are heard the cries of the wounded and dying. It is as though the earth itself has suffered an injury akin to yours, is it not?'

He had expressed a feeling I had not known to be mine until that moment, and my voice trembled as I said, 'It is exactly.'

'Exactly,' he said. 'For that reason I said *correction* rather than *restoration*. Restoration is never possible. Change is the first law of life.'

'Yes, of course,' I said, trying to get down to brass tacks.

Mr Clubb hitched his buttock more comprehensively onto the desk. 'What will happen will indeed happen, but we prefer our clients to acknowledge from the first that, apart from human desires being a messy business, outcomes are full of surprises. If you choose to repay one disaster with an equal and opposite disaster, we would reply, in our country fashion, There's a calf that won't suck milk.'

I said, 'I know I can't pay my wife back in kind, how could I?'

'Once we begin,' he said, 'we cannot undo our actions.'

'Why should I want them undone?' I asked.

Mr Clubb drew up his legs and sat cross-legged before me. Mr Cuff placed a meaty hand on my shoulder. 'I suppose there is no dispute,' said Mr Clubb, 'that the injury you seek to redress is the adulterous behavior of your spouse.'

Mr Cuff's hand tightened on my shoulder.

'You wish that my partner and myself punish your spouse.'

'I didn't hire you to read her bedtime stories,' I said.

Mr Cuff twice smacked my shoulder, painfully, in what I took to be approval.

'Are we assuming that her punishment is to be of a physical nature?' asked Mr Clubb. His partner gave my shoulder another all-too-hearty squeeze.

'What other kind is there?' I asked, pulling away from Mr Cuff's hand.

The hand closed on me again, and Mr Clubb said, 'Punishment of a mental or psychological nature. We could, for example, torment her with mysterious telephone calls and anonymous letters. We could use any of a hundred devices to make it impossible for her to sleep. Threatening incidents could be staged so often as to put her in a permanent state of terror.'

'I want physical punishment,' I said.

'That is our constant preference,' he said. 'Results are swifter and more conclusive when physical punishment is used. But again, we have a wide spectrum from which to choose. Are we looking for mild physical pain, real suffering, or something in between, on the order of, say, broken arms or legs?'

I thought of the change in Marguerite's eyes when I named the —— Hotel. 'Real suffering.'

Another bone-crunching blow to my shoulder from Mr Cuff and a wide, gappy smile from Mr Clubb greeted this remark. 'You, sir, are our favorite type of client,' said Mr Clubb. 'A fellow who knows what he wants and is unafraid to put it into words. This suffering, now, did you wish it in brief or extended form?'

'Extended,' I said. 'I must say that I appreciate your thoughtfulness in consulting with me like this. I was not quite sure what I wanted of you when first I requested your services, but you have helped me become perfectly clear about it.'

'That is our function,' he said. 'Now, sir. The extended form of real suffering permits two different conclusions, gradual cessation or termination. Which is your preference?'

I opened my mouth and closed it. I opened it again and stared at the ceiling. Did I want these men to murder my wife? No. Yes. No. Yes, but only after making sure that the unfaithful trollop understood exactly why she had to die. No, surely an extended term of excruciating torture would restore the world to proper balance. Yet I wanted the witch dead. But then I would be ordering these barnies to kill her. 'At the moment I cannot make that decision,' I said. Irresistibly, my eyes found the bottom drawer containing the files of obscene photographs. 'I'll let you know my decision after we have begun.'

Mr Cuff dropped his hand, and Mr Clubb nodded with exaggerated, perhaps ironic slowness. 'And what of your rival, the seducer, sir? Do we have any wishes in regard to that gentleman, sir?'

The way these fellows could sharpen one's thinking was truly remarkable. 'I most certainly do,' I said. 'What she gets, he gets. Fair is fair.'

'Indeed, sir,' said Mr Clubb, 'and, if you will permit me, sir, only fair is fair. And fairness demands that before we go any deeper into the particulars of the case we must examine the evidence as presented to yourself, and when I speak of fairness, sir, I refer to fairness particularly to yourself, for only the evidence seen by your own eyes can permit us to view this matter through them.'

Again, I looked helplessly down at the bottom drawer. 'That will not be necessary. You will find my wife at our country estate, Green . . .'

My voice trailed off as Mr Cuff's hand ground into my shoulder while he bent down and opened the drawer.

'Begging to differ,' said Mr Clubb, 'but we are now and again in a better position than the client to determine what is necessary. Remember, sir, that while shame unshared is toxic to the soul, shame shared is the beginning of health. Besides, it only hurts for a little while.'

Mr Cuff drew the files from the drawer.

'My partner will concur that your inmost wish is that we examine the evidence,' said Mr Clubb. 'Else you would not have signaled its location. We would prefer to have your explicit command to do so, but in the absence of explicit, implicit serves just about as well.'

I gave an impatient, ambiguous wave of the hand, a gesture they cheerfully misunderstood.

'Then all is . . . how do you put it, sir? "All is . . ."'

'All is in order, all is in train,' I muttered.

'Just so. We have ever found it beneficial to establish a common language with our clients, in order to conduct ourselves within terms enhanced by their constant usage in the dialogue between us.' He took the files from Mr Cuff's hands. 'We shall examine the contents of these folders at the table across the room. After the examination has been completed, my partner and I shall deliberate. And then, sir, we shall return for further instructions.'

They strolled across the office and took adjoining chairs on the near side of the table, presenting me with two identical wide, black-clothed backs. Their hats went to either side, the files between them. Attempting unsuccessfully to look away, I lifted my receiver and asked my secretary who, if anyone, had called in the interim and what appointments had been made for the morning.

Mr Clubb opened a folder and leaned forward to inspect the topmost photograph.

My secretary informed me that Marguerite had telephoned from the road with an inquiry concerning my health. Mr Clubb's back and shoulders trembled with what I assumed was the shock of disgust. One of the

327

scions was due at two p.m., and at four a cryptic gentleman would arrive. By their works shall ye know them, and Mrs Rampage proved herself a diligent soul by asking if I wished her to place a call to Green Chimneys at three o'clock. Mr Clubb thrust a photograph in front of Mr Cuff. 'I think not,' I said. 'Anything else?' She told me that Gilligan had expressed a desire to see me privately – meaning, without the Skipper – sometime during the morning. A murmur came from the table. 'Gilligan can wait,' I said, and the murmur, expressive, I had thought, of dismay and sympathy, rose in volume and revealed itself as amusement.

They were chuckling – even chortling!

I replaced the telephone and said, 'Gentlemen, your laughter is insupportable.' The potential effect of this remark was undone by its being lost within a surge of coarse laughter. I believe that something else was at that moment lost . . . some dimension of my soul . . . an element akin to pride . . . akin to dignity . . . but whether the loss was for good or ill, then I could not say. For some time, in fact an impossibly lengthy time, they found cause for laughter in the wretched photographs. My occasional attempts to silence them went unheard as they passed the dread images back and forth, discarding some instantly and to others returning for a second, a third, even a fourth and fifth perusal.

At last the barnies reared back, uttered a few nostalgic chirrups of laughter, and returned the photographs to the folders. They were still twitching with remembered laughter, still flicking happy tears from their eyes, as they sauntered, grinning, back across the office and tossed the files onto my desk. 'Ah me, sir, a delightful experience,' said Mr Clubb. 'Nature in all her lusty romantic splendor, one might say. Remarkably stimulating, I could add. Correct, sir?'

'I hadn't expected you fellows to be stimulated to mirth,'

I grumbled, ramming the foul things into the drawer and out of view.

'Laughter is merely a portion of the stimulation to which I refer,' he said. 'Unless my sense of smell has led me astray, a thing I fancy it has yet to do, you could not but feel another sort of arousal altogether before these pictures, am I right?'

I refused to respond to this sally but felt the blood rising to my cheeks. Here they were again, the slugs and maggots.

'We are all brothers under the skin,' said Mr Clubb. 'Remember my words. Shame unshared poisons the soul. And besides, it only hurts for a little while.'

Now I could not respond. What was the 'it' that hurt only for a little while – the pain of cuckoldry, the mystery of my shameful response to the photographs, or the horror of the barnies knowing what I had done?

'You will find it helpful, sir, to repeat after me: *It only hurts for a little while*.'

'It only hurts for a little while,' I said, and the naive phrase reminded me that they were only barnies after all.

'Spoken like a child,' Mr Clubb most annoyingly said, 'in, as it were, the tones and accents of purest innocence,' and then righted matters by asking where Marguerite might be found. Had I not mentioned a country place named Green . . . ?

'Green Chimneys,' I said, shaking off the unpleasant impression that the preceding few seconds had made upon me. 'You will find it at the end of —— Lane, turning right off —— Street just north of the town of ——. The four green chimneys easily visible above the hedge along —— Lane are your landmark, though as it is the only building in sight you can hardly mistake it for another. My wife left our place in the city just after ten this morning, so she should be getting there . . .' I looked at my watch.

'. . . in thirty to forty-five minutes. She will unlock the front gate, but she will not relock it once she has passed through, for she never does. The woman does not have the self-preservation of a sparrow. Once she has entered the estate, she will travel up the drive and open the door of the garage with an electronic device. This door, I assure you, will remain open, and the door she will take into the house will not be locked.'

'But there are maids and cooks and laundresses and bootboys and suchlike to consider,' said Mr Cuff. 'Plus a majordomo to conduct the entire orchestra and go around rattling the doors to make sure they're locked. Unless all of these parties are to be absent on account of the annual holiday.'

'My servants have the month off,' I said.

'A most suggestive consideration,' said Mr Clubb. 'You possess a devilish clever mind, sir.'

'Perhaps,' I said, grateful for the restoration of the proper balance. 'Marguerite will have stopped along the way for groceries and other essentials, so she will first carry the bags into the kitchen, which is the first room to the right off the corridor from the garage. Then I suppose she will take the staircase upstairs and air out her bedroom.' I took pen and paper from my topmost drawer and sketched the layout of the house. 'She may go around to the library, the morning room, and the drawing room, opening the shutters and a few windows. Somewhere during this process, she is likely to use the telephone. After that, she will leave the house by the rear entrance and take the path along the top of the bluff to a long, low building that looks like this.'

I drew in the outlines of the studio in its nest of trees above the Hudson. 'It is a recording studio I had built for her convenience. She may well plan to spend the entire afternoon inside it. You will know if she is there by the lights.' I saw Marguerite smiling to herself as she fitted her key into the lock on the studio door, saw her let herself in and reach for the light switch. A wave of emotion rendered me speechless.

Mr Clubb rescued me by asking, 'It is your feeling, sir, that when the lady stops to use the telephone she will be placing a call to that energetic gentleman?'

'Yes, of course,' I said, only barely refraining from adding *you dolt*. 'She will seize the earliest opportunity to inform him of their good fortune.'

He nodded with an extravagant caution I recognized from my own dealings with backward clients. 'Let us pause to see all 'round the matter, sir. Would the lady wish to leave a suspicious entry in your telephone records? Isn't it more likely that the person she telephones will be you, sir? The call to the athletic gentleman will already have been placed, according to my way of seeing things, either from the roadside or the telephone in the grocery where you have her stop to pick up her essentials.'

Though disliking these references to Leeson's physical condition, I admitted that he might have a point.

'In that case, sir, and I know that a mind as quick as yours has already overtaken mine, you would want to express yourself with the utmost cordiality when the missus calls again, so as not to tip your hand in even the slightest way. But that, I'm sure, goes without saying, after all you have been through, sir.'

Without bothering to acknowledge this, I said, 'Shouldn't you fellows be leaving? No sense in wasting time, after all.'

'Precisely why we shall wait here until the end of the day,' said Mr Clubb. 'In cases of this unhappy sort, we find it more effective to deal with both parties at once, acting in concert when they are in prime condition to be taken by surprise. The gentleman is liable to leave his place of work at the end of the day, which implies to me that he is unlikely to appear at your lovely country place

331

at any time before seven this evening or, which is more likely, eight. At this time of the year, there is still enough light at nine o'clock to enable us to conceal our vehicle in the grounds, enter the house, and begin our business. At eleven o'clock, sir, we shall call with our initial report and request additional instructions.'

I asked the fellow if he meant to idle away the entire afternoon in my office while I conducted my business.

'Mr Cuff and I are never idle, sir. While you conduct your business, we will be doing the same, laying out our plans, refining our strategies, choosing our methods and the order of their use.'

'Oh, all right,' I said, 'but I trust you'll be quiet about it.'

At that moment, Mrs Rampage buzzed to say that Gilligan was before her, requesting to see me immediately, proof that bush telegraph is a more efficient means of spreading information than any newspaper. I told her to send him in, and a second later Morning Gilligan, pale of face, dark hair tousled but not as yet completely wild, came treading softly toward my desk. He pretended to be surprised that I had visitors and pantomimed an apology which incorporated the suggestion that he depart and return later. 'No, no,' I said, 'I am delighted to see you, for this gives me the opportunity to introduce you to our new consultants, who will be working closely with me for a time.'

Gilligan swallowed, glanced at me with the deepest suspicion, and extended his hand as I made the introductions. 'I regret that I am unfamiliar with your work, gentlemen,' he said. 'Might I ask the name of your firm? Is it Locust, Bleaney, Burns or Charter, Carter, Maxton, and Coltrane?'

By naming the two most prominent consultancies in our industry, Gilligan was assessing the thinness of the ice beneath his feet: LBB specialized in investments, CCM&C

in estates and trusts. If my visitors worked for the former, he would suspect that a guillotine hung above his neck; if the latter, the Skipper was liable for the chop. 'Neither,' I said. 'Mr Clubb and Mr Cuff are the directors of their own concern, which covers every aspect of the trade with such tactful professionalism that it is known to but the few for whom they will consent to work.'

'Excellent,' Gilligan whispered, gazing in some puzzlement at the map and floor plan atop my desk. 'Tip-top.'

'When their findings are given to me, they shall be given to all. In the meantime, I would prefer that you say as little as possible about the matter. Though change is a law of life, we wish to avoid unnecessary alarm.'

'You know that you can depend on my silence,' said Morning Gilligan, and it was true, I did know that. I also knew that his alter ego, Afternoon Gilligan, would babble the news to everyone who had not already heard it from Mrs Rampage. By six p.m., our entire industry would be pondering the information that I had called in a consultancy team of such rarified accomplishments *that they chose to remain unknown but to the very few*. None of my colleagues could dare admit to an ignorance of Clubb & Cuff, and my reputation, already great, would increase exponentially.

To distract him from the floor plan of Green Chimneys and the rough map of my estate, I said, 'I assume some business brought you here, Gilligan.'

'Oh! Yes – yes – of course,' he said, and with a trace of embarrassment brought to my attention the pretext for his being there, the ominous plunge in value of an overseas fund in which we had advised one of his musicians to invest. Should we recommend selling the fund before more money was lost, or was it wisest to hold on? Only a minute was required to decide that the musician should retain his share of the fund until next quarter, when we anticipated a general improvement, but both Gilligan and I were aware that this recommendation call could easily have been handled by telephone. Soon he was moving toward the door, smiling at the barnies in a pathetic display of false confidence.

The telephone rang a moment after the detectives had returned to the table. Mr Clubb said, 'Your wife, sir. Remember: the utmost cordiality.' Here was false confidence, I thought, of an entirely different sort. I picked up the receiver to hear Mrs Rampage tell me that my wife was on the line.

What followed was a banal conversation of the utmost *duplicity*. Marguerite pretended that my sudden departure from the dinner table and my late arrival at the office had caused her to fear for my health. I pretended that all was well, apart from a slight indigestion. Had the drive up been peaceful? Yes. How was the house? A little musty, but otherwise fine. She had never quite realized, she said, how very large Green Chimneys was until she walked around in it, knowing she was going to be there alone. Had she been out to the studio? No, but she was looking forward to getting a lot of work done over the next three or four days and thought she would be working every night, as well. (Implicit in this remark was the information that I should be unable to reach her, the studio being without a telephone.) After a moment of awkward silence, she said, 'I suppose it is too early for you to have identified your traitor.' It was, I said, but the process would begin that evening. 'I'm so sorry you have to go through this,' she said. 'I know how painful the discovery was for you, and I can only begin to imagine how angry you must be, but I hope you will be merciful. No amount of punishment can undo the damage, and if you try to exact retribution you will only injure yourself. The man is going to lose his job and his reputation. Isn't that punishment enough?' After a few meaningless pleasantries the conversation had clearly come to an end, although we still had yet to say good-bye.

Then an odd thing happened to me. I nearly said, *Lock all the doors and windows tonight and let no one in.* I nearly said, *You are in grave danger and must come home.* With these words rising in my throat, I looked across the room at Mr Clubb and Mr Cuff. Mr Clubb winked at me. I heard myself bidding Marguerite farewell, and then heard her hang up her telephone.

'Well done, sir,' said Mr Clubb. 'To aid Mr Cuff and myself in the preparation of our inventory, can you tell us if you keep certain staples at Green Chimneys?'

'Staples?' I said, thinking he was referring to foodstuffs.

'Rope?' he asked. 'Tools, especially pliers, hammers, and screwdrivers? A good saw? A variety of knives? Are there by any chance firearms?'

'No firearms,' I said. 'I believe all the other items you mention can be found in the house.'

'Rope and tool chest in the basement, knives in the kitchen?'

'Yes,' I said, 'precisely.' I had not ordered these barnies to murder my wife, I reminded myself; I had drawn back from that precipice. By the time I went into the executive dining room for my luncheon, I felt sufficiently restored to give Charlie-Charlie that ancient symbol of approval, the thumbs-up sign.

3

When I returned to my office the screen had been set in place, shielding from view the detectives in their preparations but in no way muffling the rumble of comments and laughter they brought to the task. 'Gentlemen,' I said in a voice loud enough to be heard behind the screen – a most unsuitable affair decorated with a pattern of ocean liners, martini glasses, champagne bottles, and cigarettes – 'you must modulate your voices, as I have business to conduct here as well as you.' There came a somewhat softer rumble of acquiescence. I took my seat to discover my bottom desk drawer pulled out, the folders absent. Another roar of laughter jerked me once again to my feet.

I came around the side of the screen and stopped short. The table lay concealed beneath drifts and mounds of yellow legal paper covered with lists of words and drawings of stick figures in varying stages of dismemberment. Strewn through the yellow pages were the photographs, loosely divided into those in which either Marguerite or Graham Leeson provided the principal focus. Crude genitalia had been drawn, without reference to either party's actual gender, over and atop both of them. Aghast, I began gathering up the defaced photographs. 'I must insist . . .' I said. 'I really must insist, you know . . .'

Mr Clubb immobilized my wrist with one hand and extracted the photographs with the other. 'We prefer to work in our time-honored fashion,' he said. 'Our methods may be unusual, but they are ours. But before you take up the afternoon's occupations, sir, can you tell us if items of the handcuff order might be found in the house?'

'No,' I said. Mr Cuff pulled a yellow page before him and wrote *handcuffs*.

'Chains?' asked Mr Clubb.

'No chains,' I said, and Mr Cuff added *chains* to his list.

'That is all for the moment,' said Mr Clubb, and released me.

I took a step backward and massaged my wrist, which stung as if from rope burn. 'You speak of your methods,' I said, 'and I understand that you have them. But what can be the purpose of defacing my photographs in this grotesque fashion?'

'Sir,' said Mr Clubb in a stern, teacherly voice, 'where you speak of defacing, we use the term *enhancement*. Enhancement is a tool we find vital to the method known by the name of Visualization.'

I retired defeated to my desk. At five minutes before two, Mrs Rampage informed me that the Skipper and our scion, a thirty-year-old inheritor of a great family fortune named Mr Chester Montfort de M——, awaited my pleasure. Putting Mrs Rampage on hold, I called out, 'Please do give me absolute quiet, now. A client is on his way in.'

First to appear was the Skipper, his tall, rotund form as alert as a pointer's in a grouse field as he led in the taller, inexpressibly languid figure of Mr Chester Montfort de M——, a person marked in every inch of his being by great ease, humor, and stupidity. The Skipper froze to gape horrified at the screen, but Montfort de M—— continued around him to shake my hand and say, 'Have to tell you, I like that thingamabob over there immensely. Reminds me of a similar thingamabob at the Beeswax Club a few years ago, whole flocks of girls used to come tumbling out. Don't suppose we're in for any unicycles and trumpets today, eh?'

The combination of the raffish screen and our client's unbridled memories brought a dangerous flush to the Skipper's face, and I hastened to explain the presence of top-level consultants who preferred to pitch tent on-site, as it were, hence the installation of a screen, all the above in the service of, well, *service*, an all-important quality we . . .

'By Kitchener's mustache,' said the Skipper. 'I remember the Beeswax Club. Don't suppose I'll ever forget the night Little Billy Pegleg jumped up and . . .' The color darkened on his cheeks, and he closed his mouth.

From behind the screen, I heard Mr Clubb say, 'Visualize *this*.' Mr Cuff chuckled.

The Skipper recovered himself and turned his sternest glare upon me. 'Superb idea, consultants. A white-glove inspection tightens up any ship.' His veiled glance toward the screen indicated that he had known of the presence of our 'consultants' but, unlike Gilligan, had restrained himself from thrusting into my office until given legitimate reason. 'That being the case, is it still quite proper that these people remain while we discuss Mr Montfort de M——'s confidential affairs?'

'Quite proper, I assure you,' I said. 'The consultants and I prefer to work in an atmosphere of complete co-operation. Indeed, this arrangement is a condition of their accepting our firm as their client.'

'Indeed,' said the Skipper.

'Top of the tree, are they?' said Mr Montfort de M——. 'Expect no less of you fellows. Fearful competence. *Terrifying* competence.'

Mr Cuff's voice could be heard saying, 'Okay, visualize *this*.' Mr Clubb uttered a high-pitched giggle.

'Enjoy their work,' said Mr Montfort de M——.

'Shall we?' I gestured to their chairs. As a young man whose assets equaled two to three billion dollars (depending on the condition of the stock market, the value of real estate in half a dozen cities around the world, global warming, forest fires, and the like), our client was as catnip to the ladies, three of whom he had previously married and divorced after siring a child upon each, resulting in a great interlocking complexity of trusts, agreements, and contracts, all of which had to be re-examined on the occasion of his forthcoming wedding to a fourth young woman, named like her predecessors after a semiprecious stone. Due to the perspicacity of the Skipper and myself, each new nuptial altered the terms of those previous so as to maintain our client's liability at an unvarying level. Our computers had enabled us to generate the documents well before his arrival, and all Mr Montfort de M—— had to do was listen to the revised terms and sign the papers, a task that generally induced a slumberous state except for those moments when a prized asset was in transition.

'Hold on, boys,' he said ten minutes into our explanations, 'you mean Opal has to give the racehorses to Garnet, and in return she gets the teak plantation from Turquoise, who gets Garnet's ski resort in Aspen? Opal is crazy about those horses.'

I explained that his second wife could easily afford the purchase of a new stable with the income from the plantation. He bent to the task of scratching his signature on the form. A roar of laughter erupted behind the screen. The Skipper glanced sideways in displeasure, and our client looked at me blinking. 'Now to the secondary trusts,' I said. 'As you will recall, three years ago –'

My words were cut short by the appearance of a chuckling Mr Clubb clamping an unlighted cigar in his mouth, a legal pad in his hand, as he came toward us. The Skipper and Mr Montfort de M—— goggled at him, and Mr Clubb nodded. 'Begging your pardon, sir, but some queries cannot wait. Pickax, sir? Dental floss? Awl?'

'No, yes, no,' I said, and then introduced him to the other two men. The Skipper appeared stunned, Mr Montfort de M—— cheerfully puzzled.

'We would prefer the existence of an attic,' said Mr Clubb.

'An attic exists,' I said.

'I must admit my confusion,' said the Skipper. 'Why is a consultant asking about awls and attics? What is dental floss to a consultant?'

'For the nonce, Skipper,' I said, 'these gentlemen and I must communicate in a form of cipher or code, of which these are examples, but soon –'

'Plug your blowhole, Skipper,' broke in Mr Clubb. 'At the moment you are as useful as wind in an outhouse, always hoping you will excuse my simple way of expressing myself.'

Sputtering, the Skipper rose to his feet, his face rosier by far than during his involuntary reminiscence of what Little Billy Pegleg had done one night at the Beeswax Club.

'Steady on,' I said, fearful of the heights of choler to

which indignation could bring my portly, white-haired, but still powerful junior.

'Not on your life,' bellowed the Skipper. 'I cannot brook . . . cannot tolerate . . . If this ill-mannered dwarf imagines excuse is possible after . . .' He raised a fist. Mr Clubb said, 'Pish tosh,' and placed a hand on the nape of the Skipper's neck. Instantly, the Skipper's eyes rolled up, the color drained from his face, and he dropped like a sack into his chair.

'Hole in one,' marveled Mr Montfort de M———. 'Old boy isn't dead, is he?'

The Skipper exhaled uncertainly and licked his lips.

'With my apologies for the unpleasantness,' said Mr Clubb, 'I have only two more queries at this juncture. Might we locate bedding in the aforesaid attic, and have you an implement such as a match or a lighter?'

'There are several old mattresses and bed frames in the attic,' I said, 'but as to matches, surely you do not . . .'

Understanding the request better than I, Mr Montfort de M——— extended a golden lighter and applied an inch of flame to the tip of Mr Clubb's cigar. 'Didn't think that part was code,' he said. 'Rules have changed? Smoking allowed?'

'From time to time during the workday my colleague and I prefer to smoke,' said Mr Clubb, expelling a reeking miasma across the desk. I had always found tobacco nauseating in its every form, and in all parts of our building smoking had, of course, long been prohibited.

'Three cheers, my man, plus three more after that,' said Mr Montfort de M———, extracting a ridged case from an inside pocket, an absurdly phallic cigar from the case. 'I prefer to smoke, too, you know, especially during these deadly conferences about who gets the pincushions and who gets the snuffboxes.' He submitted the object to a circumcision, *snick-snick*, and to my horror set it alight. 'Ashtray?' I dumped paper clips from a crystal oyster shell and slid it toward him. 'Mr Clubb, is it? Mr Clubb, you are a fellow of wonderful accomplishments, still can't get over that marvelous whopbopaloobop on the Skipper, and I'd like to ask if we could get together some evening, cigars and cognac kind of thing.'

'We prefer to undertake one matter at a time,' said Mr Clubb. Mr Cuff appeared beside the screen. He, too, was lighting up eight or nine inches of brown rope. 'However, we welcome your appreciation and would be delighted to swap tales of derring-do at a later date.'

'Very, very cool,' said Mr Montfort de M——, 'especially if you could teach me how to do the whopbopaloobop.'

'This is a world full of hidden knowledge,' Mr Clubb said. 'My partner and I have chosen as our sacred task the transmission of that knowledge.'

'Amen,' said Mr Cuff.

Mr Clubb bowed to my awed client and sauntered off. The Skipper shook himself, rubbed his eyes, and took in the client's cigar. 'My goodness,' he said. 'I believe . . . I can't imagine . . . heavens, is smoking permitted again? What a blessing.' With that, he fumbled a cigarette from his shirt pocket, accepted a light from Mr Montfort de M——, and sucked in the fumes. Until that moment I had not known that the Skipper was an addict of nicotine.

For the remainder of the hour a coiling layer of smoke like a low-lying cloud established itself beneath the ceiling and increased in density as it grew toward the floor while we extracted Mr Montfort de M——'s careless signature on the transfers and assignments. Now and again the Skipper displaced one of a perpetual chain of cigarettes from his mouth to remark upon the peculiar pain in his neck. Finally I was able to send client and junior partner on their way with those words of final benediction, 'All is in order, all is in train,' freeing me at last to stride about my office flapping a copy of *Institutional Investor* at the cloud, a remedy our fixed windows made more symbolic than actual. The barnies further defeated the effort by wafting ceaseless billows of cigar effluvia over the screen, but as they seemed to be conducting their business in a conventionally businesslike manner I made no objection and retired in defeat to my desk for the preparations necessitated by the arrival in an hour of my next client, Mr Arthur 'This Building Is Condemned' C——, the most cryptic of all the cryptic gentlemen.

So deeply was I immersed in these preparations that only a polite cough and the supplication of 'Begging your pardon, sir' brought to my awareness the presence of Mr Clubb and Mr Cuff before my desk. 'What is it now?' I asked.

'We are, sir, in need of creature comforts,' said Mr Clubb. 'Long hours of work have left us exceeding dry in the region of the mouth and throat, and the pressing sensation of thirst has made it impossible for us to maintain the concentration required to do our best.'

'Meaning a drink would be greatly appreciated, sir,' said Mr Cuff.

'Of course, of course,' I said. 'I'll have Mrs Rampage bring in a couple of bottles of water. We have San Pellegrino and Evian. Which would you prefer?'

With a smile almost menacing in its intensity, Mr Cuff said, 'We prefer drinks when we drink. *Drink* drinks, if you take my meaning.'

'For the sake of the refreshment found in them,' said Mr Clubb, ignoring my obvious dismay. 'I speak of refreshment in its every aspect, from relief to the parched tongue, taste to the ready palate, warmth to the inner man, and to the highest of refreshments, that of the mind and soul. We prefer bottles of gin and bourbon, and while any decent gargle would be gratefully received, we have, like all men who partake of grape and grain, our favorite tipples. Mr Cuff is partial to J. W. Dant bourbon, and I enjoy a drop of Bombay gin. A bucket of ice would not go amiss, and

I could say the same for a case of ice-cold Old Bohemia beer. As a chaser.'

'You consider it a good idea to consume alcohol before embarking on . . .' I sought for the correct phrase. 'A mission so delicate?'

'We consider it an essential prelude. Alcohol inspires the mind and awakens the imagination. A fool dulls both by overindulgence, but up to that point, which is a highly individual matter, there is only enhancement. Through history, alcohol has been known for its sacred properties, and the both of us know that during the sacrament of Holy Communion, priests and reverends happily serve as bartenders, passing out free drinks to all comers, children included.'

'Besides that,' I said after a pause, 'I suppose you would prefer not to be compelled to quit my employment after we have made such strides together.'

'We are on a great journey,' he said.

I placed the order with Mrs Rampage, and fifteen minutes later into my domain entered two ill-dressed youths laden with the requested liquors and a metal bucket in which the necks of beer bottles protruded from a bed of ice. I tipped the louts a dollar apiece, which they accepted with a boorish lack of grace. Mrs Rampage took in this activity with none of the revulsion for the polluted air and spirituous liquids I had anticipated.

The louts slouched away; the chuckling barnies disappeared from view with their refreshments; and, after fixing me for a moment of silence, her eyes alight with an expression I had never before observed in them, Mrs Rampage ventured the amazing opinion that the recent relaxation of formalities should prove beneficial to the firm as a whole and added that, were Mr Clubb and Mr Cuff responsible for the reformation, they had already justified their reputation and would assuredly enhance my own.

'You believe so,' I said, noting with momentarily delayed satisfaction that the effects of Afternoon Gilligan's indiscretions had already begun to declare themselves.

Employing the tactful verbal formula for *I wish to speak exactly half my mind and no more*, Mrs Rampage said, 'May I be frank, sir?'

'I depend on you to do no less,' I said.

Her carriage and face became what I can only describe as girlish – years seemed to drop away from her. 'I don't want to say too much, sir, and I hope you know how much everyone understands what a privilege it is to be a part of this firm.' Like the Skipper but more attractively, she blushed. 'Honest, I really mean that. Everybody knows that we're one of the two or three companies best at what we do.'

'Thank you,' I said.

'That's why I feel I can talk like this,' said my ever-less-recognizable Mrs Rampage. 'Until today, everybody thought if they acted like themselves, the way they really were, you'd fire them right away. Because, and maybe I shouldn't say this, maybe I'm way out of line, sir, but it's because you always seem, well, so proper you could never forgive a person for not being as dignified as you are. Like the Skipper is a heavy smoker and everybody knows it's not supposed to be permitted in this building, but a lot of companies here let their top people smoke in their offices as long as they're discreet because it shows they appreciate those people, and that's nice because it shows that if you get to the top you can be appreciated, too, but here the Skipper has to go all the way to the elevator and stand outside with the file clerks if he wants a cigarette. And in every other company I know the partners and important clients sometimes have a drink together and nobody thinks they're committing a terrible sin. You're a religious man, sir, we look up to you so much, but I think you're going to find that people will respect you even more once it gets out that you've loosened the rules a little bit.' She gave me a look in which I read that she feared having spoken too freely. 'I just wanted to say that I think you're doing the right thing, sir.'

What she was saying, of course, was that I was widely regarded as pompous, remote, and out of touch. 'I had not known that my employees regarded me as a religious man,' I said.

'Oh, we all do,' she said with almost touching earnestness. 'Because of the hymns.'

'The hymns?'

'The ones you hum to yourself when you're working.'

'Do I, indeed? Which ones?'

'"Jesus Loves Me", "The Old Rugged Cross", "Abide with Me", and "Amazing Grace", mostly. Sometimes "Onward, Christian Soldiers".'

Here, with a vengeance, were Temple Square and Scripture Street! Here was the Youth Bible Study Center, where the child-me had hours on end sung these same hymns during our Sunday school sessions! I did not know what to make of the knowledge that I hummed them to myself at my desk, but it was some consolation that this unconscious habit had at least partially humanized me to my staff.

'You didn't know you did that? Oh, sir, that's so *cute*!'

Sounds of merriment from the far side of the office rescued Mrs Rampage from the fear that this time she had truly overstepped the bounds, and she made a rapid exit. I stared after her for a moment, at first unsure how deeply I ought to regret a situation in which my secretary found it possible to describe myself and my habits as *cute*, then resolved that it probably was, or eventually would be, for the best. 'All is in order, all is in train,' I said to myself. 'It only hurts for a little while.' With that, I took my seat once more to continue delving into the elaborations of Mr 'This Building Is Condemned' C——'s financial life.

Another clink of bottle against glass and ripple of laughter brought with them the recognition that this particular client would never consent to the presence of unknown 'consultants'. Unless the barnies could be removed for at least an hour, I should face the immediate loss of a substantial portion of my business.

'Fellows,' I cried, 'come up here now. We must address a serious problem.'

Glasses in hand, cigars nestled into the corners of their mouths, Mr Clubb and Mr Cuff sauntered into view. Once I had explained the issue in the most general terms, the detectives readily agreed to absent themselves for the required period. Where might they install themselves? 'My bathroom,' I said. 'It has a small library attached, with a desk, a worktable, leather chairs and sofa, a billiard table, a large-screen cable television set, and a bar. Since you have not yet had your luncheon, you may wish to order whatever you like from the kitchen.'

Five minutes later, bottles, glasses, hats, and mounds of paper arranged on the bathroom table, the bucket of beer beside it, I exited through the concealed door as Mr Clubb ordered up from my doubtless astounded chef a meal of chicken wings, french fries, onion rings, and T-bone steaks, medium well. With plenty of time to spare, I immersed myself again in details, only to be brought up short by the recognition that I was humming, none too quietly, that most innocent of hymns, 'Jesus Loves Me'. Then, precisely at the appointed hour, Mrs Rampage informed me of the arrival of my client and his associates, and I bade her bring them through.

A sly, slow-moving whale encased in an exquisite double-breasted black pinstripe, Mr 'This Building Is Condemned' C—— advanced into my office with his customary hauteur and offered me the customary nod of the head while his three 'associates' formed a human breakwater in the center of the room. Regal to the core, he affected not to notice Mrs Rampage sliding a black leather chair out of the middle distance and around the side of the desk until it was in position, at which point he sat himself in it without looking down. Then he inclined his slablike head and raised a small, pallid hand. One of the 'associates' promptly moved to hold the door for Mrs Rampage's departure. At this signal, I sat down, and the two remaining henchmen separated themselves by a distance of perhaps eight feet. The third closed the door and stationed himself by his general's right shoulder. These formalities completed, my client shifted his close-set obsidian eyes to mine and said, 'You well?'

'Very well, thank you,' I replied, according to ancient formula. 'And you?'

'Good,' he said. 'But things could be better.' This, too, followed long-established formula. His next words were a startling deviation. He took in the stationary cloud and the corpse of Montfort de M——'s cigar rising like a monolith from the reef of cigarette butts in the crystal shell and, with the first genuine smile I had ever seen on his pockmarked, small-featured face, said, 'I can't believe it, but one thing just got better already. You eased up on the stupid no-smoking rule which is poisoning this city, good for you.'

'It seemed,' I said, 'a concrete way in which to demonstrate our appreciation for the smokers among those clients we most respect.' When dealing with the cryptic gentlemen, one must not fail to offer intervallic allusions to the spontaneous respect in which they are held.

'Deacon,' he said, employing the sobriquet he had given me on our first meeting, 'you being one of a kind at your job, the respect you speak of is mutual, and besides that, all surprises should be as pleasant as this here.' With that, he snapped his fingers at the laden shell, and as he produced a ridged case similar to but more capacious than Mr Montfort de M——'s, the man at his shoulder whisked the impromptu ashtray from the desk, deposited its contents in the *poubelle*, and repositioned it at a point on the desk precisely equidistant from us. My client opened the case to expose the six cylinders contained within, removed one, and proffered the remaining five to me. 'Be my guest, Deacon,' he said. 'Money can't buy better Havanas.'

'Your gesture is much appreciated,' I said. 'However, with all due respect, at the moment I shall choose not to partake.'

Distinct as a scar, a vertical crease of displeasure appeared on my client's forehead, and the ridged case and its five inhabitants advanced an inch toward my nose. 'Deacon, you want me to smoke alone?' asked Mr 'This Building Is Condemned' C——. 'This stuff, if you were ever lucky enough to find it at your local cigar store, which that lucky believe me you wouldn't be, is the best of of the best, straight from me to you as what you could term a symbol of the cooperation and respect between us, and at the commencement of our business today it would please me greatly if you would do me the honor of joining me in a smoke.'

As they say or, more accurately, as they used to say, needs must when the devil drives, or words to that effect. 'Forgive me,' I said, and drew one of the fecal things from the case. 'I assure you, the honor is all mine.'

Mr 'This Building Is Condemned' C—— snipped the rounded end from his cigar, plugged the remainder in the center of his mouth, then subjected mine to the same operation. His henchman proffered a lighter, and Mr 'This Building Is Condemned' C—— bent forward and surrounded himself with clouds of smoke, in the manner of Bela Lugosi materializing before the brides of Dracula. The henchman moved the flame toward me, and for the first time in my life I inserted into my mouth an object that seemed as large around as the handle of a baseball bat, brought it to the dancing flame, and drew in that burning smoke from which so many other men before me had derived pleasure.

Legend and common sense alike dictated that I should sputter and cough in an attempt to rid myself of the noxious substance. Nausea was in the cards, also dizziness. It is true that I suffered a degree of initial discomfort, as if my tongue had been lightly singed or seared, and the sheer unfamiliarity of the experience – the thickness of the tobacco tube, the texture of the smoke, as dense as chocolate – led me to fear for my well-being. Yet, despite the not altogether unpleasant tingling on the upper surface of my tongue, I expelled my first mouthful of cigar smoke with the sense of having sampled a taste every bit as delightful as the first sip of a properly made martini. The thug whisked away the flame, and I drew in another mouthful, leaned back, and released a wondrous quantity of smoke. Of a surprising smoothness, in some sense almost cool rather than hot, the delightful taste defined itself as heather, loam, morel mushrooms, venison, and some distinctive spice akin to coriander. I repeated the process, with results even more pleasurable – this time I tasted a hint of black butter sauce. 'I can truthfully say,' I told my client, 'that never have I met a cigar as fine as this one.'

'You bet you haven't,' said Mr 'This Building Is Condemned' C——, and on the spot presented me with three more of the precious objects. With that, we turned to the tidal waves of cash and the interlocking corporate shells, each protecting another series of interconnected shells that concealed yet another, like Chinese boxes.

The cryptic gentlemen one and all appreciated certain ceremonies, such as the appearance of espresso coffee in thimble-sized porcelain cups and an accompanying assortment of *biscotti* at the halfway point of our meditations. Matters of business being forbidden while coffee and cookies were dispatched, the conversation generally turned to the conundrums posed by family life. Since I had no family to speak of, and, like most of his kind, Mr 'This Building Is Condemned' C—— was richly endowed with grandparents, parents, uncles, aunts, sons, daughters, nephews, nieces, and grandchildren, these remarks on the genealogical tapestry tended to be monologic in nature, my role in them limited to nods and grunts. Required as they were more often by the business of the cryptic gentlemen than was the case in other trades or professions, funerals were also an ongoing topic. Taking tiny sips of his espresso and equally maidenish nibbles from his favorite sweetmeats (Hydrox and Milano), my client favored me with the expected praises of his son, Arthur Jr (Harvard graduate school, English lit.), lamentations over his daughter, Fidelia (thrice-married, never wisely), hymns to his grandchildren (Cyrus, Thor, and Hermione, respectively the genius, the dreamer, and the despot), and then proceeded to link his two unfailing themes by recalling the unhappy behavior of Arthur Jr at the funeral of my client's uncle and a principal figure in his family's rise to an imperial eminence, Mr Vincente 'Waffles' C——.

The anecdote called for the beheading and ignition of another magnificent stogie, and I greedily followed suit.

'Arthur Jr's got his head screwed on right, and he's got the right kinda family values,' said my client. 'Straight A's all through school, married a stand-up dame with money of her own, three great kids, makes a man proud. Hard worker. Got his head in a book morning to night, human-encyclopedia-type guy, up there at Harvard, those professors, they love him. Kid knows how you're supposed to act, right?'

I nodded and filled my mouth with another fragrant draft.

'So he comes to my uncle Vincente's funeral all by himself, which troubles me. On top of it doesn't show the proper respect to old Waffles, who was one hell of a man, there's guys still pissing blood on account of they looked at him wrong forty years ago, on top of that, I don't have the good feeling I get from taking his family around to my friends and associates and saying, So look here, this here is Arthur Jr, my Harvard guy, plus his wife, Hunter, whose ancestors I think got here even before that rabble on the *Mayflower*, plus his three kids – Cyrus, little bastard's even smarter than his dad, Thor, the one's got his head in the clouds, which is okay because we need people like that, too, and Hermione, who you can tell just by looking at her she's mean as a snake and is gonna wind up running the world someday. So I say, Arthur Jr, what the hell happened, everybody else get killed in a train wreck or something? He says, No, Dad, they just didn't wanna come, these big family funerals, they make 'em feel funny, they don't like having their pictures taken so they show up on the six o'clock news. Didn't wanna come, I say back, what kinda shit is that, you shoulda made 'em come, and if anyone took their pictures when they didn't want, we can take care of that, no trouble at all. I go on like this, I even say, What good is Harvard and all those books if they don't make you any smarter than this, and finally Arthur Jr's mother tells me, Put a cork in it, you're not exactly helping the situation here.

'So what happens then? Insteada being smart like I should, I go nuts on account of I'm the guy who pays the bills, that Harvard up there pulls in the money better than any casino I ever saw, and you wanna find a real good criminal, get some Boston WASP in a bow tie, and all of a sudden nobody listens to me! I'm seeing red in a big way here, Deacon, this is my uncle Vincente's funeral, and insteada backing me up his mother is telling me I'm not *helping*. I yell, You wanna help? Go up there and bring back his wife and kids, or I'll send Carlo and Tommy to do it. All of a sudden I'm so mad I'm thinking these people are insulting me, how can they think they can get away with that, people who insult me don't do it twice – and then I hear what I'm thinking, and I do what she said and put a cork in it, but it's too late, I went way over the top and we all know it.

'Arthur Jr takes off, and his mother won't talk to me for the whole rest of the day. Only thing I'm happy about is I didn't blow up where anyone else could see it. Deacon, I know you're the type guy wouldn't dream of threatening his family, but if the time ever comes, do yourself a favor and light up a Havana instead.'

'I'm sure that is excellent advice,' I said.

'Anyhow, you know what they say, it only hurts for a little while, which is true as far as it goes, and I calmed down. Uncle Vincente's funeral was beautiful. You woulda thought the Pope died. When the people are going out to the limousines, Arthur Jr is sitting in a chair at the back of the church reading a book. Put that in your pocket, I say, wanna do homework, do it in the car. He tells me it isn't homework, but he puts it in his pocket and we go out to the cemetery. His mother looks out the window the whole time we're driving to the cemetery, and the kid starts reading again. So I ask what the hell is it, this book he can't put down? He tells me but it's like he's speaking some foreign language, only word I understand is "the", which happens a lot when your kid reads a lot of fancy books, half the titles make no sense to an ordinary person. Okay, we're out there in Queens, goddamn graveyard the size of Newark, FBI and reporters all over the place, and I'm thinking maybe Arthur Jr wasn't so wrong after all, Hunter probably hates having the FBI take her picture, and besides that little Hermione probably woulda mugged one of 'em and stole his wallet. So I tell Arthur Jr I'm sorry about what happened. I didn't really think you were going to put me in the same grave as Uncle Waffles, he says, the Harvard smart-ass. When it's all over, we get back in the car, and out comes the book again. We get home, and he disappears. We have a lot of people over, food, wine, politicians, old-timers from Brooklyn, Chicago people, Detroit people, LA people, movie directors, cops, actors I never heard of, priests, bishops, the guy from the Cardinal. Everybody's asking me, Where's Arthur Jr? I go upstairs to find out. He's in his old room, and he's still reading that book. I say, Arthur Jr, people are asking about you, I think it would be nice if you mingled with our guests. I'll be right down, he says, I just finished what I was reading. Here, take a look, you might enjoy it. He gives me the book and goes out of the room. So I'm wondering – what the hell *is* this, anyhow? I take it into the bedroom, toss it on the table. About ten-thirty, eleven, everybody's gone, kid's on the shuttle back to Boston, house is cleaned up, enough food in the refrigerator to feed the whole bunch all over again, I go up to bed. Arthur Jr's mother still isn't talking to me, so I get in and pick up the book. Herman Melville is the name of the guy who wrote it. The story the kid was reading is called "Bartleby the Scrivener". I decide I'll try it. What the hell, right? You're an educated guy, you ever read that story?'

'A long time ago,' I said. 'A bit . . . *odd*, isn't it?'

'Odd? That's the most terrible story I ever read in my whole life! This dud gets a job in a law office and decides he doesn't want to work. Does he get fired? He does not. This is a story? You hire a guy who won't do the job, what do you do, pamper the asshole? At the end, the dud ups and disappears and you find out he used to work in the dead-letter office. Is there a point here? The next day I call up Arthur Jr, say could he explain to me please what the hell that story is supposed to mean? Dad, he says, it means what it says. Deacon, I just about pulled the plug on Harvard right then and there. I never went to any college, but I do know that nothing means what it says, not on this planet.'

353

This reflection was accurate when applied to the documents on my desk, for each had been encoded in a systematic fashion that rendered their literal contents deliberately misleading. Another code had informed both of my recent conversations with Marguerite. 'Fiction is best left to real life,' I said.

'Someone shoulda told that to Herman Melville,' said Mr Arthur 'This Building Is Condemned' C——.

Mrs Rampage buzzed me to advise that I was running behind schedule and inquire about removing the coffee things. I invited her to gather up the debris. A door behind me opened, and I assumed that my secretary had responded to my request with an alacrity remarkable even in her. The first sign of my error was the behavior of the three other men in the room, until this moment no more animated than marble statues. The thug at my client's side stepped forward to stand behind me, and his fellows moved to the front of my desk. 'What the hell is this shit?' said the client, unable, because of the man in front of him, to see Mr Clubb and Mr Cuff. Holding a pad bearing one of his many lists, Mr Clubb gazed in mild surprise at the giants flanking my desk and said, 'I apologize for the intrusion, sir, but our understanding was that your appointment would be over in an hour, and by my simple way of reckoning you should be free to answer a query as to steam irons.'

'What the hell *is* this shit?' said my client, repeating his original question with a slight tonal variation expressive of gathering dismay.

I attempted to salvage matters. 'Please allow me to explain the interruption. I have employed these men as consultants, and as they prefer to work in my office, a condition I of course could not permit during our business meeting, I temporarily relocated them in my washroom, outfitted with a library adequate to their needs.'

'Fit for a king, in my opinion,' said Mr Clubb.

At that moment the other door into my office, to the left of my desk, opened to admit Mrs Rampage, and my client's guardians inserted their hands into their suit jackets and separated with the speed and precision of a dance team.

'Oh, my,' said Mrs Rampage. '*Excuse* me. Should I come back later?'

'Not on your life, my darling,' said Mr Clubb. 'Temporary misunderstanding of the false-alarm sort. Please allow us to enjoy the delightful spectacle of your feminine charms.'

Before my wondering eyes, Mrs Rampage curtsied and hastened to my desk to gather up the wreckage.

I looked toward my client and observed a detail of striking peculiarity, that although his half-consumed cigar remained between his lips, four inches of cylindrical ash had deposited a gray smear on his necktie before coming to rest on the shelf of his belly. He was staring straight ahead with eyes grown to the size of quarters. His face had become the color of raw piecrust.

Mr Clubb said, 'Respectful greetings, sir.'

The client gargled and turned upon me a look of unvarnished horror.

Mr Clubb said, 'Apologies to all.' Mrs Rampage had already bolted. From unseen regions came the sound of a closing door.

Mr 'This Building Is Condemned' C—— blinked twice, bringing his eyes to something like their normal dimensions. With an uncertain hand but gently, as if it were a tiny but much-loved baby, he placed his cigar in the crystal shell. He cleared his throat; he looked at the ceiling. 'Deacon,' he said, gazing upward. 'Gotta run. My next appointment musta slipped my mind. What happens when you start to gab. I'll be in touch.' He stood, dislodging the ashen cylinder to the carpet, and motioned his goons to the outer office.

4

Of course at the earliest opportunity I interrogated my detectives about this turn of events, and while they moved their mountains of paper, bottles, buckets, glasses, hand-drawn maps, and other impedimenta back behind the screen, I continued the questioning. No, they averred, the gentleman at my desk was not a gentleman whom previously they had been privileged to look upon, acquaint themselves with, or encounter in any way whatsoever. They had never been employed in any capacity by the gentleman. Mr Clubb observed that the unknown gentleman had been wearing a conspicuously handsome and well-tailored suit.

'That is his custom,' I said.

'And I believe he smokes, sir, a noble high order of cigar,' said Mr Clubb with a glance at my breast pocket. 'Which would be the sort of item customarily beyond the dreams of honest laborers such as ourselves.'

'I trust that you will permit me,' I said with a sigh, 'to offer you the pleasure of two of the same.' No sooner had the offer been accepted, the barnies back behind their screen, than I buzzed Mrs Rampage with the request to summon by instant delivery from the most distinguished cigar merchant in the city a box of his finest. 'Good for you, boss!' whooped the new Mrs Rampage.

I spent the remainder of the afternoon brooding upon the reaction of Mr Arthur 'This Building Is Condemned' C—— to my 'consultants'. I could not but imagine that his hasty departure boded ill for our relationship. I had seen terror on his face, and he knew that *I* knew what I had seen. An understanding of this sort is fatal to that nuance-play critical alike to high-level churchmen and their outlaw counterparts, and I had to confront the possibility that my client's departure had been of a permanent nature. Where Mr 'This Building Is Condemned' C—— went, his colleagues of lesser rank, Mr Tommy 'I Believe in Rainbows' B——, Mr Anthony 'Moonlight Becomes You' M——, Mr Bobby 'Total Eclipse' G——, and their fellow archbishops, cardinals, and papal nuncios would assuredly follow. Before the close of the day, I would send a comforting fax informing Mr 'This Building Is Condemned' C—— that the consultants had been summarily released from employment. I would be telling only a 'white' or provisional untruth, for Mr Clubb and Mr Cuff's task would surely be completed long before my client's return. All was in order, all was in train, and as if to put the seal upon the matter, Mrs Rampage buzzed to inquire if she might come through with the box of cigars. Speaking in a breathy timbre I had never before heard from anyone save Marguerite in the earliest, most blissful days of our marriage, Mrs Rampage added that she had some surprises for me, too. 'By this point,' I said, 'I expect no less.' Mrs Rampage *giggled*.

The surprises, in the event, were of a reassuring practicality. The good woman had wisely sought the advice of Mr Montfort de M——, who, after recommending a suitably aristocratic cigar emporium and a favorite cigar, had purchased for me a rosewood humidor, a double-bladed cigar cutter, and a lighter of antique design. As soon as Mrs Rampage had been instructed to compose a note of gratitude embellished in whatever fashion she saw fit, I arrayed all but one of the cigars in the humidor, decapitated that one, and set it alight. Beneath a faint touch of fruitiness like the aroma of a blossoming pear tree, I met in successive layers the tastes of black olives, aged Gouda cheese, pine needles, new leather, miso soup, either sorghum or brown sugar, burning peat, library paste, and myrtle leaves. The long finish intriguingly combined Bible paper and sunflower seeds. Mr Montfort de M—— had chosen well, though I regretted the absence of black butter sauce.

Feeling comradely, I strolled across my office toward

the merriment emanating from the far side of the screen. A superior cigar should be complemented by a worthy liquor, and in the light of what was to transpire during the evening I considered a snifter of Mr Clubb's Bombay gin not inappropriate. 'Fellows,' I said, tactfully announcing my presence, 'are preparations nearly completed?'

'That, sir, they are,' said one or the other of the pair.

'Welcome news,' I said, and stepped around the screen. 'But I must be assured –'

It was as if the detritus of New York City's half dozen filthiest living quarters had been scooped up, shaken, and dumped into my office. Heaps of ash, bottles, shoals of papers, books with stained covers and broken spines, battered furniture, broken glass, refuse I could not identify, refuse I could not even *see*, undulated from the base of the screen, around and over the table, heaping itself into landfill-like piles here and there, and washed against the plate-glass windows. A jagged, five-foot opening gaped in a smashed pane. Their derbies perched on their heads, islanded in their chairs, Mr Clubb and Mr Cuff leaned back, feet up on what must have been the table.

'You'll join us in a drink, sir,' said Mr Clubb, 'by way of wishing us success and adding to the pleasure of that handsome smoke.' He extended a stout leg and kicked rubble from a chair. I sat down. Mr Clubb plucked an unclean glass from the morass and filled it with Dutch gin, or *jenever*, from one of the minaret-shaped stone flagons I had observed upon my infrequent layovers in Amsterdam, the Netherlands. Mrs Rampage had been variously employed during the barnies' sequestration. Then I wondered if Mrs Rampage might not have shown signs of intoxication during our last encounter.

'I thought you drank Bombay,' I said.

'Variety is, as they say, life's condiment,' said Mr Clubb, and handed me the glass.

I said, 'You have made yourselves quite at home.'

'I thank you for your restraint,' said Mr Clubb. 'In which sentiment my partner agrees, am I correct, Mr Cuff?'

'Entirely,' said Mr Cuff. 'But I wager you a C-note to a see-gar that a word or two of explanation is in order.'

'How right that man is,' said Mr Clubb. 'He has a genius for the truth I have never known to fail him. Sir, you enter our work space to come upon the slovenly, the careless, the unseemly, and your response, which we comprehend in every particular, is to recoil. My wish is that you take a moment to remember these two essentials: one, we have, as aforesaid, our methods, which are ours alone, and two, having appeared fresh on the scene, you see it worse than it is. By morning tomorrow, the cleaning staff shall have done its work.'

'I suppose you have been Visualizing.' I quaffed *jenever*.

'Mr Cuff and I,' he said, 'prefer to minimize the risk of accidents, surprises, and such by the method of rehearsing our, as you might say, performances. These poor sticks, sir, are easily replaced, but our work once under way demands completion and cannot be duplicated, redone, or undone.'

I recalled the all-important guarantee. 'I remember your words,' I said, 'and I must be assured that you remember mine. I did not request termination. During the course of the day my feelings on the matter have intensified. Termination, if by that term you meant –'

'Termination is termination,' said Mr Clubb.

'*Ex*termination,' I said. 'Cessation of life due to external forces. It is not my wish, it is unacceptable, and I have even been thinking that I overstated the degree of physical punishment appropriate in this matter.'

'"Appropriate"?' said Mr Clubb. 'When it comes to desire, "appropriate" is a concept without meaning. In the sacred realm of desire, "appropriate", being meaningless, does not exist. We speak of your inmost wishes, sir, and desire is an extremely *thingy* sort of thing.'

I looked at the hole in the window, the broken bits of furniture and ruined books. 'I think,' I said, 'that permanent injury is all I wish. Something on the order of blindness or the loss of a hand.'

Mr Clubb favored me with a glance of humorous irony. 'It goes, sir, as it goes, which brings to mind that we have but an hour more, a period of time to be splendidly improved by a superior Double Corona such as the fine example in your hand.'

'Forgive me,' I said. 'And might I then request . . . ?' I extended the nearly empty glass, and Mr Clubb refilled it. Each received a cigar, and I lingered at my desk for the required term, sipping *jenever* and pretending to work until I heard sounds of movement. Mr Clubb and Mr Cuff approached. 'So you are off,' I said.

'It is, sir, to be a long and busy night,' said Mr Clubb. 'If you take my meaning.'

With a sigh I opened the humidor. They reached in, snatched a handful of cigars apiece, and deployed them into various pockets. 'Details at eleven,' said Mr Clubb.

A few seconds after their departure, Mrs Rampage informed me that she would be bringing through a fax communication just received.

The fax had been sent me by Chartwell, Munster, and Stout, a legal firm with but a single client, Mr Arthur 'This Building Is Condemned' C——. Chartwell, Munster, and Stout regretted the necessity to inform me that their client wished to seek advice other than my own in his financial affairs. A sheaf of documents binding me to silence as to all matters concerning the client would arrive for my signature the following day. All records, papers, computer disks, and other data were to be referred posthaste to their offices. I had forgotten to send my intended note of client-saving reassurance.

5

What an abyss of shame I must now describe, at every turn what humiliation. It was at most five minutes past six p.m. when I learned of the desertion of my most valuable client, a turn of events certain to lead to the loss of his cryptic fellows and some forty percent of our annual business. Gloomily I consumed my glass of Dutch gin without noticing that I had already far exceeded my tolerance. I ventured behind the screen and succeeded in unearthing another stone flagon, poured another measure, and gulped it down while attempting to demonstrate numerically that (a) the anticipated drop in annual profit could not be as severe as feared and (b) if it were, the business could continue as before, without reductions in salary, staff, or benefits. Despite ingenious feats of juggling, the numbers denied (a) and mocked (b), suggesting that I should be fortunate to retain, not lose, forty percent of present business. I lowered my head to the desk and tried to regulate my breathing. When I heard myself rendering an off-key version of 'Abide with Me', I acknowledged that it was time to go home, got to my feet, and made the unfortunate decision to exit through the general offices on the theory that a survey of my presumably empty realm might suggest the sites of pending amputations.

I tucked the flagon under my elbow, pocketed the five or six cigars remaining in the humidor, and passed through Mrs Rampage's chamber. Hearing the abrasive music of the cleaners' radios, I moved with exaggerated care down the corridor, darkened but for the light spilling from an open door thirty feet before me. Now and again, finding myself unable to avoid striking my shoulder against the wall, I took a medicinal swallow of *jenever*. I drew up to the open door and realized that I had come to Gilligan's quarters. The abrasive music emanated from his sound system. *We'll get rid of that, for starters*, I said to myself, and straightened up for a dignified navigation past his doorway. At the crucial moment I glanced within to observe my jacketless junior partner sprawled, tie undone, on his sofa beside a scrawny ruffian with a quiff of lime-green hair and attired for some reason in a skintight costume involving zebra stripes and many chains and zippers. Disreputable creatures male and female occupied themselves in the background. Gilligan shifted his head, began to smile, and at the sight of me turned to stone.

'Calm down, Gilligan,' I said, striving for an impression of sober paternal authority. I had recalled that my junior had scheduled a late appointment with his most successful musician, a singer whose band sold millions of records year in and year out despite the absurdity of their name, the Dog Turds or the Rectal Valves, something of that sort. My calculations had indicated that Gilligan's client, whose name I recalled as Cyril Futch, would soon become crucial to the maintenance of my firm, and as the beaky little rooster coldly took me in I thought to impress upon him the regard in which he was held by his chosen financial planning institution. 'There is, I assure you, no need for alarm, no, certainly not, and in fact, Gilligan, you know, I should be honored to seize this opportunity of making the acquaintance of your guest, whom it is our pleasure to assist and advise and whatever.'

Gilligan reverted to flesh and blood during the course of this utterance, which I delivered gravely, taking care to enunciate each syllable clearly in spite of the difficulty I was having with my tongue. He noted the bottle nestled into my elbow and the lighted cigar in the fingers of my right hand, a matter of which until that moment I had been imperfectly aware. 'Hey, I guess the smoking lamp is lit,' I said. 'Stupid rule anyhow. How about a little drink on the boss?'

Gilligan lurched to his feet and came reeling toward me.

All that followed is a montage of discontinuous imagery. I recall Cyril Futch propping me up as I communicated our devotion to the safeguarding of his wealth, also his dogged insistence that his name was actually Simon Gulch or Sidney Much or something similar before he sent me toppling onto the sofa; I see an odd little fellow with a tattooed head and a name like Pus (there was a person named Pus in attendance, though he may not have been the one) accepting one of my cigars and eating it; I remember inhaling from smirking Gilligan's cigarette and drinking from a bottle with a small white worm lying dead at its bottom and snuffling up a white powder recommended by a female Turd or Valve; I remember singing 'The Old Rugged Cross' in a state of partial undress. I told a face brilliantly lacquered with makeup that I was 'getting a feel' for 'this music'. A female Turd or Valve, not the one who had recommended the powder but one in a permanent state of hilarity I found endearing, assisted me into my limousine and on the homeward journey experimented with its many buttons and controls. Atop the town-house steps, she removed the key from my fumbling hand gleefully to insert it into the lock. The rest is welcome darkness.

6

A form of consciousness returned with a slap to my face, the muffled screams of the woman beside me, a bowler-hatted head thrusting into view and growling, 'The shower for you, you damned idiot.' As a second assailant whisked her away, the woman, whom I thought to be Marguerite, wailed. I struggled against the man gripping my shoulders, and he squeezed the nape of my neck.

When next I opened my eyes, I was naked and quivering beneath an onslaught of cold water within the marble confines of my shower cabinet. Charlie-Charlie Rackett leaned against the open door of the cabinet and regarded me with ill-disguised impatience. 'I'm freezing, Charlie-Charlie,' I said. 'Turn off the water.'

Charlie-Charlie thrust an arm into the cabinet and became Mr Clubb. 'I'll warm it up, but I want you sober,' he said. I drew myself up into a ball.

Then I was on my feet and moaning while I massaged my forehead. 'Bath time all done now,' called Mr Clubb. 'Turn off the wa-wa.' I did as instructed. The door opened, and a bath towel unfurled over my left shoulder.

Side by side on the bedroom sofa and dimly illuminated by the lamp, Mr Clubb and Mr Cuff observed my progress toward the bed. A black leather satchel stood on the floor between them. 'Gentlemen,' I said, 'although I cannot presently find words to account for the condition in which you found me, I trust that your good nature will enable you to overlook . . . or ignore . . . whatever it was that I must have done . . . I cannot quite recall the circumstances.'

'The young woman has been dispatched,' said Mr Clubb, 'and you need never fear any trouble from that direction, sir.'

'The young woman?' I remembered a hyperactive figure playing with the controls in the back of the limousine. A fragmentary memory of the scene in Gilligan's office returned to me, and I moaned aloud.

'None too clean, but pretty enough in a ragamuffin way,' said Mr Clubb. 'The type denied a proper education in social graces. Rough about the edges. Intemperate in language. A stranger to discipline.'

I groaned – to have introduced such a creature to my house!

'A stranger to honesty, too, sir, if you'll permit me,' said Mr Cuff. 'It's addiction turns them into thieves. Give them half a chance, they'll steal the brass handles off their mothers' coffins.'

'Addiction?' I said. 'Addiction to what?'

'Everything, from the look of the bint,' said Mr Cuff. 'Before Mr Clubb and I sent her on her way, we retrieved these items doubtless belonging to you, sir.' While walking toward me he removed from his pockets the following articles: my wristwatch, gold cuff links, wallet, the lighter of antique design given me by Mr Montfort de M——, likewise the cigar cutter and the last of the cigars I had purchased that day. 'I thank you most gratefully,' I said, slipping the watch on my wrist and all else save the cigar into the pockets of my robe. It was, I noted, just past four o'clock in the morning. The cigar I handed back to him with the words, 'Please accept this as a token of my gratitude.'

'Gratefully accepted,' he said. Mr Cuff bit off the end, spat it onto the carpet, and set the cigar alight, producing a nauseating quantity of fumes.

'Perhaps,' I said, 'we might postpone our discussion until I have had time to recover from my ill-advised behavior. Let us reconvene at . . .' A short period was spent pressing my hands to my eyes while rocking back and forth. 'Four this afternoon?'

'Everything in its own time is a principle we hold dear,' said Mr Clubb. 'And this is the time for you to down aspirin and Alka-Seltzer, and for your loyal assistants to relish the hearty breakfasts the thought of which sets our stomachs to growling. A man of stature and accomplishment like yourself ought to be able to overcome the effects of too much booze and attend to business, on top of the simple matter of getting his flunkies out of bed so they can whip up the bacon and eggs.'

'Because a man such as that, sir, keeps ever in mind that business faces the task at hand, no matter how lousy it may be,' said Mr Cuff.

'The old world is in flames,' said Mr Clubb, 'and the new one is just being born. Pick up the phone.'

'All right,' I said, 'but Mr Moncrieff is going to *hate* this. He worked for the Duke of Denbigh, and he's a terrible snob.'

'All butlers are snobs,' said Mr Clubb. 'Three fried eggs apiece, likewise six rashers of bacon, home fries, toast, hot coffee, and for the sake of digestion a bottle of your best cognac.'

Mr Moncrieff picked up his telephone, listened to my orders, and informed me in a small, cold voice that he would speak to the cook. 'Would this repast be for the young lady and yourself, sir?'

With a wave of guilty shame that intensified my nausea, I realized that Mr Moncrieff had observed my unsuitable young companion accompanying me upstairs to the bedroom. 'No, it would not,' I said. 'The young lady, a client of mine, was kind enough to assist me when I was taken ill. The meal is for two male guests.' Unwelcome memory returned the spectacle of a scrawny girl pulling my ears and screeching that a useless old fart like me didn't deserve her band's business.

'The phone,' said Mr Clubb. Dazedly I extended the receiver.

'Moncrieff, old man,' he said, 'amazing good luck, running into you again. Do you remember that trouble the Duke had with Colonel Fletcher and the diary? . . . Yes, this is Mr Clubb, and it's delightful to hear your voice again . . . He's here, too, couldn't do anything without him . . . I'll tell him . . . Much the way things went with the Duke, yes, and we'll need the usual supplies . . . Glad to hear it . . . The dining room in half an hour.' He handed the telephone back to me and said to Mr Cuff, 'He's looking forward to the pinochle, and there's a first-rate Pétrus in the cellar he knows you're going to enjoy.'

I had purchased six cases of 1928 Château Pétrus at an auction some years before and was holding it while its already immense value doubled, then tripled, until perhaps a decade hence, when I would sell it for ten times its original cost.

'A good drop of wine sets a man right up,' said Mr Cuff. 'Stuff was meant to be drunk, wasn't it?'

'You know Mr Moncrieff?' I asked. 'You worked for the Duke?'

'We ply our humble trade irrespective of nationality and borders,' said Mr Clubb. 'Go where we are needed, is our motto. We have fond memories of the good old Duke, who showed himself to be quite a fun-loving, spirited fellow, sir, once you got past the crust, as it were. Generous, too.'

'He gave until it hurt,' said Mr Cuff. 'The old gentleman cried like a baby when we left.'

'Cried a good deal before that, too,' said Mr Clubb. 'In our experience, high-spirited fellows spend a deal more tears than your gloomy customers.'

'I do not suppose you shall see any tears from me,' I said. The brief look that passed between them reminded me of the complicitous glance I had once seen fly like a live spark between two of their New Covenant forbears, one gripping the hind legs of a pig, the other its front legs and a knife, in the moment before the knife opened the pig's throat and an arc of blood threw itself high into the air. 'I shall heed your advice,' I said, 'and locate my analgesics.' I got on my feet and moved slowly to the bathroom. 'As a matter of curiosity,' I said, 'might I ask if you have classified me into the high-spirited category, or into the other?'

'You are a man of middling spirit,' said Mr Clubb. I opened my mouth to protest, and he went on, 'But something may be made of you yet.'

I disappeared into the bathroom. *I have endured these moon-faced yokels long enough*, I told myself. *Hear their story, feed the bastards, then kick them out.*

In a condition more nearly approaching my usual self,

I brushed my teeth and splashed water on my face before returning to the bedroom. I placed myself with a reasonable degree of executive command in a wing chair, folded my pin-striped robe about me, inserted my feet into velvet slippers, and said, 'Things got a bit out of hand, and I thank you for dealing with my young client, a person with whom in spite of appearances I have a professional relationship only. Now let us turn to our real business. I trust you found my wife and Leeson at Green Chimneys. Please give me an account of what followed.'

'Things got a bit out of hand,' said Mr Clubb. 'Which is a way of describing something that can happen to us all, and for which no one can be blamed. Especially Mr Cuff and myself, who are always careful to say right smack at the beginning, as we did with you, sir, what ought to be so obvious as to not need saying at all, that our work brings about permanent changes which can never be undone. Especially in the cases when we specify a time to make our initial report and the client disappoints us at the said time. When we are let down by our client, we must go forward and complete the job to our highest standards with no rancor or ill will, knowing that there are many reasonable explanations of a man's inability to get to a telephone.'

'I don't know what you mean by this self-serving double-talk,' I said. 'We had no arrangement of that sort, and your effrontery forces me to conclude that you failed in your task.'

Mr Clubb gave me the grimmest possible suggestion of a smile. 'One of the reasons for a man's failure to get to a telephone is a lapse of memory. You have forgotten my informing you that I would give you my initial report at eleven. At precisely eleven o'clock I called, to no avail. I waited through twenty rings, sir, before I abandoned the effort. If I had waited through a hundred, sir, the result would have been the same, on account of your decision to put yourself into a state where you would have had trouble remembering your own name.'

'That is a blatant lie,' I said, then remembered. The fellow had in fact mentioned in passing something about reporting to me at that hour, which must have been approximately the time when I was regaling the Turds or Valves with 'The Old Rugged Cross'. My face grew pink. 'Forgive me,' I said. 'I am in error, it is just as you say.'

'A manly admission, sir, but as for forgiveness, we extended that quantity from the git-go,' said Mr Clubb. 'We are your servants, and your wishes are our sacred charge.'

'That's the whole ball of wax in a nutshell,' said Mr Cuff, giving a fond glance to the final inch of his cigar. He dropped the stub onto my carpet and ground it beneath his shoe. 'Food and drink to the fibers, sir,' he said.

'Speaking of which,' said Mr Clubb. 'We will continue our report in the dining room, so as to dig into the feast ordered up by that wondrous villain Reggie Moncrieff.'

Until that moment it had never quite occurred to me that my butler possessed, like other men, a Christian name.

7

'A great design directs us,' said Mr Clubb, expelling morsels of his cud. 'We poor wanderers, you and me and Mr Cuff and the milkman too, only see the little portion right in front of us. Half the time we don't even see that in the right way. For sure we don't have a Chinaman's chance of understanding it. But the design is ever-present, sir, a truth I bring to your attention for the sake of the comfort in it. Toast, Mr Cuff.'

'Comfort is a matter cherished by all parts of a man,' said Mr Cuff, handing his partner the toast rack. 'Most particularly that part known as his soul, which feeds upon the nutrient adversity.'

I was seated at the head of the table, flanked by Mr Clubb and Mr Cuff. The salvers and tureens before us overflowed, for Mr Moncrieff, who after embracing each barnie in turn and entering into a kind of conference or huddle, had summoned from the kitchen a banquet far surpassing their requests. Besides several dozen eggs and perhaps two packages of bacon, he had arranged a mixed grill of kidneys, lambs' livers and lamb chops, and strip steaks, as well as vats of oatmeal and a pasty concoction he described as 'kedgeree – as the old Duke fancied it'.

Sickened by the odors of the food, also by the mush visible in my companions' mouths, I tried again to extract their report. 'I don't believe in the grand design,' I said, 'and I already face more adversity than my soul finds useful. Tell me what happened at the house.'

'No mere house, sir,' said Mr Clubb. 'Even as we approached along —— Lane, Mr Cuff and I could not fail to respond to its magnificence.'

'Were my drawings of use?' I asked.

'Invaluable.' Mr Clubb speared a lamb chop and raised it to his mouth. 'We proceeded through the rear door into your spacious kitchen or scullery. Wherein we observed evidence of two persons having enjoyed a dinner enhanced by a fine wine and finished with a noble champagne.'

'Aha,' I said.

'By means of your guidance, Mr Cuff and I located the lovely staircase and made our way to the lady's chamber. We effected an entry of the most praiseworthy silence, if I may say so.'

'That entry was worth a medal,' said Mr Cuff.

'Two figures lay slumbering upon the bed. In a blamelessly professional manner we approached, Mr Cuff on one side, I on the other. In the fashion your client of this morning called the whopbopaloobop, we rendered the parties in question even more unconscious than previous, thereby giving ourselves a good fifteen minutes for the disposition of instruments. We take pride in being careful workers, sir, and like all honest craftsmen we respect our tools. We bound and gagged both parties in timely fashion. Is the male party distinguished by an athletic past?' Alight with barnieish glee, Mr Clubb raised his eyebrows and washed down the last of his chop with a mouthful of cognac.

'Not to my knowledge,' I said. 'I believe he plays a little racquetball and squash, that kind of thing.'

He and Mr Cuff experienced a moment of mirth. 'More like weightlifting or football, is my guess,' he said. 'Strength and stamina. To a remarkable degree.'

'Not to mention considerable speed,' said Mr Cuff with the air of one indulging a tender reminiscence.

'Are you telling me that he got away?' I asked.

'No one gets away,' said Mr Clubb. 'That, sir, is gospel. But you may imagine our surprise when for the first time in the history of our *consultancy*' – and here he chuckled – 'a gentleman of the civilian persuasion managed to break his bonds and free himself of his ropes whilst Mr Cuff and I were engaged in the preliminaries.'

'Naked as jaybirds,' said Mr Cuff, wiping with a greasy hand a tear of amusement from one eye. 'Bare as newborn lambie-pies. There I was, heating up the steam iron I'd just fetched from the kitchen, sir, along with a selection of knives I came across in exactly the spot you described, most grateful I was, too, squatting on my haunches without a care in the world and feeling the first merry tingle of excitement in my little soldier –'

'What?' I said. 'You were naked? And what's this about your little soldier?'

'Hush,' said Mr Clubb, his eyes glittering. 'Nakedness is a precaution against fouling our clothing with blood and other bodily products, and men like Mr Cuff and myself take pleasure in the exercise of our skills. In us, the inner and the outer man are one and the same.'

'Are they, now?' I said, marveling at the irrelevance of this last remark. It then occurred to me that the remark might have been relevant after all – most unhappily so.

'At all times,' said Mr Cuff, amused by my having missed the point. 'If you wish to hear our report, sir, reticence will be helpful.'

I gestured for him to go on.

'As said before, I was squatting in my birthday suit by the knives and the steam iron, not a care in the world, when I heard from behind me the patter of little feet. *Hello*, I say to myself, *what's this?* and when I look over my shoulder here is your man, bearing down on me like a steam engine. Being as he is one of your big, strapping fellows, sir, it was a sight to behold, not to mention the unexpected circumstances. I took a moment to glance in the direction of Mr Clubb, who was busily occupied in another quarter, which was, to put it plain and simple, the bed.'

Mr Clubb chortled and said, 'By way of being in the line of duty.'

'So in a way of speaking I was in the position of having to settle this fellow before he became a trial to us in the performance of our duties. He was getting ready to tackle me, sir, which was what put us in mind of football being in his previous life, tackle the life out of me before he rescued the lady, and I got hold of one of the knives. Then, you see, when he came flying at me that way all I had to do was give him a good jab in the bottom of the throat, a matter which puts the fear of God into the bravest fellow. It concentrates all their attention, and after that they might as well be little puppies for all the harm they're likely to do. Well, this boy was one for the books, because for the first time in I don't know how many similar efforts, a hundred –'

'I'd say double at least, to be accurate,' said Mr Clubb.

'– in at least a hundred, anyhow, avoiding immodesty, I underestimated the speed and agility of the lad, and instead of planting my weapon at the base of his neck stuck him in the side, a manner of wound which in the case of your really *aggressive* attacker, who you come across in about one out of twenty, is about as effective as a slap with a powder puff. Still, I put him off his stride, a welcome sign to me that he had gone a bit loosey goosey over the years. Then, sir, the advantage was mine, and I seized it with a grateful heart. I spun him over, dumped him on the floor, and straddled his chest. At which point I thought to settle him down for the evening by taking hold of a cleaver and cutting off his right hand with one good blow.

'Ninety-nine times out of a hundred, sir, chopping off a hand will take the starch right out of a man. He settled down pretty well. It's the shock, you see, shock takes the mind that way, and because the stump was bleeding like a bastard, excuse the language, I did him the favor of cauterizing the wound with the steam iron because it was good and hot, and if you sear a wound there's no way that bugger can bleed anymore. I mean, the *problem* is *solved*, and that's a fact.'

'It has been proved a thousand times over,' said Mr Clubb.

'Shock being a healer,' said Mr Cuff. 'Shock being a balm like salt water to the human body, yet if you have too much of shock or salt water, the body gives up the ghost. After I seared the wound, it looked to me like he and his body got together and voted to take the next bus to what is generally considered a better world'. He held up an index finger and stared into my eyes while forking kidneys into his mouth. 'This, sir, is a *process*. A *process* can't happen all at once, and every reasonable precaution was taken. Mr Clubb and I do not have, nor ever have had, the reputation for carelessness in our undertakings.'

'And never shall.' Mr Clubb washed down whatever was in his mouth with half a glass of cognac.

'Despite the *process* under way,' said Mr Cuff, 'the gentleman's left wrist was bound tightly to the stump. Rope was again attached to the areas of the chest and legs, a gag went back into his mouth, and besides all that I had the pleasure of whapping my hammer once and once only on the region of his temple, for the purpose of keeping him out of action until we were ready for him in case he was not boarding the bus. I took a moment to turn him over and gratify my little soldier, which I trust was in no way exceeding our agreement, sir.' He granted me a look of the purest innocence.

'Continue,' I said, 'although you must grant that your tale is utterly without verification.'

'Sir,' said Mr Clubb, 'we know one another better than that.' He bent over so far that his head disappeared beneath the table, and I heard the undoing of a clasp. Resurfacing, he placed between us on the table an object wrapped in one of the towels Marguerite had purchased for Green Chimneys. 'If verification is your desire, and I intend no reflection, sir, for a man in your line of business has grown out of the habit of taking a fellow at his word, here you have wrapped up like a birthday present the finest verification of this portion of our tale to be found in all the world.'

'And yours to keep, if you're taken that way,' said Mr Cuff.

I had no doubts whatsoever concerning the nature of the trophy set before me, and therefore I deliberately composed myself before pulling away the folds of toweling. Yet for all my preparations the spectacle of the actual trophy itself affected me more greatly than I would have thought possible, and at the very center of the nausea rising within me I experienced the first faint stirrings of enlightenment. *Poor man*, I thought, *poor mankind*.

I refolded the material over the crablike thing and said, 'Thank you. I meant to imply no reservations concerning your veracity.'

'Beautifully said, sir, and much appreciated. Men like ourselves, honest at every point, have found that persons in the habit of duplicity often cannot understand the truth. Liars are the bane of our existence. And yet, such is the nature of this funny old world, we'd be out of business without them.'

Mr Cuff smiled up at the chandelier in rueful appreciation of the world's contradictions. 'When I replaced him on the bed, Mr Clubb went hither and yon, collecting the remainder of the tools for the job at hand.'

'When you say you replaced him on the bed,' I broke in, 'is it your meaning —'

'Your meaning might differ from mine, sir, and mine, being that of a fellow raised without the benefits of a literary education, may be simpler than yours. But bear in mind that every guild has its legacy of customs and traditions which no serious practitioner can ignore without thumbing his nose at all he holds dear. For those brought up into our trade, physical punishment of a female subject invariably begins with the act most associated in the feminine mind with humilation of the most rigorous sort. With males the same is generally true. Neglect this step, and you lose an advantage which can never be regained. It is the foundation without which the structure cannot stand, and the foundation must be set in place even when conditions make the job distasteful, which is no picnic, take my word for it.' He shook his head and fell silent.

'We could tell you stories to curl your hair,' said Mr Clubb. 'Matter for another day. It was on the order of nine-thirty when our materials had been assembled, the preliminaries taken care of, and business could begin in earnest. This is a moment, sir, ever cherished by professionals such as ourselves. It is of an eternal freshness.

You are on the brink of testing yourself against your past achievements and those of masters gone before. Your skill, your imagination, your timing and resolve will be called upon to work together with your hard-earned knowledge of the human body, because it is a question of being able to sense when to press on and when to hold back, of, I can say, having that instinct for the right technique at the right time you can acquire only through experience. During this moment you hope that the subject, your partner in the most intimate relationship which can exist between two people, owns the spiritual resolve and physical capacity to inspire your best work. The subject is our instrument, and the nature of the instrument is vital. Faced with an out-of-tune, broken-down piano, even the greatest virtuoso is up Shit Creek without a paddle. Sometimes, sir, our work has left us tasting ashes for weeks on end, and when you're tasting ashes in your mouth you have trouble remembering the grand design and your wee part in that majestical pattern.'

As if to supplant the taste in question and without benefit of knife and fork, Mr Clubb bit off a generous portion of steak and moistened it with a gulp of cognac. Chewing with loud smacks of the lips and tongue, he thrust a spoon into the kedgeree and began moodily slapping it onto his plate while seeming for the first time to notice the Canalettos on the walls.

'We started off, sir, as well as we ever have,' said Mr Cuff, 'and better than most times. The fingernails was a thing of rare beauty, sir, the fingernails was prime. And the hair was on the same transcendent level.'

'The fingernails?' I asked. 'The hair?'

'Prime,' said Mr Clubb with a melancholy spray of food. 'If they could be done better, which they could not, I should like to be there as to applaud with my own hands.'

I looked at Mr Cuff, and he said, 'The fingernails and

the hair might appear to be your traditional steps two and three, but they are in actual fact steps one and two, the first procedure being more like basic groundwork than part of the performance work itself. Doing the fingernails and the hair tells you an immense quantity about the subject's pain level, style of resistance, and aggression/passivity balance, and that information, sir, is your virtual bible once you go past step four or five.'

'How many steps are there?' I asked.

'A novice would tell you fifteen,' said Mr Cuff. 'A competent journeyman would say twenty. Men such as us know there to be at least a hundred, but in their various combinations and refinements they come out into the thousands. At the basic or kindergarten level, they are, after the first two: foot soles; teeth; fingers and toes; tongue; nipples; rectum; genital area; electrification; general piercing; specific piercing; small amputation; damage to inner organs; eyes, minor; eyes, major; large amputation; local flaying; and so forth.'

At mention of 'tongue', Mr Clubb had shoved a spoonful of kedgeree into his mouth and scowled at the paintings directly across from him. At 'electrification', he had thrust himself out of his chair and crossed behind me to scrutinize them more closely. While Mr Cuff continued my education, he twisted in his chair to observe his partner's actions, and I did the same.

After 'and so forth', Mr Cuff fell silent. The two of us watched Mr Clubb moving back and forth in evident agitation before the paintings. He settled at last before a depiction of a regatta on the Grand Canal and took two deep breaths. Then he raised his spoon like a dagger and drove it into the painting to slice beneath a handsome ship, come up at its bow, and continue cutting until he had deleted the ship from the painting. 'Now that, sir, is local flaying,' he said. He moved to the next picture, which gave a view of the Piazzetta. In seconds he had sliced all the canvas from the frame. 'And that, sir, is what is meant by general flaying.' He crumpled the canvas in his hands, threw it to the ground, and stamped on it.

'He is not quite himself,' said Mr Cuff.

'Oh, but I am, I am myself to an alarming degree, I am,' said Mr Clubb. He tromped back to the table and bent beneath it. Instead of the second folded towel I had anticipated, he produced his satchel and used it to sweep away the plates and serving dishes in front of him. He reached within and slapped down beside me the towel I had expected. 'Open it,' he said. I unfolded the towel. 'Are these not, to the last particular, what you requested, sir?'

It was, to the last particular, what I had requested. Marguerite had not thought to remove her wedding band before her assignation, and her . . . I cannot describe the other but to say that it lay like the egg perhaps of some small shore bird in the familiar palm. Another portion of my eventual enlightenment moved into place within me, and I thought: *Here we are, this is all of us, this crab and this egg.* I bent over and vomited beside my chair. When I had finished, I grabbed the cognac bottle and swallowed greedily, twice. The liquor burned down my throat, struck my stomach like a branding iron, and rebounded. I leaned sideways and, with a dizzied spasm of throat and guts, expelled another reeking contribution to the mess on the carpet.

'It is a Roman conclusion to a meal, sir,' said Mr Cuff.

Mr Moncrieff opened the kitchen door and peeked in. He observed the mutilated paintings and the objects nested in the striped towel and watched me wipe a string of vomit from my mouth. He withdrew for a moment and reappeared holding a tall can of ground coffee, wordlessly sprinkled its contents over the evidence of my distress, and vanished back into the kitchen. From the depths of my wretchedness, I marveled at the perfection of this display of butler decorum.

I draped the toweling over the crab and the egg. 'You are conscientious fellows,' I said.

'Conscientious to a fault, sir,' said Mr Cuff, not without a touch of kindness. 'For a person in the normal way of living cannot begin to comprehend the actual meaning of that term, nor is he liable to understand the fierce requirements it puts on a man's head. And so it comes about that persons in the normal way of living try to back out long after backing out is possible, even though we explain exactly what is going to happen at the very beginning. They listen, but they do not hear, and it's the rare civilian who has the common sense to know that if you stand in a fire you must be burned. And if you turn the world upside down, you're standing on your head with everybody else.'

'Or,' said Mr Clubb, calming his own fires with another deep draft of cognac, 'as the Golden Rule has it, what you do is sooner or later done back to you.'

Although I was still one who listened but could not hear, a tingle of premonition went up my spine. 'Please go on with your report,' I said.

'The responses of the subject were all one could wish,' said Mr Clubb. 'I could go so far as to say that her responses were a thing of beauty. A subject who can render you one magnificent scream after another while maintaining a basic self-possession and not breaking down is a subject highly attuned to her own pain, sir, and one to be cherished. You see, there comes a moment when they understand that they are changed for good, they have passed over the border into another realm, from which there is no return, and some of them can't handle it and turn, you might say, sir, to mush. With some it happens right at the foundation stage, a sad disappointment because thereafter all the rest of the work could be done by the crudest apprentice. It takes some at the nipples stage, and at the genital stage quite a few more. Most of them comprehend irreversibility during the piercings, and by the stage of small amputation ninety percent have shown you what they are made of. The lady did not come to the point until we had begun the eye work, and she passed with flying colors, sir. But it was then the male upped and put his foot in it.'

'And eye work is delicate going,' said Mr Cuff. 'Requiring two men, if you want it done even close to right. But I couldn't have turned my back on the fellow for more than a minute and a half.'

'Less,' said Mr Clubb. 'And him lying there in the corner meek as a baby. No fight left in him at all, you would have said. You would have said, that fellow there is not going to risk so much as opening his eyes until his eyes are opened for him.'

'But up he gets, without a rope on him, sir,' said Mr Cuff, 'which you would have said was beyond the powers of a fellow who had recently lost a hand.'

'Up he gets and on he comes,' said Mr Clubb. 'In defiance of all of Nature's mighty laws. Before I know what's what, he has his good arm around Mr Cuff's neck and is earnestly trying to snap that neck while beating Mr Cuff about the head with his stump, a situation which compels me to set aside the task at hand and take up a knife and ram it into his back a fair old number of times. The next thing I know, he's on *me*, and it's up to Mr Cuff to peel him off and set him on the floor.'

'And then, you see, your concentration is gone,' said Mr Cuff. 'After something like that, you might as well be starting all over again at the beginning. Imagine if you are playing a piano about as well as ever you did in your life, and along comes another piano with blood in its eye and jumps on your back. It was pitiful, that's all I can say about it. But I got the fellow down and jabbed him here and there until he was still, and then I got the one item we count on as a surefire last resort for incapacitation.'

'What is that item?' I asked.

'Dental floss,' said Mr Clubb. 'Dental floss cannot be overestimated in our line of work. It is the razor wire of everyday life, and fishing line cannot hold a candle to it, for fishing line is dull, but dental floss is both *dull* and *sharp*. It has a hundred uses, and a book should be written on the subject.'

'What do you do with it?' I asked.

'It is applied to a male subject,' he said. 'Applied artfully and in a manner perfected only over years of experience. The application is of a lovely *subtlety*. During the process, the subject must be in a helpless, preferably an unconscious, position. When the subject regains the first fuzzy inklings of consciousness, he is aware of no more than a vague discomfort like unto a form of tingling, similar to when a foot has gone to sleep. In a wonderfully short period of time, that discomfort builds itself up, ascending to mild pain, *severe* pain, and outright agony. Then it goes past agony. The final stage is a mystical condition I don't think there is a word for which, but it closely resembles ecstasy. Hallucinations are common. Out-of-body experiences are common. We have seen men speak in tongues, even when tongues were, strictly speaking, organs they no longer possessed. We have seen wonders, Mr Cuff and I.'

'That we have,' said Mr Cuff. 'The ordinary civilian sort of fellow can be a miracle, sir.'

'Of which the person in question was one, to be sure,' said Mr Clubb. 'But he has to be said to be in a category all by himself, a man in a million you could put it, which is the cause of my mentioning the grand design ever a mystery to us who glimpse but a part of the whole. You see, the fellow refused to play by the time-honored rules. He was in an awesome degree of suffering and torment, sir, but he would not do us the favor to lie down and quit.'

'The mind was not right,' said Mr Cuff. 'Where the proper mind goes to the spiritual, sir, as just described, this was that one mind in *ten* million, I'd estimate, which moves to the animal at the reptile level. If you cut off the head of a venomous reptile and detach it from the body, that head will still attempt to strike. So it was with our boy. Bleeding from a dozen wounds. Minus one hand. Seriously concussed. The dental floss murdering all possibility of thought. Every nerve in his body howling like a banshee. Yet up he comes with his eyes red and the foam dripping from his mouth. We put him down again, and I did what I hate, because it takes all feeling away from the body along with the motor capacity, and cracked his spine right at the base of the head. Or would have, if his spine had been a normal thing instead of solid steel in a thick india-rubber case. Which is what put us in mind of weightlifting, sir, an activity resulting in such development about the top of the spine you need a hacksaw to get even close to it.'

'We were already behind schedule,' said Mr Clubb, 'and with the time required to get back into the proper frame of mind, we had at least seven or eight hours of work ahead of us. And you had to double that, because while we could knock the fellow out, he wouldn't have the decency to *stay* out more than a few minutes at a time. The natural thing, him being only the secondary subject, would have been to kill him outright so we could get on with the real job, but improving our working conditions by that fashion would require an amendment to our contract. Which comes under the heading of Instructions from the Client.'

'And it was eleven o'clock,' said Mr Cuff.

'The exact time scheduled for our conference,' said Mr Clubb. 'My partner was forced to clobber the fellow into senselessness, how many times was it, Mr Cuff, while I prayed for our client to do us the grace of answering his phone during twenty rings?'

'Three times, Mr Clubb, three times exactly,' said Mr Cuff. 'The blow each time more powerful than the last, which, combined with his having a skull made of granite, led to a painful swelling of my hand.'

'The dilemma stared us in the face,' said Mr Clubb. 'Client unreachable. Impeded in the performance of our duties. State of mind, very foul. In such a pickle, we could do naught but obey the instructions given us by our hearts. *Remove the gentleman's head*, I told my partner, *and take care not to be bitten once it's off*. Mr Cuff took up an axe. Some haste was called for, the fellow just beginning to stir again. Mr Cuff moved into position. Then from the bed, where all had been lovely silence but for soft moans and whimpers, we hear a god-awful yowling ruckus of the most desperate and importunate protest. It was of a sort to melt the heart, sir. Were we not experienced professionals who enjoy pride in our work, I believe we might have been persuaded almost to grant the fellow mercy, despite his being a pest of the first water. But now those heart-melting screeches reach the ears of the pest and rouse him into movement just at the moment Mr Cuff lowers the boom, so to speak.'

'Which was an unfortunate bit of business,' said Mr Cuff. 'Causing me to catch him in the shoulder, causing him to rear up, causing me to lose my footing what with all the blood on the floor, then causing a tussle for possession of the axe and myself suffering several kicks to the breadbasket. I'll tell you, sir, we did a good piece of work when we took off his hand, for without the nuisance of a stump really being useful only for leverage, there's no telling what that fellow might have done. As it was, I had the devil's own time getting the axe free and clear, and once I had done, any chance of making a neat, clean job of it was long gone. It was a slaughter and an act of butchery with not a bit of finesse or sophistication to it, and I have to tell you, such a thing is both an embarrassment and an outrage to men like ourselves. Turning a subject into hamburger by means of an axe is a violation of all our training, and it is not why we went into this business.'

'No, of course not, you are more like artists than I had imagined,' I said. 'But in spite of your embarrassment, I suppose you went back to work on . . . on the female subject.'

'We are not *like* artists,' said Mr Clubb, 'we *are* artists, and we know how to set our feelings aside and address our chosen medium of expression with a pure and patient attention. In spite of which we discovered the final and insurmountable frustration of the evening, and that discovery put paid to all our hopes.'

'If you discovered that Marguerite had escaped,' I said, 'I believe I might almost, after all you have said, be –'

Glowering, Mr Clubb held up his hand. 'I beg you not to insult us, sir, as we have endured enough misery for one day. The subject had escaped, all right, but not in the simple sense of your meaning. She had escaped for all eternity, in the sense that her soul had taken leave of her body and flown to those realms at whose nature we can only make our poor, ignorant guesses.'

'She died?' I asked. 'In other words, in direct contradiction of my instructions, you two fools killed her. You love to talk about your expertise, but you went too far, and she died at your hands. I want you incompetents out of my house immediately. Begone. Depart. This minute.'

Mr Clubb and Mr Cuff looked into each other's eyes, and in that moment of private communication I saw an encompassing sorrow that utterly turned the tables on me: before I was made to understand how it was possible, I saw that the only fool present was myself. And yet the sorrow included all three of us, and more besides.

'The subject died, but we did not kill her,' said Mr Clubb. 'We did not go, nor have we ever gone, too far. The subject chose to die. The subject's death was an act of suicidal will. While you are listening, sir, is it possible, sir, for you to open your ears and hear what I am saying? She who might have been in all of our long experience the noblest, most courageous subject we ever will have the good fortune to be given witnessed the clumsy murder of her lover and decided to surrender her life.'

'Quick as a shot,' said Mr Cuff. 'The simple truth, sir, is that otherwise we could have kept her alive for about a year.'

'And it would have been a rare privilege to do so,' said Mr Clubb. 'It is time for you to face facts, sir.'

'I am facing them about as well as one could,' I said. 'Please tell me where you disposed of the bodies.'

'Within the house,' said Mr Clubb. Before I could protest, he said, 'Under the wretched circumstances, sir, including the continuing unavailability of the client and the enormity of the personal and professional letdown felt by my partner and myself, we saw no choice but to dispose of the house along with the telltale remains.'

'Dispose of Green Chimneys?' I said, aghast. 'How could you dispose of Green Chimneys?'

'Reluctantly, sir,' said Mr Clubb. 'With heavy hearts and an equal anger. With the same degree of professional unhappiness experienced previous. In workaday terms, by means of combustion. Fire, sir, is a substance like shock and salt water, a healer and a cleanser, though more drastic.'

'But Green Chimneys has not been healed,' I said. 'Nor has my wife.'

'You are a man of wit, sir, and have provided Mr Cuff and myself many moments of precious amusement. True, Green Chimneys has not been healed, but cleansed it has been, root and branch. And you hired us to punish your wife, not heal her, and punish her we did, as well as possible under very trying circumstances indeed.'

'Which circumstances include our feeling that the job ended before its time,' said Mr Cuff. 'Which circumstance is one we cannot bear.'

'I regret your disappointment,' I said, 'but I cannot accept that it was necessary to burn down my magnificent house.'

'Twenty, even fifteen years ago, it would not have been,' said Mr Clubb. 'Nowadays, however, that contemptible alchemy known as Police Science has fattened itself up into such a gross and distorted breed of sorcery that a single drop of blood can be detected even after you scrub and scour until your arms hurt. It has reached the hideous point that if a constable without a thing in his head but the desire to imprison honest fellows employed in an ancient trade finds two hairs at what is supposed to be a crime scene, he waddles along to the laboratory and instantly a loathsome sort of wizard is popping out to tell him that those same two hairs are from the heads of Mr Clubb and Mr Cuff, and I exaggerate, I know, sir, but not by much.'

'And if they do not have our names, sir,' said Mr Cuff, 'which they do not and I pray never will, they ever after have our particulars, to be placed in a great universal file against the day when they *might* have our names, so as to look back into that cruel file and commit the monstrosity of unfairly increasing the charges against us. It is a malignant business, and all sensible precautions must be taken.'

'A thousand times I have expressed the conviction,' said Mr Clubb, 'that an ancient art ought not be against the law, nor its practitioners described as criminals. Is there a name for our so-called crime? There is not. GBH they call it, sir, for Grievous Bodily Harm, or, even worse, Assault. We do not Assault. We induce, we instruct, we instill. Properly speaking, these cannot be crimes, and those who do them cannot be criminals. Now I have said it a thousand times and one.'

'All right,' I said, attempting to speed this appalling conference to its end, 'you have described the evening's unhappy events. I appreciate your reasons for burning down my splendid property. You have enjoyed a lavish meal. All remaining is the matter of your remuneration, which demands considerable thought. This night has left me exhausted, and after all your efforts, you, too, must be in need of rest. Communicate with me, please, in a day or two, gentlemen, by whatever means you choose. I wish to be alone with my thoughts. Mr Moncrieff will show you out.'

The maddening barnies met this plea with impassive stares and stoic silence, and I renewed my silent vow to give them nothing – not a penny. For all their pretensions, they had accomplished naught but the death of my wife and the destruction of my country house. Rising to my feet with more difficulty than anticipated, I said, 'Thank you for your efforts on my behalf.'

Once again, the glance that passed between them implied that I had failed to grasp the essentials of our situation.

'Your thanks are gratefully accepted,' said Mr Cuff, 'though, dispute it as you may, they are premature, as you know in your soul. Yesterday morning we embarked upon a journey of which we have yet more miles to go. In consequence, we prefer not to leave. Also, setting aside the question of your continuing education, which if we do not address will haunt us all forever, residing here with you for a sensible period out of sight is the best protection from law enforcement we three could ask for.'

'No,' I said, 'I have had enough of your education, and I need no protection from officers of the law. Please, gentlemen, allow me to return to my bed. You may take the rest of the cognac with you as a token of my regard.'

'Give it a moment's reflection, sir,' said Mr Clubb. 'You have announced the presence of high-grade consultants and introduced these same to staff and clients both. Hours later, your spouse meets her tragic end in a conflagration destroying your upstate manor. On the very same night also occurs the disappearance of your greatest competitor, a person certain to be identified before long by a hotel employee as a fellow not unknown to the late spouse. Can you think it wise to have the high-grade consultants vanish right away?'

I did reflect, then said, 'You have a point. It will be best if you continue to make an appearance in the office for a time. However, the proposal that you stay here is ridiculous.' A wild hope, utterly irrational in the face of the grisly evidence, came to me in the guise of doubt. 'If Green Chimneys has been destroyed by fire, I should have been informed long ago. I am a respected figure in the town of ——, personally acquainted with its chief of police, Wendall Nash. Why has he not called me?'

'Oh, sir, my goodness,' said Mr Clubb, shaking his head and smiling inwardly at my folly, 'for many reasons. A small town is a beast slow to move. The available men have been struggling throughout the night to rescue even a jot or tittle portion of your house. They will fail, they have failed already, but the effort will keep them busy past dawn. Wendall Nash will not wish to ruin your night's sleep until he can make a full report.' He glanced at his wristwatch. 'In fact, if I am not mistaken . . .' He tilted his head, closed his eyes, and raised an index finger. The telephone in the kitchen began to trill.

'He has done it a thousand times, sir,' said Mr Cuff, 'and I have yet to see him strike out.'

Mr Moncrieff brought the instrument through from the kitchen, said, 'For you, sir,' and placed the receiver in my waiting hand. I uttered the conventional greeting, longing to hear the voice of anyone but . . .

'Wendall Nash, sir,' came the chief's raspy, high-pitched drawl. 'Calling from up here in ——. I hate to tell you this, but I have some awful bad news. Your place Green Chimneys started burning sometime around midnight last night, and every man jack we had got put on the job and the boys worked like dogs to save what they could, but sometimes you can't win no matter what you do. Me personally, I feel terrible about this, but, tell you the truth, I never saw a fire like it. We nearly lost two men, but it looks like they're going to come out of it okay. The rest of our boys are still out there trying to save the few trees you got left.'

'Dreadful,' I said. 'Please permit me to speak to my wife.'

A speaking silence followed. 'The missus is not with you, sir? You're saying she was inside there?'

'My wife left for Green Chimneys yesterday morning. I spoke to her there in the afternoon. She intended to work in her studio, a separate building at some distance from the house, and it is her custom to sleep in the studio when working late.' Saying these things to Wendall Nash, I felt almost as though I were creating an alternative world, another town of —— and another Green Chimneys, where another Marguerite had busied herself in the studio, and there gone to bed to sleep through the commotion. 'Have you checked the studio? You are certain to find her there.'

'Well, I have to say we didn't, sir,' he said. 'The fire took that little building pretty good, too, but the walls are still standing and you can tell what used to be what, furnishingwise and equipmentwise. If she was inside it, we'd of found her.'

'Then she got out in time,' I said, and instantly it was the truth: the other Marguerite had escaped the blaze and now stood, numb with shock and wrapped in a blanket, unrecognized amidst the voyeuristic crowd always drawn to disasters.

'It's possible, but she hasn't turned up yet, and we've been talking to everybody at the site. Could she have left with one of the staff?'

'All the help is on vacation,' I said. 'She was alone.'

'Uh-huh,' he said. 'Can you think of anyone with a serious grudge against you? Any enemies? Because this was not a natural-type fire, sir. Someone set it, and he knew what he was doing. Anyone come to mind?'

'No,' I said. 'I have rivals, but no enemies. Check the hospitals and anything else you can think of, Wendall, and I'll be there as soon as I can.'

'You can take your time, sir,' he said. 'I sure hope we find her, and by late this afternoon we'll be able to go through the ashes.' He said he would give me a call if anything turned up in the meantime.

'Please, Wendall,' I said, and began to cry. Muttering a consolation I did not quite catch, Mr Moncrieff vanished with the telephone in another matchless display of butler politesse.

'The practice of hoping for what you know you cannot have is a worthy spiritual exercise,' said Mr Clubb. 'It brings home the vanity of vanity.'

'I beg you, leave me,' I said, still crying. 'In all decency.'

'Decency lays heavy obligations on us all,' said Mr Clubb. 'And no job is decently done until it is done completely. Would you care for help in getting back to the bedroom? We are ready to proceed.'

I extended a shaky arm, and he assisted me through the corridors. Two cots had been set up in my room, and a neat array of instruments – 'staples' – formed two rows across the bottom of the bed. Mr Clubb and Mr Cuff positioned my head on the pillows and began to disrobe.

8

Ten hours later, the silent chauffeur aided me in my exit from the limousine and clasped my left arm as I limped toward the uniformed men and official vehicles on the far side of the open gate. Blackened sticks that had been trees protruded from the blasted earth, and the stench of wet ash saturated the air. Wendall Nash separated from the other men, approached, and noted without comment my garb of gray homburg hat, pearl-gray cashmere topcoat, heavy gloves, woolen charcoal-gray pin-striped suit, sunglasses, and malacca walking stick. It was the afternoon of a midsummer day in the upper eighties. Then he looked more closely at my face. 'Are you, uh, are you sure you're all right, sir?'

'In a manner of speaking,' I said, and saw him blink at the oozing gap left in the wake of an incisor. 'I slipped at the top of a marble staircase and tumbled down all forty-six steps, resulting in massive bangs and bruises, considerable physical weakness, and the persistent sensation of being uncomfortably cold. No broken bones, at least nothing major.' Over his shoulder I stared at four isolated brick towers rising from an immense black hole in the ground, all that remained of Green Chimneys. 'Is there news of my wife?'

'I'm afraid, sir, that——' Nash placed a hand on my shoulder, causing me to stifle a sharp outcry. 'I'm sorry, sir. Shouldn't you be in the hospital? Did your doctors say you could come all this way?'

'Knowing my feelings in this matter, the doctors insisted I make the journey.' Deep within the black cavity, men in bulky orange space suits and space helmets were sifting through the sodden ashes, now and then dropping unrecognizable nuggets into heavy bags of the same color. 'I gather that you have news for me, Wendall,' I said.

'Unhappy news, sir,' he said. 'The garage went up with

the rest of the house, but we found some bits and pieces of your wife's little car. This here was one incredible hot fire, sir, and by hot I mean *hot*, and whoever set it was no garden-variety firebug.'

'You found evidence of the automobile,' I said. 'I assume you also found evidence of the woman who owned it.'

'They came across some bone fragments, plus a small portion of a skeleton,' he said. 'This whole big house came down on her, sir. These boys are experts at their job, and they don't hold out hope for finding a whole lot more. So if your wife was the only person inside . . .'

'I see, yes, I understand,' I said, staying on my feet only with the support of the malacca cane. 'How horrid, how hideous that it should all be true, that our lives should prove such a *littleness* . . .'

'I'm sure that's true, sir, and that wife of yours was a, was what I have to call a special kind of person who gave pleasure to us all, and I hope you know that we all wish things could of turned out different, the same as you.'

For a moment I imagined that he was talking about her recordings. Then I understood that he was laboring to express the pleasure he and the others had taken in what they, no less than Mr Clubb and Mr Cuff but much, much more than I, had perceived as her essential character.

'Oh, Wendall,' I said into the teeth of my sorrow, 'it is not possible, not ever, for things to turn out different.'

He refrained from patting my shoulder and sent me back to the rigors of my education.

9

A month – four weeks – thirty days – seven hundred and twenty hours – forty-three thousand, two hundred minutes – two million, five hundred and ninety-two thousand seconds – did I spend under the care of Mr

Clubb and Mr Cuff, and I believe I proved in the end to be a modestly, moderately, middlingly satisfying subject, a matter in which I take an immodest and immoderate pride. 'You are little in comparison to the lady, sir,' Mr Clubb once told me while deep in his ministrations, 'but no one could say that you are nothing.' I, who had countless times put the lie to the declaration that they should never see me cry, wept tears of gratitude. We ascended through the fifteen stages known to the novice, the journeyman's further five, and passed, with the frequent repetitions and backward glances appropriate for the slower pupil, into the artist's upper eighty, infinitely expandable by grace of the refinements of his art. We had the little soldiers. We had *dental floss*. During each of those forty-three thousand, two hundred minutes, throughout all two million and nearly six hundred thousand seconds, it was always deepest night. We made our way through perpetual darkness, and the utmost darkness of the utmost night yielded an infinity of textural variation, cold, slick dampness to velvety softness to leaping flame, for it was true that no one could say I was nothing.

Because I was not nothing, I glimpsed the Meaning of Tragedy.

Each Tuesday and Friday of these four sunless weeks, my consultants and guides lovingly bathed and dressed my wounds, arrayed me in my warmest clothes (for I never after ceased to feel the blast of arctic wind against my flesh), and escorted me to my office, where I was presumed much reduced by grief as well as by certain household accidents attributed to grief.

On the first of these Tuesdays, a flushed-looking Mrs Rampage offered her consolations and presented me with the morning newspapers, an inch-thick pile of faxes, two inches of legal documents, and a tray filled with official-looking letters. The newspapers described the fire and eulogized Marguerite; the increasingly threatening faxes declared Chartwell, Munster, and Stout's intention to ruin me professionally and personally in the face of my continuing refusal to return the accompanying documents along with all records having reference to their client; the documents were those in question; the letters, produced by the various legal firms representing all my other cryptic gentlemen, deplored the (unspecified) circumstances necessitating their clients' universal desire for change in re financial management. These lawyers also desired all relevant records, disks, etc., etc., urgently. Mr Clubb and Mr Cuff roistered behind their screen. I signed the documents in a shaky hand and requested Mrs Rampage to have these shipped with the desired records to Chartwell, Munster, and Stout. 'And dispatch all these other records, too,' I said, handing her the letters. 'I am now going in for my lunch.'

Tottering toward the executive dining room, now and then I glanced into smoke-filled offices to observe my much-altered underlings. Some of them appeared, after a fashion, to be working. Several were reading paperback novels, which might be construed as work of a kind. One of the Skipper's assistants was unsuccessfully lofting paper airplanes toward his wastepaper basket. Gilligan's secretary lay asleep on her office couch, and a records clerk lay sleeping on the file room floor. In the dining room, Charlie-Charlie Rackett hurried forward to assist me to my accustomed chair. Gilligan and the Skipper gave me sullen looks from their usual lunchtime station, an unaccustomed bottle of Scotch whisky between them. Charlie-Charlie lowered me into my seat and said, 'Terrible news about your wife, sir.'

'More terrible than you know,' I said.

Gilligan took a gulp of whisky and displayed his middle finger, I gathered to me rather than Charlie-Charlie.

'Afternoonish,' I said.

'Very much so, sir,' said Charlie-Charlie, and bent closer to the brim of the homburg and my ear. 'About that little request you made the other day. The right men aren't nearly so easy to find as they used to be, sir, but I'm still on the job.'

My laughter startled him. 'No squab today, Charlie-Charlie. Just bring me a bowl of tomato soup.'

I had partaken of no more than two or three delicious mouthfuls when Gilligan lurched up beside me. 'Look here,' he said, 'it's too bad about your wife and everything, I really mean it, honest, but that drunken act you put on in my office cost me my biggest client, not to forget that you took his girlfriend home with you.'

'In that case,' I said, 'I have no further need of your services. Pack your things and be out of here by three o'clock.'

He listed to one side and straightened himself up. 'You can't mean that.'

'I can and do,' I said. 'Your part in the grand design at work in the universe no longer has any connection with my own.'

'You must be as crazy as you look,' he said, and unsteadily departed.

I returned to my office and gently lowered myself into my seat. After I had removed my gloves and accomplished some minor repair work to the tips of my fingers with the tape and gauze pads thoughtfully inserted by the detectives into the pockets of my coat, I slowly drew the left glove over my fingers and became aware of feminine giggles amid the coarser sounds of male amusement behind the screen. I coughed into the glove and heard a tiny shriek. Soon, though not immediately, a blushing Mrs Rampage emerged from cover, patting her hair and adjusting her skirt. 'Sir, I'm so sorry, I didn't expect . . .' She was staring at my right hand, which had not as yet been inserted into its glove.

'Lawnmower accident,' I said. 'Mr Gilligan has been released, and I should like you to prepare the necessary papers. Also, I want to see all of our operating figures for the past year, as significant changes have been dictated by the grand design at work in the universe.'

Mrs Rampage flew from the room. For the next several hours, as for nearly every remaining hour I spent at my desk on the Tuesdays and Fridays thereafter, I addressed with a carefree spirit the details involved in shrinking the staff to the smallest number possible and turning the entire business over to the Skipper. Graham Leeson's abrupt disappearance greatly occupied the newspapers, and when not occupied as described I read that my arch rival and competitor had been a notorious Don Juan, i.e., a compulsive womanizer, a flaw in his otherwise immaculate character held by some to have played a substantive role in his sudden absence. As Mr Clubb had predicted, a clerk at the —— Hotel revealed Leeson's sessions with my late wife, and for a time professional and amateur gossip-mongers alike speculated that he had caused the disastrous fire. This came to nothing. Before the month had ended, Leeson sightings were reported in Monaco, the Swiss Alps, and Argentina, locations accommodating to sportsmen – after four years of varsity football at the University of Southern California, Leeson had won an Olympic silver medal in weightlifting while earning his MBA at Wharton.

In the limousine at the end of each day, Mr Clubb and Mr Cuff braced me in happy anticipation of the lessons to come as we sped back through illusory sunlight toward the real darkness.

10

The Meaning of Tragedy

Everything, from the designs of the laughing gods down to the lowliest cells in the human digestive tract, is changing all the time, every particle of being large and small is eternally in motion, but this simple truism, so transparent on its surface, evokes immediate headache and stupefaction when applied to itself, not unlike the sentence 'Every word that comes out of my mouth is a bald-faced lie.' The gods are ever laughing while we are always clutching our heads and looking for a soft place to lie down, and what I beheld in my momentary glimpses of the meaning of tragedy preceding, during, and after the experience of *dental floss* was so composed of paradox that I can state it only in cloud or vapor form, as:

The meaning of tragedy is: *All is in order, all is in train.*
The meaning of tragedy is: *It only hurts for a little while.*
The meaning of tragedy is: *Change is the first law of life.*

11

So it took place that one day their task was done, their lives and mine were to move forward into separate areas of the grand design, and all that was left before preparing my own departure was to stand, bundled up against the nonexistent arctic wind, on the bottom step and wave farewell with my remaining hand while shedding buckets and bathtubs of tears with my remaining eye. Chaplinesque in their black suits and bowlers, Mr Clubb and Mr Cuff ambled cheerily toward the glittering avenue and my bank, where arrangements had been made for the transfer into their hands of all but a small portion of my private fortune by my private banker, virtually his final act in that capacity. At the distant corner, Mr Clubb and Mr Cuff, by then only tiny figures blurred by my tears, turned, ostensibly to bid farewell, actually, as I knew, to watch as I mounted my steps and went back within the house, and with a salute I honored this last painful agreement between us.

A more pronounced version of the office's metamorphosis had taken place inside my town house, but with the relative ease practice gives even to one whose step is halting, whose progress is interrupted by frequent pauses for breath and the passing of certain shooting pains, I skirted the mounds of rubble, the dangerous loose tiles, more dangerous open holes in the floor, and the regions submerged under water and toiled up the resilient staircase, moved with infinite care across the boards bridging the former landing, and made my way into the former kitchen, where broken pipes and limp wires protruding from the lathe marked the sites of those appliances rendered pointless by the gradual disappearance of the household staff. (In a voice choked with feeling, Mr Moncrieff, Reggie Moncrieff, Reggie, the last to go, had informed me that his final month in my service had been 'as fine as my days with the Duke, sir, every bit as noble as ever it was with that excellent old gentleman'.) The remaining cupboard yielded a flagon of *jenever*, a tumbler, and a Monte Cristo torpedo, and with the tumbler filled and the cigar alight I hobbled through the devastated corridors toward my bed, there to gather my strength for the ardors of the coming day.

In good time, I arose to observe the final appointments of the life soon to be abandoned. It is possible to do up one's shoelaces and knot one's necktie as neatly with a single hand as with two, and shirt buttons eventually become a breeze. Into my traveling bag I folded a few modest essentials atop the flagon and the cigar box, and into a pad of shirts nestled the black lucite cube prepared at my request by my instructor-guides and containing, mingled with the ashes of the satchel and its contents, the few bony nuggets rescued from Green Chimneys. The traveling bag accompanied me first to my lawyer's office, where I signed papers making over the wreckage of the town house to the European gentleman who had purchased it sight unseen as a 'fixer upper' for a fraction of its (considerably reduced) value. Next I visited the melancholy banker and withdrew the pittance remaining in my accounts. And then, glad of heart and free of all unnecessary encumbrance, I took my place in the sidewalk queue to await transportation by means of a kindly kneeling bus to the great terminus where I should employ the ticket reassuringly lodged within my breast pocket.

Long before the arrival of the bus, a handsome limousine crawled past in the traffic, and glancing idly within, I observed Mr Chester Montfort de M—— smoothing the air with a languid gesture while in conversation with the two stout, bowler-hatted men on his either side. Soon, doubtless, he would begin his instructions in the whopbopaloobop.

12

What is a pittance in a great city may be a modest fortune in a hamlet, and a returned prodigal might be welcomed far in excess of his true deserts. I entered New Covenant quietly, unobtrusively, with the humility of a new convert uncertain of his station, inwardly rejoicing to see all unchanged from the days of my youth. When I purchased a dignified but unshowy house on Scripture Street, I announced only that I had known the village in my childhood, had traveled far, and now in my retirement wished no more than to immerse myself in the life of the community, exercising my skills only inasmuch as they might be requested of an elderly invalid. How well the aged invalid had known the village, how far and to what end had he traveled, and the nature of his skills remained unspecified. Had I not attended daily services at the Temple, the rest of my days might have passed in pleasant anonymity and frequent perusals of a little book

I had obtained at the terminus, for while my surname was so deeply of New Covenant that it could be read on a dozen headstones in the Temple graveyard, I had fled so early in life and so long ago that my individual identity had been entirely forgotten. New Covenant is curious – intensely curious – but it does not wish to pry. One fact and one only led to the metaphoric slaughter of the fatted calf and the prodigal's elevation. On the day when, some five or six months after his installation on Scripture Street, the afflicted newcomer's faithful Temple attendance was rewarded with an invitation to read the Lesson for the Day, Matthew 5:43–48, seated amid numerous offspring and offspring's offspring in the barnie-pews for the first time since an unhappy tumble from a hayloft was Delbert Mudge.

My old classmate had weathered into a white-haired, sturdy replica of his own grandfather, and although his hips still gave him considerable difficulty his mind had suffered no comparable stiffening. Delbert knew my name as well as his own, and though he could not connect it to the wizened old party counseling him from the lectern to embrace his enemies, the old party's face and voice so clearly evoked the deceased lawyer who had been my father that he recognized me before I had spoken the whole of the initial verse. The grand design at work in the universe once again could be seen at its mysterious business: unknown to me, my entirely selfish efforts on behalf of Charlie-Charlie Rackett, my representation to his parole board and his subsequent hiring as my spy, had been noted by all of barnie-world. I, a child of Scripture Street, had become a hero to generations of barnies! After hugging me at the conclusion of the fateful service, Delbert Mudge implored my assistance in the resolution of a fiscal imbroglio that threatened his family's cohesion. I of course assented, with the condition that my services should be free of charge. The Mudge imbroglio proved elementary, and soon I was performing similar services for other barnie-clans. After listening to a half dozen accounts of my miracles while setting broken barnie-bones, New Covenant's physician visited my Scripture Street habitation under cover of night, was prescribed the solution to his uncomplicated problem, and sang my praises to his fellow townies. Within a year, by which time all New Covenant had become aware of my 'tragedy' and consequent 'reawakening', I was managing the Temple's funds as well as those of barn and town. Three years later, our reverend having in his ninety-first year, as the Racketts and Mudges put it, 'woke up dead', I submitted by popular acclaim to appointment in his place.

Daily, I assume the honored place assigned me. Ceremonious vestments assure that my patchwork scars remain unseen. The lucite box and its relics are interred deep within the sacred ground beneath the Temple where I must one day join my predecessors – some bony fragments of Graham Leeson reside there, too, mingled with Marguerite's more numerous specks and nuggets. Eye patch elegantly in place, I lean forward upon the malacca cane and, while flourishing the stump of my right hand as if in demonstration, with my ruined tongue whisper what I know none shall understand, the homily beginning, *It only* . . . To this I append in silent exhalation the two words concluding that little book brought to my attention by an agreeable murderer and purchased at the great grand station long ago, these: *Ah, humanity!*